UNDER THE NET

Iris Murdoch was born in Dublin in 1919 of Anglo-Irish parents. She went to Badminton School, Bristol, and read classics at Somerville College, Oxford. During the war she was an Assistant Principal at the Treasury, and then worked with UNRRA in London, Belgium and Austria. She held a studentship in Philosophy at Newnham College, Cambridge, and then in 1948 she returned to Oxford where she became a Fellow of St Anne's College. Until her death in February 1999, she lived with her husband, the teacher and critic John Bayley, in Oxford. Awarded the CBE in 1976, Iris Murdoch was made a DBE in the 1987 New Year's Honours List. In the 1997 PEN Awards she received the Gold Pen for Distinguished Service to Literature.

Since her writing debut in 1954 with *Under the Net*, Iris Murdoch has written twenty-six novels, including the Booker Prize-winning *The Sea, the Sea* (1978) and most recently *The Green Knight* (1993) and *Jackson's Dilemma* (1995). Other literary awards include the James Tait Black Memorial Prize for *The Black Prince* (1973) and the Whitbread Prize for *The Sacred and Profane Love Machine* (1974). Her works of philosophy include *Sartre: Romantic Rationalist*, *Metaphysics as a Guide to Morals* (1992) and *Existentialists and Mystics* (1997). She has written several plays including *The Italian Girl* (with James Saunders) and *The Black Prince*, adapted from her novel of the same name. Her volume of poetry, *A Year of Birds*, which appeared in 1978, has been set to music by Malcolm Williamson.

ALSO BY IRIS MURDOCH

Fiction

The Flight from the Enchanter
The Sandcastle
The Bell
A Severed Head
An Unofficial Rose
The Unicorn
The Italian Girl
The Red and the Green
The Time of the Angels
The Nice and the Good
Bruno's Dream
A Fairly Honourable Defeat
An Accidental Man
The Black Prince
The Sacred and Profane Love Machine
A Word Child
Henry and Cato
The Sea, The Sea
Nuns and Soldiers
The Philosopher's Pupil
The Good Apprentice
The Book and the Brotherhood
The Message to the Planet
The Green Knight
Jackson's Dilemma
Something Special

Non-Fiction

Acastos: Two Platonic Dialogues
Metaphysics as a Guide to Morals
Existentialists and Mystics

Iris Murdoch

UNDER THE NET

WITH AN INTRODUCTION BY
Kiernan Ryan

VINTAGE

Published by Vintage 2003

2 4 6 8 10 9 7 5 3 1

First published in Great Britain in 1954 by
Chatto & Windus

First published by
Vintage in 2002

Vintage
Random House, 20 Vauxhall Bridge Road,
London SW1V 2SA

Random House Australia (Pty) Limited
20 Alfred Street, Milsons Point, Sydney
New South Wales 2061, Australia

Random House New Zealand Limited
18 Poland Road, Glenfield,
Auckland 10, New Zealand

Random House (Pty) Limited
Endulini, 5A Jubilee Road, Parktown 2193,
South Africa

The Random House Group Limited Reg. No. 954009
www.randomhouse.co.uk

A CIP catalogue record for this book
is available from the British Library

ISBN 0 099 45844 6

Papers used by Random House are natural, recyclable
products made from wood grown in sustainable forests.
The manufacturing processes conform to the environ-
mental regulations of the country of origin

Printed and bound in Great Britain by
Cox & Wyman Limited, Reading, Berkshire

To

RAYMOND QUENEAU

All, all of a piece throughout:
Thy Chase had a Beast in view:
Thy Wars brought nothing about;
Thy Lovers were all untrue.
'Tis well an Old Age is out,
And time to begin a New.

DRYDEN: THE SECULAR MASQUE

INTRODUCTION

IT'S HARD TO think of a modern British novelist who made a bolder, more brilliant debut than Iris Murdoch did with *Under the Net*. When the novel was first published in 1954, it was immediately apparent that a remarkable new writer had arrived on the scene, a writer already in full command of the art to which she was to devote the rest of her creative life. No one had conjured up a world quite like that before, entrancing the imagination with a flawless fusion of the mundane and the marvellous, laughter and lyricism, farce and philosophy. It was the first novel by Iris Murdoch I happened to read, three decades after it launched her career, and it remains far and away my favourite. Its prodigiously gifted author went on to write twenty-five more novels, many of which were bigger, more ambitious affairs, and several of which won prestigious literary prizes. But she never wrote a better novel than the one that made her name.

In a nutshell, *Under the Net* is Jake Donaghue's account of how he became the writer who wrote *Under the Net*. It's Murdoch's portrait of the artist as a restless, feckless, penniless young man on a quest to find out what he thinks, who he loves, and where his life is heading. When we meet him at the start of the novel, Jake, who scrapes a living as a hack translator of French fiction, has just returned to London from Paris to learn that he and his sidekick, Finn, have been turfed out of his girlfriend's flat to fend for themselves and find someone else to sponge off. After entrusting his manuscripts to the care of the mysterious, chain-smoking Mrs

Tinckham, who broods over her cat-filled cornershop 'like an earth goddess surrounded by incense', Jake embarks on a frantic odyssey that catapults him all over London and back to Paris, before restoring him at the end of the book to the bosom of Mrs Tinckham, much the wiser for his adventures and poised to pen the novel that we've just finished reading.

En route to his recognition of his destiny, Jake entangles himself in a bizarre erotic comedy of errors. His compulsive pursuit of his erstwhile lover, the singer Anna Quentin, across the capital and across the Channel, leads to the discovery that Anna is in love not with him but with his friend Hugo, who in turn is infatuated with Anna's sister, the glamorous film star, Sadie, who has eyes, it transpires, only for Jake. His equally compulsive pursuit of the enigmatic Hugo, a fire-works manufacturer turned film magnate, whose philosophy of silence has obsessed Jake for years, is the core of our hero's parallel search for the truth, for a take on life that will equip him to make sense of things. That search brings him into the orbit of two characters whose world views compete with Hugo's for Jake's intellectual allegiance: Dave Gellman, a freelance utilitarian philosopher peddling a 'peculiar brand of linguistic analysis', who provides the homeless Jake and Finn with a bolt-hole, and Lefty Todd, leader of the New Independent Socialist Party, to whose cause Hugo ends up committing his fortune.

It's Jake's relationship with Hugo that takes us to the heart of his tale and the explanation of its tantalising title. Jake first meets Hugo when the two of them are cooped up in a country house as guinea pigs in a cold-cure experiment. He swiftly realizes that he is in the presence of an extraordinary individual – 'the most purely objective and detached person I had ever met' – and falls completely under his spell. What's so spellbinding about Hugo is his unswerving honesty and truthfulness. In the course of their marathon discussions, Hugo proves himself to be immune to the lure of theoretical abstraction. It's the intractable specificity of things that enthrals him, not the specious propositions that we foist on them to make them fit our conceptual systems. 'For Hugo', Jake recalls, 'each thing was astonishing, delightful, complicated and mysterious. During these conversations I began to see the whole world anew.' In Hugo's view, indeed, 'The whole language is a machine for making falsehoods', because it can never depict things exactly as they are. Every time we speak, we lie, and only in silence or in action can we come close to telling the truth. Jake is inspired to turn their conversations into a fictional dialogue, which he publishes under the apt title *The Silencer*, undeterred by his guilty awareness that the mere existence of the book is a betrayal of Hugo's convictions.

The essence of those convictions is summed up by Hugo's surrogate, 'Annandine', in the extract from *The Silencer* to which Jake treats us in Chapter 6:

> the movement away from theory and generality is the movement toward truth. All theorising is flight. We must be ruled by the situation itself and this is unutterably particular. Indeed it is something to which we can never get close enough, however hard we may try as it were to crawl under the net.

The net under which we try to crawl is, of course, the net of language – the web of words that divides us from the unutterable particularity of the world and the immediacy of our experience. Hugo's position clearly leaves human beings, unless they are prepared to succumb to silence, in something of a bind, condemning them to a travesty of the truth whenever they open their mouths or put pen to paper. But it leaves no one in a more acute quandary than the novelist, the whole point of whose existence is to spin yarns out of words, to catch the truth of life in the toils of narrative. As 'Annandine' observes:

> I know that nothing consoles and nothing justifies except a story – but that doesn't stop all stories from being lies. Only the greatest men can speak and still be truthful. Any artist knows this obscurely; he knows that a theory is death, and that all expression is weighted with theory. Only the strongest can rise against that weight.

In *Under the Net* Iris Murdoch, in the guise of Jake Donoghue, proves herself strong enough to rise against that weight, using the power of words to spring us from the prisonhouse of language, the falsehood of fiction to unlock the truth of experience. The whole novel is a paradoxical vindication of its own impossible art.

To qualify as an adept of that art, Jake has to find his way out of the maze of misconceptions in which his egotism has stranded him. He starts off in a trance of distraction, just short of accepting that 'the present age was not one in which it was possible to write a novel'. A rootless drifter through a demi-monde of artists, drinkers, club owners and starlets, 'a sort of professional Unauthorized Person' plagued by 'shattered nerves', whose cause he is disinclined to divulge, Jake freely confesses that he hates solitude but fears intimacy: 'The substance of my life is a private conversation with myself which to turn into a dialogue would be equivalent to self-destruction.' From this slough of self-absorption the picaresque plot of *Under the Net* conspires to deliver him. Jake's impetuous personality and misreading of everyone around him propel him headlong into one absurd predicament after another, from each of which he contrives to extricate himself. His assumption that his impulsive craving for Anna is reciprocated maroons him in the prop room of an avant-garde mime theatre, transfixed by the eyes of a stuffed snake and a rocking-horse; his belief that Sadie has connived with Sacred Sammy the bookie to cheat him of his share in a movie deal provokes him to kidnap Sammy's latest acquisition, Marvellous Mister Mars, the canine movie star; and his conviction that Hugo despises him for publishing *The Silencer*, and that he is Jake's rival for Anna's affections, compels him to stalk his estranged mentor first to his film studio, where they are embroiled in a political riot that destroys the set, and finally to a hospital ward in the dead of night, where Jake is forced at last to crawl under the net of his misprisions and face up to reality.

With 'a wrench which dislocated past, present, and future', he realizes that he has got everything wrong all along, that he's guilty 'of having conceived things as I pleased and not as they were'. His solipsism has made him misconstrue the motives and emotions of everyone close to him by viewing them through the filter of self-serving fantasies. But now 'a pattern in my mind was suddenly scattered and the pieces of it went flying about me like birds'. Jake's fantasy of Anna fades 'like a sorcerer's apparition', to be replaced by his apprehension of her singularity and otherness:

It seemed as if, for the first time, Anna really existed now as a separate being and not as a part of myself. To experience this was extremely painful. Yet as I tried to keep my eyes fixed upon where she was I felt toward her a sense of initiative which was perhaps after all one of the guises of love. Anna was something which had to be learnt afresh. When does one ever know a human being? Perhaps only after one has realized the impossibility of knowledge and renounced the desire for it and finally ceased to feel even the need of it. But then what one achieves is no longer knowledge, it is simply a kind of co-existence; and this too is one of the guises of love.

This is the fundamental wisdom that suffuses Iris Murdoch's fiction from *Under the Net* onward. True virtue, true goodness, true love flow from respect for the strangeness and the mystery of other people and the world that surrounds us. They flow from the refusal to inflict our own designs on them, to deny their innate elusiveness, their impenetrable quiddity. When Jake reaches this realization, he is ready to write, ready to forge a fable that will look at the world afresh instead of projecting his illusions upon it. The novel's cryptic epigraph, from Dryden's 'The Secular Masque', makes perfect sense from this vantage point, distilling as it does the essence of Jake's experience:

All, all of a piece throughout:
Thy Chase had a Beast in view:
Thy Wars brought nothing about;
Thy Lovers were all untrue.
'Tis well an Old Age is out,
And time to begin a New.

The palpable proof of Jake's metamorphosis, and the imaginative embodiment of Murdoch's artistic creed, is *Under the Net* itself. Every page bears witness to its author's appetite for astonishment. Sometimes it's a matter of capturing, through the exquisite precision of the wording, the miracle concealed in the commonplace: 'An ever-increasing family of tabbies, sprung from one enormous matriarch, sit about upon the counter and on the empty shelves, somnolent and contemplative, their amber eyes narrowed and winking in the sun, a reluctant slit of liquid in an expanse of hot fur.' (The phrase 'a reluctant slit of liquid' is a perfect example of the paradoxical power of words to transport us beyond language to touch the thing itself.) At other times it's a matter of employing that precision to define the psychological enigma that puts a person beyond the reach of definition: 'To anyone who will take the trouble to become attached to her she will immediately give a devoted, generous, imaginative and completely uncapricious attention, which is still a calculated avoidance of self-surrender.' And as often as not, it's a question of framing those uncanny moments when the realm of fairy tale and the realm of the quotidian converge: 'amid the enchanting chaos of silks and animals and improbable objects that seemed to rise almost to her waist she looked like a very wise mermaid rising out of a motley coloured sea.'

No one and nothing in *Under the Net* is invulnerable to enchantment, to the casual alchemy that transmutes the real into the surreal at every turn: 'Occasionally a bird flew along between the windows and the wall, but looking always more like a false bird on a string than a real bird that would fly away somewhere else.' Even the leader of the New Independent Socialist Party cannot escape transfiguration: 'as we came up to him I was impressed by his enormous eyes, which looked at us sad and round and luminous as the eyes of a wombat or a Rouault Christ.' As the irreverent coupling of Christ with a hirsute marsupial suggests, people and their predicaments in this novel are frequently presented as *funny* in both senses of the word: funny because they are peculiar and funny because they make us laugh. *Under the Net* reverberates with delighted laughter at the sheer queerness of its characters and the ludicrous scrapes they wind up in. One-line deadpan gags abound: 'No man who has faced the Liffey can be appalled by the dirt of another river', observes Jake, as he and Finn strip off for an illicit midnight dip in the Thames. Not surprisingly, given Murdoch's birth in the fair city through which the Liffey runs, the humour often exhibits a distinctively Irish penchant for the preposterous. When he tracks Hugo down to the set where his studio is filming the epic tale of Catiline's conspiracy, Jake debates whether he should get togged up in a toga and smuggle himself in with the extras: 'But I decided that really there was no reason why I should have to attire myself like an ancient Roman in order to find Hugo, especially as this would mean surrendering my trousers to another person, an act of which I have a primitive terror.'

Jake's progress is punctuated by a series of epiphanies, dreamlike moments of transcendent illumination that mark stages in the emancipation of his mind and enshrine the latent strangeness of the world. Three of these moments stand out as especially memorable. The first is the description of Jake's ecstatic moonlit swim in the Thames: 'The whole expanse of water was running with light. It was like swimming in quicksilver.' The second is the phantasmagorical scene on the film-set, in which the police fight a pitched battle with nationalists and revolutionaries in a replica of ancient Rome, while above them sways a banner with the words 'SOCIALIST POSSIBILITY' printed on it in enormous letters and 'a superhuman voice' is shouting 'NO ONE IS TO LEAVE'. And the third, which plays such a decisive part in Jake's sentimental education, is his frenetic pursuit of Anna through the swirling Parisian crowds celebrating the fall of the Bastille, a chase that ends in bewilderment in the dark wood of the Tuileries:

> I ran along calling Anna's name. But now suddenly the wood seemed to be full of statues and lovers. Every tree had blossomed with a murmuring pair and every vista mocked me with a stone figure. Slim forms were flitting

along the avenues and pallid oblique faces caught the small light which penetrated through the forest. The din from the Concorde echoed along the tops of the trees. I cannoned into a tree trunk and hurt my shoulder. I sped along the colonnade toward a motionless figure which confronted me with marble eyes. I looked about me and called again. But my voice was caught up in the velvet of the night like a knife-thrust caught in a cloak.

When *Under the Net* first appeared, much was made of its supposed affinities with the novels and plays of the Angry Young Men being published around the same time, particularly Kingsley Amis's *Lucky Jim*, John Wain's *Hurry on Down*, Philip Larkin's *Jill*, and John Osborne's *Look Back in Anger* itself. Half a century on, however, it's plain that, beyond the statutory streak of post-war disaffection Jake shares with the heroes of these works, he's a distant cousin of theirs at best, and that the novel's deepest debts are European rather than English. Murdoch makes no secret of how much *Under the Net* owes to the fiction of the French surrealist Raymond Queneau, to whom the book is dedicated, and the novels of Samuel Beckett. Indeed, when Jake is given his marching orders in the opening chapter, the first things he packs are Beckett's *Murphy* (1938) and Queneau's *Pierrot Mon Ami* (1943). Anyone familiar with these novels will immediately recognize the precursors of Jake in their protagonists and the seeds of some of Murdoch's scenes in Murphy's and Pierrot's adventures. Jake's hijacking of the superstar alsatian Mister Mars, for example, recalls Pierrot's journey with a van full of circus animals; while his job as a hospital cleaner is clearly an *hommage* to Murphy's spell as a male nurse at the Magdalen Mental Mercyseat. Jean-Paul Sartre's seminal existentialist novel *La Nausée* (1938) can also be glimpsed in the interstices of *Under the Net* (Murdoch's first published book was a study of the philosopher, *Sartre: Romantic Rationalist* (1953)), though Jake's sense of alienation rarely touches the depths of anguish plumbed by Sartre's hero, Roquentin.

Murdoch patently learned a lot from these authors, but

they had nothing to teach her about turning what she'd looted from them to her own inimitable account. Even Jake's obligatory existentialist brooding on the void at the heart of the human condition can't stifle his creator's incorrigible zest for life, which pulses through the book from beginning to end. 'I felt neither happy nor sad, only rather unreal, like a man shut in a glass', Jake reflects in the final chapter, as he looks down at the crowds in Oxford Street and ponders the import of what he has undergone:

> Events stream past us like these crowds and the face of each is seen only for a minute. What is urgent is not urgent forever but only ephemerally. All work and all love, the search for wealth and fame, the search for truth, life itself, are made up of moments which pass and become nothing. Yet through this shaft of nothings we drive onward with that miraculous vitality that creates our precarious habitations in the past and the future.

In *Under the Net* everything ends up dancing to Iris Murdoch's tune, swept up in her jig of joy at what the last words of the novel call 'the wonders of the world'.

KIERNAN RYAN
2002

One

WHEN I saw Finn waiting for me at the corner of the street I knew at once that something had gone wrong. Finn usually waits for me in bed, or leaning up against the side of the door with his eyes closed. Moreover, I had been delayed by the strike. I hate the journey back to England anyway; and until I have been able to bury my head so deep in dear London that I can forget that I have ever been away I am inconsolable. So you may imagine how unhappy it makes me to have to cool my heels at Newhaven, waiting for the trains to run again, and with the smell of France still fresh in my nostrils. On this occasion too the bottles of cognac which I always smuggle had been taken from me by the Customs, so that when closing time came I was utterly abandoned to the torments of a morbid self-scrutiny. The invigorating objectivity of true contemplation is something which a man of my temperament cannot achieve in unfamiliar towns in England, even when he has not also to be worrying about trains. Trains are bad for the nerves at the best of times. What did people have nightmares about before there were trains? So all this being considered, it was an odd thing that Finn should be waiting for me in the road.

As soon as I saw Finn I stopped and put the cases down. They were full of French books and very heavy. I shouted "Hey!" and Finn came slowly on. He never makes haste. I find it hard to explain to people about Finn. He isn't exactly my servant. He seems often more like my manager. Sometimes I support him, and sometimes he supports me; it depends. It's somehow clear that we aren't equals. His name is Peter O'Finney, but you needn't mind about that, as he is always called Finn, and he is a sort of remote cousin of mine, or so he used to claim, and I never

7

troubled to verify this. But people do get the impression
that he is my servant, and I often have this impression too,
though it would be hard to say exactly what features of the
situation suggest it. Sometimes I think it is just that Finn is
a humble and self-effacing person and so automatically
takes second place. When we are short of beds it is always
Finn who sleeps on the floor, and this seems thoroughly
natural. It is true that I am always giving Finn orders, but
this is because Finn seems not to have many ideas of his
own about how to employ his time. Some of my friends
think that Finn is cracked, but this is not so; he knows very
well indeed what he is about.

When Finn came up to me at last I indicated one of the
cases for him to carry, but he did not pick it up. Instead
he sat down on it and looked at me in a melancholy way.
I sat down on the other case, and for a little while we were
silent. I was tired, and reluctant to ask Finn any questions;
he would tell all soon enough. He loves trouble, his own
or other people's without discrimination, and what he particularly likes is to break bad news. Finn is rather handsome in a sad lanky fashion, with straight drooping brownish
hair and a bony Irish face. He is a head taller than me (I
am a short man), but he stoops a little. As he looked at me
so sadly my heart sank.

"What is it?" I said at last.

"She's thrown us out," said Finn.

I could not take this seriously; it was impossible.

"Come now," I said kindly to Finn. "What does this
really mean?"

"She's throwing us out," said Finn. "Both of us, now,
to-day."

Finn is a carrion crow, but he never tells lies, he never
even exaggerates. Yet this was fantastic.

"But why?" I asked. "What have we done?"

"It's not what we've done, it's what she's after doing,"
said Finn. "She's going to get married to a fellow."

This was a blow. Yet even as I flinched I told myself, well, why not? I am a tolerant and fair-minded

man. And next moment I was wondering, where can we go?

"But she never told me anything," I said.

"You never asked anything," said Finn.

This was true. During the last year I had become un-interested in Magdalen's private life. If she goes out and gets herself engaged to some other man whom had I to thank but myself?

"Who is this person?" I asked.

"Some bookie fellow," said Finn.

"Is he rich?"

"Yes, he has a car," said Finn. This was Finn's criterion, and I think at that time it was mine too.

"Women give me heart disease," Finn added. He was no gladder than I was at being turned out.

I sat there for a moment, feeling a vague physical pain in which portions of jealousy and wounded pride were compounded with a profound sense of homelessness. Here we were, sitting in Earls Court Road on a dusty sunny July morning on two suitcases, and where were we to go next? This was what always happened. I would be at pains to put my universe in order and set it ticking, when suddenly it would burst again into a mess of the same poor pieces, and Finn and I be on the run. I say my uni-verse, not ours, because I sometimes feel that Finn has very little inner life. I mean no disrespect to him in saying this; some have and some haven't. I connect this too with his truthfulness. Subtle people, like myself, can see too much ever to give a straight answer. Aspects have always been my trouble. And I connect it with his aptness to make objective statements when these are the last things that one wants, like a bright light on one's headache. It may be, though, that Finn misses his inner life, and that that is why he follows me about, as I have a complex one and highly differentiated. Anyhow, I count Finn as an in-habitant of my universe, and cannot conceive that he has one containing me; and this arrangement seems restful for both of us.

It was more than two hours till opening time, and I could hardly face the thought of seeing Magdalen at once. She would expect me to make a scene, and I didn't feel energetic enough to make a scene, quite apart from not knowing anyway what sort of scene I ought to make. That would need some thinking out. There is nothing like being ousted for making one start to specify what it is one is being ousted from. I wanted time to reflect on my status.

"Would you like a cup of coffee in Lyons'?" I said to Finn hopefully.

"I would not," said Finn; "I'm destroyed already waiting for you to come back, and herself wishing me at the devil. Come on now and see her." And he started off down the street. Finn never refers to people otherwise than by pronouns or vocatives. I followed him slowly, trying to work out who I was.

Magdalen lived in one of those repulsive heavy-weight houses in Earls Court Road. She had the top half of the house; and there I had lived too for more than eighteen months, and Finn as well. Finn and I lived on the fourth floor in a maze of attics, and Magdalen lived on the third floor, though I don't say we didn't see a lot of each other, at any rate at first. I had begun to feel that this was my home. Sometimes Magdalen had boy friends, I didn't mind and I didn't enquire. I preferred it when she had, as then I had more time for work, or rather for the sort of dreamy un-lucrative reflexion which is what I enjoy more than anything in the world. We had lived there as snug as a pair of walnuts in their shells. We had also lived there practically rent-free, which was another point. There's nothing that irritates me so much as paying rent.

Magdalen, I should explain, is a typist in the city, or she was at the time of the earlier events related in this story. This hardly describes her, however. Her real em-ployment is to be herself, and to this she devotes a tremen-dous zeal and artistry. Her exertions are directed along the lines suggested to her by women's magazines and the cinema, and it is due simply to some spring of native and incorruptible vitality in her that she has not succeeded in rendering herself quite featureless in spite of having made the prevailing conventions of seduction her constant study. She is not beautiful: that is an adjective which I use sparingly; but she is both pretty and attractive. Her prettiness lies in her regular features and fine complexion, which she covers over with a peach-like mask of make-up until all is as smooth and inexpressive as alabaster. Her hair is permanently waved in whatever fashion is declared to be the most becoming. It is a dyed gold. Women think that beauty lies in approximation to a harmonious norm. The only reason why they fail to make themselves indistinguishably similar is that they lack the time and the money and the technique. Film stars, who have all these, *are* indistinguishably similar. Magdalen's attractiveness lies in her eyes, and in the vitality of her manner and expression. The eyes are the one part of the face which nothing can disguise, or at any rate nothing which has been invented yet. The eyes are the mirror of the soul, and you can't paint them over or even sprinkle them with gold dust. Magdalen's are big and grey and almond-shaped, and glisten like pebbles in the rain. She makes a lot of money from time to time, not by tapping on the typewriter, but by being a photographer's model; she is everyone's idea of a pretty girl.

Magdalen was in the bath when we arrived. We went into her sitting-room, where the electric fire and the little piles of nylon stockings and silk underwear and the smell of face-powder made a cosy scene. Finn slumped on to the tousled divan in the way she always asked him not to. I went to the bathroom door and shouted "Madge!"

The splashing ceased, and she said, "Is that you, Jake?" The cistern was making an infernal noise.

"Yes, of course, it's me. Look, what is all this?"

"I can't hear you," said Magdalen. "Wait a moment."

"What is all this?" I shouted. "All this about your

marrying a bookie? You can't do this without consulting me!"

I felt I was making a passable scene outside the bathroom door. I even banged on the panel.

"I can't hear a word," said Madge. This was untrue; she was playing for time. "Jake, dear, do put the kettle on and we'll have some coffee. I'll be out in a minute."

Magdalen swept out of the bathroom with a blast of hot perfumed air just as I was making the coffee, but dodged straight into her dressing-room. Finn got up hastily from the divan. We lit cigarettes and waited. Then after a long time Magdalen emerged resplendent, and stood before me. I stared at her in quiet amazement. A marked change had taken place in her whole appearance. She was wearing a tight silk dress, of an expensive and fussy cut, and a great deal of rather dear-looking jewellery. Even the expression on her face seemed to have altered. Now at last I was able to take in what Finn had told me. Walking down the road I had been too full of self-concern to reflect upon the oddness and enormity of Madge's plan. Now its cash value was before me. It was certainly unexpected. Madge was used to consort with tedious but humane city men, or civil servants with Bohemian tastes, or at worst with literary hacks like myself. I wondered what curious fault in the social stratification should have brought her into contact with a man who could inspire her to dress like that. I walked slowly round her, taking it all in.

"What do you think I am, the Albert Memorial?" said Magdalen.

"Not with those eyes," I said, and I looked into their speckled depths.

Then an unaccustomed pain shot through me and I had to turn away. I ought to have taken better care of the girl. This metamorphosis must have been a long time preparing, only I had been too dull to see it. A girl like Magdalen can't be transformed overnight. Someone had been hard at work.

Madge watched me curiously. "What's the matter?" she asked. "Are you ill?"

I spoke my thought. "Madge, I ought to have looked after you better."

"You didn't look after me at all," said Madge. "Now someone else will."

Her laughter had a cutting edge, but her eyes were troubled, and I felt an impulse to make her, even at this late stage, some sort of rash proposal. A strange light, cast back over our friendship, brought new things into relief, and I tried in an instant to grasp the whole essence of my need of her. I took a deep breath, however, and followed my rule of never speaking frankly to women in moments of emotion. No good ever comes of this. It is not in my nature to make myself responsible for other people. I find it hard enough to pick my own way along. The dangerous moment passed, the signal was gone, the gleam in Magdalen's eye disappeared and she said, "Give me some coffee." I gave her some.

"Now look, Jakie," she said, "you understand how it is. I want you to move your stuff out as soon as poss, to-day if you can. I've put all your things in your room."

She had too. Various objects of mine which usually decorated the sitting-room were missing. Already I felt I didn't live there any more.

"I don't understand how it is," I said, "and I shall be interested to hear."

"Yes, you must take *everything*," said Magdalen. "I'll pay for the taxi if you like." Now she was as cool as a lettuce.

"Have a heart, Madge," I said. I was beginning to worry about myself again, and felt a lot better. "Can't I go on living upstairs? I'm not in the way." But I knew this was a bad idea.

"Oh, Jake!" said Madge. "You are an imbecile!" This was the kindest remark she had made yet. We both relaxed.

All this time Finn had been leaning against the door,

looking abstractedly into the middle distance. Whether he was listening or not it was hard to tell.

"Send him away," said Magdalen. "He gives me the creeps."

"Where can I send him to?" I asked. "Where can we either of us go? You know I've got no money."

This was not strictly true, but I always pretend as a matter of policy to be penniless, one never knows when it may not turn out to be useful for this to be taken for granted.

"You're adults," said Magdalen. "At least, you're supposed to be. You can decide that for yourselves."

I met Finn's dreamy gaze. "What shall we do?" I asked him.

Finn sometimes has ideas, and after all he had had more time to reflect than I had.

"Go to Dave's," he said.

I could see nothing against that, so I said "Good!" and shouted after him, "Take the cases!" for he had shot off like an arrow. I sometimes think he doesn't care for Magdalen. He came back and took one of them and vanished.

Magdalen and I looked at each other like boxers at the beginning of the second round.

"Look here, Madge," I said, "you can't turn me out just like that."

"You arrived just like that," said Madge.

It was true. I sighed.

"Come here," I told her, and held out my hand. She gave me hers, but it remained as stiff and unresponsive as a toasting-fork, and after a moment or two I released it.

"Don't make a scene, Jakie," said Madge.

I couldn't have made even a little one at that moment. I felt weak, and lay down on the divan.

"Eh, eh!" I said gently. "So you're putting me out, and all for a man that lives on other people's vices."

"We all live on other people's vices," said Madge with an air of up-to-date cynicism which didn't suit her. "I

do, you do, and you live on worse ones than he does."
This was a reference to the sort of books I sometimes
translated.

"Who is this character, anyway?" I asked her.

Madge scanned me, watching for the effect. "His name,"
she said, "is Starfield. You may have heard of him." A
triumphant look blazed without shame in her eye.

I hardened my face to make it expressionless. So it was
Starfield, Samuel Starfield, Sacred Sammy, the diamond
bookmaker. To describe him as a bookie had been a bit
picturesque on Finn's part, although he still had his offices
near Piccadilly and his name in lights. Starfield now did a
bit of everything in those regions where his tastes and his
money could take him: women's clothes, night clubs, the
film business, the restaurant business.

"I see," I said. I wasn't going to put on a show for
Madge. "Where did you meet him? I ask this question
in a purely sociological spirit."

"I don't know what that means," said Madge. "If you
must know, I met him on a number eleven bus." This
was clearly a lie. I shook my head over it.

"You're enlisting for life as a mannequin," I said. "You'll
have to spend all your time being a symbol of conspicuous
wealth." And it occurred to me as I said it that it mightn't
be such a bad life at that.

"Jake, will you get out!" said Magdalen.

"Anyhow," I said, "you aren't going to live *here* with
Sacred Sam, are you?"

"We shall need this flat," said Magdalen, "and I want
you out of it now."

I thought her answer was evasive. "Did you say you were
getting *married*?" I asked. I began to have the feeling of
responsibility again. After all, she had no father, and I felt
in loco parentis. It was about the only locus I had left.
And it seemed to me, now that I came to think of it, somehow fantastically unlikely that Starfield would marry a girl
like Magdalen. Madge would do to hang fur coats on as
well as any other female clothes-horse. But she wasn't flashy,

any more than she was rich or famous. She was a nice
healthy English girl, as simple and sweet as May Day at
Kew. But I imagined Starfield's tastes as being more exotic
and far from matrimonial. "*Yes*," said Madge with emphasis, still as fresh as cream. "And now will you start pack-
ing?" She had a bad conscience, though, I could see from
the way she avoided my eye.

She started fiddling with the bookshelves, saying, "I think
there are some books of yours here," and she took out
Murphy and *Pierrot Mon Ami*.

"Making room for comrade Starfield," I said. "Can he
read? And by the way, does he know I exist?"

"Well, yes," said Magdalen evasively, "but I don't want
you to meet. That's why you must pack up at once. From
to-morrow onward Sammy will be here a lot."

"One thing's certain," I said, "I can't move everything
in a day. I'll take some things now, but I'll have to come
back to-morrow." I hate being hurried. "And don't forget," I added fervently, "that the radiogram is *mine*." My
thoughts kept reverting to Lloyds Bank Limited.

"Yes, dear," said Madge, "but if you come back after
to-day, telephone first, and if it's a man, ring off."

"This disgusts me," I said.

"Yes, dear," said Madge. "Shall I order a taxi?"

"No!" I shouted, leaving the room.

"If you come back when Sammy's here," Magdalen called
after me up the stairs, "he'll break your neck."

*   *   *

I took the other suitcase, and packed up my manuscripts in a brown-paper parcel, and left on foot. I needed
to think, and I can never think in a taxi for looking at the
cash meter. I took a number seventy-three bus, and went
to Mrs Tinckham's. Mrs Tinckham keeps a newspaper
shop in the neighbourhood of Charlotte Street. It's a
dusty, dirty, nasty-looking corner shop, with a cheap
advertisement board outside it, and it sells papers in
various languages, and women's magazines, and Westerns

and Science fiction and Amazing Stories. At least these
articles are displayed for sale in chaotic piles, though I have
never seen anyone buy anything in Mrs Tinckham's shop
except ice cream, which is also for sale, and the *Evening
News*. Most of the literature lies there year after year, fading
in the sun, and is only disturbed when Mrs Tinckham herself has a fit of reading, which she does from time to time,
and picks out some Western, yellow with age, only to
declare halfway through that she's read it before but had
quite forgotten. She must by now have read the whole of
her stock, which is limited and slow to increase. I've seen
her sometimes looking at French newspapers, though she
professes not to know French, but perhaps she is just looking at the pictures. Besides the ice-cream container there is
a little iron table and two chairs, and on a shelf above there
are red and green non-alcoholic drinks in bottles. Here I
have spent many peaceful hours.

Another peculiarity of Mrs Tinckham's shop is that it is
full of cats. An ever-increasing family of tabbies, sprung
from one enormous matriarch, sit about upon the counter
and on the empty shelves, somnolent and contemplative,
their amber eyes narrowed and winking in the sun, a reluctant slit of liquid in an expanse of hot fur. When I come
in, one often leaps down and onto my knee, where it sits
for a while in a sedate objective way, before slinking into
the street and along by the shop fronts. But I have never
met one of these animals further than ten yards away
from the shop. In the midst sits Mrs Tinckham herself,
smoking a cigarette. She is the only person I know who
is literally a chain-smoker. She lights each one from the
butt of the last; how she lights the first one of the day remains to me a mystery, for she never seems to have any
matches in the house when I ask her for one. I once
arrived to find her in great distress because her current
cigarette had fallen into a cup of coffee and she had no
fire to light another. Perhaps she smokes all night, or perhaps there is an undying cigarette which burns eternally in
her bedroom. An enamel basin at her feet is filled, usually

to overflowing, with cigarette ends; and beside her on the counter is a little wireless which is always on, very softly and inaudibly, so that a sort of murmurous music accompanies Mrs Tinckham as she sits, wreathed in cigarette smoke, among the cats.

I came in and sat down as usual at the iron table, and lifted a cat from the nearest shelf on to my knee. Like a machine set in motion it began to purr. I gave Mrs Tinckham my first spontaneous smile of the day. She is what Finn calls a funny old specimen, but she has been very kind to me, and I never forget kindness.

"Well, now, back again," said Mrs Tinckham, laying aside *Amazing Stories,* and she turned the wireless down a bit more until it was just a mumble in the background.

"Yes, unfortunately," I said. "Mrs Tinck, what about a glass of something?"

For a long time I have kept a stock of whiskey with Mrs Tinckham in case I ever need a medicinal drink, in quiet surroundings, in central London, out of hours. By now they were open, but I needed the soothing peace of Mrs Tinckham's shop, with the purring cat and the whispering wireless and Mrs Tinckham like an earth goddess surrounded by incense. When I first devised this plan I used to mark the bottle after every drink, but this was before I knew Mrs. Tinckham well. She is equal to a law of nature in respect of her reliability. She can keep counsel too. I once overheard one of her odder-looking clients, who had been trying to pump her about something, shout out, "You are pathologically discreet!" and this is how she is. I suspect indeed that this is the secret of Mrs Tinckham's success. Her shop serves as what is known as an "accommodation address", and is a rendezvous for people who like to be very secretive about their affairs. I sometimes wonder how much Mrs Tinckham knows about the business of her customers. When I am away from her I feel sure that she cannot be so naïve as not to have some sort of appreciation of what is going on under her nose. When I am with her, she looks so plump and vague, and blinks in a way so much like one of her cats, that I am filled with doubt. There are moments when, out of the corner of my eye, I seem to see a look of acute intelligence upon her face; but however fast I turn about I can never surprise any expression there except one of beaming and motherly solicitude and more or less vacant concern. Whatever may be the truth, one thing is certain, that no one will ever know it. The police have long ago given up questioning Mrs Tinckham. It was time lost. However much or little she knows, she has never, in my experience, displayed either for profit or for effect any detailed acquaintance with the little world that circulates round her shop. A woman who does not talk is a jewel in velvet. I am devoted to Mrs Tinckham.

She filled a *papier mâché* beaker with whiskey and passed it over the counter. I have never seen her take a drink of any kind herself.

"No brandy this time, dear?" she asked.

"No, the damned Customs took it," I said, and as I had a gulp at the whiskey I added, "Devil take them!" with a gesture which embraced the Customs, Madge, Starfield, and my bank manager.

"What's the matter, dear? Times bad again, are they?" said Mrs Tinckham, and as I looked into my drink I could see her gaze flicker with awareness.

"People are a trial and a trouble, aren't they?" she added, in that voice which must have greased the way to many a confession.

I am sure that people talk enormously to Mrs Tinckham. I have come in sometimes and felt this unmistakably in the atmosphere. I have talked to her myself; and in the lives of many of her customers she probably figures as the only completely trustworthy confidant. Such a position could hardly help but be to some extent lucrative, and Mrs Tinckham certainly has money, for she once lent me ten pounds without a murmur, but I am sure that gain is not Mrs Tinckham's chief concern. She just loves to know everybody's business, or rather to know about their lives, since "business" suggests an interest narrower and less humane than the one which I now felt, or imagined that I felt, focused with some intensity upon me. In fact the truth about her naïvety, or lack of it, may lie somewhere between the two, and she lives, perhaps, in a world of other people's dramas, where fact and fiction are no longer clearly distinguished.

There was a soft murmuring, which might have been the wireless or might have been Mrs Tinckham casting a spell in order to make me talk to her : a sound like the gentle winding of a delicate line on which some rare fish precariously hangs. But I gritted my teeth against speech. I wanted to wait until I could present my story in a more dramatic way. The thing had possibilities, but as yet it lacked form. If I spoke now there was always the danger of my telling the truth; when caught unawares I usually tell the truth, and what's duller than that? I met Mrs Tinckham's gaze, and although her eyes told nothing I was sure she knew my thoughts.

"People and money, Mrs Tinck," I said. "What a happy place the world would be without them."

"And sex," said Mrs Tinck. We both sighed.

"Had any new kittens lately?" I asked her.

"Not yet," said Mrs Tinckham, "but Maggie's pregnant again. Soon you'll have your pretty little ones, won't you, yes!" she said to a gross tabby on the counter.

"Any luck this time, do you think?" I asked.

Mrs Tinckham was always trying to persuade her tabbies to mate with a handsome Siamese who lived further down the street. Her efforts, it is true, consisted only of carrying the creatures to the door, and pointing out the elegant male with such remarks as, "Look at that lovely pussy there!"— and so far nothing had come of it. If you have ever tried to direct a cat's attention to anything you will know how difficult this is. The beast will look everywhere but where your finger points.

"Not a chance," said Mrs Tinckham bitterly. "They

all dote on the black-and-white Tom at the horse-meat
shop. Don't you, you pretty girl, yes," she said to the
expectant tabby, who stretched out a heavy luxurious
paw, and unsheathed its claws into a pile of *Nouvelles
Litiéraires*.

I began to undo my parcel upon the table. The cat
jumped from my knee and sidled out of the door. Mrs
Tinckham said, "Ah, well," and reached out for *Amazing
Stories*.

I glanced hastily through the manuscripts. Once before,
in a rage, Magdalen had torn up the first sixty stanzas of
an epic poem called *And Mr Oppenheim Shall Inherit the
Earth*. This dated from the time when I had ideals. At
that time too it had not yet become clear to me that the
present age was not one in which it was possible to write
an epic. At that time I naïvely imagined that there was no
reason why one should not attempt to write anything that
one felt inclined to write. But nothing is more paralysing
than a sense of historical perspective, especially in literary
matters. At a certain point perhaps one ought simply to
stop reflecting. I had contrived in fact to stop myself just
short of the point at which it would have become clear
to me that the present age was not one in which it was
possible to write a novel. But to return to *Mr Oppenheim*;
my friends had criticized the title because it sounded anti-
Semitic, though of course Mr Oppenheim simply sym-
bolized big business, but Madge didn't tear it up for that,
but out of pique, because I broke a lunch date with her
to meet a woman novelist. The latter was a dead loss,
but I came back to find *Mr Oppenheim* in pieces. This was
in the old days. But I feared that the performance might
have been repeated. Who knows what thoughts were
passing through that girl's mind while she was deciding to
throw me out? There's nothing like a woman's doing
you an injury for making her incensed against you. I
know myself how exasperating it is of other people to put
themselves in positions where you have to injure them. So
I scanned the stuff with care.

Everything seemed to be in order, except that one item was missing. That was the typescript of my translation of *Le Rossignol de Bois*. This *Wooden Nightingale* was Jean Pierre Breteuil's last book but two. I had done it straight on to the typewriter; I've translated so much of Jean Pierre's stuff now, it's just a matter of how fast I can type. I can't be bothered with carbons—I have no manual skill and you know what carbons are—so there was only one copy. I had no fears for this though, as I knew that if Magdalen had wanted to destroy something she would have destroyed one of my own things and not a translation. I made a mental note to collect it next time; it was probably in the bureau downstairs. *Le Rossignol* would be a best-seller, and that meant money in my pocket. It's about a young composer who is psychoanalysed and then finds that his creative urge is gone. I enjoyed this one, though it's bad best-selling stuff like everything that Jean Pierre writes.

Dave Gellman says I specialize in translating Breteuil because that's the sort of book I wish I could write myself, but this is not so. I translate Breteuil because it's easy and because it sells like hot cakes in any language. Also, in a perverse way, I just enjoy translating, it's like opening one's mouth and hearing someone else's voice emerge. The last but one, *Les Pierres de l'Amour*, which I had read in Paris, was undoubtedly another winner. Then there was a very recent novel called *Nous Les Vainqueurs*, which I hadn't read. I decided to see my publisher and get an advance on *The Wooden Nightingale*; and I would try to sell him an idea I had in Paris about a collection of French short stories translated and introduced by me. That was what my suitcases were full of. It would keep the wolf at a distance. Anything rather than original work, as Dave says. I reckoned I had about seventy pounds in the bank. But clearly the immediate and urgent problem was to find a cheap and sympathetic place in which to live and work now that Earls Court Road was closed to me.

You may be thinking that it was rather unkind of Magdalen to throw me out with so little ceremony, and you may think too that it was soft of me to take it so quietly. But in fact Magdalen is not a tough. She is a bright, sensual person, simple and warm-hearted, and ready to oblige anyone provided this doesn't put her to any trouble; and which of us could say more? For myself, I had a bad conscience about Madge. I said just now that I lived practically rent-free. Well, this wasn't quite true; in fact, I'd lived entirely rent-free. This thought annoyed me a little. It's bad for one's *locus standi* to live on a woman's charity. Also, I knew that Madge wanted to get married. She hinted as much to me more than once; and I think she would have married me at that. Only I had wanted otherwise. So on both these counts I felt I had no rights at all at Earls Court Road, and only myself to thank if Madge looked for security elsewhere; though I think I was quite objective in judging Sacred Sammy to be no cert, but a pretty long shot.

At this point perhaps I should say a word about myself. My name is James Donaghue, but you needn't bother about that, as I was in Dublin only once, on a whiskey blind, and saw daylight only twice, when they let me out of Store Street police station, and then when Finn put me on the boat for Holyhead. That was in the days when I used to drink. I am something over thirty and talented, but lazy. I live by literary hack-work, and a little original writing, as little as possible. One can live by writing these days, if one does it pretty well all the time, and is prepared to write anything which the market asks for. I mentioned before that I am a short man, but slight and neatly built would describe me better. I have fair hair and sharp elfish features. I am good at Judo, but don't care for boxing. What is more important for the purposes of this tale, I have shattered nerves. Never mind how I got them. That's another story, and I'm not telling you the whole story of my life. I have them; and one effect of this is that I can't bear being alone for long. That's why Finn is so useful to me. We sit together for hours, sometimes without uttering a word. I am thinking perhaps about God, freedom and immortality. What Finn would be thinking about I don't know. But more than this, I hate living in a strange house, I love to be protected. I am therefore a parasite, and live usually in my friends' houses. This is financially convenient also. I am not unwelcome because my habits are quiet and Finn can do odd jobs.

It was certainly something of a problem to know where to go next. I wondered if Dave Gellman would harbour us. I fondled the idea, though I suspected it was no good. Dave is an old friend, but he's a philosopher, not the kind that tells you about your horoscope and the number of the beast, but a real one like Kant and Plato, so of course he has no money. I felt perhaps I oughtn't to make demands on Dave. Also he's a Jew, a real dyed-in-the-wool Jew, who fasts and believes that sin is unredeemable and is shocked at the story about the woman who broke the alabaster vase of very precious ointment and at a lot of other stories in the New Testament. It's not this I mind, but the way he argues interminably with Finn about the Trinity and the unimportance of sentiments and the notion of charity. There's no concept Dave hates so much as the concept of charity, which seems to him equivalent to a sort of spiritual cheating. According to Dave, this notion simply makes for indirectness and the idea that one can get away with anything. Human beings have to live by clear practical rules, he says, and not by the vague illumination of lofty notions which may seem to condone all kinds of extravagance. Dave is one of the few people with whom Finn talks at length. I should explain that Finn is a lapsed Catholic, but Methodist by temperament, or so it seems to me, and he testifies passionately to Dave. Finn is always saying he will go back to Ireland to be in a country which really has religion, but he never goes. So I thought it might not be very restful chez Dave. I prefer it when Finn doesn't talk too much. I used to talk a lot with Dave myself about abstract things. I was pleased when I first got to know him to hear that he was a philosopher, and I thought that he might tell me some important truths. At that time I used to read Hegel and Spinoza, though I confess I never understood them much, and I hoped to be able to discuss them with Dave. But somehow we never seemed to get anywhere, and most of our conversations consisted of my saying something and Dave saying he didn't understand what I meant and I saying it again and Dave getting very impatient. It took me some time to realize that when Dave said he didn't understand, what he meant was that what I said was nonsense. Hegel says that Truth is a great word and the thing is greater still. With Dave we never seemed to get past the word; so finally I gave up. However, I am very fond of Dave and we have plenty of other things to talk about, so I didn't dismiss the idea of going to live with him. It was the only idea I had. When I had at last come to this conclusion I unpacked some of my books and left them together with the parcel of manuscripts under Mrs Tinckham's counter. Then I left the shop and went to Lyons'.

Two

THERE are some parts of London which are necessary and others which are contingent. Everywhere west of Earls Court is contingent, except for a few places along the river. I hate contingency. I want everything in my life to have a sufficient reason. Dave lived west of Earls Court, and this was another thing I had against him. He lived off the Goldhawk Road, in one of those reddish black buildings which for some reason are called mansions. It was in such contexts, in my dark London childhood, that I first learnt the word, and it has ruined many pieces of prose for me since, including some Biblical ones. I think that Dave doesn't mind much about his surroundings. Being a philosopher, he is professionally concerned with the central knot of being (though he would hate to hear me use this phrase), and not with the loose ends that most of us have to play with. Also, since he is Jewish he can feel himself to be a part of History without making any special effort. I envy him that. For myself, I find I have to work harder and harder every year to keep in with History. So Dave can afford to have a contingent address. I wasn't sure that I could.

Dave's mansions are tall, but they are overhung by a huge modern hospital, with white walls, which stands next to them. A place of simplicity and justification, which I pass with a *frisson*. Now as I came up the dark stained-glass staircase to Dave's flat I heard a hum of voices. This displeased me. Dave knows far too many people. His life is a continual *tour de force* of intimacy. I myself would think it immoral to be intimate with more than four people at any given time. But Dave seems to be on intimate terms with more than a hundred. He has a large and clinging acquaintance among artists and intellectuals, and he knows many left-wing political people too, including oddities such as Lefty Todd, the leader of the New Independent Socialist Party, and others of even greater eccentricity. Then there are his pupils, and the friends of his pupils, and the ever-growing horde of his ex-pupils. No one whom Dave has taught seems ever to lose touch with him. I find this, in a way, hard to understand, since as I have indicated Dave was never able to communicate anything to me when we talked about philosophy. But perhaps I am too much the incorrigible artist, as he once exclaimed. This reminds me to add that Dave disapproves of the way I live, and is always urging me to take a regular job.

Dave does extra-mural work for the University, and collects about him many youths who have a part-time interest in truth. Dave's pupils adore him, but there is a permanent fight on between him and them. They aspire like sunflowers. They are all natural metaphysicians, or so Dave says in a tone of disgust. This seems to me a wonderful thing to be, but it inspires in Dave a passion of opposition. To Dave's pupils the world is a mystery; a mystery to which it should be reasonably possible to discover a key. The key would be something of the sort that could be contained in a book of some eight hundred pages. To find the key would not necessarily be a simple matter, but Dave's pupils feel sure that the dedication of between four and ten hours a week, excluding University vacations, should suffice to find it. They do not conceive that the matter should be either more simple or more complex than that. They are prepared within certain limits to alter their views. Many of them arrive as theosophists and depart as Critical Realists or Bradleians. It is remarkable how Dave's criticism seems so often to be purely catalytic in its action. He blazes upon them with the destructive fury of the sun, but instead of shrivelling up their metaphysical pretensions, achieves merely their metamorphosis from one rich stage into another. This curious fact makes me think that perhaps after all Dave is, in spite of himself, a good teacher. Occasionally he succeeds in converting some peculiarly receptive youth to his own brand of linguistic analysis; after which as often as not the youth loses interest in philosophy altogether. To watch Dave at work on these young men is like watching someone prune a rose bush. It is all the strongest and most luxuriant shoots which have to come off. Then later perhaps there will be blossoms; but not philosophical ones, Dave trusts. His great aim is to dissuade the young from philosophy. He always warns me off it with particular earnestness.

I hesitated at the door. I hate entering a crowded room and feeling a whole gallery of faces focused upon me. I felt tempted to go away again; but at last, making an inward gesture of detachment, I went in. The room was full of young men, all talking at once and drinking cups of tea, but I needn't have troubled about the faces, as no one paid any attention to my entry except Dave himself. He was sitting in a corner a little apart from the *mêlée*, and raised his hand when he saw me with the dignified gesture of a patriarch greeting the appearance of an expected sign. Not that Dave is a patriarchal Hebrew to look at. He is fattish and baldish with merry brown eyes and podgy hands, a slightly guttural voice and an imperfect command of English. Finn was sitting near him on the floor with his back to the wall and his legs stretched out like the victim of an accident.

I made my way past several beardless youths, stepped over Finn and shook hands with Dave. I gave Finn a friendly kick and seated myself on the edge of the table. A youth handed me a cup of tea automatically, talking back over his shoulder as he did so. Ought brings you back to is in the end. Yes, but what sort of is?

"I see it still goes on," I said.

"A natural human activity," said Dave with a slight frown. Then he looked at me amiably.

"I hear you are in a kettle of fish," he said, raising his voice somewhat above the din.

"Might call it so," I said cautiously, sipping my tea. I never overdo my troubles to Dave, for he is so often sarcastic and unsympathetic about them.

"If I would be you," said Dave, "I would take a proper job." He pointed to the white wall of the hospital which loomed very close outside the window.

"There they want always orderlies," he said. "You might even be a nurse. Or you could do something for part time."

Dave was constantly making this suggestion; I can't think why, as there were few pieces of advice which, on the face of it, I was less likely to follow. I think he did it partly to annoy me. At other times he would press upon me the desirability of being a probation officer or a factory inspector or a teacher in an elementary school.

I looked at the wall of the hospital. "To save my soul," I said.

"Not therefore!" said Dave scornfully. "Always you are thinking of your soul. Precisely it is not to think of your soul, but to think of other people."

I could see that there was something in this, though I didn't need Dave to point it out, and I couldn't see that there was anything to be done about it at the moment. Finn threw me a cigarette. In a mild way he always tried to protect me from Dave. The immediate problem was to find a sympathetic place to live, and until this was fixed nothing else mattered. I have to keep on writing if I'm to make ends meet, and when I am homeless I can settle down to nothing.

When I'd finished my tea I set off on a quiet tour of Dave's flat. Living-room, Dave's bedroom, spare room, bathroom and kitchen. I inspected the spare room with care. It also looked out onto the wall of the hospital, which at this point seemed to stand even closer. The room was painted a sickly golden brown and was spartan in its appointments. At the moment it was strewn with Finn's belongings. It could be worse. As I was examining the wardrobe, Dave came in. He knew very well what was in my mind.

"No, Jake," he said. "Definitely not."

"Why not?"

"We must not be two nervous wrecks living together."

"You old python!" I said. Dave is not a nervous wreck,

but as tough as an old boot. I didn't argue though, because I was a little off the idea myself because of Jehovah and the Trinity. "Since you're turning me out," I said, "you are in duty bound to make a constructive suggestion."

"You were never in, Jake," said Dave, "but I will try to think." Dave knows my requirements. We went back to the other room and the din broke over us again.

"You should try the ladies, not?"

"Not," I said. "I've had the ladies."

"Sometimes you make me sick, Jake."

"I can't help my psychology. After all, freedom is only an idea."

"It's in the third *Critique*," Dave shouted to someone across the room.

"Which ladies, anyway?" I asked.

"I don't know your women," said Dave, "but if you paid a few visits someone might give you an idea."

I felt that Dave would be more pleased to see me when I had established myself elsewhere. Finn, who was lying with his head under the table, suddenly said, "Try Anna Quentin." Finn sometimes has the most extraordinary intuitions.

This name stuck into me like a dart. "How can I?" I said. "Nothing could be more impossible," I added.

"Ah, you are still so," said Dave.

"I am not so at all," I said. "Anyway I have no notion where she is." And I turned away from them toward the window. I don't like people reading things in my face.

"He's off!" said Dave, who knows me well.

"Suggest something else," I said.

"I suggest you are a big fool," said Dave. "Society should take you by the neck and shake you and make you do a sensible job. Then in your evenings you would have the possibility to write a great book."

I could see that Dave was in one of his bad moods. The noise was mounting. With my foot I pushed my suitcase under the table beside Finn.

"Can I leave this here?"

How do you know which is your real self anyway? some-one was asking.

"You can leave them both here," said Dave.

"I'll ring up later," I said. And I left them.

*   *   *

I was still in some pain from the name that Finn had uttered. But in the midst of the pain a queer melody had been set going; a little flute that piped me to be away. It was not of course that I had the slightest intention of looking for Anna, but I wanted to be alone with the thought of her. I am not a mystic about women. I like the women in novels by James and Conrad who are so peculiarly flower-like and who are described as "guileless, profound, confident and trustful". That "profound" is good; fluttering white hands and as deep as the sea. But I have never met any of these women in real life. I like to read about them, but then I like to read about Pegasus and Chrysaor. The women that I know are often inexperienced, inarticulate, credulous and simple; but I see no reason to call them deep because they manifest qualities which would make us call men self-absorbed. Or if they are cunning they deceive themselves and others in much the same way as men do. It is the same deception that we are all involved in; except in so far as women are always a little more unbalanced by the part they have to act. Like high-heeled shoes which shift the inward organs in the course of time. Few things disgust me more than these pretended profundities.

Yet I had found Anna deep. I cannot think what it is about her that would justify me in calling her mysterious, and yet she always seemed to me to be an unfathomable being. Dave once said to me that to find a person inexhaustible is simply the definition of love, so perhaps I loved Anna. She has a husky-speaking voice and a tenderly moulded face which is constantly lit by a warm intent glow from within. It is a face full of yearning, yet poised upon itself without any trace of discontent. She has heavy brown hair which is piled up in curving archaic coils, or was when I knew her first. All that was a long time ago. Anna is six years older than I am, and when I first met her she did a singing act with her sister Sadie. Anna provided the voice and Sadie provided the flash. Anna has a contralto voice that would break your heart even over the radio; and she makes little gestures while she sings which make her quite irresistible face to face. She seems to throw the song into your heart, at least this was what she did to me the first time I heard her, and I never got over it.

Anna is about as like her sister as a sweet blackbird is like some sort of rather dangerous tropical fish, and later on the act broke up. This was partly I think because they couldn't stand each other, and partly because their ambitions diverged. About this period, if you remember, British films were passing through a critical phase. The Bounty Belfounder Company had just been set up, and old Phantasifilms Ltd. had come into new hands. But neither company seemed able to discover any new stars, although there were the usual old faithfuls, and time and again some youngster would receive the routine press fanfare and then pass away in the course of one picture with the noise and the brevity of a firework. Phantasifilms evidently decided that human beings were bad box office and started on their series of animal pictures, and they did make one or two discoveries in the animal kingdom: notably of course the Alsatian, Mister Mars, whose sentimental escapes probably saved them from bankruptcy. Bounty Belfounder was from the start a much more successful concern, and it was in this region that Sadie soon set about selling her talents; and Sadie, as you know, did turn out to be a star.

A star is a curious phenomenon. It is not at all the same thing as a good screen actress; it is not even a matter of charm or beauty. What makes the star is some quality of surface and *éclat*. Sadie had *éclat;* or so the public thought, though personally I still prefer the word "flash". You will have gathered that I am not keen on Sadie. Sadie is glossy and dazzling. She is younger than Anna and has Anna's features, only smaller and tighter, as if someone had started to shrink her head but had never got beyond the first stage. She has a speaking voice not unlike Anna's, only with the husky note made more metallic. Not chestnut husks but rusty iron. Some people find this very fascinating too. She can't sing.

Anna never tried to get into films. I don't know why; she always seemed to me to have much greater potentialities than Sadie. But perhaps her façade had a certain superficial lack of definiteness. You need to be a vessel with a sharp prow to get into the film world. After she parted from Sadie, Anna did a certain amount of more serious singing; but she lacked the training necessary to take her far in the world. When I last heard of her she was singing folksongs in a night club, and that sort of combination expressed her very well.

Anna used to live in a tiny service flat off the Bayswater Road, very much overlooked by other houses, and I would go there often to see her. I was greatly attached to her, but I could see even then that her character was not all that it should be. Anna is one of those women who cannot bear to reject any offer of love. It is not exactly that it flatters her. She has a talent for personal relations, and she yearns for love as a poet yearns for an audience. To anyone who will take the trouble to become attached to her she will immediately give a devoted, generous, imaginative and completely uncapricious attention, which is still a calculated avoidance of self-surrender. This is no doubt another reason why she never went into films; her private life must be an almost full-time activity. This has the sad result too that her existence is one long act of disloyalty; and when I knew her she was constantly involved in secrecy and lying in order to conceal from each of her friends the fact that she was so closely bound to all the others. Or sometimes she would try another technique, that of deadening, by small and steady shocks, the sharpness of jealousy, until in the end the victim became resigned to the liberal scope of her affections, while remaining just as much her slave as ever. I don't care for this; and I saw through Anna very rapidly. Yet my interpretation of her never robbed her of her mystery, nor did her emotional promiscuity ever turn me against her. Perhaps this was because I so constantly felt, like the warm breeze that blows from a longed-for island bringing to the seafarer the scent of flowers and fruit, the strength and reality of her tenderness for me. I knew that it was very possible that it was with exactly this charm that she held all her admirers. But it made no difference.

You may wonder whether I ever thought of marrying Anna. I did think of it. But marriage remains for me an Idea of Reason, a concept which may regulate but not constitute my life. I cannot help, whenever I consider a woman, using the possibility of marriage as an illuminating hypothesis which is not in any serious sense an instrument of the actual. With Anna, however, I did come near to taking the thing seriously; and that, although I'm sure she would never have said yes, was perhaps why I let myself drift away from her in the end. I hate solitude, but I am afraid of intimacy. The substance of my life is a private conversation with myself which to turn into a dialogue would be equivalent to self-destruction. The company which I need is the company which a pub or a café will provide. I have never wanted a communion of souls. It's already hard enough to tell the truth to oneself. But communion of souls was Anna's special subject. Also, Anna had a taste for tragedy which made me nervous. She always had her eye lifting for heavy drama. She took life intensely and very hard. Whereas I think it is foolish to take life so, as if you were to provoke a dangerous animal which will break your bones in the end in any case. So when Anna went to France to sing French folksongs in French night clubs I said to her vaguely that I would look her up when she returned, but she knew I wouldn't and I knew she knew. That was some years ago, and I'd had a peaceful time since then, especially at Earls Court Road.

When I left Dave's I walked to Shepherd's Bush and boarded an eighty-eight bus and sat in the front seat on top,

and some of the reflexions which I have recorded above
were passing through my mind. It's not easy to find someone whom one has mislaid for years in London, particularly
if she belongs to the sort of milieu that Anna belonged to, but
clearly the first thing to do is to look in the telephone book.
So I got off at Oxford Circus and went into the Under-
ground. When I left Goldhawk Road I had no intention of
looking for Anna, but by the time I was passing Bond Street
it really seemed that there was nothing else in the world that
was worth doing. Indeed, it was unclear to me how I had
managed to exist without her for so long. But I am like that.
For long times I settle down, and in these times I would not
stir a finger to lift a guinea a yard off. When I am fixed I am
immobile. But when I am unfixed I am volatile, and then I
fly at random from point to point like a firecracker or one
of Heisenberg's electrons until I settle down again in another
safe place. Also I had a curious faith in Finn's intuition. It
often happened that Finn made some unexpected suggestion
which when I followed it up turned out to have been just the
thing. I could see that the Earls Court Road phase of my
life was over, and that that peace of mind was gone beyond
recall. Madge had forced a crisis on me; well, I would
explore it, I would even exploit it. Who can tell what day
may not inaugurate a new era? I picked up the London
phone book L to R.

The phone book told me nothing; I wasn't surprised. I
then rang up two theatre agencies who didn't know Anna's
whereabouts, and the B.B.C., who did but wouldn't say.
I thought of trying to get hold of Sadie at the Belfounder
studio, but I didn't want Sadie to know that I was looking
for Anna. I suspected Sadie of having been a little sweet
on me at one time; at any rate she was always rather unpleasant in the old days about my being fond of Anna,
although I know that some women regard all men as their
personal property, and I thought it possible that she
wouldn't tell me where Anna was even if she knew. Anyway,
since Sadie had become so famous I had seen nothing of her,
and I didn't imagine that she would welcome any attempt

on my part to renew the acquaintance, particularly if she had been aware that I had been aware of what I conjectured to have been the state of her feelings. By now it was about opening time. It seemed useless to start ringing up the night clubs at this hour, so there was nothing to be done but to work Soho. There is always someone in Soho who knows what one wants to discover; it's just a matter of finding him. Also there was always the possibility of my running into Anna herself. My fates are such that as soon as I interest myself in a thing a hundred accidents happen which are precisely relevant to that thing. But I rather hoped that I wouldn't meet Anna first in a public place, for my mind had already begun to run very much upon this meeting.

I usually keep clear of Soho, partly because it's so bad for the nerves and partly because it's so expensive. It's expensive not so much because the nervous tension makes one drink continually as because of the people who come and take one's money away. I am very bad at refusing people who ask me for money. I can never think of a reason why if I have more ready cash than they have I should not be bound to give them some at least of what I have. I give with resentment but without hesitation. By the time I had worked my way along Brewer Street and Old Compton Street and up Greek Street as far as the Pillars of Hercules most of the money in my pocket had been taken away by various acquaintances. I was feeling extremely nervous by this time, not only because of Soho but because of imagining whenever I entered a pub that I should find Anna inside. I had been to these pubs a hundred times in the last few years without this thought coming into my head; but now suddenly the whole of London had become an empty frame. Every place lacked her and expected her. I began to drink spirits.

When I found myself short of money I crossed the street to cash a cheque at one of my afternoon drinking clubs that lay close by; and it was there that at last I picked up the trail. I asked the barman if he knew where Anna was to be found these days. He replied yes, he thought that she was running some sort of little theatre in Hammersmith. He searched under the bar and produced a card which bore the words *The Riverside Theatre,* and an address on Hammersmith Mall. The barman said he didn't know whether she was still there, but that that's where she was some months ago. She had left him this card to give to some gentleman who had never turned up. I might as well have it now, the barman said. I took it, and went into the street with my heart pounding. It needed serious reflexion on the state of my finances to prevent me from taking a taxi to Hammersmith. But I ran all the way to Leicester Square station.

Three

THE address I had been given was on that part of the
Mall that lies between the Doves and the Black Lion.
On Chiswick Mall the houses face the river, but on that
piece of Hammersmith Mall which is relevant to my tale
they turn their backs to the river and pretend to be an
ordinary street. Chiswick Mall is a lazy hazy collection of
houses and greenery that looks dreamily out on to the water,
but Hammersmith Mall is a labyrinth of waterworks and
laundries with pubs and Georgian houses in between, which
sometimes face the river and sometimes back it. The number to which I had been directed turned out to be a house
standing a little by itself, with its back to the river and its
front on a quiet piece of street, and an opening beside it
where some steps led down to the water.

By now I was in no such hurry. I looked at the house
with suspicious curiosity, and it seemed to be looking
back at me. It was a brooding self-absorbed sort of house,
fronted by a small ragged garden and a wall shoulder
high. The house was square, with rows of tall windows,
and had preserved a remnant of elegance. I approached
the iron gate in the wall. It was then that I observed a
poster which was fixed on the other side of the gate.
It was a home-made poster whose colours were running
a bit, so that it had a rather sad appearance. I deciphered
it. It said:

RIVERSIDE MIMING THEATRE

Re-opening on August 1st with a luxurious and fanciful
production of Ivan Lazemnikov's great farce MARISHKA.
Members only. The audience is requested to laugh softly
and not to applaud.

I stared at this object for some time. I don't know why,
but it struck me as queer. Finally, with a slow crescendo

in the region of the heart I pushed open the gate, which
was a little rusty, and walked up to the house. The windows gleamed blackly, like eyes behind dark glasses. The
door was newly painted. I did not look for a bell, but
tried the handle at once. The door opened quietly and I
stepped on tiptoe into the hall. An oppressive silence
surged out of the place like a cloud. I closed the door
and shut out all the little noises of the river front. Now
there was nothing but the silence.

I stood perfectly still for a while until my breathing became more regular, and until I could see my way in the
dark hall. As I did these things I was asking myself why I
was behaving in such an odd way, but the possible proximity
of Anna confused me completely, so that I couldn't think
but could only perform the little series of actions which
suggested themselves with a feeling of inevitability. I walked
slowly down the hall, planting my feet with care on a long
black sound-absorbing rug. When I came to the stairs I
glided up them; I suppose my feet touched the steps. I
could hear no sound.

I found myself on a broad landing, with a carved wooden
balustrade behind me and several doors in front of me.
Everything seemed neat and nicely appointed. The carpets
were thick, and the woodwork as clean as an apple. I looked
about me. It didn't occur to me to doubt that Anna was
somewhere near, any more than it occurred to me to call her
name or utter any other sound. I moved to the nearest door
and opened it wide. Then I got a shock that stiffened me
from head to toe.

I was looking straight into seven or eight pairs of staring
eyes, which seemed to be located a few feet from my face.
I stepped back hastily, and the door swung to again with a
faint click which was the first sound I had heard since I
entered the house. I stood still for a moment in utter incomprehension, my scalp prickling. Then I seized the
handle firmly and opened the door again, stepping as I
did so into the doorway. The faces had moved, but were
still turned towards me; and then in an instant I under-

stood. I was in the gallery of a tiny theatre. The gallery, sloping and foreshortened, seemed to give immediately onto the stage; and on the stage were a number of actors, moving silently to and fro, and wearing masks which they kept turned toward the auditorium. These masks were a little larger than life, and this fact accounted for the extraordinary impression of closeness which I had received when I first opened the door. My perceptual field now adjusted itself, and I looked with fascinated interest and surprise upon the strange scene.

The masks were not attached to the face, but mounted upon a rod which the actor held in his right hand and skilfully maintained in parallel to the footlights, so that no hint of the actor's real features could be seen. Most of the masks were made full face, but two of them, which were worn by the only two women on the scene, were made in profile. The mask features were grotesque and stylized, but with a certain queer beauty. I noticed particularly the two female masks, one of them sensual and serene, and the other nervous, watchful, hypocritical. These two masks had the eyes filled in, but the male masks had empty eyes through which the eyes of the actors gleamed oddly. All were dressed in white, the men in white peasant shirts and breeches, and the women in plain ankle-length white robes caught in at the waist. I wondered if this was Lazemnikov's great farce *Marishka*; both *Marishka* and its author were equally strange to me.

The actors meanwhile were continuing to execute their movements in the extraordinary silence which seemed to keep the whole house spellbound. I saw that they were wearing soft close-fitting slippers and that the stage was carpeted. They moved about the stage with gliding or slouching movements, turning their masked heads from side to side, and I observed something of that queer expressiveness of neck and shoulder in which Indian dancers excel. Their left hands performed a variety of simple conventional gestures. I had never seen mime quite like this before. The effect was hypnotic. What was going on was not clear to

me, but it seemed that a huge burly central figure, wearing
a mask which expressed a sort of humble yearning stupidity,
was being mocked by the other players. I examined the two
women carefully, wondering if either of them was Anna;
but I was certain that neither was. I should have known her
at once. Then my attention was caught by the burly simpleton. For some time I stared at the mask, with its grotesque
immobility and the flash of eyes behind it. A sort of force
seemed to radiate from those eyes which entered into me
with a gentle shock. I stared and stared. There was something about that hulking form that seemed vaguely
familiar.

At that moment, with one of the movements, the stage
creaked, and the backcloth shivered slightly. This sound
brought me to myself, and brought with it the sudden alarming realization that the actors could see me. On tiptoe I
moved back onto the landing and closed the door. The
silence was over me like a great bell, but the whole place
throbbed with a soundless vibration which it took me a
moment to recognize as the beating of my own heart. I
turned now to look at the other doors. One at the far end
of the landing had a little notice on it. I read, in large letters,
Props Room, and underneath in smaller letters, *Miss
Quentin*. I closed my eyes for a moment and stilled my
breathing. Then I knocked.

The sound echoed strangely. Then a husky voice said:
"Come in."

I stepped into the room. It was a long narrow room with
large windows opening onto the river, and it was filled to
overflowing with a sort of multicoloured chaos which I
couldn't at the first moment take in. In the midst of this
Anna sat writing at a desk with her back to me. I shut the
door behind me as she turned slowly. For a long moment
we looked at each other in silence. Like a filling glass I felt
my soul rise into my eyes; and in the intense equilibrium of
the meeting we both experienced almost a moment of
contemplation. Anna got up and said "Jake!" Then I saw
her.

She was plumper and had not defended herself against time. There was about her a sort of wrecked look which was infinitely touching. Her face, which I remembered as round and smooth as an apricot, was become just a little tense and drawn, and her neck now revealed her age. The great brown eyes, which once opened so blandly upon the world, seemed narrowed, and where Anna had used to draw a dark line upward at their corners the years had sketched in a little sheaf of wrinkles. Tresses of hair which had escaped from the complex coronet curled about her neck, and I could see streaks of grey. I looked upon the face that I had known so well and now that for the first time I saw its beauty as mortal I felt that I had never loved it so dearly. Anna took in my glance, and then with an instinctive gesture she took refuge behind her hands.

"What brings you here, Jake?" said Anna.

The spell was broken. "I wanted to see you," I said; and now I was anxious just to avoid looking at her and to collect my wits. I looked around the room. An astonishing medley of objects lay about in piles which in places reached up to the ceiling. The contents of the room had a sort of strange cohesion and homogeneity, and they seemed to adhere to the walls like the contents of a half-empty jam jar. Yet here was every kind of thing. It was like a vast toy shop that had been hit by a bomb. In my first glance I noticed a French horn, a rocking-horse, a set of red-striped tin trumpets, some Chinese silk robes, a couple of rifles, Paisley shawls, teddy bears, glass balls, tangles of necklaces and other jewellery, a convex mirror, a stuffed snake, countless toy animals, and a number of tin trunks out of which multi-coloured costumes trailed. Exquisite and expensive playthings lay enlaced with the gimcrack contents of Christmas crackers. I sat down on the nearest seat, which happened to be the back of the rocking-horse, and surveyed the scene.

"What is this extraordinary place?" I said. "What are you doing these days, Anna?"

"Oh, this and that," said Anna. She had always used to

say this when she didn't want to tell me something. I could see she was nervous, and as she talked she kept picking things up, now a piece of ribbon, or now a ball or a long band of Brussels lace.

"How did you find this place?" she asked. I told her.

"Why did you come?"

I didn't want to embark on a routine series of questions and answers. What did it matter why I had come? I didn't know myself.

"I've been turned out of a place where I live." This wasn't very explicit, but I couldn't think of anything to tell but the truth.

"Oh!" said Anna.

Then she asked, "What have you been doing all these years?"

I wished I had something impressive to say, but again I could think of nothing but the truth. "I've done some translating and some broadcasting," I said. "I've managed."

But I could see Anna wasn't really listening to my replies. She picked up a pair of red gloves, and pulled one of them on, smoothing out the fingers and averting her eyes from me.

"Seen any of our old friends, lately?" she asked.

I felt I really couldn't answer this. "Who cares about our old friends?" I said.

What is more tormenting than a meeting after a long time, when all the words fall to the ground like dead things, and the spirit that should animate them floats disembodied in the air? We both felt its presence.

"You look just the same, Jake," said Anna. It was true. I still look much as I did when I was twenty-four.

She added, "I wish I did!"

"You look lovely," I said.

Anna laughed, and picked up a wreath of artificial flowers. "What a mess this place is!" she said. "I keep meaning to tidy it."

"It's lovely too," I said.

"Well, if you call *this* lovely!" said Anna.

All this time she avoided my eye. In a moment we should be talking soberly like two old acquaintances. I wasn't going to allow this. I looked at her, and amid the enchanting chaos of silks and animals and improbable objects that seemed to rise almost to her waist she looked like a very wise mermaid rising out of a motley coloured sea; but in a moment she would have escaped me. The strangeness of the whole day was suddenly present to me with a kind of impetus; and immediately I had an idea. In the old days the living-room of Anna's Bayswater flat had been so surrounded by other windows that there was only one corner of the room, low down on the floor, which was not overlooked. So if I wanted to kiss Anna this was the only place where I could do it. At that time too I had, in a not entirely disinterested fashion, been teaching Anna some Judo, and one of our customs had been that when I came in I would seize her and throw her down into this corner to be kissed. The memory of this rose in me now like an inspiration and I advanced upon her. I took her wrist, and for an instant saw her eyes wide with alarm, very close to mine, and then in a moment I had thrown her, very carefully, onto a pile of velvet costumes in the corner of the room. My knee sank into the velvet beside her, and straightaway a mass of scarves, laces, tin trumpets, woolly dogs, fancy hats and other objects came cascading down on top of us until we were half buried. I kissed Anna.

Her eyes were still wide and her lips parted and for a moment she lay stiffly in my arms like a great doll. Then she began to laugh, and I laughed too, and we both laughed enormously with pleasure and relief. I felt her sigh and relax, and her body became rounded and pliant, and we looked into each other's faces and smiled a long smile of confidence and recognition.

"Darling Anna!" I said. "However have I existed without you!" I pulled some embroidered silk up behind her head to make a pillow. She threw her back into it and regarded me and then drew me closer.

"I want to tell you all sorts of things, Jake," said Anna, "but I don't know whether I can now. I'm terribly glad to see you. You can see that, can't you?" She looked into my eyes and I felt the old warm spicy breeze blowing. Of course I couldn't doubt it.

"You crook!" I said.

Anna laughed at me as she had always done. "So some girl has thrown you out!" said Anna. She always counter-attacked.

"You know you could have had me forever if you'd wanted me," I said. I wasn't going to let her get away with it, and what I said was more or less true after all.

"I loved you," I added.

"Oh, love, love!" said Anna. "How tired I am of that word. What has love ever meant to me but creaking stairs in other people's houses? What use has all this love ever been that men forced on me? Love is persecution. All I want is to be left alone to do some loving on my own account."

I contemplated her coolly, framing her head in my arms. "You wouldn't be so careless of it if you'd ever lacked the love of others," I said.

She met my look now, and there was something detached and theoretical in her eye which I had never noticed there before.

"No really, Jake," she said. "This talk of love means very little. Love is not a feeling. It can be tested. Love is action, it is silence. It's not the emotional straining and scheming for possession that you used to think it was."

This seemed to me very foolish talk. "But love *is* concerned with possession," I said. "If you knew anything about unsatisfied love, you'd know this."

"No," said Anna strangely. "Unsatisfied love is concerned with understanding. Only if it is all, all understanding, can it remain love while being unsatisfied."

I was not listening to this serious speech because my attention had been caught by the word "silence".

"What is this place, Anna?" I asked.

"That's one of the things that would be hard to explain, Jakie," said Anna, and I could feel her hands seeking each other in the small of my back. She locked me to her, then she said, "It's a little experiment."

This phrase grated on me. It didn't sound like Anna at all. There was some other voice here. I thought I would pick my way round this.

"What about your singing?" I asked.

"Oh, I've given up singing," said Anna. "I shan't sing any more." Her glance fled away over my shoulder and she withdrew her hands.

"Why in heaven's name not, Anna?"

"Well," said Anna, and I could still sense the curious artificiality in her tone, "I don't care for that way of earning a living. The sort of singing I do is so"—she searched for the word—"ostentatious. There's no truth in it. One's just exploiting one's charm to seduce people."

I took her by the shoulders and shook her. "You don't believe what you're saying!" I cried.

"I do, Jake!" Anna looked up at me almost imploringly.

"How about the theatre?" I asked. "How does that come in?"

"This is pure art," said Anna. "It's very simple and it's very pure."

"Anna, who's been getting at you?" I asked her.

"Jake," said Anna, "you were always like that. As soon as I said anything that surprised you, you said that someone had been getting at me!"

During the last part of our conversation she had laid her hand upon my shoulder so that her wrist watch was just in sight, and I could see her gaze passing lightly over it from time to time. I felt furious.

"Stop looking at your watch!" I said. "You haven't seen me for years. You can spare me a little time now!"

I guessed that Anna had it in mind that very soon our tête-à-tête would be interrupted. Our interview had a schedule of which Anna was continuously aware. All Anna's life worked to schedule; like a nun, she would have been lost without her watch. I took the wrist with the watch upon it, and twisted it until I heard her gasp. She faced me now with an intensity and a bright silent defiance which I remembered and loved from long ago. We regarded each other so for a moment. We knew each other very well. I kept her pinioned, but released the tension enough for us to kiss. Her body was tense again, but now it was as if my grip had communicated to it some positive force, and it was like a rigid missile to which I clung as we hurtled through space. I kissed her stiffened neck and shoulder.

"Jake, you're hurting me," said Anna.

I let her go and lay heavily upon her breasts, completely limp. She stroked my hair. We lay so in silence for a long time. The universe came to rest like a great bird.

"You're going to say that I must go," I said.

"You must," said Anna, "or rather, I must. Now get up, please."

I got up, and I felt as if I were rising from sleep. I looked down on Anna. She lay amid the coloured debris like a fairy-tale princess tumbled from her throne. The silks were at hip and breast. A long tress of hair had escaped. She lay still for a moment, receiving my gaze, her foot arching with consciousness of it.

"Where's your crown?" I asked.

Anna searched under the pile and produced a gilded coronet. We laughed. I helped her up and we dusted bits of tinsel, gold dust and loose spangles off her dress.

While Anna did her hair I ranged about the room, examining everything. I suddenly felt quite at ease now. I knew that I should see Anna again.

"You must explain about this place," I said. "Who acts here?"

"Mainly amateurs," said Anna. "Some of my friends. But it's a quite special technique."

"Yes, I could see that," I said.

Anna turned on me. "So you went into the theatre?"

"Yes, just for an instant. Did it matter? It looked very impressive," I said. "Is it something Indian?"

"There are connexions with India," said Anna, "but it's really something on its own." I could see she was thinking of something else.

"Well, that's a prop you'll hardly need much!" I said, pointing to the thundersheet.

A thundersheet, in case you don't know, is a thin piece of metal, a couple of yards square, which when shaken produces a mysterious rumbling noise not unlike thunder. I went up to it.

"Don't touch it!" said Anna. "Yes, we're going to sell that."

"Anna, did you mean it about singing?" I asked.

"Yes," said Anna, "it's corrupt," she said. I had again the curious feeling of seeing someone in the grip of a theory.

"Only very simple things can be said without falsehood," she added.

"What I saw in that theatre wasn't simple," I told her.

Anna spread her hands. "What did you want me for?" she asked.

This question brought me back to reality. I said cautiously, "I wanted to see you. You know that. But I've also got a problem about somewhere to live. Perhaps you can advise me. I suppose I couldn't live here," I asked, "in an attic or something?"

Anna shivered. "No," she said, "that would be impossible."

We looked at each other, both thinking fast.

"When shall I see you again?" I asked.

Anna's face was rigid and withdrawn. "Jake," she said, "you must leave me alone for a while. I have a lot of things to think about."

"So have I," I said. "We might think together."

She smiled a pale smile. "If I need you I'll call for you," she said. "And I may need you."

"I hope you will," I said, and I wrote Dave's address for her on a piece of paper. "I give you notice that if a long time passes without my being needed I shall appear whether I'm needed or not."

Anna was looking at her watch again.

"May I write to you?" I asked. In my experience women who have any interest at all in keeping a hand on you will rarely refuse this. It binds without compromising. Anna, who knew my thoughts on this topic, as on most others, eyed me, and we both smiled.

"I don't mind," she said. "A letter to the theatre finds me."

She was picking up her things now and frowning slightly. It occurred to me that the problem that preoccupied her was how to get me out of the building without being seen.

"I haven't anywhere to sleep to-night," I told her : my first lie. "May I stay here?"

Anna eyed me again, wondering how much I knew about what she was thinking. She considered it.

"All right," she said. "Stay here—and don't come down with me now. Only you must promise not to prowl around and to leave the place early to-morrow." I promised.

"Suggest where I can live, Anna," I said.

I thought that now that she'd come as far as letting me stay the night she might relent in the matter of an attic. Anna set her desk in order and locked the drawers.

"Look," she said. "You might try Sadie. She's going to the States and she wants a caretaker to look after her flat. You might just do." She scribbled down an address.

I took it with reserve. "Are you friends with Sadie now?" I asked.

Anna laughed a bit impatiently. "She's my sister. We put up with each other. You could go and see her anyway— this idea might just work." And she looked at me doubtfully.

"Well, let's meet to-morrow and discuss it some more," I suggested.

This decided Anna. "No," she said. "You go and see Sadie—and don't come back here unless I summon you."

She turned to go. I took her hand, and then embraced her

with immense tenderness. She returned the embrace. We parted.

I heard no sound after the door closed, and for some time I stood as one enchanted in the middle of the room. During my talk with Anna it had become quite dark in the room, but outside it was still a late blue summer evening that made the trees and the river vibrate with colour. Some little while later I heard the sound of a car starting. I went to the window, and by leaning out a little could command a piece of the roadway. As I looked out a luxurious black Alvis purred round the corner and up toward the main road. I wondered if Anna was inside. For the moment I hardly cared. As for her ambiguous dismissal of me, I was used to this. Most of the women I know behave in this way, and I have become accustomed to asking no questions, and even to thinking no questions. We all live in the interstices of each other's lives, and we would all get a surprise if we could see everything. I knew that there was a man in it somewhere; there always was where Anna was concerned. But that speculation could wait.

I was glad to be alone. I had had what was for me an intolerably eventful day—and now for a long time I leaned on the window sill, looking down toward Hammersmith Bridge. The river murmured past, carrying with it the last fragments of daylight, and finally it became a dark gulf of unseen movement. I thought over my meeting with Anna. She had said some strange things, but it was not on these that I was brooding. I was remembering the way she moved her hands, her nervous gestures as she fingered now a ball and now a necklace, the curve of her thigh as she lay on the floor, the grey locks in her hair, the weariness at her neck. All this called up what seemed to me to be a new love, a hundred times more profound than the old one. I was deeply moved. Yet at the same time I took the thing with a grain of salt. I had often known myself to be moved in the past, and little had come of it. What was certain was that something had remained intact of that which there had formerly been between us; and it could not be but that the passage of time had somehow made this remnant the more precious. I thought with some satisfaction of our interview and how splendidly Anna had responded to all the old cues.

Street lamps were lighted now on the bridge, and far away the dark river ran into a crackle of light. I turned back into the room and stumbled my way to the door. I clicked the electric-light switch, and somewhere in the corner a lamp went on, buried under a covering of gauzy materials. Anna had asked me not to prowl; but it had been rather a vague prohibition, and I thought that just a little prowling might be in order. I felt a great desire to stand again in the little theatre; indeed, it had been largely for this that I had asked Anna on the spur of the moment to let me stay. By the dim light I found the switch on the landing, and closing the door of the props room behind me I went to the door of the theatre. I would not have been surprised to find the silent mime still in progress there in the dark. I tried the door, but it was locked. I tried the other doors on the landing and then the doors in the hall-way downstairs. To my great exasperation they were all locked. Then the stillness of the place began to choke me like a mist, and a sudden panic came over me in case I should come back and find the door of the props room locked too. I ran noiselessly up the stairs again and bounded into the room. The lamp still burnt dimly and all was as before. I thought of going outside and trying to get into the auditorium from the road, but some spirit forbade me to leave the house. I removed two or three layers of textiles from the lamp and surveyed the room. It looked, in this half light, more fantastic than ever. I wandered about for a while, picking up the objects which Anna had handled. My gaze kept returning to the thunder-sheet and I felt a nervous urge to rush up to it and strike it. I thought of all the superb noise that lay asleep there, and how I could make the whole house rock with it. I made myself almost sweat with nervousness imagining it. But something compelled me to silence, and I even walked about on tiptoe.

After a while I began to have an uneasy feeling of being observed. I am very sensitive to observation, and often have this feeling not only in the presence of human beings but in that of small animals. Once I even traced the source of it to a large spider whose mysterious eyes were fixed upon me. In my experience the spider is the smallest creature whose gaze can be felt. I now began to search around to see what it could be that was looking at me. I could find no living thing, but eventually I came upon a set of masks, similar to those I had seen on the stage, whose slanting eyes were turned mournfully in my direction. No doubt I had noticed them unconsciously as I was rambling about the room. I now examined them with care and was struck by the unnerving beauty of their design, and the serenity which was expressed by even the more unpleasant ones. They were made of a light wooden material, and slightly painted, some full face and some in profile. There was something a trifle oriental in their mood, something which spoke more even perhaps in the subtly curving mouth than in the slanting eyes. One or two of them distantly reminded me of Indian Buddhas I had seen. They were all a bit larger than life. I found them very alarming objects indeed and put them down nervously after a little while. They clattered dully as I released them and that made me start and experience the silence anew. Then I began to discern that the room was full of eyes, the big vacant eyes of the rocking-horse, the beady eyes of teddy bears, the red eyes of the stuffed snake, the eyes of dolls and puppets and gollywogs. I began to feel extremely uneasy. I took the remaining pieces of gauze off the lamp, but even then it gave precious little light. Something in the far corner subsided softly. I sat down cross-legged in the middle of the floor and tried to think about something realistic.

I took from my pocket the piece of paper which Anna had given me. It bore an address in Welbeck Street. I looked at it, and wondered to myself, in a spirit of prediction rather than intention, whether I would ever present myself at Sadie's door. I felt reluctant to, for the reasons already mentioned. On the other hand, the whole matter looked different now that it was Anna who had suggested that I should see Sadie. If Anna and Sadie were friends, then to consort with Sadie was one way of keeping in touch with Anna. Also I was curious, now that I reflected on the matter, to see how Sadie would receive me. Finally, few people are so free of earthly vanity as not to find it pleasant, other things being equal, to be on matey terms with someone whose face is displayed all over London on posters twelve feet high. It then struck me how absolutely splendid it would be if Sadie did in fact go away and leave me in possession of a luxurious rent-free flat with a central address. This seemed so highly desirable that it was certainly worth risking a rebuff to obtain. It began to seem to me very likely indeed that I would at least investigate the situation at Welbeck Street.

When I had reached this purely inductive conclusion about my future movements I felt better and at once began to be very sleepy. The floor was so encumbered with objects that I had to set to work to clear myself a space. A strip of stained white carpet began to emerge. Then I looked about for something to use as a blanket. There was no lack of textiles. In the end I selected a bearskin complete with snout and claws. I didn't switch out the light, but covered the lamp up again with gauzy stuffs until it gave only a faint glow. I didn't want to risk waking up later and finding myself alone in the dark in such a room. Then I thrust my hands and feet into the bear's paws and let the great snarling snout fall over my forehead. It made a snug sleeping-suit. Before I finally curled up I thought some more about Anna and about what in the world she could be up to. I could believe that this theatre was Anna's creation; and yet clearly there was some other mind at work as well, and some of the things which Anna had said were certainly not her own. It also occurred to me to wonder where the money had come from. At last I yawned and stretched myself out. An oriental shawl served me as a pillow. Soft objects were falling onto my feet. Then there was stillness. Sleep never forsakes me or makes me wait for long after it is bidden. Almost at once I fell asleep.

Four

THE next day round about ten o'clock I was walking down Welbeck Street. I was in a bad temper. By daylight the whole project seemed very much less attractive. I felt that to be snubbed by a film star would put me in a bad state of mind for months. But I regarded the matter as something which had been decided and which now simply had to be carried out. I often use this method for deciding difficult cases. In stage one I entertain the thing purely as a hypothesis, and in stage two I count my stage one thinking as a fixed decision on which there is no going back. I recommend this technique to any of you who are not good at making decisions. I felt a certain temptation to return to the theatre to see if I could find Anna again, but I was afraid of offending her. So there was nothing to be done but to get over with seeing Sadie.

Sadie's flat was on the third floor, and I found the door open. A naïve char appeared who told me that Miss Quentin was not at home. She then informed me that Miss Quentin was at the hairdresser, and she named an expensive Mayfair establishment. I had taken the precaution of mentioning that I was Miss Quentin's cousin. I thanked her and set off again towards Oxford Street. I have often visited women in hairdressing establishments and the idea held no terrors for me. Indeed I find that women are often especially charitable and receptive if one visits them at the hairdresser, perhaps because they like being able to show off some captive member of the male sex to so many other women when the latter are not so fortunate as to have their male retainers by them. To play this role, however, one must be presentable, and so I went straightaway to a barber's and had a good shave. After that I bought myself a new tie in a shop in Oxford Street and threw away my other tie. As I mounted the heavily perfumed stairway of Sadie's hair-dresser and caught a glimpse of myself in a mirror I thought that I looked a fine figure of a man.

Women's hairdressers obey some obscure law of nature which rules that, contrary to what is the case in other spheres, the more expensive the firm the less is the privacy given to the clients. Shop girls in Putney can have their hair done in the seclusion of a curtained cubicle, but wealthy women in Mayfair have to sit exposed in rows and watch each other being metamorphosed. I found myself in a big room where elegant heads were in various stages of assembly. A row of well-dressed backs were presented to me, and as I looked up and down searching for Sadie, I felt myself under observation in a dozen rose-tinted mirrors. I couldn't see her anywhere. I started to glide along one of the rows, look-ing into each mirror, and seeing here a young face and there an old one looking at me from under crimped and plastered locks. Each pair of eyes met mine with a questioning look until I began to feel like a prince in a fairy tale. I was glad I had thought of investing in the new tie. At the end of the row there were several figures whose heads were covered by purring electric driers. Here at last I met in the mirror a pair of eyes which were unmistakably Sadie's.

I stopped and put my hands on the back of her chair. I stood a while and looked gravely into these eyes while their owner returned my glance first with casualness, then with hostility, and at last with dawning recognition.

Sadie gave a little scream. "Jake!" she cried.

I could feel we were being looked at. I began to be pleased that I'd come.

"Hello, Sadie!" I said, and I didn't have to fake my delighted smile.

"My *dear* creature," said Sadie, "I haven't seen you for centuries! How lovely! Were you looking for me?"

I said that I was, and I fetched a chair and sat just behind her shoulder. We grinned at each other in the mirror. I thought we were a fine-looking pair. Sadie looked very handsome, even with her hair in a net, and if anything younger than ever. Even allowing for the rosy glass, her complexion was exquisite, and her brown eyes were absolutely blazing with vitality. I quite involuntarily put my hand on her arm.

"You charming fellow!" said Sadie. "What sports do you devise these days? Tell me all!"

There was an affectation in her voice and manner which struck me as new. Also she spoke in a curiously loud and ringing tone so that what she said echoed audibly all the way down the room. The explanation of this occurred to me in a moment; she was partly deafened by the purr of the drier and didn't realize how loudly she was speaking.

I replied, also raising my voice, "Oh, I'm still at the old writing game. Books, books, you know. I've got about three on hand at the moment. And publishers will keep pestering me."

"You always were such a clever chap, Jake," Sadie shouted admiringly.

Silence reigned throughout the rest of the shop except for the whispering voices of a few assistants, and I could feel every ear strained in our direction. I thought it impossible that there was anyone in the room who didn't know who Sadie was. I settled down to enjoy the conversation.

"How's life treating you?" I asked.

"Oh, it's too utterly boring," said Sadie. "I'm simply worn out with work. On the set from dawn to dusk. I've only just managed to escape to get my hair done here in peace. I've quarrelled with the hairdresser at the studio. I'm so tired, I quarrel with everyone these days." She cast me an enticing smile.

"When are you going to have dinner with me, Sadie?" I asked.

"Oh, darling," said Sadie, "I'm tied up for days and days. Someone's even coming to fetch me away from this place. You must come round some time and have a drink at my flat."

I calculated quickly. Sadie's days probably were heavily mortgaged and this might be my only opportunity of talking with her for some time. So if I was going to raise the ticklish subject it had better be done now.

"Listen, Sadie," I said, lowering my voice.

"What's that, darling?" shouted Sadie from under the drier.

"Listen!" I shouted back. "I gather that you want to let your flat while you're away."

I couldn't bring myself, in front of such an audience, to put the matter less delicately. I hoped that Sadie would pick it up with tact.

Sadie's response was even more amiable than I had bargained for. "My dear boy," she said, "don't speak of letting. I want a caretaker, in fact I want a bodyguard—and you can take on from now if you like."

"Well, I'd be very glad," I said. "The lease of my present place has just expired and I'm pretty well on the streets."

"Then, my dear, you must come at once," roared Sadie. "You'll be most enormously useful if you can just be around the place a little. You see, I'm being persecuted by the most frightful man."

This sounded interesting. I could feel the ears being pricked up all round us. I laughed in a masculine way.

"Well, I suppose I'm fairly tough," I said. "I don't mind keeping an eye on things, provided I can get some work done too." Already I had visions of something even better than Earls Court Road.

"My dear, it's an enormous flat," said Sadie. "You can have a suite of rooms. I'll just feel so much safer if you can come and stay there till I go away. This fellow is quite madly in love with me. He keeps calling and trying to get in at all hours, and when he doesn't call he rings up, and I'm just a nervous wreck."

"You won't start being afraid of me, I suppose?" I said, leering at her in the glass. Sadie went off into peals of laughter. "Jake, darling, no, you're just too utterly harmless!" she called out.

I didn't so much care for this turn in the conversation.

Out of the corner of my eye I could see several elegantly dressed women craning their necks to get a look at me. I felt we should change the subject.

"Who is this intolerable person?" I asked.

"I'm afraid it's the big chief himself, it's Belfounder," said Sadie. "So you can just imagine how embarrassing it all is. I'm simply beside myself."

At the utterance of this name I nearly fell off my chair. The room spun round and round, and I seemed to be seeing Sadie through a cloud. This altered everything. With an enormous effort I kept my face composed, but my stomach was rearing inside me like a wild cat. I wanted nothing now but to get away and think over this astonishing news.

"Are you sure?" I said to Sadie.

"My sweet boy, I know my own boss," said Sadie.

"I mean, sure that he loves you," I said.

"He's absolutely demented about me," said Sadie. "By the way," she said, "how did you know I wanted a caretaker?"

"Anna told me," I said. I was beyond caution now.

Sadie's eye glittered in the mirror. "So you're seeing Anna again," said Sadie.

I hate that sort of remark. "You know Anna and I are old friends," I said.

"Yes, but you haven't been seeing her for ages, have you?" said Sadie, still at the top of her voice.

I began to dislike the conversation very much indeed. I just wanted to get away.

"I've been in France for a considerable time," I said.

I didn't imagine Sadie had any close knowledge of Anna's doings. I could see Sadie's face focused now into a look of intelligent venom. She looked like a beautiful snake; and the curious fantasy came to me that if I were to look under the drier at the real face and not at the reflexion I should see there some terrible old witch.

"Well, you call on me next Tuesday, early," said Sadie, "and I'll install you. I mean it about this bodyguard act."

"That'll be splendid, Sadie dear," I said automatically, "I'll be sure to come." And I rose.

"I have to see my publisher," I explained.

We exchanged smiles, and I strode out of the place, followed by a large number of fascinated female eyes.

*   *   *

I omitted to mention earlier that I am acquainted with Belfounder. As my acquaintance with Hugo is the central theme of this book, there was little point in anticipating it. You will hear more than enough on this subject in the pages that follow. I had better start by explaining something about Hugo himself and then I will tell you of the circumstances in which I first met him and something of the early days of our friendship. Hugo's original name was not Belfounder. His parents were German, and his father adopted the name Belfounder when he came to live in England. He found it, I believe, on a tombstone in a Cotswold churchyard, and he thought that it would be good for business. It evidently was, for Hugo in due course inherited a flourishing armaments factory, and the firm of Belfounder and Baermann, Small-arms, Ltd. Unfortunately for the firm, Hugo was at that time an ardent pacifist; and after various upheavals, in the course of which the Baermann faction withdrew, Hugo was left with a small concern which came to be called Belfounder's Lights and Rockets Ltd. He had contrived to convert the armaments factory into a rocket factory; and here for some years he concerned himself with the manufacture of rockets, Very lights, small commercial dynamite, and fireworks of all kinds.

It started out, as I say, a small concern. But somehow money always stuck to Hugo, he simply couldn't help making it; and within a short time he was extremely rich and prosperous, almost as prosperous as his father had been. (No one can be quite as prosperous as an armaments manufacturer.) He always lived simply, however, and at the time I first got to know him he used to work on and off as a craftsman in his own factory. His speciality was set pieces.

As you probably know, the creation of a set piece is a highly skilled affair, calling for both manual dexterity and creative ingenuity. The peculiar problems of the set piece delighted Hugo and inspired him: the trigger-like relation of the parts, the contrasting appeal of explosion and colour, the blending of pyrotechnical styles, the methods for combining *éclat* with duration, the perennial question of the coda. Hugo treated the set piece as if it were a symphony; he despised the vulgarity of representational pieces. "Fireworks are *sui generis*," he once said to me. "If you must compare them to another art, compare them to music."

There was something about fireworks which absolutely fascinated Hugo. I think what pleased him most about them was their impermanence. I remember his holding forth to me once about what an *honest* thing a firework was. It was so patently just an ephemeral spurt of beauty of which in a moment nothing more was left. "That's what all art is really," said Hugo, "only we don't like to admit it. Leonardo understood this. He deliberately made the Last Supper perishable." The enjoyment of fireworks, according to Hugo, ought to be an education in the enjoyment of all worldly splendour. "You pay your money," said Hugo, "and you get an absolutely momentary pleasure with no nonsense about it. No one talks cant about fireworks."

Unfortunately he was wrong, and his theories turned out to be his own undoing as a craftsman. Hugo's set pieces began to be in enormous demand. No smart house-party or public festival was complete without one. They were even exported to America. Then the newspapers began to talk, and to refer to them as works of art, and to classify them into styles. This so much disgusted Hugo that it paralysed his work. After a while he began to conceive a positive hatred for set pieces, and after a while he abandoned them altogether.

It was through the common cold that I first met Hugo. This was in a period when I was particularly short of cash, and things went very ill indeed with me until I discovered an incredibly charitable arrangement whereby I could get free board and lodging in exchange for being a guinea pig in a cold-cure experiment. The experiment was going forward at a delightful country house where one could stay indefinitely and be inoculated with various permutations of colds and cures. I dislike having a cold, and the cures never seemed to work when they tried them on me; but on the other hand it was free, and one got fairly used to working with a cold, which was good practice for ordinary life. I managed to get a lot of writing done, at least up to the time when Hugo appeared.

The controllers of this charitable scheme used to propose to the victims that they be domiciled in pairs since, as they observed in the prospectus, few people can tolerate complete solitude. I don't care for solitude myself, as you know, but after a few tries I came to dislike even more the company of garrulous fools, and when I returned to this admirable place for a second season I asked to be allowed to live alone. The limited and protected isolation which such an institution offers in fact suits me quite well. This was granted; and I was hard at work, and battling too with a particularly appalling cold, when it was announced to me that the accommodation problem was now such that I must after all accept a companion. I had no choice but to agree, and I looked with very ill favour upon the enormous shaggy personage who then shambled in, put his things on the bed, and sat down at the other table. I grunted some sort of ungracious greeting, and then returned to my work, to make it clear that I was no fit companion for a chatterbox. I was further irritated by the fact that whereas I had only the cold, my companion was given both the cold and the cure, so that while I was choking and sneezing and using up a sackful of paper handkerchiefs, he remained in complete possession of his human dignity, and looking the picture of health. It was never clear to me on what principle the distribution of inoculations was made, though it always seemed that I got more than my fair share of colds.

I had feared that my companion would chatter, but it

was soon plain that there was no such danger. Two days passed during which we did not exchange a single word. He seemed, indeed, absolutely unaware of my presence. He neither read nor wrote, but spent most of his time sitting at the table and looking out of the window across the pleasant parkland that surrounded the house. He sometimes mumbled to himself and said things half under his breath. He bit his nails prodigiously and once he produced a pen-knife and absently chipped holes in the furniture until one of the attendants took it from him. I thought at first that perhaps he was mentally deficient. During the second day I even began to feel a little nervous of him. He was extremely large, both stout and tall, with very wide shoulders and enormous hands. His huge head was usually sunk low between his shoulders, while his brooding gaze traced around the room or across the countryside a line which seemed to be suggested by none of the ordinary objects which lay in his field of vision. He had dark rather matted hair and a big shapeless mouth which opened every now and then, occasionally emitting a semi-articulate sound. Once or twice he began humming to himself, but broke off abruptly on each occasion—and this was the nearest he seemed to get to acknowledging my presence.

By the evening of the second day I was completely unable to go on with my work. Devoured by mingled nervousness and curiosity, I sat too looking out of my window, and blowing my nose, and wondering how to set about establishing the human contact which was by now become an absolute necessity. It ended up with my asking him, with undiplomatic abruptness, for his name. He had been introduced to me when he arrived, but I had paid no attention then. He turned toward me a very gentle pair of dark eyes and said his name : Hugo Belfounder. He added: "I thought you didn't want to talk." I said that I was not at all averse to talking, that I had just been rather immersed in something when he arrived, and I begged his pardon if I had appeared churlish. It seemed to me, even from the way he spoke, that he was not only not mentally deficient, but was highly intelligent; and I began, almost automatically, to pack up my papers. I knew that from now on I should do no more work. I was closeted with a person of the utmost fascination.

From that moment on Hugo and I fell into a conversation the like of which I have never known. We rapidly told each other the complete story of our lives, wherein I at least achieved an unprecedented frankness. We then went on to exchange our views on art, politics, literature, religion, history, science, society and sex. We talked without interruption all day, and often late into the night. Sometimes we laughed and shouted so much that we were rebuked by the authorities, and once we were threatened with separation. Somewhere in the middle of this the current experimental session ended, but we forthwith enrolled ourselves for another consecutive one. We eventually settled down to a discussion the nature of which is to some extent germane to my present story.

Hugo has often been called an idealist. I would prefer to call him a theoretician, though he is a theoretician of a peculiar kind. He lacked both the practical interests and the self-conscious moral seriousness of those who are usually dubbed idealists. He was the most purely objective and detached person I had ever met—only in him detachment showed less like a virtue and more like a sheer gift of nature, a thing of which he was quite unaware. It was something which was expressed in his very voice and manner. I can picture him now, as I so often saw him during those conversations, leaning far forward in his chair and biting his knuckles as he picked up some hot-headed remark of mine. He was, in discussion, very slow. He would open his mouth slowly, shut it again, open it again, and at last venture a remark. "You mean . . ." he would say, and then he would rephrase what I had said in some completely simple and concrete way, which sometimes illuminated it enormously, and sometimes made nonsense of it entirely. I don't mean that he was always right. Often he failed utterly to understand me. It didn't take me long to discover that I had a much wider general knowledge than he on most of the subjects we discussed. But he would very quickly realize when we were, from his point of view, at a dead end, and he would say: "Well, I can say nothing about that," or "I'm afraid that here I don't understand you at all, not at all," with a finality which killed the topic. From first to last it was Hugo, not I, who conducted the conversation.

He was interested in everything, and interested in the theory of everything, but in a peculiar way. Everything had a theory, and yet there was no master theory. I have never met a man more destitute than Hugo of anything which could be called a metaphysic or general *Weltanschauung*. It was rather perhaps that of each thing he met he wanted to know the *nature*—and he seemed to approach this question in each instance with an absolute freshness of mind. The results were often astonishing. I remember a conversation which we had once about translating. Hugo knew nothing about translating, but when he learnt that I was a translator he wanted to know what it was like. I remember him going on and on, asking questions such as: What do you mean when you say that you think the meaning in French? How do you know you're thinking it in French? If you see a picture in your mind how do you know it's a French picture? Or is it that you say the French word to yourself? What do you see when you see that the translation is exactly right? Are you imagining what someone else would think, seeing it for the first time? Or is it a kind of feeling? What kind of feeling? Can't you describe it more closely? And so on and so on, with a fantastic patience. This sometimes became very exasperating. What seemed to me to be the simplest utterance soon became, under the repeated pressure of Hugo's "You mean", a dark and confused saying of which I no longer myself knew the meaning. The activity of translating, which had seemed the plainest thing in the world, turned out to be an act so complex and extraordinary that it was puzzling to see how any human being could perform it. Yet at the same time Hugo's enquiries rarely failed to throw an extraordinary amount of light on whatever he concerned himself with. For Hugo each thing was astonishing, delightful, complicated and mysterious. During these conversations I began to see the whole world anew.

During the early part of my discussions with Hugo I kept trying to "place" him. Once or twice I asked him directly whether he held this or that general theory—which he always denied with the air of one who has been affronted by a failure of taste. And indeed it seemed to me later that to ask such questions of Hugo showed a peculiar insensitivity to his unique intellectual and moral quality. After a while I realized that Hugo held no general theories whatsoever. All his theories, if they could be called theories, were particular. But still I had the feeling that if I tried hard enough I could come somehow to the centre of his thought; and after a while my passion became to discuss with Hugo not so much politics or art or sex, but what it was that was so peculiar in Hugo's approach to politics or art or sex. At last we did have a conversation which seemed to me to touch on something central to Hugo's thought, if Hugo's thought could be said at all to have anything so figurative as a centre. He himself would probably have denied this; or rather, I'm not sure that he would have known what it meant for thoughts to have an orientation. We arrived at the point in question by way of a discussion about Proust. From Proust we were led on to discuss what it meant to describe a feeling or a state of mind. Hugo found this very puzzling, as indeed he found everything very puzzling.

"There's something fishy about describing people's feelings," said Hugo. "All these descriptions are so dramatic."

"What's wrong with that?" I said.

"Only," said Hugo, "that it means that things are falsified from the start. If I say afterwards that I felt such and such, say that I felt 'apprehensive'—well, this just isn't true."

"What do you mean?" I asked.

"I didn't feel this," said Hugo. "I didn't feel anything of

that kind at the time at all. This is just something I say afterwards."

"But suppose I try hard to be accurate," I said.

"One can't be," said Hugo. "The only hope is to avoid saying it. As soon as I start to describe, I'm done for. Try describing anything, our conversation for instance, and see how absolutely instinctively you . . ."

"Touch it up?" I suggested.

"It's deeper than that," said Hugo. "The language just won't let you present it as it really was."

"Suppose then," I said, "that one were offering the description at the time."

"But don't you see," said Hugo, "that just gives the thing away. One couldn't give such a description at the time without seeing that it was untrue. All one could say at the time would be perhaps something about one's heart beating. But if one said one was apprehensive this could only be to try to make an impression—it would be for *effect*, it would be a lie."

I was puzzled by this myself. I felt that there was something wrong in what Hugo said, and yet I couldn't see what it was. We discussed the matter a bit further, and then I told him, "But at this rate almost everything one says, except things like 'Pass the marmalade' or 'There's a cat on the roof', turns out to be a sort of lie."

Hugo pondered this. "I think it is so," he said with seriousness.

"In that case one oughtn't to talk," I said.

"I think perhaps one oughtn't to," said Hugo, and he was deadly serious. Then I caught his eye, and we both laughed enormously, thinking of how we had been doing nothing else for days on end.

"That's colossal!" said Hugo. "Of course one does talk. But," and he was grave again, "one does make far too many concessions to the need to communicate."

"What do you mean?"

"All the time when I speak to you, even now, I'm saying not *precisely* what I think, but what will impress you and make you respond. That's so even between us—and how much more it's so where there are stronger motives for deception. In fact, one's so used to this one hardly sees it. The whole language is a machine for making falsehoods."

"What would happen if one *were* to speak the truth?" I asked. "Would it be possible?"

"I know myself," said Hugo, "that when I really speak the truth the words fall from my mouth absolutely dead, and I see complete blankness in the face of the other person."

"So we never really communicate?"

"Well," he said, "I suppose *actions* don't lie."

It took us about half a dozen cold-cure sessions to reach this point. We had arranged by now to have the cold alternately, so that whatever intellectual diminution was entailed by it should be shared equally between us. Hugo had insisted on this; though I would willingly have had all the colds myself, partly because of a protective feeling I was developing toward Hugo, and partly because Hugo made such an infernal noise when he had the cold. I don't know why it didn't dawn on us earlier that we didn't have to stay in the cold-cure establishment in order to continue our talks. Perhaps we were afraid of breaking the continuity. I don't know when it would have occurred to us to leave of our own volition; but eventually we were turned out by the authorities, who feared that if we went on having colds much longer we might do some permanent injury to our health.

By this time I was completely under Hugo's spell. He himself never appeared to notice the extent of the impression he made on me. In conversation he was completely without any sort of desire to score points, and although he often silenced me, he seemed unaware of having done so. It was not that I always agreed with him. His failure to grasp certain kinds of ideas often filled me with annoyance. But it was as if his very mode of being revealed to me how hopelessly my own vision of the world was blurred by generality. I felt like a man who, having vaguely thought that flowers are all much the same, goes for a walk with a

botanist. Only this simile doesn't fit Hugo either, for a
botanist not only notices details but classifies. Hugo only
noticed details. He never classified. It was as if his vision
were sharpened to the point where even classification was
impossible, for each thing was seen as absolutely unique. I
had the feeling that I was meeting for the first time an almost completely truthful man; and the experience was turning out to be appropriately upsetting. I was but the more
inclined to attribute a spiritual worth to Hugo in proportion
as it would never have crossed his mind to think of himself
in such a light.

When we were turned out of the cold-cure establishment
I had nowhere to live. Hugo suggested that I should come
and live with him, but some instinct of independence forbade this. I felt that Hugo's personality could very easily
swallow mine up completely, and much as I admired him
I didn't want this to happen. So I declined his offer. I had
in any case to go to France about this time to see Jean Pierre,
who was making a fuss about one of the translations, so our
conversation was interrupted for a while. During this interval Hugo returned to work at the Rocket Factory, and
began to develop his great ingenuity with set pieces, and
generally resumed the pattern of his London life. His
attempts to break out of this pattern always took some
eccentric form or other; his inability to take a normal comfortable expensive holiday was the nearest thing to a neu-
rotic trait that I ever discovered in him. When I got back
from Paris I took a cheap room in Battersea, and Hugo and
I resumed our talks. We would meet on Chelsea Bridge
after Hugo's day's work, and wander along the Chelsea
embankment, or make the round of the pubs in the King's
Road, talking ourselves to exhaustion.

Some time previous to this, however, I had made a move
which turned out to be fatal. The conversation of which I
have given a small extract above had interested me so much
that I had made a few notes of it just to remind myself.
When I glanced at these notes again after a little while they
looked very scrappy and inadequate, so I added to them a

bit, just to make them a better reminder. Then later still when I looked them up it struck me that the argument as it stood on paper didn't make sense. So I added some more, to make it look intelligible, still drawing on my memory. Then when I read the thing through it began to occur to me that it was rather good. I'd never seen anything quite like it. I ran through it again and made it look a bit more elegant. After all, I am a natural writer; and since the thing was now on paper it might as well look decent. So I polished it up quite a lot and then began to fill in the preliminary conversation as well. This conversation I found wasn't so clear in my memory, and in reconstructing it I drew on a number of different occasions.

Of course, I didn't tell Hugo about this. I intended the thing as a private and personal record for myself, so there was no point in telling him. In fact, I knew in my heart that the creation of this record was a sort of betrayal of everything which I imagined myself to have learnt from Hugo. But this didn't stop me. Indeed, the thing began to have for me the fascination of a secret sin. I worked on it constantly. I now expanded it to cover a large number of our conversations, which I presented not necessarily as I remembered them to have occurred, but in a way which fitted in with the plan of the whole. A quite considerable book began to take shape. I kept it in the form of a dialogue between two characters called Tamarus and Annandine. The curious thing was that I could see quite clearly that this work was from start to finish an objective justification of Hugo's attitude. That is, it *was* a travesty and falsification of our conversations. Compared with them it was a pretentious falsehood. Even though I wrote it only for myself, it was clearly written for effect, written to impress. Some of the most illuminating moments of our talk had been those which, if recorded, would have sounded the flattest. But these I could never bring myself to record with the starkness which they had had in reality. I was constantly supplying just that bit of shape, that hint of relation, which the original had lacked. Yet though I saw

the thing quite plainly as a travesty I didn't like it any
the less for that.

Then one day I couldn't resist showing it to Dave Gellman. I thought it might impress him. It did. He immediately wanted to discuss it with me. Not much came of this,
however, as I found myself quite incapable of discussing
Hugo's ideas with Dave. Greatly as I was moved by these
ideas, I was totally unable to reproduce them in talk with
anyone else. When I tried to explain some notion of Hugo's
it sounded flat and puerile, or else quite mad, and I soon
gave up the attempt. After that Dave rather lost interest in
the book; nothing is true or important for Dave which
can't be maintained in an oral discussion. However, he
had during this time, and contrary to my instructions,
showed the book, which he had taken home to finish, to one
or two other people who were also very impressed by it.

Since I knew how much the whole project would dis-
please him, I had felt myself bound to conceal Hugo's
identity. I had presented the thing to Dave as a dramatic
exercise, rather remotely based on conversations which I had
had with a variety of people. But now in a little while I
found myself being regarded in certain circles as a kind of
sage, and many of my friends pressed me to let them see the
manuscript. Eventually I did show it to a few more people
and began to get used to the idea that it should circulate a
little. All this time I was still working on it, and drawing
additional matter from my current conversations with Hugo.
I had continued to keep my friendship with Hugo completely secret from all my other friends. I did this at first
out of a jealous desire to keep my remarkable find to myself,
and later on also because I feared that Hugo might discover
my treachery.

People were now constantly suggesting to me that I
should publish the thing, at which I just laughed. But
the notion was attractive to me all the same. It was attractive at first in the way something can attract one when one
knows one will never do it. As publication was so absolutely out of the question I felt it was quite safe to

brood upon it in imagination. I thought what a remarkable book it would make, how original, how astonishing, how illuminating. I amused myself inventing titles for it. I would sit holding the manuscript in my hands, and then I would fancy it reproduced a thousand-fold. I suffered continually at that time from a fear of losing the manuscript, and although I typed out two or three copies I still felt it very likely that somehow or other they would all be destroyed and the thing lost forever—which I couldn't help thinking would be a pity. Then one day a publisher approached me directly with a proposal for its publication.

This took me by surprise. I had never been spontaneously approached by a publisher before and such condescension rather turned my head. It occurred to me that if this book were a success, which I couldn't doubt, this might smooth my way considerably in the literary world. It's easier to sell junk when you're known than works of genius when you're unknown. If I could leap to fame in this way my career as a writer would be made. I set this idea aside, telling myself that the project was an impossible one. I couldn't palm off Hugo's ideas as my own. Most of all, I couldn't use material drawn from my intimacy with Hugo to present the public with a work which would fill Hugo himself with repulsion and disgust. But the idle dreams of publication which I had nourished earlier now unmasked themselves as a real will. I became obsessed with the notion that I would publish. A sort of fatality drew me towards it. I saw all my past acts as leading inevitably to this end. I remember a drunken evening during which I passed in fantasy through every stage of the process which should bring the dialogue into print. By then the idea had too great a reality in imagination for it to be long before it should become actual. I rang up the publisher at his home.

He knew of my reluctances, and arrived early the next morning with the contract, which I signed with a flourish of abandon and a splitting headache. After he had gone I took out the manuscript and looked at it as one looks at the woman for whom one has lost one's honour. I entitled it

The Silencer and added an author's preface to the effect that I owed many of the ideas contained therein to a friend who should be nameless, but that I had no reason to believe that he would approve of the form in which I was presenting them. Then I sent the thing away and left it to its fate.

While this crisis had been gathering, Hugo had begun to put his money into films. He started to do this in a vaguely philanthropic way, in order to give the British film industry a leg up. But then it all began to interest him, and by the time Bounty Belfounder was founded Hugo knew his way about pretty well in the film world. He was in fact a remarkable man of business. He inspired universal confidence and had an iron nerve. Bounty Belfounder went ahead like wildfire. It had an experimental stage, if you remember, largely I think inspired by Hugo himself, when it produced a lot of silent films of the kind which used to be called "expressionist"; but it soon settled down to making quite ordinary films, with occasional experimental departures. Hugo didn't talk to me much about his film ventures, though we were seeing each other frequently all this time. I think he was a little ashamed of being so successful. I, on the contrary, felt proud of him for being so versatile, and took an especial pleasure in going to the cinema to see, before the credit titles, the familiar shot of City Spires, and hear the crescendo of City Bells, while the words *Presented by HUGO BELFOUNDER* grew solemnly upon the screen.

At first my secret activity had seemed to make no difference at all to my friendship with Hugo. Our talks continued, with all their old freshness and spontaneity, and our subject matter was inexhaustible. As the book grew and gained strength, however, it seemed to drain some of the blood away from my other intimacy. It began to constitute itself a rival. What had seemed at first an innocent *suppressio veri* began to grow into a very poisonous *suggestio falsi*. The knowledge that I was deceiving Hugo took the frankness out of my responses to him even in fields quite unconnected with this particular deception. Hugo never seemed to notice anything, however, and I continued to take great pleasure in his company. But when at last I had signed the contract and the book had gone away to the publisher I felt I could hardly any more look Hugo in the face. After a day or two I got used to seeing him, even under these conditions, but an awful melancholy began to hang over our association. I knew now that our friendship was doomed.

I wondered whether I dared, even at this stage, tell Hugo the truth. Once or twice I felt myself on the brink of a confession. But each time I drew back. I was unable to face his scorn and anger. But what most deterred me was the feeling that after all the thing was still not totally irrevocable. I could still go to the publisher and ask to be released from my contract. By offering him some pecuniary compensation I could probably even now get out of the thing altogether. But at the thought of this my heart sank. My only consolation lay in a dreadful fatalism—and the notion that I was still a free agent, and that the crime could still be avoided, was too intensely painful to entertain. The mere idea that Hugo might demand that I withdraw the book caused me such distress that I could not bring myself even to contemplate telling him of my action; and this was not because I had any longer a desire to see the book in print. The sweetness of this prospect had been killed for some time now by my desolation at the thought of losing Hugo. It was just that I could console myself with nothing except the dreadful certainty, which I hugged closer to myself every day, that the die was cast.

I fell during this period into such a melancholy that, although I saw Hugo as often as ever, I found it extremely difficult to talk to him. I would sometimes sit for hours in his presence, silent except for such brief responses as were needed to keep him talking. Hugo soon noticed my depression and questioned me about it. I feigned illness; and the more worried and solicitous Hugo became concerning my condition, the greater grew my torment. He started sending me presents of fruit and books, tins of glucose and iron tonic, and implored me to see a doctor; and indeed by this time I had made myself really ill.

On the day when the book was to be published I was beside myself. I had an appointment to meet Hugo that evening, on the bridge as usual. By about midday I felt that evidence of my treachery must be displayed in every bookshop in London. I thought it likely that Hugo would not yet have seen the book. But it could only be a matter of a short time before he would see it, as he often went into bookshops. Our appointment was at five-thirty. I spent the afternoon drinking brandy—and about five o'clock I went out into Battersea Park. A sort of calm had descended on me, as I knew now that I should not meet Hugo that day, or any other day ever again. A tragic fascination drew me to the riverside, from which I could see the bridge. Hugo appeared punctually and waited. I sat on a seat and smoked two cigarettes. Hugo walked up and down. After a while longer I saw him cross the bridge to the south bank and I knew he was going to my lodgings. I lighted another cigarette. Half an hour later I saw him walk slowly back across the bridge and disappear.

I then returned to my room, gave in my notice, packed up my things, and left immediately by taxi. About a week later a letter from Hugo was forwarded to me in which he enquired what had happened to me and asked me to get in touch with him. I left the letter unanswered. Hugo is not a great hand at letter-writing and finds it very hard to express himself on paper at all. I received no more letters. Meanwhile *The Silencer* was being treated to a few luke-warm reviews. Such reviewers as undertook to say anything about it at all had clearly found it unintelligible. One of them labelled it "pretentious and obscurantist". But on the whole no one paid much attention to it. It was a quiet flop. So far from its opening to me a career of literary fame, it did my reputation considerable harm, and I came to be regarded as a solemn highbrow with no powers of entertainment; and that in quarters where I had been at some pains to build up a quite other impression.

I cared very little about this, however. I was anxious only to forget the whole business and to live the relationship with Hugo out of my system altogether. *The Silencer* went through only one edition which, after being conspicuously remaindered in Charing Cross Road, mercifully disappeared from the market. I didn't retain a copy myself, and just wished most heartily that all could be as if the accursed book had never been. I stopped going to the cinema, and avoided looking at the more sensational dailies which tended to feature Hugo's activities. It was about now that Finn turned up and attached himself to me, and gradually my life took on a new pattern and the powerful image of Hugo began to fade. Nothing had interrupted the fading process until the moment when Sadie so unexpectedly mentioned Hugo's name in the hairdresser's shop.

Five

I WALKED down the street in a daze. I bought a packet of cigarettes and went into a milk bar to think things over. The mention of Hugo's name was in itself quite enough to upset me considerably, and for a while I was in such pain that I couldn't put the matter to myself clearly at all. What did seem to emerge, as far as my present situation was concerned, was that Hugo's involvement in the affair made it quite out of the question for me to accept Sadie's offer or to have anything more to do with Sadie at all. My immediate impulse was simply to run away. After a while, however, I began to feel calm enough to find the situation rather interesting; and then, as I reflected more and more upon it, it became clear to me that Sadie simply couldn't be telling the truth. I knew from of old that Sadie was a notorious liar and would tell any falsehood to procure herself even a quite temporary advantage. Also the sheer improbability of Hugo being in love with Sadie was, when I considered it, overwhelming. Hugo was never very forward with women, and tended anyway to admire the quiet home-keeping types. I just couldn't see him behaving in the way Sadie had described. That there was some stratagem going forward which involved Hugo was very possible; but a more likely explanation of it was that Sadie was up to some professional caper which Hugo was trying to circumvent. I knew nothing about the film world, but I imagined it to be in a continuous ferment of personal intrigue. Indeed, it was even possible that it was Sadie who was in love with Hugo and was trying to entangle him in some way. This, when it occurred to me, seemed a very plausible hypothesis indeed. I knew, from Sadie's conduct toward myself, how easily she was impressed by men whom she imagined to be intellectuals; and whereas Hugo was not at all the man to love Sadie, Sadie was just the woman to be in love with Hugo.

When I had come to this conclusion I felt better. Somehow the idea of Hugo gone on Sadie had been extremely distasteful to me. This still, however, failed to illuminate a course of action for me. What was I to do? If I accepted Sadie's offer I would seem to be enrolling myself on the wrong side in some sort of obscure battle with Hugo; and if I accepted the offer with the full intention of helping Hugo if possible and outwitting Sadie, this savoured of double-dealing. I still had besides a strong inclination to keep clear of the thing altogether, as I didn't dare even to imagine with what sort of a head I could bring myself to face Hugo, should that dread necessity ever arise. On the other hand, I felt that by now I was somehow involved myself, and I couldn't help being fascinated by the way things had fallen out, and wondering what on earth would happen next. Some fate which I would not readily deny was leading me back to Hugo.

I thought the matter to and fro and up and down, and the morning passed without my having made a decision. I was becoming quite exhausted by the suspense, so I decided that, since work was out of the question in view of my nervous and excited condition, I might as well pass the afternoon in a useful routine way by going and fetching the radiogram from Earls Court Road. At this I found myself ruefully reflecting that while I was likely to get my neck broken at Welbeck Street by Hugo I was likely to get it broken at Earls Court Road by Sacred Sammy. I went to the telephone.

There was no reply from Madge's number, so I judged that the coast was clear and set off. I still had my key to the flat and I let myself in, wondering what was the best place to store the radiogram, whether at Dave's or at Mrs Tinckham's. I bounded into the sitting-room, and was well inside the door when I saw a man standing on the other side of the room with a bottle in his hand. It needed but one glance to tell me that this was Sacred Sammy. He was dressed in tweeds and had the look of an outdoor man who had lived too much by electric light. He had a heavy reddish face and a powerful spread of nose. His hair was only slightly grey. He held his head well and the bottle by the neck. He looked at me now with a calm bland dangerous look. It was evident to me that he knew who I was. I hesitated. Sammy has his name in lights, but he used to be a real race-course bookie, and there was no doubt that he was a tough customer. I estimated the distance between us and took a step back. Then I took off my belt. It was a heavy leather belt with a strong brass buckle. This was only a feint. I have seen Guardsmen do this before a fight and it's an impressive gesture. I had no intention of using it as a weapon, but prevention is better than a *fracas* and Sammy, who perhaps didn't know that I was a Judo expert, might have it in mind to start something. If he came at me I had already planned to give him an old-fashioned flying mare.

While I was performing these manœuvres I saw Sammy's face soften into a look of affected incomprehension.

"What do you think you're doing?" he asked.

I wasn't quite ready for this, and felt let down. "Don't you want to fight?" I replied, with irritation.

Sammy stared at me, and then broke into a roar of laughter. "My, my!" he said. "Whatever gave you that idea. You're Donaghue, aren't you? Here, have a lotion." And quick as a flash he put a glass of whiskey into my free hand. You can imagine what a fool I felt, with the whiskey in one hand and my belt in the other.

When I had reorganized myself, I said, hoping that I didn't sound sheepish, "I suppose you're Starfield?" I felt thoroughly at a loss. I suspected that it ought to be up to me whether we fought or not. I certainly didn't want to fight, but I had let Sammy get the initiative now, and no mistake, and I hated that too.

"That's me," said Sammy, "and you're young Donaghue. Well, what a fire-eater!" and he went off into another explosion of laughter. I took a gulp of the whiskey and put on my belt, endeavouring to wear the expression of one who, contrary to appearances, is master of the situation. The films provide one with useful conventions of this kind. I looked Sammy up and down with deliberation. He was rather a handsome creature in the style already indicated. There was a crude power in him, and I set myself to see the Sammy whom Madge saw. It wasn't difficult. He had humorous triangular blue eyes, which noticed my scrutiny with amusement and returned it with mock seriousness.

"You're quite a young fellow!" said Sammy. "You know, I could never get much out of Madge about you." He re-filled my glass.

"I expect you're fed up about being fired out," he added in a completely unprovocative tone.

"Look here, Starfield," I said, "there are some things a gentleman can't discuss coolly. If you want to fight, good. If not, shut up. I've come here to fetch some of my things, not to chat with you." I was pleased not to be feeling afraid of him, and I hoped he was aware of it, but I knew that my speech would have sounded better if I hadn't been drinking the man's whiskey. It also occurred to me at that moment that Sammy might dispute my ownership of the radiogram.

"You're a touchy fellow," said Sammy. "Don't be in such a hurry. I want to look at you. It's not every day I meet a writer chap who talks on the radio."

I suspected he was mocking, but the mere thought that Sammy might find me a romantic figure amused me so much that I laughed, and Sammy laughed too in sympathy. He seemed to want me to like him. I was drinking my second glass of whiskey and beginning to think that perhaps after all Sammy was rather a peach.

"Where did you meet Madge?" I asked. I wasn't going to let him make all the running.

"Where did she tell you I met her?" Sammy countered.

"On a number eleven bus."

Sammy let out his roar. "Not likely!" he said. "Catch me riding on a bus! No, we met at a party some film people were giving."

I raised my eyebrows.

"Yes, boy, she was just beginning to get around." Sammy wagged his finger at me. "Never let them out of your sight, that's the only way!"

This mixture of triumph and solicitude nauseated me. "Magdalen is a free agent," I said coldly.

"Not any more she isn't!" said Sammy.

I looked at him with sudden loathing. "Look here," I said, "are you really going to marry Madge?"

Sammy took this as an expression of friendly incredulity from a well-wisher. "Why not?" he said. "Isn't she a beautiful girl? Isn't she a turn up for the book? She hasn't got a wooden leg, has she?" and he dug me in the ribs so violently that the whiskey splashed onto the carpet.

"I don't mean that," I said. "I mean do you *intend* to marry her?"

"Oh, you're asking about my *intentions*," said Sammy. "That's a body blow! You ought to have brought your shotgun!" He roared with laughter again. "Here," he said, "let's finish the bottle."

By now I had just sufficient whiskey in me not to care much one way or the other.

"It's your affair," I said.

"It is. Believe you me," said Sammy, and we left it at that.

Sammy now began to rummage in his pockets. "There's something I'd like to give you, young fellow," he said. I watched suspiciously. He produced his cheque-book with an ostentatious flourish and opened his fountain pen.

"Well, now," he said, "shall we say a hundred pounds, shall we say two hundred?"

I was open-mouthed. "Whatever for?" I asked.

"Well, let's say for removal expenses," said Sammy, and winked.

For a moment I was completely baffled. Then it dawned on me that I was being bought off! How had such an idea got into Sammy's head? It took but another moment to conclude that Magdalen must have put it there. This further proof of the tortuousness of Madge's mind left me gasping.

This must have been her strange notion of how to put a good thing in my way. I was both extremely affronted and extremely touched. I smiled at Sammy with a sort of gentleness.

"No," I said, "I couldn't possibly take money."

"Why not?" said Sammy.

"First, because I really have no claims on Madge," I said. I thought he might understand this point better, so I put it first. "And secondly because I don't belong to a social class that takes money in a situation like this."

Sammy eyed me as one eyes a clever debater.

"First you say there's no situation," he said, "and then you say it's not a situation where you take money. Let's be grown up about it. I know the conventions as well as you do. But what do chaps like you care about your social class? Chaps like you are always short of money. If you don't take the cash you'll regret it to-morrow." And he began to write a cheque.

My awareness that his hypothetical statement was true added but the more passion to my cries of "No! I won't take it! I don't want it!"

Sammy looked at me with an interested *ad hominem* look. "But I've done you an injury," he said in an explanatory tone. "I wouldn't feel straight with my conscience if you didn't take something."

He sounded really concerned for me, and I began to wonder what sort of picture Madge had given him.

"What makes you so damned sure you've injured me?" I asked.

"Well, your being so set on marrying Madge," said Sammy.

I took a deep breath. This rather had me cornered. It seemed a disloyalty to Madge to declare that nothing was further from my mind than the idea of marrying her—especially as it now occurred to me that Madge might well have been using my alleged aspirations as a lever to make up Sammy's mind. In any case, I could see that Sammy was determined not to believe a denial.

"Well, maybe I am injured," I said grudgingly.

"That's a generous fellow!" cried Sammy, delighted. "And now let's say a couple of hundred quid!"

I wondered what to do. Sammy's curious ethical code did seem to demand a settlement. I needed the money. What prevented the closure of this mutually rewarding deal? My principles. Surely there must be some way round. In similar fixes I have rarely failed to find one.

"Don't interrupt, Starfield," I said, "I'm thinking." Then I had an idea.

The mid-day edition of the *Evening Standard* was lying on the floor at our feet. I turned to the back page and looked at my watch. It was 2.35. Racing that day was at Salisbury and Nottingham.

"I suggest," I said, "that you tell me a winner in the three o'clock race, and that you phone the bet for me to your own firm or wherever you keep your betting account. If that goes down we'll increase the stake for the three-thirty and so on for the rest of the afternoon. We'll aim at making fifty pounds, and you agree to stand the loss if any."

Sammy was overjoyed. "Done!" he said. "What a sportsman! But we'll make a sight more than fifty pounds. I know to-day's card like my own daughter. It's a poem."

We spread the paper out on the rug.

"Little Grange will win the three o'clock at Salisbury," said Sammy. "A cert, but odds on. We'll ginger it up by joining it with Queen's Rook in the three-thirty."

I was beginning to feel cautious; already I had the feeling that Sammy was gambling with my money.

"But suppose Queen's Rook doesn't win!" I said. "It's not fun I want, it's cash. Let's put something on Little Grange alone."

"Nonsense," said Sammy. "What's the use of caution when you know your onions? Hold onto your hat, my boy, while I just get the office on the blower. Hello, hello! Is that Andy? This is Sam."

"Keep the stake down, keep the stake down," I was saying to him.

"My private account," Sammy was saying. "Sure, I don't hold with gambling!" in reply to some witticism of Andy's. "This is for a friend who's done me a good turn."

He winked a triangular eye at me, and in a moment he had placed forty pounds in a win double, Little Grange and Queen's Rook. While that was cooking we turned our attention to the Nottingham card. The three o'clock at Nottingham was a selling plate.

"Not interesting," said Sammy. "That's a race for horses with three legs, we'll steer clear of it. But the rest of the day's a wedding present. Let's make it really exciting and have a treble. Saint Cross in the three-thirty, Hal Adair in the four o'clock, and Peter of Alex in the four-thirty. I don't care for the four o'clock at Salisbury. That leaves the four-thirty at Salisbury, and that'll be won by either Dagenham or Elaine's Choice."

"Well, put it on each way, for heaven's sake," I said.

I poured myself out another stiff glass. I am not a natural gambler.

Sammy was on the phone staking twenty pounds at Nottingham. Then he was asking for the winner of the three o'clock race at Salisbury. I sat down on the floor. Sammy stood to lose more money than I had in the bank. My nerves were vibrating like the strings of a harp. I wished I'd never suggested it.

"Stop looking green," said Sammy. "It's only money! And just guess who won the three o'clock. Little Grange at two to one on!"

This made it worse. "But it's a double," I said. "Doubles never work. It's just a way of losing more than one's stake."

"Shut up," said Sammy, "and leave the worrying to me. If you can't stand it you can go and sit on the landing."

He was working out on a piece of paper how much we were going to win. "Queen's Rook won't lose," said Sammy, "but we're covered anyway by the four-thirty. Twenty-five quid each way on the two of them just to please you.

There's security for you! You put it down and you pick it up!"

I was working out how much we were going to lose. This was easier and could be done in the head. I made it a hundred and sixty pounds. I was tempted to go away and leave Sammy to it, but dignity forbade me to desert him in what was after all my own enterprise. Besides this, the question was academic, since too much whiskey on an empty stomach had by now immobilized me completely. My legs felt as if they were stuffed with straw. I groaned. Sammy was ringing up about the next race. Queen's Rook had been beaten by a head but Saint Cross had won at Nottingham.

This was worse than anything. "Confound you," I said, "why didn't you do what I told you about Little Grange? Now we're forty pounds down and we haven't even won anything on Saint Cross."

"That just makes it better sport," said Sammy. "Believe you me, to-day's your lucky day. What's to-day? Wednesday? Well, Wednesday's your lucky day. It's years since I've really gambled," said Sammy, "I'd quite forgotten the feeling!" He was rubbing his hands with hideous zest.

"You know, boy," he said, "it does me good to meet someone like you now and then. Makes me realize the value of money!"

When the four o'clock race at Nottingham was won by Hal Adair, cool channels of sweat ran down my back and sides. I didn't feel it was my lucky day, and even Sammy was showing signs of strain. He drank what remained of the whiskey and told me that the trouble with me was that I didn't take a thing like this in the right spirit.

"Getting cash is like taming a lion," said Sammy. "Never let it see that you care."

My head, after describing gentle circles, subsided onto the carpet, carrying the rest of my trunk with it. I turned my face under the sofa. "Filthy lucre! Filthy lucre!" I could hear Sammy saying, with the voice of a man cursing the woman he has ruined. When 4.30 approached, the atmosphere was electric. Sammy was on the phone before the race was even started, but I hardly listened, I was too busy wondering how I would raise the money to pay him back. I decided that if I gave him the radiogram we'd be approximately quits.

I could hear Sammy saying, "Come on, Andy, look sharp. I've got a friend here who's biting the furniture."

Then I heard Sammy swearing. "What is it?" I asked languidly.

"Elaine's Choice didn't run," said Sammy, "and Dagenham was fourth."

"What about Nottingham?" I asked without interest.

"Wait," said Sammy, who was glued to the phone again. I began to roll gently under the sofa.

Then I heard him shout, "By God, we've done it! I said you had a lucky face!" I rolled out again and my torso regained the vertical.

"Peter of Alex at nine to two!" shouted Sammy. "Quick, open another bottle!"

We both struggled with the bottle, broke a glass, and sat on the floor laughing like mad things and toasting each other. The room was beginning to undulate gently about me and I wasn't sure that I knew what was happening. Sammy was shouting, "Well done the old firm!" and "Can I pick them or can I pick them!" and checking his sums.

"Look," he said, "Saint Cross was at seven to two, that makes ninety pounds on Hal Adair at two to one on, that makes a hundred and thirty-five pounds on Peter of Alex at nine to two, that makes seven hundred and twenty-two pounds ten. Considering the meetings, it's decent odds. What did I tell you? Better than scribbling, what?" Sammy waved the bottle in the air.

"Wait a moment," I said. "There's the forty pounds that went down on Queen's Rook and there's the each way bet at Salisbury."

"Oh, forget it!" said Sammy. "Remember the bookie wins every day. That's why I've enjoyed this so much."

"No, you damn well stick to the agreement!" I shouted. What was left of my honour was at stake.

After some more shouting Sammy agreed to the deduction. "All right, Donaghue," he said. "That makes six hundred and thirty-three pounds ten. I'll write the cheque now. The money'll go into my account." He produced his cheque-book again.

This sobered me up. I had a curious sense of being back at the beginning, only now Sammy was offering me three times as much. I couldn't credit it, now that the excitement was over, that Sammy could really have won so much cash just by saying things into the telephone.

I told Sammy this and he laughed at me. "Your trouble is," he said, "you're too used to sweating blood for money. But that's not the way to get it. Just lie on your back and whistle and it'll come." Eventually we agreed that Sammy should wait to send me the cheque until he had received the account showing his winnings. That would convince me that the transaction was real. He exclaimed a lot about how decent it was of me to trust him, and I gave him Dave's address and staggered up to go. Sammy ordered me a taxi. He was so far from disputing my claim to the radiogram that I think he would have let me take away the whole flat and helped me to carry it down the stairs. We stowed the radiogram beside the taxi-driver and then took leave of each other with many exclamations of regard. "That was good sport!" said Sammy. "We must do it another day!"

The taxi took me to the Goldhawk Road, and the taxi-driver conveyed both me and the radiogram up the stairs. I burst in on Dave and Finn, laughing like a lunatic. When they asked me what was so funny I told them I was going to take a job as Sadie's bodyguard—and this when I explained it certainly seemed funny enough. I said nothing about either Hugo or Sammy. Finn and Dave received my project, the latter with sarcasm, the former with expectant interest. I think I am a constant source of entertainment to Finn. After that I went to bed and fell into a drunken sleep.

Six

IT was about 9.15, on the appointed morning, when I reached Welbeck Street, as I had to go first to Mrs Tinckham's to collect my manuscripts. I found the door open and Sadie fretting and fuming about the hall.

"My dear creature," she said, "thank heavens you've come. When I say dawn to dusk I mean dawn to dusk. You've made me madly late. Never mind, don't look like that, come in. I see you've brought enough scribbling-paper to last a year. That's just as well. Listen, I want you, just for to-day and to-morrow, to stay here *all* day. Do you mind? I'll feel better if I know someone's here all the time. There's oceans to drink and the fridge is just full of salmon and raspberries and things. Don't invite your friends in though, there's an angel. If Belfounder or anybody telephones just say in a stern masculine voice that I'm out indefinitely. There's an utter darling. Now I must absolutely run."

"When'll you be back?" I asked, rather overwhelmed by these instructions.

"Oh, late to-night," said Sadie. "Don't wait up. Just choose yourself one of the spare rooms. The beds are all made." Then she kissed me with considerable enthusiasm and went away.

When the door had closed and there was silence in the large sunlit flat except for distant street noises, I stretched out my arms luxuriously and set out to survey the domain. Rugs from Kazakstan and Afghanistan and the Caucasus shifted softly underfoot on the parquet flooring. Rosewood and satinwood and mahogany curved and splayed and tapered in surfaces which glowered with care and quality. Tiny jade objects squatted on white mantel-shelves. Damask curtains stirred gently in the summer breeze. Sadie had come a long way since the days of the Quentin sisters. Here and there, under china animals or French paper-weights, were neat piles of letters or press cuttings or thousand-franc notes. I prowled quietly around, whistling to myself. Several Georgian cut-glass decanters, with enamel labels round their necks, stood on a low table; and in a cupboard I found a vast number of half-empty bottles of sherry, port, vermouth, pernod, gin, whiskey and brandy. In the kitchen there was a good deal of hock and claret in one of the cupboards, and the larder was filled with various *pâtés*, small sausages, and crab and jellied chicken in tins. I found about twelve kinds of biscuits, but no sign of any bread. In the fridge was salmon, raspberries and considerable quantities of butter, milk and cheese.

I went back to the sitting-room and poured myself out a long drink of Italian vermouth and soda water, to which I added some ice from the fridge. I took a cigarette from a little Sèvres casket that perched on gilded feet. Then I sank gently into a deep armchair and let my sense of time be stilled into a long regular undulation which seemed to pass through my body like a sigh. It was a hot day. The windows opened upon the distant intermittent murmur of London. My head was empty and my limbs were leaden with content. After a long time I reached out for some of my manuscripts and began to sort them. As I was looking at them all thought of Sadie and of the recent tumult was already far away. It diminished to a pinpoint and disappeared. I stretched out my legs, crumpling an exquisitely golden yellow and midnight blue striped Kazak rug into folds at my feet. If sleep could have come to me now it would have been one deep cascade of refreshment and peace. But I lay wakeful and soon ceased to turn over the typed and scribbled pages. I let them slide to the floor.

It was some time later again, and my eye was wandering along a low white bookshelf on the other side of the room. On top of this at intervals were Worcester and Dresden figures. I surveyed these, and my glance came lazily back along the top row of books. Then suddenly I stiffened and leapt up as if I'd been stabbed, scattered foolscap and typing-paper to the right and left. I strode to the bookcase. There, right in the centre, was a copy of *The Silencer*. I hadn't seen one for years. It even had its paper cover on. I looked at it with repulsion and fascination. Then I pulled it out, telling myself how foolish I was to be so moved at seeing the paltry work again; and as I held it in my hand I began to feel suddenly no longer repulsed but affectionate and protective toward it, and curious. I sat down crosslegged on the floor beside the bookshelves and opened it.

It's always a strange experience to read one's own writings again after an interval. They so rarely fail to impress. As I turned the pages of this curious journal I felt that the years which separated me from the moment of its creation had given it a strange independence. It was like meeting as an adult someone whom one knew long ago as a child. It wasn't that I liked the thing any better, but that now it somehow stood alone; and the idea crossed my mind that now at last it might be possible to make peace with it. I started to read at random.

TAMARUS: But ideas are like money. There must be an accepted coin which circulates. Concepts which are used for communication are justified by success.

ANNANDINE: That's near to saying that a story is true if enough people believe it.

TAMARUS: Of course I don't mean that. If I use an analogy or invent a concept part of what must be tested when the success is tested is whether by this means I can draw attention to real things in the world. Any concept can be misused. Any sentence *can* state a falsehood. But words themselves don't tell lies. A concept may have limitations but these won't mislead if I expose them in my use of it.

ANNANDINE: Yes, that's the grand style of lying. Put down your best half truth and call it a lie, but let it stand all the same. It will survive when your qualifications have been forgotten, even by yourself.

TAMARUS: But life has to be lived, and to be lived it has to be understood. This process is called civilization. What you say goes against our very nature. We•are rational animals in the sense of theory-making animals.

ANNANDINE: When you've been most warmly involved in life, when you've most felt yourself to be a man, has a theory ever helped you? Is it not then that you meet with things themselves naked? Has a theory helped you when you were in doubt about what to do? Are not these very simple moments when theories are shilly-shallying? And don't you realize this very clearly at such moments?

TAMARUS: My answer is twofold. Firstly that I may not reflect upon theories, but I may be expressing one all the same. Secondly that there are theories abroad in the world, political ones for instance, and so we have to deal with them in our thoughts, and that at moments of decision too.

ANNANDINE: If by expressing a theory you mean that some-one else could make a theory about what you do, of course that is true and uninteresting. What I speak of is the real decision as we experience it; and here the move-ment away from theory and generality is the movement toward truth. All theorizing is flight. We must be ruled by the situation itself and this is unutterably particular. Indeed it is something to which we can never get close enough, however hard we may try as it were to crawl under the net.

TAMARUS: That may be. But what about my other point?

ANNANDINE: It is true that theories may often be a part of a situation that one has to contend with. But then all sorts of obvious lies and fantasies may be a part of such a situation; and you would say that one must be good at detecting and shunning lies, and not that one must be good at lying.

TAMARUS: So you would cut all speech, except the very simplest, out of human life altogether. To do this would be to take away our very means of understanding our-selves and making life endurable.

ANNANDINE: Why should life be made endurable? I know that nothing consoles and nothing justifies except a story —but that doesn't stop all stories from being lies. Only the greatest men can speak and still be truthful. Any artist knows this obscurely; he knows that a theory is death, and that all expression is weighted with theory. Only the strongest can rise against that weight. For most of us, for almost all of us, truth can be attained, if at all, only in silence. It is in silence that the human spirit touches the divine. This was something which the ancients understood. Psyche was told that if she spoke about her pregnancy her child would be a mortal; if she kept silent it would be a god.

I read this thoughtfully. I had quite forgotten that I had managed to put up even as good a show as that against Hugo. I now found Hugo's arguments very much less impressive, and there occurred to me instantly a variety of ways in which the position of Tamarus might be strengthened. When I had written the dialogue I had obviously been far too bemused by Hugo. I decided then and there that I would confiscate the book for my own use and read the whole of it with great care, and revise my views. The possibility even occurred to me of a sequel. But I shook my head over it at once. There remained the fact that Annandine was but a broken-down caricature of Hugo. Hugo would never even have used words such as "theory" or "generality". I had not achieved more than the most shadowy expression of Hugo's point of view.

While I was thinking these thoughts a little stream was running softly somewhere in my mind, a little stream of reminiscence. What was it? Something was asking to be remembered. I held the book gently in my hands, and followed without haste the course of my reverie, waiting for the memory to declare itself. I wondered idly why Sadie should possess a copy of the book. It was not the sort of thing which could conceivably interest her. I turned to the beginning and looked inside the cover. The name written there was not Sadie's but Anna's. I looked at it for a moment, still holding the book very gently, and the memory that I had been seeking took hold of my whole consciousness with the force of a hurricane.

What the piece of dialogue had been trying to remind me of were the words which Anna had uttered at the Mime

Theatre; the words which I had felt were not her own. They were not her own. They were Hugo's. They were an echo, a travesty, of Hugo, just as my own words were an echo and a travesty of him. When I had heard Anna speak it had not occurred to me to connect what she said with the real Hugo; and when I had thought about Hugo I had not been reminded of Anna. It was my own wretched copy of Hugo's attitude which suddenly made clear to me the source from which Anna too must have derived the principles which she spoke of, and of which the theatre itself was an expression. It did not occur to me to imagine that Anna could have got her ideas from my book. The book was not a strong enough or a pure enough instrument to impress so simple and unspeculative a mind as Anna's. There was no doubt about it. Anna's ideas were simply an expression of Hugo in a debased medium, just as my own ideas were such an expression in yet another medium; and the two expressions, in a curious way, had striking points of resemblance to each other rather than to the original.

My head was spinning. I replaced the book and leaned back against the shelves. I had a sense of everything falling into place to make a pattern which I had not yet had the time to survey. So Hugo was acquainted with Anna. There was no reason in nature why he should not be, since he knew Sadie. But the thought of Hugo knowing Anna was new to me and profoundly disturbing. I had always taken care to insulate very carefully that part of my life which concerned Hugo. I had first met Anna before I had parted from Hugo, though it was after this that I had come to know her well. I had spoken to her of Belfounder, rather vaguely, as someone whom I had used to know a little, before he became so grand. I probably gave her the impression that Hugo had dropped me. As for the book, I had never shown her a copy, or mentioned it to her except as a piece of juvenilia and something of no interest at all. I always referred to it as if it had been published many years before and already buried and forgotten.

A cloud of questions buzzed about me. When had Anna

obtained the book? How much did she know of my treach-
erous behaviour to Hugo? What was the significance of the
Mime Theatre? What were the relations between Hugo
and Anna? What things might they not have said to each
other about myself? I covered my mouth at the enormity
of the possibilities which now began to unfold. Suddenly
Sadie's behaviour began to make sense too—and in an
instant it was clear to me that it was not Sadie that Hugo
was in love with but Anna. Hugo was become yet another
of those to whom Anna gave that modicum of tolerant and
mildly affectionate attention which was needed to keep
them in a state of frenzy. Anna, of course, was very much
more the sort of girl whom Hugo would be likely to love.
This was the situation which was driving Sadie furious with
jealousy and perhaps inspiring the very hostilities which
Hugo was now engaged in countering, and I apparently
employed in some obscure way to further. Or it might be
that Hugo was interested in Welbeck Street simply because
he thought to find Anna there. There were a hundred
possibilities.

This also explained the Mime Theatre. This doubtless
was some fantasy of Hugo's which he had recruited Anna,
against her will maybe, to realize. That she had picked up
in the process a crude version of his ideas was not surprising.
Anna was sensitive and Hugo was impressive. Perhaps indeed the theatre was designed to catch Anna's interest and
attention, and to be ultimately the gilded cage which would
imprison her. I was reminded of the silent expressionism of
Hugo's early films. The speechless purity of the mime might
well have become a genuine obsession for Hugo. But the
beautiful theatre itself, this was a house for Anna, a house
which Hugo had built and in which Anna would be queen.
An uneasy queen; I recalled her restlessness, her nervousness,
when I had seen her at the theatre. She was clearly not
at peace in the role which Hugo had created for her. Then
I had another revelation. There came back to me with
immense vividness the burly masked figure whom I had
seen upon the stage in the tiny theatre, the figure that had

at once seemed to me strangely familiar; and it was clear to me then, without a shadow of doubt, that that figure had been Hugo himself.

At that very moment the telephone rang. My heart sprang within me and fell like a bird striking a window pane. I started to my feet. I had not the slightest doubt but that the caller was Hugo. I looked at the phone as if it had been a rattlesnake. I lifted the receiver and said "Hello!" in an assumed voice, hoarse and trembling.

At the other end of the wire Hugo said hesitantly, "I'm so sorry. I wonder if I could possibly speak to Miss Quentin, if she's there?"

I stood there paralysed, without an idea of what to say to him. Then I said, "Listen, Hugo, it's Jake Donaghue here. I want to see you as soon as possible about something very important." There was dead silence. Then I said, "Could you come here to Sadie's? I'm alone here. Or shall I come where you are?" In the middle of this sentence Hugo replaced the receiver.

Then I was in a complete frenzy. I shouted into the phone and hurled it down. I tore my hair and cursed at the top of my voice. I stamped up and down the room scattering the rugs to right and left. It took me a good ten minutes to calm down and start wondering what it was exactly that I was so upset about. I felt that now I must see Hugo at once, instantly, at any cost, within the hour if possible. Until I had seen Hugo the world would stand still. I was not in the least clear about what I wanted to see Hugo for. It was just essential, that was all, and I would be in anguish until it was done. I seized the phone book. I knew that Hugo had moved from his former house, and I had taken care not to know anything of his present abode. I turned the pages with trembling fingers. Yes, he was in the book; a Holborn address and a City number. With a stampeding heart I dialled the number. There was no reply.

Then I sat quietly wondering what to do next. I decided that I should go first of all straight to the address given in the phone book, in case he should nevertheless be there, and

that I should then seek him if need be at the Bounty Belfounder studio. If Hugo had been looking for Sadie it was
unlikely that he was at the studio, since that was where Sadie
herself was. On the other hand, the Miss Quentin he had
asked for might have been Anna. So there was really no
knowing whether or not he mightn't be at the studio. In any
case the first thing to do was to go to Holborn to see if he
was hiding there and just not answering the phone. Of
course he would have been sure to guess, if he had telephoned from his home, that I would ring him back there
immediately.

Then I began to imagine with what feelings of disgust
and dislike he must have put down the receiver after I had
announced my identity. He could not even bring himself to
speak to me for a moment. I put these thoughts away, they
were too painful, and I began to set the rugs straight and
tidy up my things. It occurred to me then that Sadie had
especially asked me to stay in the flat all day. I countered
this, however, with the reflexion that after all I was going
out to hunt for Hugo, and it was against an incursion from
Hugo that I was supposed to be defending the place. So that
what I was doing could just count as aggressive rather than
defensive tactics having the same end in view, viz. the
deflection of Hugo from Welbeck Street. If I could find
Hugo and occupy him with myself I would be simply ful-
filling Sadie's wishes in another way. With that I strode to
the door. I took a farewell look around the flat, and then
turned the handle.

Nothing happened. I turned the handle again. The door
was stuck fast. The Yale lock turned all right, but there was
a lock of another design, with no key in it, lower down the
door—and this evidently was locked. I examined the bolts,
but they were all drawn back. I shook the door and pulled
at it with all my strength. It was quite certain that it was
locked and the key was gone. I was locked in. When this
was clear beyond a shadow of doubt I made my way to the
kitchen and tried the kitchen door, which gave onto a fire
escape. This was locked too.

I then examined the windows. The only one that offered me any hope was the kitchen window, which was separated from the door by a few feet. A daring fellow could have leapt from there onto the fire escape. I judged the distance, looked at the drop, and decided that I was not a daring fellow. I had no head for heights. That consideration bore equally against the drainpipe in the front of the house. I began to search the flat, looking in drawers and boxes to see if I could find a key; but I did this without much hope of success. I was of course perfectly certain that Sadie had done this on purpose. She wanted me, for reasons of her own, to hold the fort all day, and her method of making sure that I did so was to keep me a prisoner. The fact that she had been right in anticipating that I should want to desert my post didn't make me any the less incensed against her. It was indeed equally clear that with this incident my relations with Sadie must terminate.

When I had given up the search for the key my final bid was to try to pick the lock of the kitchen door. It was a simple lock. I am in general not too bad at picking locks, a skill which was taught to me by Finn, who is very good at it. But I could make nothing of this one, largely because I couldn't find a suitable tool. The best thing to pick a lock with is a firm piece of wire or a stout hairpin. I could find neither of these in the flat, so I soon gave up altogether. Now that it was inescapably plain to me that I was a prisoner, and that there was nothing to be done but to wait for Sadie to come back, I felt perfectly calm and quiet though perhaps morose might have described it better. I packed up all my belongings in readiness for a quick move. I was resolved to be short with Sadie. Also I was still determined to set off at the very moment of my liberation to look for Hugo. I rang Hugo's number again but got no reply. I thought of telephoning elsewhere for assistance, but on reflexion I decided that there was no one to whom I felt inclined to speak frankly of my predicament. I poured myself out a half tumbler of gin, and sat down and laughed very considerably.

After that I began to feel hungry. It was after two o'clock. I went into the kitchen and made myself a long luxurious meal, consisting of *pâté de foie gras*, salmon, jellied chicken and tinned asparagus, raspberries, Roquefort and orange juice. I decided that, in spite of the enormity of Sadie's crime, I would not drink her wine. I found some brandy in one of the cupboards and sat a long time over that, regretting only that Sadie didn't smoke cigars. When thoughts of Hugo and Anna had begun to disturb me excessively I washed up all the plates. After that I began to feel moody, and went to one of the front windows which gave onto Welbeck Street and leaned out, watching the traffic and the people passing by.

I had been leaning there some little while, and I was singing a French song to myself and wondering gloomily what on earth I'd say to Sadie when she came back, when I saw two familiar figures coming down the other side of the street. It was Finn and Dave. When they saw me they began to make signals in a conspiratorial fashion.

"It's all right," I called out, "I'm alone."

They came across, and Dave said "Good! We were afraid the Queen of Sheba might be there!"

They both looked up at me grinning. I was extremely glad to see them.

"So!" said Dave, who was pleased with himself, "are you enjoying to be a bodyguard? Have you guarded well?"

Finn smiled up at me with his usual amiability, but I could see that on this occasion his sympathies were with Dave. They both seemed to find the situation vastly funny. I wondered what they'd think in a moment.

"I've had a quiet day," I said with dignity. "I've done some work."

"Shall we ask him what his work was?" said Dave to Finn. I could see I was in for a bad half-hour.

"Well, if you've done your day's work," said Dave, "why not come out and have a drink. It is nearly time that they are open. Unless you'd rather invite us in. Or are you not allowed to have followers?"

"I can't come out," I said calmly, "and I can't ask you in either."

"Why not?" asked Dave.

"Because I'm locked in," I said.

Finn and Dave looked at each other, and then they collapsed helplessly. Dave sat down on the kerb choking with laughter and Finn leaned weakly against the lamp-post. They rocked. I waited coolly for the paroxysm to be over, humming softly to myself. Dave at last lifted his head and after several attempts managed to say to Finn, "But that settles it!" and they were both off again.

"Look here," I said, impatiently, "stop laughing and get on with getting me out of here."

"He wants to get *out*!" cried Dave. "But haven't you tried? What about that drainpipe? It looks perfectly easy, doesn't it, Finn?" And they doubled up again.

"I've tried everything," I said. "Now shut up and do what I say. I suggest Finn picks the lock of the kitchen door. You can get up by a fire escape at the back. I'd have done it myself only Sadie doesn't use hairpins."

"We don't use hairpins either," said Dave, "but if you like we'll carry a petition to Sadie."

"Finn," I said, "will you help me out of this place?"

"I will surely," said Finn, "but I've nothing with me."

"Well, go and find something!" I shouted.

By now our somewhat bizarre conversation had attracted a good deal of attention in the street and I didn't want to prolong it. Eventually it was agreed that Finn should walk round the neighbouring streets until he found a hairpin, and then come back to deal with the door. Even in these days one doesn't have to walk far in the streets of London before coming on a hairpin, if one happens to be looking for one. My only fear was that Finn would forget what he was supposed to be doing and go into a pub. I know myself that nothing is so hypnotic as walking along with one's eyes on the pavement.

When this had been settled I closed the window firmly. I

felt that further conversation with Dave would be unprofitable at that moment. In a few minutes, however, I could hear him banging on the kitchen door, and I had to go and converse with him out of the kitchen window simply to keep him quiet. He then kept up for some quarter of an hour a stream of irritating *badinage*, full of more or less fantastic suggestions to the effect that if I'd had an ounce of spirit I might have escaped by crawling along ledges, climbing onto the roof, tying the sheets together, and other things of a similar kind, to which I answered somewhat curtly. At last I heard Finn coming bounding up the fire escape. He had found a beautiful hairpin, and it didn't take him more than half a minute to deal with the lock. Dave and I watched him with admiration. When the door was open Dave and Finn wanted to come in and look round, but I hustled them quickly down the steps. I was not sorry to be spared the interview with Sadie, and had no wish to have her arriving back on us just at this stage. Before I left I stuffed my pockets with biscuits. I asked myself if I belonged to a social class that would pinch two tins of *pâté de foie gras* from a woman guilty of making an illegal detention, and decided that I did. I took a last sad look at the Afghans and Kazaks, and seized my belongings and went.

When we were in the street I hailed a taxi at once. Finn and Dave were both in the highest spirits, and had clearly no intention of being parted from me. I think they felt that if they hung onto me they'd be in for an entertaining evening, of which they were loath to be cheated. I on my side wasn't yet entirely certain what I was going to do, and felt my usual need of moral support, so I let them pile into the taxi after me. We went first to Mrs Tinckham's shop, where I left my suitcase and the manuscripts.

"Now, where do we go?" asked Dave, his round face shining with glee, like a small boy before a picnic.

"We're going to look for Belfounder," I said.

"You mean the film fellow," said Finn. "The fellow you used to know a long time ago?"

"Him," I said, and refused to be pumped further, so that

Dave had to entertain Finn for the rest of the journey with a wealth of more or less insulting conjecture.

I didn't listen to them. I was beginning to feel very nervous now that the prospect of an interview with Hugo was looming over me like an iceberg. I had really very little idea about what I wanted to say to Hugo. It wasn't exactly that I needed to see him to find out about his feelings for Anna. I felt as confident that I had diagnosed these correctly as I was that the simpleton on the stage at the Mime Theatre had been Hugo, and that it had been Hugo who had driven Anna away afterwards in the big black Alvis. I wanted of course much more to discover Hugo's state of mind toward myself. Not that I was in any real doubt about this either; it was certain that Hugo must regard me with a most comprehensible dislike and contempt. But this condition I might by my own efforts alter. Yet it was not even for this that I wanted to see Hugo. During the afternoon it had crossed my mind that Hugo might have a great deal more to teach me; the more so, as my own perspective had altered since the days of our earlier talks. I had seen this in a flash when I had re-read, after so long, a piece of the dialogue. My appetite for Hugo's conversation was not blunted. There might be more speech between us yet. Was it this then that made me seek him with such a feverish urgency? It seemed to me that after all I just wanted to see him because I wanted to see him. The bullfighter in the ring cannot explain why it is that he wants to touch the bull. Hugo was my destiny.

Seven

THE taxi stopped and we got out. Dave paid. Hugo
lived, it appeared, right up above Holborn Viaduct, in
a flat perched on top of some office buildings. A door
opened on a stone stairway, and a painted board showed
us, together with the names of commercial and legal firms,
his name, Belfounder. The taxi drove off and left us standing alone on the Viaduct. If you have ever visited the City
of London in the evening you will know what an uncanny
loneliness possesses these streets which during the day are so
busy and noisy. The Viaduct is a dramatic viewpoint. But
although we could see for a long way, not only toward Holborn and Newgate Street, but also along Farringdon Street,
which swept below us like a dried-up river, we could see no
living being. Not a cat, not a copper. It was a warm evening, cloudlessly and brilliantly blue, and the place was mute
around us, walled in by a distant murmur which may have
been the sound of traffic or else the summery sigh of the declining sun. We stood still. Even Finn and Dave were impressed.

"You wait here," I told them, "and if I don't come out in
a few minutes you can go away."

But they were not pleased with this. "We'll just see you
up the stairs," said Dave. "You can trust us to become
scarce at the moment you will wish." I think they hoped to
catch a glimpse of Hugo.

I wasn't at all sure whether I could trust them, but I
didn't argue, and we started in Indian file up the stone steps.
I felt nothing now but a blank determination. We plodded
on up the stairway, past the locked-up offices of gown-
makers and oath-takers. When we had reached about the
fourth floor a strange sound began to make itself heard. We
stopped and looked at each other.

"What is it?" said Finn.

None of us could say. We walked up a little further on tiptoe. The sound came from the top of the building; it began to define itself as a continuous high-pitched chatter.

"He's giving a party!" I said with a sudden inspiration.

"It's women!" said Dave. "Film stars, I expect. Come on!"

We proceeded with caution; only another bend of the stairs separated us from Hugo's door. I pushed the two of them back and went up alone. The door was ajar. The noise was now deafening. I threw my shoulders back and walked in.

I found myself in a completely empty room. There was another door opposite to me. I walked quickly across and opened it. The next room was empty too. As I stepped back through the doorway I banged into Finn and Dave.

"It's birdies," said Finn. It was. Hugo's flat occupied a corner position, and was skirted on the outside by a high parapet. A sloping roof jutted out over the window so as almost to touch the parapet; and in the deep angle under the roof there were hundreds of starlings. We could see them fluttering at the windows and jumping up and down between the glass and the parapet as if they had been in a cage. Their noise must have been inaudible from the street or perhaps we confused it with the general hum of London. Here it was overwhelming. I felt enormous confusion and enormous relief. There was no sign of Hugo.

Dave was at the window making futile attempts to drive the birds away.

"Leave them alone," I said. "They live here."

I looked about me with curiosity. The second room was Hugo's bedroom, and was furnished with the sparse simplicity characteristic of the Hugo I had known. It contained nothing but an iron bed, rush-bottomed chairs, a chest of drawers and a tin trunk with a glass of water on top of it. The first and larger room, however, revealed a new Hugo. A Turkey carpet covered the entire floor, and mirrors, settees and striped cushions made an idle and elegant scene. A number

of original paintings hung on the walls. I identified two
small Renoirs, a Minton and a Miro. I whistled slightly
over these. I could not remember that Hugo had ever been
particularly interested in painting. There were very few
books. It struck me as charmingly typical of Hugo that he
should go out and leave the door ajar upon this treasure
house.

Finn was watching the birds. If one could have ignored
their deafening chatter, they were a pretty sight, as they
scrambled and fluttered and jostled each other, spreading
their serrated wings, framed in each window as if they were
part of the decoration of the room. As I looked at them I
was wondering whether I should not just settle down here
and wait for Hugo to come back.

But at that moment Dave, who had been prowling around
on his own account, called out "Look at this!" He was
pointing to a note which was pinned onto the door and
which we had failed to notice as we came in. It read simply:
Gone to the pub.

Dave was already out on the landing. "For what do we
wait?" he asked. He looked like a man who wanted a drink.
Once the idea had been put into his head, Finn began to
look like one too.

I hesitated. "We don't know which pub," I said.

"It'll be the nearest one, obviously," said Dave, "or one
of the nearest ones. We can make a tour."

He and Finn were off down the stairs. I glanced quickly
about the landing. Another door showed me a bathroom
and a small kitchen. The kitchen window gave onto a flat
roof, across which I could see the windows and sky-lights
of other office buildings. This was all there was to Hugo's
domain. I gave the starlings a farewell look, left the door of
Hugo's sitting-room as I had found it, and followed Finn
and Dave down the stairs.

We stood beside the iron lions on the Viaduct. The intense light of evening fell upon the spires and towers of St
Bride to the south, St James to the north, St Andrew to
the west, and St Sepulchre, and St Leonard Foster and St

Mary-le-Bow to the east. The evening light quieted the houses and the abandoned white spires. Farringdon Street was still wide and empty.

"Which way?" asked Dave.

I know the City well. We could either go westward to the King Lud and the pubs of Fleet Street, or we could go eastward to the less frequented alley-twisted and church-dominated pubs of the City. I conjured up Hugo's character.

"East," I said.

"Which is east?" Finn asked.

"Come on!" I said.

We strode past St Sepulchre and straight into the Viaduct Tavern, which is a Meux's house. A glance round the bars satisfied me that Hugo wasn't there, and I was about to go when Finn and Dave started protesting.

"I remember," said Dave, "you once before told me that it was bad form to drink in a pub you didn't know the name of, or to enter a pub without drinking."

Finn said, "It brings bad luck."

"However that may be," said Dave, "I want a drink. What is yours, Finn?"

If other things had been equal I would have wanted a drink too, and as it was a hot night I joined the others in a pint, drinking which I stood apart thinking about Hugo. We got the pint down fast and I gave them orders to march. Averting my eyes from the Old Bailey, I led them across the road.

There was a sleek Charrington's house called the Magpie and Stump. Running ahead of them I took in the scene at a glance and was out again before they could reach the door. "No good!" I cried. "We'll try the next." I could see that the alcohol would involve us in a *rallentando* and I wanted to get as far as possible while the going was good.

Finn and Dave passed me at the double and dodged into the George. The George is an agreeable Watney's house with peeling walls and an ancient counter with one of those cut-glass and mahogany superstructures through which the barman peers like an enclosed ecclesiastic. There was no Hugo.

"This is no use," I said to Dave, as we raised our three tankards. "He may be anywhere."

"Don't throw in," said Dave. "You can always go back to the flat."

This was true; and in any case an intolerable restlessness devoured me. If I had to kill the evening until Hugo's return I might as well kill it searching for Hugo as any other way. I spread out in my mind the environs of the Cathedral. Then I concluded an agreement with Finn and Dave that we should only patronize every other pub. Finally I turned my attention to making them move. When we emerged I made toward Ludgate Hill, and turned up the hill toward St Paul's. There was a Younger's house on the hill, but Hugo wasn't in it. The next stop was Short's in St Paul's Churchyard. We had a drink there, and I debated privately whether we shouldn't turn back to Fleet Street; but having betted on the east side I didn't now want to give up. Besides, I felt reluctant to risk meeting Hugo in a Fleet Street milieu, where our personal drama might be spoilt by drunken journalists. I led my company down Cheapside.

The evening was by now well advanced. The darkness hung in the air but spread out in a suspended powder which only made the vanishing colours more vivid. The zenith was a strong blue, the horizon a radiant amethyst. From the darkness and shade of St Paul's Churchyard we came into Cheapside as into a bright arena, and saw framed in the gap of a ruin the pale neat rectangles of St Nicholas Cole Abbey, standing alone away to the south of us on the other side of Cannon Street. In between the willow herb waved over what remained of streets. In this desolation the coloured shells of houses still raised up filled and blank squares of wall and window. The declining sun struck on glowing bricks and flashing tiles and warmed the stone of an occasional fallen pillar. As we passed St Vedast the top of the sky was vibrating into a later blue, and turning into what used to be Freeman's Court we entered a Henekey's house.

Here our agreement broke down, largely because of the operation of the *rallentando* referred to earlier. I was beginning to think by now that it was unlikely that we should meet Hugo, but that we might as well complete the circle. As we went back across Cheapside and turned down Bow Lane they were putting the street lights on. Yellow light from swinging lamps in alleyways fell upon the white walls, revealing ancient names, and darkened the upper air toward night. We noticed a few stars which looked as if they had been there a long time. We turned into the old Tavern in Watling Street. This was just the sort of pub Hugo liked; but he was not therein. As we drank I told the other two that we should visit the Skinners' Arms and then double back to Ludgate Circus.

They had no objection. "So long," Finn said, "as we don't have to waste too much of the good time in walking." I pulled them out and we approached the Skinners' Arms. This pub stands at the junction of Cannon Street and Queen Victoria Street, under the shadow of St Mary, Aldermary. We rolled in.

When we were well inside the door and I had satisfied myself that Hugo wasn't there, Dave gripped my arm and said, "There's someone here I'd like you to meet."

At the end of the long bar, leaning against the counter, was a slim pale individual wearing a red bow-tie. He saluted Dave, and as we came up to him I was impressed by his enormous eyes, which looked at us sad and round and luminous as the eyes of a wombat or a Rouault Christ.

"Meet Lefty Todd," said Dave, and uttered my name too.

We shook hands. I had of course heard a great deal about the eccentric leader of the New Independent Socialists, but I had never met him before and I studied him now with considerable interest.

"What are you doing here?" he said to Dave. His exhausted anaemic look contrasted with the vigour and abruptness of his speech, and as he spoke he waved vaguely to Finn as if he knew him. Finn is someone who never gets introduced.

"Ask Donaghue," said Dave.

"What are you doing here?" said Lefty to me.

I don't like being asked direct questions, and on such occasions I usually lie. "We've been visiting a friend at the office of the *Star*," I said.

"Who?" said Lefty. "I know everyone at the *Star*."

"A man called Higgins," I said, "he's new."

Lefty stared at me. "All right," he said, and turned back to Dave. "You don't often come to these parts," he said.

"I suppose you've been putting the *Independent Socialist* to bed," said Dave.

"It's not strictly in bed yet," said Lefty. "I've left it to the others!"

He turned back to me. "I've heard of you."

I was still feeling annoyed. I didn't make the *gauche* error of replying to this remark, when uttered by a famous person, with "I've heard of you too." Instead I replied, "What have you heard?" This often disconcerts.

Lefty was not disconcerted. He pondered for a moment and then said, "That you are a talented man who is too lazy to work and that you hold left-wing opinions but take no active part in politics."

This was plain enough. "You were not misinformed," I told him.

"About the former," said Lefty, "I don't care a damn, but I'd like to ask you a few questions about the latter. Have you got time?" He showed me the dial of his watch.

I felt a bit confused by the former and the latter, as well as by the brusqueness of his manner and the amount of beer I had drunk. "You mean you want to talk to me about politics?"

"About *your* politics."

Dave and Finn had drifted away and were sitting in the far corner.

"Why not?" I said.

Eight

"WELL, now, let's get clear about where we stand, shall we?" said Lefty. "What political experience have you had in the past?"

"I was in the Y.C.L. once," I said, "and now I'm in the Labour Party."

"Well, we know what *that* means, don't we?" said Lefty. "Practical experience nil. But do you at least keep up to date in a theoretical way? Do you study the political scene?" He spoke with the brisk cheerfulness of a physician.

"Scarcely," I said.

"Could you say at all clearly why you've given up?"

I spread out my hands. "It's hopeless . . ."

"Ah," said Lefty, "that's the one thing you mustn't say. That's the sin against the Holy Ghost. Nothing's ever hopeless. Is it, Dave?" he said to Dave, who at that moment was at the counter buying another drink.

"Nothing except trying to shut you up," said Dave.

"Would you say that you cleared out because you didn't care what happened or because you didn't know what to do?" Lefty asked me.

"These two things connect," I said, and would have said more about this only Lefty cut me short.

"How right you are," he said. "I was just going to say it myself. So that you admit that you care?"

"Of course," I said, "but . . ."

"Well, it's the chink in the dam," said he. "If you can care at all you can care absolutely. What other moral problem is there in this age?"

"Being loyal to one's friends and behaving properly to women," I answered quick as a flash.

"You're wrong," said Lefty. "It's the whole framework

109

that's at stake. What's the use of preventing a man from stumbling when he's on a sinking ship?"

"Because if he breaks his ankle he won't be able to swim," I suggested.

"But why try to save him from breaking his ankle if you can try to save him from losing his life?"

"Because I know how to do the former but not the latter," I told him rather testily.

"Well, let's see, shall we?" said Lefty, who had lost none of his eagerness.

He opened a brief-case and produced a pile of pamphlets which he flicked through rapidly.

"This is the one for you," he said, and held it up in front of me as if it were a mirror. In large letters on the cover was the question: Why have *you* LEFT POLITICS? and under-neath: LEFT POLITICS needs *you*! At the bottom it said: price 6d. I began to fumble in my pocket.

"No, you take it away, it's a present," said Lefty; "in fact, we never sell these things. But if there's a price on it people feel they've made a good bargain, and then they read it. You look it over when you've got a quiet time to-morrow." And he thrust it inside my coat.

"Now, are you a socialist?"

"Yes," I said.

"Certain?"

"Yes."

"Good. Mind you, we don't yet know what this means, but so far so good. Now, what features of the present situa-tion make you feel that it's hopeless to fight for socialism?"

"It's not exactly that I feel it's hopeless . . ." I began.

"Come, come," said Lefty, "we've confessed to the illness, haven't we? Let's get on towards the cure."

"All right," I said, "it's this. English socialism is perfectly worthy, but it's not socialism. It's welfare capitalism. It doesn't touch the real curse of capitalism, which is that work is deadly."

"Good, good!" said Lefty. "Let's take it slowly now. What was the most profound thing Marx ever said?"

I was beginning to be annoyed by this question and answer method. He asked each question as if there was one precise answer to it. It was like the catechism. "Why should any one thing be the most profound?" I asked.

"You're right, Marx said a lot of profound things," said Lefty, not deigning to notice my annoyance. "For instance, he said that consciousness doesn't found being, but social being is the foundation of consciousness."

"Mind you, we don't yet know what this means . . ." I said.

"Oh, yes we do!" said Lefty, "and it doesn't mean what some mechanistically minded Marxists think it means. It doesn't mean that society develops mechanically and ideologies just tag along. What's crucial in a revolutionary era? Why, consciousness. And what is its chief characteristic? Why, precisely not just to reflect social conditions but to reflect *on* them—within limits, mind you, within limits. That's why you intellectuals are important. Now what would you say was the future of a body like NISP?"

"To get more votes than any other party and make you Prime Minister."

"Not a bit of it!" said Lefty triumphantly.

"Well, what is its future?" I asked.

"I don't know," said Lefty.

I felt it was unfair of him suddenly to throw in a question to which he didn't know the answer.

"But that's the essence of it!" he went on. "People accuse us of being irresponsible. But those people just don't understand our role. Our role is to explore the socialist consciousness of England. To increase its sense of responsibility. New social forms will be forced on us soon enough. But why should we sit waiting with nothing better to keep us company than social ideas drawn from the old ones?"

"Wait a moment," I said. "What about the people meanwhile? I mean the masses. *Ideas* occur to *individuals*. That's always been the trouble with the human race."

"You've put your finger on it," said Lefty. "What, you are going to say, about the famous unity of theory and practice?"

"Indeed," I said, "I could wish no greater good to England than that English socialism should become inspired and rejuvenated. But what is the use of an intellectual renaissance that doesn't move the people? Theory and practice only unite under very special circumstances."

"E.g. when?" said Lefty.

"Well," I said, "e.g. when the Bolshevik party fought for power in Russia."

"Ah," said Lefty, "you've chosen a bad example for your own argument. Why are we so impressed by the very high degree of consciousness which these people seem to have had of what they were up to? Because they succeeded. If they hadn't succeeded they'd look like a little gang of crackpots. It's in retrospect that we see the whole thing as a machine of which they understood the workings. You can't judge the unity of theory and practice in a moment-to-moment way. The principle of their disunity is important too. The trouble with you is you don't really believe in Socialist Possibility. You're a mechanist. And why are you a mechanist? I'll tell you. You call yourself a socialist, but you were brought up on Britannia rules the waves like the rest of them. You want to belong to a big show. That's why you're sorry you can't be a communist. But you can't be—and neither have you enough imagination to pull out of the other thing. So you feel hopeless. What you need is flexibility, flexibility!" Lefty pointed at me an immensely long and supple finger. "Maybe we have lost one chance to be the leaders of Europe," he said. "But the point is to deserve it. Then perhaps we'll have another one."

"And meanwhile," I said, "what about the Dialectic?"

"There you go," said Lefty. "It's like the evil eye. You don't really believe in it, yet it paralyses you. Even the adherents of the Dialectic know that the future is anyone's guess. All one can do is first reflect and then act. That's the human job. Not even Europe will go on forever. Nothing goes on forever."

Dave was at the bar again.

"Except the Jews," I said.

"Yes, you're right," said Lefty, "except the Jews."

We both looked at him.

"What?" said Dave.

"It's time now, please," said the barmaid.

"So you do recognize certain mysteries?" I asked Lefty.

"Yes, I'm an empiricist," he said.

We handed in our glasses.

By now I had enough alcohol inside me to feel despair at the prospect of having to stop drinking. Also I was beginning to take rather a fancy to Lefty.

"Can we buy a bottle of brandy here?" I asked.

"I think so," he said.

"Well, suppose we buy one and continue this discussion somewhere?" I said.

Lefty hesitated. "All right," he said, "but we'll need more than one bottle. Four half bottles of Hennessy, please, Miss," he said to the barmaid.

We emerged into Queen Victoria Street. It was a very still, hot night, burnt with stars and flooded by a moon. A few drunks reeled off and left us the scene. We stood looking toward St Paul's, each man with a brandy bottle in his pocket.

"Whither?" said Dave.

"Let me just collect my wits," said Lefty. "I have to go to the Post office and send off some letters."

It is characteristic of central London that the only thing you can buy there at any hour of the day or night is a stamp. Even a woman you can't get after about three-thirty a.m. unless you are *bien renseigné*. We set off in the direction of the General Post Office, and as we turned into King Edward Street I took a swig from my bottle. As I did so I realized I was already very drunk indeed.

The General Post Office was spacious, cavernous, bureaucratic, sober and dim. We entered hilariously, disturbing the meditation of a few clerks and of the people who are always to be found there at late hours penning anonymous letters or suicide notes. While Lefty bought stamps and despatched cables I organized the singing in round of *Great Tom is Cast,* which continued, since I never have the presence of mind necessary to stop a round once it is started, until an official turned us out. Outside we studied the fantastic letter-boxes, great gaping mouths, where one can watch the released letter falling down and down a long dark well until it lands upon a tray in a lighted room far below. This so fascinated Finn and me that we decided we must write some letters forthwith, and we returned inside and bought two letter cards. Dave said he already received more letters than he wanted and there was no sense in inviting yet more by pointless acts of correspondence. Finn said he was going to write to someone in Ireland. I started to write to Anna, pressing the card vertically against the wall of the Post Office; but I could think of nothing to say to her except *I love you,* which I wrote several times over, very badly. Then I added, *you are beautiful,* and sealed the letter. I put it well into the mouth of the box and let it go and it fell, turning over and over like an autumn leaf.

"Come on!" said Lefty.

"Where?"

"Here," he said, and led us suddenly down beside the edge of the Post Office. In a daze I saw Lefty ahead of me rising from the ground. He was on top of a wall beckoning to me. The way I felt at that moment I could have walked up the side of the *Queen Mary.* I followed, and the others followed me. A moment later we found ourselves in what seemed like a small enclosed and much overgrown garden. In the light summer darkness I discerned a fig tree which leaned across an iron gateway. Grass grew knee deep about fallen white stones. We sat. Then I realized that we were in what had once been the nave of St Leonard Foster. I lay back in the deep grass and my eyes filled with stars.

A little while later Lefty was saying to me, "What you need is to become involved. As soon as you do something and knock into people you'll begin to hate a few of them. Nothing destroys abstraction so well as hatred."

"It's true," I said lazily. "At present I hate nobody."

We spoke in low voices. Near by Finn and Dave lay murmuring to each other.

"Then you ought to be ashamed," said Lefty.

"But what could I do?" I asked him.

"That would have to be studied," said Lefty. "We treat our members scientifically. We ask about each one : where is the point of intersection of his needs and ours? What will he most like doing which will also most benefit us? Of course, we ask for a certain amount of simple routine work as well."

"Of course," I said. I was watching Orion rising through a forest of grass.

"In your case," said Lefty, "it's fortunately quite plain what you can do."

"What?"

"Write plays," said Lefty.

"I can't," I said. "Won't novels do?"

"No," said he. "Who reads novels now? Ever tried to write a play?"

"No."

"Well, the sooner you start the better. Aimed at the West End, naturally."

"It's not easy to get a play put on in the West End," I told him.

"Don't you believe it!" said Lefty. "It's just a matter of making certain routine concessions to popular taste. Before you start you can make a scientific analysis of a few recent successes. The trouble with you is you don't like hard work. Give it the right framework and then you can fill in any message you please. You'd better come round and discuss it with me some time next week. Now then, when can you come?"

Lefty produced his diary and began turning over its

thickly marked pages. I tried to think of some reason why this was impossible, but I could think of none. Orion was putting his foot into my eye.

"Tuesday, Wednesday, Thursday . . ." I said to him. "But I promise nothing."

"I'm pretty filled up," said Lefty. "What about Friday at about three-fifteen? I'm free till four, and with luck a bit longer. Come to the *Ind. Soc.* office."

"All right, all right," I said. I could see the pallor of Lefty's face turned toward me.

"You'll forget," he said. And he took out a card, and wrote down the time and place, and pushed it into my pocket.

"And now," he said to me, "perhaps you'll tell me what it was you were doing in these parts?"

This question moved me, partly because it was the first direct indication I had had that Lefty was human, and partly because it reminded me of Hugo, who had been unaccountably absent from my mind during the last few hours. I dragged myself to a sitting position. My head felt as if it were on a spring and someone were trying to pull it off. I clutched it violently with both hands.

"I was looking for Belfounder," I told him.

"Hugo Belfounder?" said Lefty, and there was a note of interest in his voice.

"Yes, do you know him?" I asked.

"I know who you mean," said Lefty.

I looked towards him, but his enormous eyes showed only as two black patches in the pallor of his face. "Did you see him this evening?" I asked.

"He didn't come into the Skinners'," said Lefty.

I wanted to ask Lefty more questions; I wondered how he saw Hugo. As a capitalist? But my head claimed all my attention for the moment.

It was a bit later again, it must have been some time after two, when Finn expressed a desire to go swimming. Lefty had been talking to Dave, and I was just getting my second wind. The night was faultlessly warm and still. As soon as

Finn suggested this idea it seemed to all of us except Dave an irresistible one. We discussed where to go. The Serpentine was too far away and so was Regent's Park, and the St James's Park area is always stiff with police. The obvious thing was to swim in the Thames.

"You'll get swept away by the tide," said Dave.

"Not if we swim when it's on the turn," said Finn. This was brilliant. But when was it on the turn?

"My diary will tell us," said Lefty. We crowded round while he struck a match. High tide at London Bridge was at two fifty-eight. It was perfect. A moment later we were climbing the wall.

"Watch out for police," said Lefty. "They'll think we're going to rob a warehouse. If you see one, pretend to be drunk."

This was rather superfluous advice.

Across a moonswept open space we followed what used to be Fyefoot Lane, where many a melancholy notice board tells in the ruins of the City where churches and where public houses once stood. Beside the solitary tower of St Nicholas we passed into Upper Thames Street. There was no sound; not a bell, not a footstep. We trod softly. We turned out of the moonlight into a dark labyrinth of alleys and gutted warehouses where indistinguishable objects loomed in piles. Scraps of newspaper blotted the streets, immobilized in the motionless night. The rare street lamps revealed pitted brick walls and cast the shadow of an occasional cat. A street as deep and dark as a well ended at last in a stone breakwater, and on the other side, at the foot of a few steps, was the moon again, scattered in pieces upon the river. We climbed over onto the steps and stood in silence for a while with the water lapping our feet.

On either side the walls of warehouses jutted out, cutting our view and sheltering the inlet where the river came to us, thick with scum and floating spars of wood, full to overflowing in the bosom of London. There was a smell as of rotten vegetables. Finn was taking off his shoes. No man who has faced the Liffey can be appalled by the dirt of another river.

"Careful," said Lefty. "Keep well down on the steps, then no one can see us from the street. Don't talk aloud, and don't dive in. There may be river police around." He pulled his shirt off.

I looked at Dave. "Are you coming in?" I asked him.

"Of course not!" he said. "I think you are all mad." And he sat down with his back to the breakwater.

My heart was beating violently. I began to undress too. Already Finn was standing pale and naked with his feet in the water. He was thrusting aside the flotsam with his foot and walking slowly down the steps. The water reached to his knees, to his buttocks, and then with a soft splash he was away and the wood was knocking upon the stone as the ripples came back.

"What an infernal row he's making!" said Lefty.

My stomach was chill and I was shivering. I pulled off my last garment. Lefty was already stripped.

"Keep it quiet," he said. "I don't want to be copped for *this*!"

We looked at each other and smiled in the darkness. He turned to the river and began edging awkwardly down, his body diminishing into the black water. The night air touched my body with a touch which was neither warm nor cold, only very soft and unexpected. My blood buzzed behind my skin with a nervous beat. Then without a sound Lefty had followed Finn. The water took my ankles in a cold clasp. As I went down I could see from the corner of my eye Dave crouched above me like a monument. Then the water was about my neck and I shot out into the open river.

The sky opened out above me like an unfurled banner, cascading with stars and blanched by the moon. The black hulls of barges darkened the water behind me and murky towers and pinnacles rose indistinctly on the other bank. I swam well out into the river. It seemed enormously wide; and as I looked up and down stream I could see on one side the dark pools under Blackfriars Bridge, and on the other the pillars of Southwark Bridge glistening under the moon. The whole expanse of water was running with light. It was like swimming in quicksilver. I looked about for Finn and Lefty, and soon saw their heads bobbing not far away. They came towards me and for a while we swam together. We had caught the tide beautifully upon the turn and there was not the least hint of a current.

I was easily the best swimmer of the three. Finn swims strongly but awkwardly, wasting his power in unnecessary movements and rolling too much from side to side. Lefty swam with neatness but without vigour. I guessed that he would soon tire. I swim excellently, giving myself to the water, and I have an effortless crawl which I can keep up indefinitely. Swimming has natural affinities with Judo. Both arts depend upon one's willingness to surrender a rigid and nervous attachment to the upright position. Both bring muscles into play throughout the whole body. Both demand, over an exceptionally wide area of bodily activity, the elimination of superfluous motion. Both resemble the dynamism of water which runs through many channels to find its own level. In fact, however, once one has learnt to control one's body and overcome the primeval fear of falling which is so deep in the human consciousness, there are few physical arts and graces which are not thereby laid open to one, or at any rate made much easier of access. I am, for instance, a good dancer and a very creditable tennis player. If it were possible for anything to console me for my lack of height, these things would console me.

Now the other two had gone back to the steps. I swam to one of the barges, and clung onto the cable for a while, throwing my head back to scan a panorama of blue-black sky and black and silver water, and stilling my body until the silence entered me with a rush. Then I climbed up the cable until I was free of the water, and clung to it like a white worm. Then I let go with my feet, and clambered down hand over hand lowering myself noiselessly back into

the river. As my legs broke the surface I could feel a gentle
and continuous pull. The tide was beginning to run out
again. I made for the steps.

Finn and Lefty were dressing in a state of smothered
hilarity. I joined them. A tension had been released, a
ritual performed. Now we should have liked to have
shouted and fought. But the necessity of silence turned our
energy into laughter. When I was dressed I felt warm, and
nearly sober, and ravenously hungry. I searched the pockets
of my mackintosh and found the biscuits and *foie gras*
which I had taken from Sadie. These were received with
quiet acclamation. We sat upon the steps which were
lengthening now as the tide receded and deposited at our
feet broken crates and tin cans and a miscellany of vege-
table refuse. I opened the tins of *pâté* with my knife and
made a distribution of biscuits. There was still some
brandy left in the bottles other than mine; but Dave
said he had had enough and resigned his rights to me.
Lefty announced that he must go soon, as the Party were
moving into a new Branch Office that morning. He offered
the rest of his bottle to Finn, and it was not refused. We
ate joyously, passing the tins from hand to hand. The
brandy was going down my throat like divine fire and
making my blood race at the speed of light.

What happened after that I'm not very sure. The rest of
the night appears in patches through the haze that hangs
over it in my memory. Lefty went away, after we had sworn
eternal friendship, and I had pledged myself to the cause of
socialist exploration. I had a long sentimental talk with
Dave about something or other, Europe perhaps. Finn, who
was even drunker than I, got mislaid. We left him somewhere with his feet in the water. Dave said some time later
that he thought it was perhaps his head that had been in the
water, so we came back to look for him but couldn't find
him. As we walked those empty streets under a paling sky
a strange sound was ringing in my ears which was perhaps
the vanishing bells of St Mary and St Leonard and St
Vedast and St Anne and St Nicholas and St John Zachary.

The coming day had thrust a long arm into the night. Astonishingly soon the daylight came, like a diffused mist, and as we were passing St Andrew-by-the-Wardrobe and I was finishing the brandy the horizon was already streaked with a clear green.

Nine

THE next thing that I remember is that we were in Covent Garden Market drinking coffee. There is an early-morning coffee-stall there for the use of the porters, but we seemed to be its only customers. It was broad daylight now and had been, I believe, for some time. We were standing in the part of the market that is devoted to flowers. Looking about me and seeing exceedingly many roses I was at once reminded of Anna. I decided I would take her some flowers that very morning, and I told Dave so. We wandered into an avenue of crated blossoms. There were so few people about and there were so many flowers that it seemed the most natural thing to help ourselves. I passed between walls of long stemmed roses still wet with the dew of the night, and gathered white ones and pink ones and saffron ones. Round a corner I met Dave laden with white peonies, their bursting heads tinged with red. We put the flowers together into an armful. As there seemed no reason to stop there, we rifled wooden boxes full of violets and anemones, and crammed our pockets with pansies, until our sleeves were drenched and we were half suffocated with pollen. Then, clutching our bouquets, we walked out of the Market and sat down on a doorstep in Long Acre.

My head was aching violently and I was very far from sober. As in a dream I heard Dave saying, "Good heavens, I forgot. I have a letter for you which came two days ago. I have it since a long time in my pocket." He thrust it towards me and I took it languidly. Then I saw that the writing upon it was Anna's.

I tore open the envelope, my fingers trembling with fear and clumsiness. The letters danced and shifted in front of my eyes. When at last they settled down what I read was the following short message: *I want to see you urgently.*

Please come to the Theatre. My head was in my hands. I
started to groan.

"What is it?" asked Dave.

"Get me a taxi," I groaned to him.

"I feel just as bad as you do," said Dave. "Get your own
bloody taxi."

So I got up and went away, taking the flowers with me,
and leaving Dave on the doorstep leaning back against the
door with his eyes closed.

I found a taxi in the Strand and told it to drive me to
Hammersmith. My heart was beating out the refrain *too
late*. I sat forward all the way and the stems of the flowers
were breaking in my hand. We were nearly there before I
noticed how deeply I had impaled myself upon the roses. I
mopped the blood with my shirt sleeve, which was still
muddy from last night. I dismissed the taxi at Hammersmith Town Hall, and walked down toward the river. I
found myself reeling against walls as I went along, and there
was a pain in my heart that almost stopped my breath.
There was the Theatre. But something strange was going
on. The door was open. I quickened my pace. Two or
three lorries stood outside. I bounded into the hall, and as
I did my feet rang upon an uncarpeted floor. I flew up the
stairs, scarcely touching the boards, and flung myself into
Anna's room.

The room was completely bare. It took me a moment to
be quite sure that it was indeed the same room. The whole
multi-coloured chaos was gone, and of it not a spangle, not
a silken thread remained. The room had been stripped and
swept. The windows stood wide open upon the river. Only
in the far corner were a pair of trestle tables with a pile of
papers upon them. I stood there sick with amazement.
Then I stepped back on to the landing. It was clear that
the transformation had affected the whole house. It hum-
med and creaked and echoed. I could hear voices in several
of the rooms and heavy boots striking on bare boards. Doors
were banging. Through every window there came in the
busy murmur of the summer morning. Violent hands had

been laid upon the house; it had been violated. With a sudden impulse I approached the door of the auditorium. I shook it, but it was still locked. Whatever secret the heart of that strange building had contained here at least it could, for a while longer, brood upon it still.

A cheerful-looking girl in blue jeans came up the stairs whistling. When she saw me standing there she said, "Oh, have you come for the retail trade figures?"

I stared at her like a maniac, and after a moment she said, "Sorry, I thought you were the man from the Paddington group."

"I was looking for one of the Theatre people," I said.

"Oh, I'm afraid they've all gone away," said the girl. She went into Anna's room.

I was still standing there, clutching the banisters with one hand and an armful of flowers with the other, when two men in corduroys passed me carrying a large wooden board. Upon the board were painted the letters NISP.

I found myself out in the street. Two more lorries had drawn up. I began to walk along the road parallel to the river. When I was level with the last lorry, one of the ones that had been there when I arrived, something inside it caught my eye. I paused and came closer. Then I was filled by a strange emotion. What the lorry contained was the contents of Anna's room. Inside this enormous box, only just held in by the high tail-board, were piled higgledy-piggledy all the treasures that I remembered. I took a quick look round. No one was watching. And in a moment I had clambered over the tail-board and slipped flowers and all, amid a rain of falling petals, into a yielding mass of toys and textiles. I looked about me. All my old friends were there: the rocking horse, the stuffed snake, the thundersheet, the masks. I looked at them all and I was filled with sorrow. As the harsh sunlight blazed in upon them they seemed but a soiled and broken chaos. The mysterious order which had reigned over their confusion in the theatre room, and which had flowed so gently and naturally from the presence of Anna in their midst, had been withdrawn. They lay now awkwardly one against another, lengthwise and cornerwise, and their magic had departed.

As I was looking at them there was a sudden jolt and the lorry started. I was pitched forward, bruising my cheek upon something hard, while a cascade of miscellaneous objects nearly buried me in the belly of the vehicle. I lay still for a while where I was, my face stuck close up against one of the leering masks, while the mouth of a tin trumpet bored into my back. Then slowly I shook myself free. The lorry was going along King Street. I wondered to myself if there was any possibilty that if I stayed in it it would take me to Anna. But I felt on reflexion extremely sure that it wouldn't. These things had the air of abandoned things, and it was more likely that they were bound for the warehouse of some auctioneer. I began slowly and sadly to pick them over, recognizing and saluting each one; and as I did so I crumbled the flowers too, spreading the petals of roses and peonies upon the gimcrack heap, with a sense that I was strewing the grave of some strange enterprise.

I was stooping to disentangle my foot from a glass necklace, when something caught my eye upon the neck of the rocking-horse, which was lying on its side half submerged in the pile. Attached to the rein there was an envelope. With startled anxiety I looked more closely. On the outside of the envelope was written the letter J. I unpinned it and with breathless haste unfolded the sheet of paper which was inside. It read: *I'm sorry I couldn't wait any longer. I have had an offer which although I don't like it I feel I have to accept. Anna.* I looked upon this, stunned, and a load of misery shifted grinding in my heart. What did it mean? Oh, why had I not come earlier! What was this offer? Perhaps Hugo . . . I wrenched my feet free from their entanglements, scattering a sharp rain of glass beads which pattered about and finally sank into holes and pockets in the swaying mountain. Amid a rending of silks I got to my knees and worked my way toward the tail-board. We were just passing the Albert Hall.

I took a last slow look at Anna's things. Half hidden by a

striped shawl I saw the gilt coronet with which I had crowned her queen of her own silent and coloured domain. I thrust my hand through the circle of the coronet, pulled it up on to my arm, and then prepared to jump. The lorry was slowing down for the traffic lights at Knightsbridge. As I got unsteadily to my feet I saw the thundersheet which was balancing awkwardly with one of its corners boring deep into the mass. I reached out and shook it with all my strength. Then I jumped. As the lorry gathered speed and turned into the Brompton Road the uncanny sound was echoing about the crossroads, making everybody stop to stare and listen. With its rumbling still in my ears I walked into Hyde Park, fell flat upon the grass, and almost immediately fell asleep.

Ten

I AWOKE what seemed to be days later and found that in fact it was only half-past eleven. It took me some time to remember why I was feeling so miserable, and I looked for several minutes at the gilt crown, which I had been clutching in my hand while I slept, without being able to recall what it was or how I came to be holding it. When the sorrowful events of the more recent past came back to me I set myself to wondering what I ought to do next. The first thing seemed to be to get myself as far as a chemist and take something for my headache. I did this. Then I quenched my raging thirst at a water fountain. The quenching of thirst is so exquisite a pleasure that it is a scandal that no amount of ingenuity can prolong it. After that I sat on a bench at Hyde Park Corner rubbing my head, and trying to make a plan.

It was by now perfectly clear to me that my previous pattern of life was gone forever. I can take a hint from the fates. What new pattern would in due course emerge I had no means of telling. Meanwhile there were certain problems which would undoubtedly give me no rest until I had at least made some attempt to solve them. I was tempted to set off again then and there for Holborn Viaduct. But on second thoughts I decided that I had better collect my wits a little before attempting to face Hugo. I was still feeling very strange. In any case it was unlikely that Hugo would be at home during the day. The former argument bore equally against my trying to find him at the studio. I had better spend the day quietly, sleep in the afternoon perhaps, and then start again hunting for Hugo. I would have much preferred to look for Anna. But I had no idea now where to start looking. Also I wanted to lay quickly to rest the terrible suspicion that where I found Hugo now I would also find Anna. This idea didn't bear thinking about and so I didn't think about it.

I then began to reflect at greater length upon the drama of the last few days, and as I did so I remembered with annoyance that in my agitation at leaving Sadie's flat I had failed to bring away with me the copy of *The Silencer* which I had resolved to confiscate for my own use. The more I thought about this the more it annoyed me. It remained to be seen whether I would ever again be able to hold a conversation with Hugo; but in any case it seemed to me that it was time for me to reassess the dialogue and decide whether it contained anything that was fit for salvage. One cannot, I felt, be so prodigal with one's past. The man who had written that curious work still lived within me and might yet write other things. It was clear that *The Silencer* was a piece of unfinished business.

Where could I get a copy? It was no use trying libraries or bookshops. The most sensible thing was to go back to Sadie's and fetch the copy from there. I didn't want to meet Sadie again. But then it was very unlikely that she would be at home. As for getting in, I could get in the way that Finn had got in. When I had thought this out it seemed to be an excellent plan. I would be doing something which was both important and absorbing, and that would keep me from worrying about Anna and Hugo. When I had quite decided this I took a seventy-three bus to Oxford Street, put Anna's crown in the Left Luggage office at Oxford Circus, drank a great deal of black coffee, and bought a packet of hairpins at Woolworths.

I am the sort of man who will prefer to walk for twenty minutes rather than wait five minutes at a bus stop for a five-minute bus ride. When I am worrying about something inactivity and waiting become a torment. But as soon as some practical scheme, however hopeless, is on foot I am content again, and shut my eyes to everything else. So as I strode now along Welbeck Street I felt that I was doing something useful, and although my heart, as well as my head, was aching, I was by no means in a frenzy. I turned

off the street, and sloping along the back alley, easily identified Sadie's fire escape. I padded up, fumbling for my hairpin. I hoped the thing would be easy.

As I approached Sadie's door, however, I heard voices
which were undoubtedly coming from her kitchen. This
was a disappointment. I stood irresolute. It occurred to me
that the speakers might be the char and her friend and that
they might be persuaded to let me in. I walked up a step or
two and thought that I caught the tones of Sadie's voice—
and I was just going to go away when I heard somebody
utter Hugo's name. Some spirit told me that this concerned
me. I thought there might be no harm in hearing a bit more.
So I ascended until, standing upright a few steps from Sadie's
landing, my head was just below the level of the frosted
glass of the door. There was laughter masculine and femin-
ine. Then I heard Sadie's voice say, "Those who don't keep
correspondence are as wax in the hands of those who do!"
There was more laughter, and a sound as of the clinking of
ice in glasses. After that the masculine voice replied. I
didn't hear what it said because I was too electrified by
recognizing it. It belonged to Sammy.

I sat down on the steps and knitted my brows. So Sammy
was a friend of Sadie's, was he? I knew instinctively that the
two of them were up to no good, and I felt a pang of concern
for Madge. It was no use, however, my trying to think it all
out on the spot especially with the head that I still had. The
only thing to do was to record a few more impressions.
There would be time for thinking later. I found that, sitting
down, I was just out of earshot; and standing up was ex-
hausting, especially if I was in for a long session. So I
crawled up the last two or three steps on to Sadie's landing
and sat down cross-legged with my back against Sadie's
door. Here I was within a couple of feet of the speakers,
but safe from observation unless they should happen to
open the door; which naturally I hoped they wouldn't
do.

Sadie was saying, "We must catch him as soon as he
reaches London. He's the sort of person who likes to be

presented with a *fait accompli*. It's just a matter of seizing the initiative."

Sammy replied, "Do you think he'll play?"

Sadie said, "Either he will or he won't. If he won't there's no harm done, and if he will . . ."

"If he will," said Sammy, "stand by for the moon!"

They laughed again. They were perhaps a bit drunk. They were certainly *tête-à-tête*.

"You're sure Belfounder won't make trouble?" Sammy asked then.

"I tell you it's a gentleman's agreement," said Sadie.

"And you're no gentleman!" said Sammy. And he nearly choked himself laughing.

By now it was clear to me that I had done right to eavesdrop. If ever two people were plotting something, Sadie and Sammy were. But what was it all about? Who was it who had to be caught in London? What did make sense was this, that Sadie was engaged in double-crossing Hugo, doubtless because she was jealous of his preference for Anna. I must hear more, I thought, and sat there with my eyes popping out. But as I did so I noticed something rather annoying. The back of Sadie's house was close to the back of a house in the next street. In fact the two houses might be said to overlook each other. The opposite house had a fire escape which was the twin of Sadie's, and between these two erections was a distance of only some fifteen feet. Now my eavesdropping position necessitated my staring straight into one of the rooms of this house. That is, my head had been turned more or less in that direction, though I had been far too preoccupied to perceive anything up to the moment when I noticed that two women were watching me closely from the room opposite. One of them wore a red pinafore, and the other was a powerful-looking woman with a hat on. I dropped my eyes, and was brought sharply back to the conversation behind me by hearing my own name mentioned.

I missed that sentence. The next one was from Sammy, who said, "As a script it certainly has everything."

"Good for Madge!" Sadie said. "She can pick a winner."

"Too bad she didn't back him too!" said Sammy: More laughter.

"You're sure he couldn't make a case?" Sammy asked.

"Not a clear one," said Sadie, "and that's all that matters. He probably has nothing in writing, and if he ever had he'll have lost it."

"He can refuse us permission to use it, though," said Sammy.

"But, don't you see," said Sadie, "that doesn't matter. All we need the thing for is to get H.K. to sign on the dotted line."

All this was of absorbing interest, though I still couldn't for the life of me see what it meant.

At this point there occurred another distraction. The two women opposite had opened their window wide and were looking at me with considerable suspicion. It is hard consistently to avoid the gaze of someone fifteen feet away who is trying to catch your eye, especially when there is nothing else in the vicinity which you can plausibly be thought to be looking at. I smiled politely.

They consulted each other. Then the one in the hat called out, "Are you all right?"

This was very unnerving. It required an iron discipline to prevent myself from getting up and running. I prayed that Sammy and Sadie hadn't heard. Meanwhile I nodded my head vigorously and directed a happy smile in the direction of the two ladies.

"Are you sure?" she asked again.

Almost in despair I nodded, and added to my smile such gestures indicative of total well-being as it is possible to perform in a sitting position with one's back against a door. I shook hands with myself, held up my thumb and index finger in the form of an O, and smiled even more emphatically.

"If you ask me, I think he's an escaped loonie," said the second woman. They retired a little from the window.

"I'm going to tell my husband," I heard one of them saying.

Sadie and Sammy were still talking. By now my ears were nearly leaving my head and gluing themselves on to the door behind me.

"What are you so nervous about?" Sadie was saying. There was no doubt who was using whom in this connivance of unsavoury characters. "Present him with the star and the script and your contracts, and we have a flying start. Belfounder hasn't anything on us legally; and if he starts making complaints I can make plenty of counter-complaints about the way I was treated. As for young Donaghue, we can buy him any day of the week." This annoyed me so much I nearly got up and banged on the door.

But at once Sammy replied, "I don't know. These fellows have funny scruples."

Good for Sammy! I thought; and I was seized forthwith by a convulsive desire to laugh, and had to prevent myself by covering my mouth violently.

The woman with the pinafore reappeared at her window, and at the same time the woman with the hat, who evidently lived in the flat above, appeared at a higher window accompanied by a man.

"There he is!" she said, pointing to me. Then they came out onto the fire escape.

"Perhaps he's deaf and dumb," said the woman with the pinafore.

"Can't you say anything?" called the man on the fire escape.

This was becoming embarrassing. I glared at him, and pointing into my mouth shook my head vigorously. I wasn't sure whether nodding wouldn't have conveyed my meaning more clearly, but the possibilities of misunderstanding were in any case so enormous that it didn't seem to matter much one way or the other.

"He's hungry," said the woman in the pinafore.

"Why don't you do something?" said the woman in the hat to her husband in that maddening way women have. I felt quite sorry for the fellow.

He scratched his head. "Why can't we just leave him alone?" he said. "He's not doing any harm."

This was such a sensible remark that I couldn't but wave to him my congratulations and fellow-feelings. The effect must have been gruesome. He recoiled.

"You can't leave him there," said the woman with the pinafore. She had come out onto the fire escape too. "He's looking straight into our rooms. Suppose the children were to see him?"

"I tell you, he's got away from somewhere!" said the woman above.

A female who was obviously a char then appeared at the kitchen door of the flat below, and had to have the whole matter explained to her. All this while I was in a cold sweat in case the hullabaloo might attract the attention of Sadie and Sammy; but they were either so drunk or else so absorbed in their plot that so far they had noticed nothing.

"I'd like to look it over again before I see H. K.," Sadie was saying. "Where is it, incidentally?"

"It's at my flat," said Sammy.

"Could we phone and have it brought over at once?" Sadie asked.

"There's no one there," said Sammy, "that is unless our new star has come. But that's unlikely." He laughed.

"You know, I think that was a terribly bad idea of yours," said Sadie. "That stuff's just out of date."

"You're jealous!" said Sammy. "Look, I'll call there this evening and bring it round then; will that do?"

"That'll do," said Sadie.

"Late!" said Sammy.

"*That*'ll do!" said Sadie.

There was laughing and scuffling. I wished them joy of each other. But most of all I wished that I could understand what in heaven's name they were up to.

"I'll leave squaring Donaghue to you," said Sammy.

"We aren't on very good terms," said Sadie. "Did I tell you I tried to employ him as a caretaker, but he cleared off?"

"With Belfounder on the rampage you'll need an armed guard," said Sammy. "But why employ an ass like Donaghue? You really have no common sense at all."

"I rather like him," said Sadie simply. This bit touched me deeply.

"Well, you look after him then," said Sammy.

"Oh, stop worrying, will you?" said Sadie. "One translation's just like another. If he won't let us use his we can buy another translation overnight. All we need is to let H. K. see it now in English. As for the Frenchman, he'd sell us his grandmother for dollars."

This set me reeling, and I was just getting to the answer when Sammy gave it to me. "It makes a nice title, doesn't it?" he said. "The *Wooden Nightingale*."

I sat there with my mouth open. But I was given no time to reflect. The scene opposite claimed my attention once more; things over there were beginning to move fast.

"Better call the police, if you ask me," said the char. "Better to let the police deal with them kind, I always think."

The house opposite stood on one side of a wide cobbled lane which gave onto Queen Anne Street. At the corner of this lane I now saw that a small crowd was collecting, attracted by the drama on the fire escape.

"Look at 'im looking down!" said the char. "'E knows what's going on!"

"You go and dial nine nine nine," said the woman in the hat to her husband.

Then the char, who had retired for a moment, reappeared armed with an extremely long cobweb brush. "Shall I poke 'im with my brush and see what 'e does?" she asked; and she forthwith mounted the fire escape and brought the brush into play, delivering me a sharp jab on the ankle.

This was too much. In any case, I had heard enough. I now had all the materials needed for the solution of the problem, and I was in mortal terror that at any moment Sadie and Sammy would come out.

With leisurely grace, under the fascinated gaze of many

eyes, I uncurled my legs, and crawled on my stomach down the first two or three steps. After that I stood up, and rubbed my limbs, which had become very stiff, and walked without haste down the fire escape.

"I told you he was mad!" said the woman in the pinafore.

"He's getting away! Do something!" said the woman in the hat.

"Oh, let him go, poor devil!" said the husband.

"Quick!" said the char. And they all hurried down the other fire escape to join the little crowd at the bottom.

When I reached the foot of the steps I took a quick look back to see if anyone had emerged from Sadie's flat. There was no one. My tormentors were standing all together in the laneway. We looked at each other in silence.

"Creep up on him slow like," said the char.

"Look out, he may be dangerous," said someone else.

They stood hesitating. I took a look behind me, the alley which led into Welbeck Street was clear. Uttering a piercing hiss I suddenly rushed forward toward them; and they scattered in terror, some retreating up the fire escape and some back down the lane. Then I doubled back into Welbeck Street and took to my heels.

Eleven

I MADE for the nearest quiet place I knew of, which happened to be the Wallace Collection, to sit down and put together the fragments of my answer. Sitting facing the cynical grin of Frans Hals's Cavalier, I laboured at it. My mind was still not working very fast. My translation of Breteuil's *Rossignol de Bois,* which I had left with Madge, had been purloined by Sammy. No, it hadn't, it had been presented to Sammy by Madge. Why? To be made a film out of. Who by? Some fellow called H. K. who knows no French. An American probably. What's in this for Sadie? Sammy sells this idea to this Yank, and sells him Sadie at the same time. What about Bounty Belfounder? Sadie walks out on them. Can they do anything about that? Apparently not, they haven't got Sadie tied up properly. What about me? If I won't play it doesn't matter tuppence once this H. K. has been sold the idea. Would Jean Pierre defend me? Of course not. He'll deal directly with where the dollars are. Anyhow, have I any rights? None. Then what am I complaining about? My typescript has been stolen. Stolen? Madge shows it to Sammy, who shows it to H. K. Stolen? What's Madge up to anyway? Madge is being double-crossed by Sammy, who ditches her for Sadie. Sammy uses Madge and Sadie uses Sammy to get her revenge on Hugo and make a fortune in dollars at the same time. I began to see the whole picture. What was so maddening was that the *Wooden Nightingale* would in fact make a marvellous film. It really had everything. Madge, in days when she imagined that it might somehow be possible to persuade me to make money, had gone on about it continually. Poor Madge! She had picked the winner, but Sadie and Sammy would hit the jackpot.

"Not if I can help it!" I exclaimed, and made for the exit.

"An entertaining story," said the Cavalier. "I applaud your decision."

What was my decision? There were no two ways about it. I must try to get back my typescript at once. To do this would be to defend my own interests, and to defend Hugo's, and, what mattered most, to do down Sadie and Sammy. That would be striking a blow for Madge too. Where was the typescript? At Sammy's flat. Where was Sammy's flat? The universal provider of information to which I had applied before told me that Sammy lived in Chelsea. It was clear that I should have to work fast. I must get hold of the typescript before this H. K. could see it. The way Sadie had referred to it suggested that it had not yet been copied. Sammy had implied that he would not be visiting his flat until the evening. He had said that it was probably empty. I rang Sammy's number and got no reply. Then I decided that I badly needed Finn.

I rang Dave's number and after some delay Finn answered, sounding rather dazed. I told him that I was glad he hadn't been drowned, and that I wanted him to come and join me as soon as he could. When he knew it was me he cursed me for a long time in Gaelic, and said that he'd been asleep. I congratulated him, and asked how soon he could get along. At last after much grumbling he said he would come to meet me in the King's Road, and there about three-quarters of an hour later we duly met. The time was then about twenty to three.

I had taken the precaution of asking Finn to bring with him an implement which we called the Master Key, which was a lock-picking tool of simple style which we had designed together on scientific principles. You may think it odd that two ordinary law-abiding citizens like myself and Finn should have troubled to provide ourselves with such an article. But we have found by experience that there are a surprising number of occasions in a society such as ours when simply in defence of one's own rights, as in the present case, one needs to get through a locked door to which one possesses no key. And after all, one may even find oneself

E*

locked out of one's house, and one can't call the Fire Brigade every time.

We telephoned again to make sure the flat was empty; and then as we walked along the road I told Finn the outline of the story. He found this so interesting that he quite got over his bad temper. It was clear, however, that he still had a dreadful hangover. He had the slightly squinting look which he gets with a hangover, and kept shaking his head as he went along. I have often asked Finn why he shakes his head when he has a hangover, and he tells me that it's to make the spots move away from in front of his eyes. It surprises me when Finn, with all his Irish training, stands up to a drinking bout less well than I do; though on this occasion it was possible that although, like the Walrus, I had got all I could, Finn had in fact, like the Carpenter, got hold of more. He has an almost psychic capacity for finding drink at all hours. Whatever the reason, he was in bad shape, while I was by now feeling fine, only a little bit weak in the stomach.

I wasn't at all sure how easy it would prove to get into Sammy's flat. Sammy was the sort of person who might easily have installed a special lock, or worse still a burglar alarm. He lived, moreover, in one of those enormous blocks of service flats, where it was possible that we might be interfered with in our work by the porter or some other busybody. When we reached the block I sent Finn round to the other side of the building to see if he could find a tradesmen's entrance, in case we were disturbed, while I walked in the front way, keeping an eye lifting for porters. We met outside Sammy's door, which was on the fourth floor. Finn said there was a decent quiet tradesmen's entrance. I told him I had seen only one porter, who sat in a glass cage near the main door and didn't look as if he was likely to move. Finn whipped out the Master Key, while I kept watch at the end of the corridor. In a minute or two Sammy's door was opening quietly and we both went in.

We found ourselves in a wide hallway. Sammy had one of the large corner flats. We tried a door, which led into the kitchen.

"We'll concentrate on the living-room and on his bedroom," I said.

"Here's his bedroom," said Finn, and started opening drawers. He lifts and replaces objects with the speed and dexterity of a factory hand on piece work; and as he puts it himself, divil a one would know that it was other than the spring breeze had touched their things. We were both gloved, of course. I watched him for a moment, and then I made for what I took to be the main living-room. The door opened right enough into a large corner room, with windows on both sides. But what I saw as I opened the door made me stop dead in my tracks.

I looked at it for a while, and then I called to Finn, "Come and have a look at this!"

He joined me. "Mother of God!" he said.

Right in the middle of the room was a shining aluminium cage, about three feet tall and five feet square. Inside the cage, growling softly and fixing us with a nervous bright eye, was a very large black-and-tan Alsatian dog.

"Can it get out?" said Finn.

I approached the cage, and as I did so the animal growled more loudly, wagging its tail vigorously at the same time in the ambiguous way dogs have.

"Be careful with the brute!" said Finn, who doesn't care for dogs. "It'll be springing out on you."

I studied the cage. "It can't get out," I said.

"Well, thank God," said Finn, who once this was clear seemed to have no further interest in the phenomenon. "Don't be teasing it now," he added, "or it'll set up a howl will bring the cops onto us."

I looked at the animal curiously; it had a kind intelligent face, and in spite of its growls it seemed to be smiling.

"Hello," I said, and thrust my hand through the bars, whereon it became silent and licked me prodigiously. I began stroking its long nose.

"And don't be acting the maggot with it either," said Finn; "we haven't got all day."

I knew that we hadn't got all day. Finn went back to

Sammy's bedroom and I began to study the living-room. I was very anxious indeed to find the typescript. I kept pausing to imagine with delight Sammy's fury on finding that it was gone. I ransacked Sammy's bureau and a chest of drawers. Then I searched through a cupboard on the landing. I looked in suitcases, and brief-cases, and under cushions and behind books, and even went through the pockets of all Sammy's coats. I came upon various interesting objects, but not the typescript. There was no sign of the thing. Finn had drawn a blank too. We searched the other rooms, but without much hope, as they looked as if they were very little used.

"Where the hell else can we look?" asked Finn.

"I'm sure he's got a secret safe," I said. The fact that the bureau was unlocked suggested this. If I knew my Sammy, he was a man with plenty to hide.

"Well, if he has it'll do us no good finding it," said Finn, "for we'll not be able to open it."

I feared he was right. But we scoured the house again, tapping the floorboards and looking behind pictures, and making sure that there was no drawer or cupboard which we had missed.

"Come on," said Finn, "let you and I be making tracks." We had been there nearly three-quarters of an hour.

I stood in the living-room cursing. "The bloody thing must be in some place," I said.

"True for you!" said Finn, "and it'll likely stay in that place." He pointed to the dial of his watch.

The dog had been watching us all the time, its bushy tail sweeping to and fro against the bars. "A fine watch-dog you are!" Finn told it.

The roof of the cage, which like its floor was made of solid aluminium, was pitched high enough to let the beast stand upright, but not high enough for it to prick its ears when standing up.

"Poor boy!" I said. "You know," I said to Finn, "it's very odd this dog being here. I've never seen anyone put a dog in a cage like that, have you?"

"I suppose it's some sort of special dog," said Finn. Then I whistled. There suddenly came back to my mind what Sammy had said about a new star; and in that moment I recognized the animal.

"Did you ever see *Red Godfrey's Revenge*?" I asked Finn, "or *Five in a Flood*?"

"Is it cracked you are?" said Finn.

"Or *Stargazers' Farm* or *Dabbling in the Dew*?"

"What are you at at all?" he said.

"It's Mister Mars!" I cried, pointing at the beast. "It's Marvellous Mister Mars, the dog star. Don't you recognize him? Sammy must have bought him for the new firm!" I was so fascinated by this discovery that I forgot all about the typescript. Nothing thrills me so much as meeting a film star in real life, and I had been a fan of Mars for years.

"Och, you're potty," said Finn, "all Alsatians look alike. Come away now before himself arrives back on us."

"But it *is* Mars!" I cried. "Aren't you Mister Mars?" I said to the dog. It pranced and wagged its tail faster than before. "There you are!" I said to Finn.

"A fat lot that tells you!" said Finn. "Aren't you Rin Tin Tin?" he said to the dog, who wagged its tail faster still.

"Well, what about this?" I said.

Inscribed unobtrusively along the top of the cage were the words: *Marvellous Mister Mars*—and on the other side *The property of Plantasifilms Ltd*.

"That bit's out of date," I said.

"I'll not dispute it then," said Finn. "I'm off," he added and made for the door.

"Oh wait!" I said, in such a tone of anguish that he stopped.

I was beginning to have a wonderful idea. While it came slowly up I held both hands pressed to my temples and kept my eyes fixed on Mister Mars, who gave one or two soft encouraging barks as if he knew what was coming into my mind.

"Finn," I said slowly, "I have an absolutely wonderful idea."

"What?" said Finn suspiciously.

"We'll kidnap the dog," I said.

Finn stared at me. "What in the world for?" he said.

"Don't you see?" I cried, and as the glorious daring and simplicity of the scheme became even plainer to me I capered about the room. "We'll hold him as a hostage, we'll exchange him for the typescript!"

Finn's look of puzzlement softened into a look of patience. He leaned against the edge of the door. "They wouldn't play," he said, speaking slowly as to a child or a lunatic, "and why should they indeed? We'll only get ourselves in trouble. And anyway, there wouldn't be time."

"I won't go away from here empty handed!" I told him.

The time element was certainly serious. But I felt a feverish desire to become an actor in this drama. It was worth taking a risk with Mars. Sammy's position over the typescript was just dubious enough to restrain him from getting tough. If I could embarrass him by detaining Mars, or even persuade him that Mars's safety was at stake, he might at least be made to parley about the typescript. In fact, I had no really clear plan in my mind at all. I am a swift intuitive type of thinker. All I knew was that I had a bargaining-point under my hand and that I would be a fool not to take advantage of it. Even if the whole manœuvre did no more than annoy and inconvenience Sammy, it would have been worth it. I explained all this to Finn as I started to examine the cage to see how it opened. Finn, who now saw that my mind was made up, shrugged his shoulders and started examining the cage too, while Mars followed us round inside, watching our movements with obvious approval.

The thing was mysterious. There was no door in it, and no locks or bolts or screws, so far as we could see. The bars fitted closely into the roof and the floor.

"Perhaps one side comes away," I said. But there was no sign of any special fastening. The whole thing was as smooth as a pebble.

"It's soldered in," said Finn.

"It can't be," I said. "Surely no one carried the thing upstairs like this."

"Well, it's some trick modern fitting," said Finn. This didn't help. "If we had a good hammer and knew where to tap it . . ." he said. But we hadn't. I battered it for some time with my shoe, but nothing gave.

"Can't we break the bars?" I suggested.

"They're as hard as the Divil's forehead," said Finn.

I went to the kitchen to look for a tool, but I couldn't find a screw-driver, let alone a crowbar. We tried a poker on the bars, but bent it without their yielding a millimetre. I was frantic. I would have sent Finn out for a file, only it was getting late. He was looking at his watch. It was ten past four. I knew he was straining to be away, though I knew too that now we were embarked on a particular enterprise he would stand by me as long as I wanted him. He was squatting there by the cage, and both he and Mars were looking up at me, Finn with the gentle look which he reserves for moments of difficulty.

"Every time I hear a noise on the stairs I have heart disease," said Finn.

I was having it too. But I wasn't going to go away without Mars. I took off my gloves; I felt that things were moving into a new phase.

"Then we'll take the cage as well," I said.

"It won't go through the door," said Finn, "and anyway someone's sure to stop us on the way out."

"We'll try," I said. "If it won't go through the door I'll promise to give up."

"You'll have no choice," said Finn.

I was certain it would go through the door. But to get it through we should have to stand it on its side. There was a bowl of water inside on the aluminium floor of the cage.

"That proves it," said Finn; "they surely put it together up here. We'll not get it away."

I took a flower vase and poured the water from the bowl into it, holding it close against the bars. Then very gently we began to tilt the cage. Mars, who had been watching us intently, now began to get very excited.

"Be careful," said Finn, "or he'll bite the hand off you." We tilted the cage until it lay entirely upon its side, and as we did so Mars slid down until he was standing on the bars which now rested on the floor. He began to bark nervously.

"Be quiet," I told him. "Think of the fix you were in in *Five in a Flood,* and it all turned out all right!"

"When we lift the cage," said Finn, "his feet will fall through the bars and he may break a leg by struggling."

This was a sensible thought. We stood and considered the problem. We were past troubling about the time. We were ready to go on now even if it meant another two hours.

"We must stretch something across the bars," I said. I seized a tablecloth, and stuffing it into the cage tried to spread it out under Mars's feet. But he immediately started to paw it and worry it.

"You'll have to fix it somehow," said Finn, "or he'll scuff it away with his feet."

"String," I said.

"That would slip off," said Finn. "What you need is something long enough to double back and tie onto itself underneath."

He disappeared and came back a moment later with a sheet. We measured the sheet against the edge of the cage.

"It's not long enough to meet underneath," said Finn.

I began trying to tie the corners of the sheet to the bars, but it was highly starched and the knots came undone at once. We looked round desperately.

"What about those curtains?" I suggested.

"We'd need a step-ladder to get them down," said Finn.

"No time," I said. I gave them a sharp tug, and the fitting came out of the wall and the curtains came down on top of us with a great clattering of rings. We detached one of them. It was extremely long. We stretched it along inside the cage, making Mars pick up his feet and stand on it. Then there was quite enough of it protruding at either end for it to meet itself if doubled back on the underside of the bars. But we had no means of getting at the underside.

"We need a jack," said Finn.

I took two chairs and put them one at each end of the cage. "Lift it onto these," I said.

We began to lift, but as we did so Mars's paws, slipping through the bars as soon as the cage left the floor, pulled the curtain into a tangle. At the same time he began to bark loudly. We put the cage down again.

I looked at Finn. He was sweating. He looked at me.

"I've just thought of something else," he said quietly.

"What is it?" I asked him.

"Even suppose we *were* to tie the two ends of the curtain together underneath," said Finn, "the knot would pull the curtain up into a rope on the inside of the bars, so it wouldn't even then be spread out under his feet. Do you see what I mean?"

I saw what he meant. We leaned pensively against the two ends of the cage.

"Perhaps after all it would be better to try twine," said Finn. "If we were to thread two pieces into the curtain rings at each end, and then make two holes . . ."

"To hell with it!" I cried. "We'll try nothing more," and I began to drag the curtain out from under Mars's feet. He forthwith seized the corner of it in his mouth and wouldn't let go.

"Get it away from him!" I told Finn.

"You do that," said Finn, "and I'll pull."

With difficulty I forced Mars's mouth open, and we rescued what remained of the curtain. After that I sat on the floor and leaning my head against the bars I began to laugh hysterically.

"I've thought of something too," I told Finn.

"What?"

"Perhaps it won't go through the door after all!"

I was laughing so much I could hardly get this out. Then Finn began to laugh too, and we both lay on the floor and laughed like maniacs until we could do nothing more but groan.

After that we started hunting for where Sammy kept his whiskey, and when we had found it we had a couple of stiff ones. Finn showed signs of wanting to settle down to this, but I led him back to the cage.

"Come on!" I told Finn briskly, "and let him do what he likes with his feet!"

We lifted the upended cage from the ground, holding it at each end by the bars. At first Mister Mars began to slip and slither; but it was soon evident that in our anxiety about his welfare we had reckoned without his own intelligence. As soon as he realized that he had nothing to stand on but the bars, he tucked up his legs and lay stretched out along the side of the cage, looking a little uncomfortable but perfectly calm. When we saw this we began to laugh again so much that we had to put the cage down.

"For heaven's sake!" I said at last, and we marched towards the door.

The cage itself was very light, and most of the weight was Mars. It wasn't difficult to carry. I held my breath. The thing jarred against the doorway.

"Steady!" I said to Finn, who was going first. He was facing me and walking backwards and I could see his eyes growing as round as saucers. We jostled it and edged it in silence. Then Finn was stepping backwards into the hallway, and the cage was sliding through the door like a piston through a cylinder. There wasn't half an inch to spare.

"We've done it!" cried Finn.

"Wait," I said, "there's the other door."

We opened the door into the corridor. The cage slid through it as if it were greased with vaseline. We put it down outside and shook hands. I stepped back into Sammy's flat, and took a last look at the living-room; it looked rather like a battle scene, but I didn't see that I could do anything about that.

I was about to close Sammy's front door, when Finn said, "Look, even if we can get out of the building, how are we going to get this thing away? The police will be asking us what we're doing."

"We'll get a taxi," I said.

"This won't go into an ordinary taxi," said Finn; "we'd have to find one with a hood that takes down."

"Then we'll hire a lorry, I don't care," I told him.

"But where'll we put it meanwhile?" said Finn.

I breathed deeply. "Look," I said, "you're right of course. You go out and find a bloody taxi whose bloody hood takes down, or a lorry, or whatever you please, if you can do it in ten minutes. If you can't, come back and we'll carry it out and be damned. I'll wait here."

"Hadn't you better wait inside?" said Finn.

We looked deep into each other's eyes. Then we picked up the cage and carried it back into Sammy's flat.

"I'll wait in the corridor," I said, "and if Sammy appears I'll just make off. If I'm not here when you come back you'll know we've had it."

We shook hands again and Finn went away. I stood in the corridor biting my knuckles and listening to every sound. The thought that even at this late moment Mars could slip through my fingers tormented me into a frenzy. I went and looked at him and talked to him through the bars. Then I went into Sammy's kitchen and found a couple of pork chops which I presented to him. Then I went back to my post in the corridor.

After about five minutes I heard feet on the stairs and was preparing to fly, but it was Finn. He looked amazingly cool.

"I've got a taxi with a hood," he said.

We lifted the cage and once more slid it out into the passage. I closed Sammy's door. Then we set off toward the stairs.

"We'll go out the back way," I said, "and avoid the porter."

"The taxi's at the front door," said Finn.

"Well then, we'll carry the damn thing round the outside of the building!"

Then Mars dropped one of his chops and I trod on it and we nearly fell down the first flight of stairs. But I was beyond caring. When we got to the ground floor we turned sharply toward the tradesmen's entrance, Finn leading the way.

When we reached the tradesmen's door we found it was locked. We had just made this discovery when a voice behind us said "Hey!" and we jumped as if we'd been shot at. It was the porter. He was a burly slow-looking man with an obstinate expression.

"Can't go out that way, you know," he said.

"Why not?" I asked.

"Because it's shut at four-thirty," he said.

"Well then, we'll go out the other way," I told him. I would have broken his neck just then to get Mars out of the building. "Pick it up!" I said to Finn. We picked it up.

"Hey! Not so fast!" said the porter and barred our way. He was chewing gum.

"We're in a hurry," I told him. "Forward march!" I said to Finn, and we started making for the main entrance, brushing the porter aside. I could see now, through the glass doors, the taxi waiting, and the taxi-driver, and it was like the sight of the promised land.

The porter went ahead of us and put his hand on the door. "Not so fast I said," he said.

"I said we were in a hurry," I said.

"I've got to know what you're doing, you know," said the porter, "and what's your authority."

"We're removing this animal from the building," I said, "and our authority is Mr Starfield. Have you any objection?"

The porter ruminated. Then at last he said, "Objection? I should just think not! Again and again I told Mr Starfield it's against the rules, I told him, to have pet animals in these flats. It's not a pet animal, he says to me, it's a performing dog. Performing dog! I says to him, it'd better not perform here or I'll have the trustees on you, I said. I've told you it's against the rules, I said. If I liked I could have you turned out, I said. And it's no good your offering me money neither. I don't want to lose my job, do I? I got to do my job, ain't I? It isn't for myself I mind, I told him. What's it to me if you bring a dog in, I told him. I don't mind for a dog any more than for a woman, I told him. But it's the rules . . ."

While this was going on we got Mars out into the street. The taxi-driver, who had lowered the hood of his taxi, began to help us to lift the cage on. It took up the whole of the back of the taxi, lying tilted with one end down almost on the floor and the other end jutting out over the hood at the back. Poor old Mars was now back on his aluminium floor, but as it was tilting at an angle of forty-five degrees he was slithered down against the bars, together with his water-bowl, which rattled madly as we adjusted the cage. He held grimly on to his remaining pork chop and this mercifully prevented him from barking.

"Poor chap!" said the taxi-driver, who was taking it all very philosophically. "He ain't very comfy. Let's try it this way." And he wanted to be at the cage again.

"Leave it!" I cried, "it's very well!"

"But now there ain't no room for you two," said the taxi-driver.

"There's plenty of room," I told him. I gave the porter half a crown. Finn got up in front beside the driver, and I climbed on top of the cage and crouched in the angle between it and the back of the driving-seat.

"That ain't much good," said the driver. "Now, if you was to put yourself . . ."

"Will you please go!" I shouted. It only remained for the taxi to fail to start. But it started. The porter waved us goodbye, and we were off toward the King's Road.

Finn turned round and looked at me and we laughed silently at each other, a long, long laugh of triumph and achievement.

"You ain't said where I'm to go to," said the driver, stopping the taxi at the King's Road.

"Go towards Fulham," I told him, "and we'll tell you

more in a minute!" I didn't want to run the risk of meeting Sammy coming back in his car from chez Sadie. We must have looked damned conspicuous. People turned and stared after us all the way along the road.

"Look," I said to Finn, "the first thing is to buy a file and let this animal out."

"The shops are shut," said Finn.

"Well, we'll knock 'em up again," I told him.

"Stop at an ironmonger's shop," I told the driver, who so far hadn't flickered an eyelid. Nothing can astonish a London taxi-driver. He stopped outside an ironmonger's in the Fulham Palace Road, and after some knocking and some argument we purchased a file.

"Now," I said to the driver, "take us to some quiet place near here where we can work on this thing without being disturbed."

The driver, who knew his London, drove us to a disused timber yard near Hammersmith Bridge and helped us to unload the cage. I should like to have dismissed him then and there, only I suspected we hadn't enough money to pay him. Finn had about three and eightpence, as usual. What he thought we were up to heaven only knows. Whatever he thought, he made no comments. Perhaps he reckoned that the more dubious our proceedings were the larger his tip was likely to be.

We settled down to work with the file, taking it in turns; but working as hard as we could it took us a good half-hour to free Mister Mars. The bars refused to bend even when they were severed at one extremity, so each of them had to be cut through twice over. Mars licked our hands while we worked, whining eagerly. He knew very well what was afoot. At last we had removed three bars, and as the file bit through the last piece of metal and the third one heeled over Mars was already struggling through the gap. I received the enormous warm sleek beast into my arms and then in a moment we were all tearing round and round the yard, dog barking and men shouting, as we celebrated his freedom.

"Mind he doesn't run away," said Finn.

I didn't believe that Mars would be so ungrateful as to want to leave us after all the trouble we had taken for him, but I was relieved all the same when he answered obediently to my "Come here, sir!"

After that we discussed the problem of what to do with the cage. Finn suggested that we should heave it into the river, but I was against this. There is nothing the London police hate so much as seeing people drop things into the river. We decided eventually to leave it where it was. It wasn't as if we really cared about covering up our tracks, or as if this were possible anyway.

As we talked, the taxi-driver was looking at the thing thoughtfully. "Unreliable," he said, "these fancy locks. Always getting jammed, ain't they?" He put his hand through the bars and pressed a spring on the underside of the roof. One of the sides of the cage immediately fell open with oily smoothness. That put an end to that discussion. Finn and I studied the face of the taxi-driver. He looked back at us guilelessly. We felt beyond making any comment.

*   *   *

"I tell you something," said Finn, "I'm tired. Can we go somewhere and rest now?"

I had no intention of resting; but I thought I had better let Finn off. Also I had a sudden desire to be alone with Mars. I gave Finn five bob, which was all I could spare, and told him to take the taxi to Goldhawk Road and get Dave to lend him the rest. He was reluctant to leave me and it took me some time to convince him that this was what I really wanted. At last the taxi drove away, and Mister Mars and I set off on foot towards Hammersmith Broadway.

As I strode along with Mars beside me I felt like a king. We kept turning to look at each other, and I could not but feel that he approved of me as much as I approved of him. I was touched by his obedience. I am always astonished when any other creature does what I tell him. It seemed to me at that moment that pinching Mars was one of the most

inspired acts of my life. It wasn't that I was thinking that
there was anything in particular that I could do with Mars.
Nothing was further from my mind just then than Sadie and
Sammy. I was just pleased to have got Mars after having
worked so hard to get him. Our heads held high, we went
together into the Devonshire Arms at Hammersmith Broadway.

Mars attracted a lot of attention. "A fine dog you have
there!" someone said to me. As I gave my order I picked
up an evening paper which was lying on the counter. It
occurred to me that now was the time to look for a clue to
the identity of H. K. This might also make clear the time-
table to which Sadie and Sammy were working. I began to
look through the paper. I didn't have to look far. A head-
line read: MOVIE MAGNATE SAILS ON THE Q.E. And underneath: *Hollywood Kingmaker Seeks Ideas in Britain*:

In one of the most luxurious cabins of the liner *Queen
Elizabeth* which docks here shortly sits a quiet little man
drinking coca-cola. His name, little known to the public, is
one to conjure with in Hollywood. Those who really know
in the movie business know that Homer K. Pringsheim is
the power behind many a throne and the maker and breaker
of many a film career. Mr Pringsheim, who lives simply and
shuns publicity, told a press conference in New York that he
went to Europe "as a tourist mainly". It is well known, however, that "H. K." as this formidable figure is affectionately
called in Los Angeles, is on the look out for new stars and
new ideas. Asked whether he favoured closer co-operation
between the British and American film industries, Mr Pringsheim said, "Well, maybe."

That made that clear anyway. I wondered what were
Sadie's means of access to H. K. and how long it would take
her to get him on the dotted line. I didn't doubt that Sadie
knew exactly what she was doing. She had probably
charmed that quiet little man on some previous visit. I
should have to work fast. It remained to discover when
exactly the *Elizabeth* docked.

I was looking through the rest of the paper to see if this was announced anywhere when I suddenly noticed a small item at the bottom of one of the pages which read as follows:

ANNA QUENTIN FOR HOLLYWOOD?

Connoisseurs of the song will be familiar with the name of Anna Quentin, distinguished blues singer and versatile vocalist. Miss Quentin's admirers, who have been regretting her recent retirement from the limelight, will hear with mixed feelings the report that she is bound for Hollywood. Miss Quentin, leaving for a short stay in Paris, refused either to confirm or deny a rumour that she had signed a long-term contract for work in America and that she would be sailing shortly in the *Liberté*. Miss Quentin is the sister of the well-known screen actress Sadie Quentin.

I studied this for about ten minutes, trying to read between the lines. Like Miss Quentin's other admirers I had mixed feelings. On the whole I felt profound relief. This Hollywood contract was undoubtedly the offer which Anna had accepted with reluctance. Possibly she had decided that the only way to deal with Hugo's importunities was flight. On the other hand, I knew that Anna would be sorry to leave Europe. For myself, my immediate feeling was that I would rather lose her to Hollywood than to Hugo. She might come back from Hollywood; and anyway it was still possible that she hadn't finally made up her mind to go. My knowledge of Anna's character suggested that if she had finally decided to do something about which she had serious misgivings she would want everyone to know about it at once.

These were my first reactions. Within about five minutes, however, of having been relieved of my greatest fear I began, like a man cured of a fever who finds that he has the toothache, to be distressed by the alternative state of affairs on its own account. It is true that I had not felt any irresistible urge to go back to the theatre and pester Anna with my attentions. But I had known that Anna was there, and

I had felt sure that before long she would summon me. As indeed she had, I remembered with pain. But Anna in the U.S.A. was very different food for thought. It occurred to me then that if I left at once I might catch her in Paris and dissuade her from going at all.

This idea was for a short while very attractive. I was interrupted in my contemplation of it by Mars, who placed a large dry paw on my knee. "Yes," I told him, "I'd forgotten you." Of course, I could always just return Mars to Sammy. If I didn't want to see the face Sammy would make I could bring Mars back to Chelsea and tie him up outside the door. Or I could turn him in at a police station if it came to that. What did I care really about the *Wooden Nightingale*? Let them have the damn thing. It then began to seem to me that pinching Mars was one of the most foolish things I had ever done. If I hadn't put myself in the wrong by doing that I might have taken a high moral line with Sadie and Sammy about the typescript—Sammy at any rate had a bad conscience about it—and soaked them for a lot of money. Also I was landed with the animal. If it wasn't for him I could drop the whole tiresome business and pursue Anna.

Yet indeed, I thought again, it would be a grave thing to go away just now. What I must certainly do was warn Hugo about Sadie's plan. Not that there was likely to be anything that Hugo could do about it; but I would not be easy until he knew. As for my instinct in joining battle with Sammy and Sadie, it had been a sound enough instinct. At the very least something unexpected had overtaken that reptilian pair; and when I reflected on the way Sammy had treated Madge I only wished I could have devised some even greater shock for him. It remained to be seen how high a value could be put on Mars from the blackmail point of view. I ate a meat pie, and Mars ate another one, and I looked at my watch. It was ten to eight. The sooner I could find Hugo the better; and in fact as soon as his burly bear-like image was risen fairly before me I was filled with a very great eagerness to see him, the more so as I felt that there was some perverse fate that was trying to keep us apart. It was spiritually necessary for me to find Hugo.

A few minutes later I was ringing up Lloyd's. The *Queen Elizabeth* docked the day after to-morrow. That wasn't too bad. I then rang Hugo's Holborn number and got no answer. I forthwith telephoned the Bounty Belfounder studio. I thought it just possible that Hugo might be still there. The studio answered and told me that in fact everyone was still on the set. Whether Mr Belfounder was still there they were not sure. He had been there earlier in the evening but had perhaps gone. This was good enough. I decided to go to the studio.

Twelve

THE Bounty Belfounder studio is situated in a suburb of Southern London where contingency reaches the point of nausea. I went as far as my money would take me in a taxi and the rest of the way by bus. This left me penniless, but I had no thoughts beyond the moment. If you have ever seen a film studio you will know how curiously in its décor the glittering and the decrepit are merged. Bounty Belfounder somewhat favoured the latter. It covered a considerable area in between a railway line and a main road and was enclosed on the road side by a very high corrugated-iron fence. The main door, which was in the centre of a strip of low temporary buildings, looked rather like the entrance to a zoo; and over it the name BOUNTY BELFOUNDER perpetually burning in neon light raised a sigh in the breasts of girls who passed it daily on their way to work in and around the Old Kent Road.

Mars and I alighted from the bus. If you have ever tried to get into a film studio you will know that the chances of your turning out to be an Unauthorized Person are very high indeed. I am myself a sort of professional Unauthorized Person; I am sure I have been turned out of more places than any other member of the English intelligentsia. As I stood now looking at the studio it began to occur to me that I might have difficulty in getting in. The main entrance consisted of a pair of iron gates which were not only closed but were guarded by no less than three men who sat in a small office overlooking the road and whose task and joy it plainly was to usher in the illustrious with fawning and to spurn the humble from the door. I knew that it was useless to approach them and ask for Hugo. So I thought I might as well make a tour of the outside of the place and see if there wasn't some more inviting way in. Already I had

attracted the attention of the Cerberi and their glances
convicted me of loitering. It also occurred to me that,
especially in this milieu, Mars might be recognized. I was
really rather of Finn's opinion that one Alsatian dog looks
much like another; but then there are some people who
can distinguish day-old chicks and Chinamen. We turned
away looking casual.

We followed the iron fence as far as the railway. It was
covered with advance publicity of the film which was
apparently being made inside at that very moment. I
remembered now having seen something about it in the
papers. It was a film about the conspiracy of Catiline which
was to be remarkable for its painstaking care in presenting
this much-disputed and doubtless misrepresented episode.
At Last! the posters announced to bewildered Londoners,
The Truth About Catiline! No less than three eminent
ancient historians were on the payroll. Sadie was playing the
part of Orestilla, Catiline's wife, whom Sallust says no good
man ever praised save for her beauty and whom Cicero
professed to believe to be not only Catiline's wife but also
his daughter. Of this latter insinuation the film makes no
mention, but the former, whether prompted by research or
by the necessities of the script, it repudiates by presenting
Orestilla as a woman with a heart of gold and moderate
reformist principles.

The place seemed to be impregnable. There might have
been a way of entering from the railway side. But I left
this as a last resort; for although I am not frightened of
motor cars I am rather nervous of trains. This I know
is illogical since, except in moments of crisis, trains run
on rails and cannot pursue you across pavements and
into shops as cars can. On this occasion, however, my
natural fears were augmented by the presence of Mars. I
vividly pictured him being run over by a train, which to
my fevered imagination seemed to be the unavoidable con-
sequence of our venturing out onto the tracks. So I turned
back toward the main gate.

Here I noticed that the three men who had taken me for

a felonious loiterer had gone, and that one man only sat
framed in the window. I looked at the gate, and as I did so
I saw inside it, standing in the studio yard, the big
black Alvis which I had last seen gliding away from the
Riverside Theatre. I was certain it was the same car. This
decided me. Somewhere on the other side of these gates was
Hugo. Without an idea in my head I approached the
window. The man looked at me questioningly. I leaned
towards him.

"I'm George's friend," I hissed, and looked fixedly into
his eyes. I mumbled the name a bit so that it might serve
equally for John or Joe or James or Jack. One or other of
these bolts evidently reached a target. The man nodded in
a rather contemptuous way and touched a lever. The gates
opened.

"Straight across the yard and on the left," he said. I
walked in.

I didn't want to attract attention to Mars by calling him;
I hoped he would have enough sense to follow me in at once.
As I could hear the gates beginning to close behind me I
couldn't help turning slightly to see what had happened to
him. But all was well. He had not only followed discreetly
at my heels, but had even lowered his tail as he passed under
the office window. Without looking back again I hurried
across the yard, past Hugo's car, and entered a labyrinth of
buildings on the other side. On my left a large door said
EXTRAS. This was doubtless the desired destination of
Joe's friend, and I wondered for a moment whether it
mightn't profit me to continue in this role. But I decided
that really there was no reason why I should have to attire
myself like an ancient Roman in order to find Hugo, especially as this would mean surrendering my trousers to
another person, an act of which I have a primitive terror.
So I went straight on and as I did so I took off my tie and
knotted one end of it onto Mars's collar. I felt ready for
anything.

In the distance I could now hear a voice holding forth
in a passionate rhetorical manner. The sound of it carried

clearly through the sensitive evening air. It was this way that I went, for I did not doubt that if I could find the centre of operations I should discover Hugo. There was no one about and no other sound to be heard. The office people had evidently gone home. With Mars padding beside me I ran down a lane of concrete buildings and then down another one. Somewhere ahead there was a great deal of light. Then I turned a corner and there opened before me the most astonishing scene.

In the background, rising up in an explosion of colour and form, was a piece of ancient Rome. On brick walls and arches and marble pillars and columns there fell the brilliantly white radiance of the arc lamps, making the buildings stand out in a relief more violent than of nature and darkening by contrast the surrounding air into a haze of twilight. Nearer to me was a forest of wooden scaffolding festooned with cables in which were perched the huge lamps themselves; and in between, mounted on steel stilts and poised on cranes, were the innumerable cameras, all eyes. Most strange of all, in the open arena in front of the city stood a crowd of nearly a thousand men in perfectly motionless silence. Their backs were turned to me and they seemed to listen enthralled to the vibrating voice of a single figure who stood raised above them on a chariot, swaying and gesticulating in the focus of the blazing light.

This doubtless was Catiline inflaming the Roman plebs. The unnatural whiteness of the light made the colours burn into my eyes and I had to turn my head away. At any other time I would have been fascinated to watch what was going on. At that moment, however, there was but one thought in my mind, that it was now almost certain that only a small distance separated me from Hugo. I began to move round behind the scaffolding, walking behind the beams of light as one walks behind a waterfall. I didn't want Hugo to see me first. And as I went the city seemed to unfold, revealing by some trick of the scene vista after vista of streets and temples and pillared market places.

I went on in a stupor, just outside the circle of colour, with the cascade of radiance on one side and the twilight on the other. Even Mars seemed under a spell, a gliding dog whose jointed legs swung to and fro without touching the earth. The passionate voice continued, pouring out an unending flood of exalted protest and appeal. Some of the words which it was uttering began now to find their way into my ears. It was saying: "And that, comrades, is the way to get rid of the capitalist system. I don't say it's the only way, but I do say it's the best way." I stopped. For all I knew Marxism might rapidly be transforming the study of ancient history; all the same, this sounded rather odd. Then in a flash I realized that the speaker was not Catiline but Lefty.

The voice ceased and the crowd started out of their immobility. In a murmur which rose to a roar and re-echoed from the façades of the artificial city they clapped and shouted, rustling and swaying and turning to one another. Here and there among them were togaed Romans, but the majority of the men were obviously engineers and technicians in blue overalls and shirt sleeves. On the far side of them I could see now, coming more fully into view as its bearers moved a little, a long banner stretched between two poles, on which was printed in enormous letters SOCIALIST POSSIBILITY. And at that moment I caught sight of Hugo.

He was standing by himself a little apart from the crowd but in the full blaze of the light. He stood upon the steps of a temple on the edge of the city, looking toward Lefty over the heads of the people. In the many angled radiance he cast no shadow and in the whiteness of the light he looked strangely pale, as if his flesh were covered with chalk. He was joining and unjoining his hands in a pensive gesture which might have been an afterthought of clapping. He stood in a characteristic way which I remembered well, his shoulders hunched and his head thrust forward, his eyes shifting sharply, stooping a little and his lips moving a little. Then he began to bite his nails. I stood rooted to the spot.

Lefty began speaking again and a deep silence at once surrounded his voice.

Hugo felt my gaze and turned slightly. Some fifteen yards only separated us. I moved from the shadow into the light. Then he saw me. For a moment we looked at each other. I felt no impulse to smile or even to move. I felt as if I looked at Hugo out of another world. Gravity and sadness fell between us like a veil and for a moment I hardly felt that he could see me, so intently was I seeing him. Then Hugo smiled and raised his hand and Mars began to tug me forward toward him. A deep distress overcame me. After the dignity of silence and absence, the vulgarity of speech. I smiled automatically and studied Hugo's face; what did it express? Friendship, contempt, indifference, irritation? It was inscrutable. I mounted the steps and stood beside him.

Hugo completed his smile and his salute, neither slowly nor in haste, and then turned back toward the meeting. As he did so he made a gesture toward Lefty which seemed to signify: "Just listen to this!"

"Hugo!" I hissed.

"Sssh!" said Hugo.

"Hugo, listen," I said, "I've got to talk to you at once. Can we go somewhere quiet?"

"Sssh," said Hugo. "Later. I want to hear this. It's colossal." He gave me a sharp sideways look and waved his hands in a deprecatory way. Lefty completed a period and a soft murmur of approval swept over the crowd.

"Hugo," I said out loud and with strong emphasis, "I've got to warn you . . ."

Silence had fallen again. Hugo shook his head at me and put his finger to his lips and gave his attention to Lefty.

I went on in a lowered voice, trying to drive the words into his ears. "Sadie is double-crossing you, she . . ."

"She always is," said Hugo. "Shut up, Jake, will you? We can talk later."

Despair overwhelmed me. I sat down on the steps at Hugo's feet. Mister Mars sat beside me. The glare of the arc lamps was boring into my left eye and Lefty's voice was piercing my head like a skewer. "Ask yourself what you really value," Lefty was saying. "You know what it says about where your treasure is your heart is." I suddenly felt that everything I had been doing lately was pointless—Anna was going to America, Sadie and Sammy were doing whatever they pleased and nothing would stop them, Madge had been deceived, I had found Hugo and he wouldn't speak to me. It only remained for me to be arrested and put in prison for stealing Mars. I put an arm round the latter's neck and he licked me sympathetically behind the ear.

Lefty seemed good for another hour. He was really a remarkable speaker. He spoke simply but without faltering. His discourse was copious and yet well ordered too. Not without flowers, it was not without force either. Although afterwards all I could remember of what he said were a few striking phrases, I had the impression at the time that a closely reasoned argument was being presented. He somehow combined the intimate tone of the popular preacher with the dramatic and inflammatory style of the demagogue. Winged by sincerity and passion, his speech fell like an arrow from above, clean and piercing. The thousand men were under his spell. Their breathing was stilled and their eyes fixed intensely upon him. For a while I watched them so. Then there was a slight shiver at the edge of the crowd. Opposite to us and behind the speaker there were a number of boards with slogans upon them. These boards now began to sway gently to and fro like corks upon a pool which is suddenly disturbed. I noticed one or two scuffles developing on the side near the main entrance. But hardly anyone looked round. Lefty absorbed them.

I looked up at Hugo. He stood like a man in a trance. I swivelled round, turning my back on the meeting and looking behind me into the streets of the ingenious city which excess of light made to glow with excess of colour. Behind it, all seemed dark. I sighed. Then I looked at

Hugo again. My despair began to give way to exasperation and I felt coming upon me that nervous impulse to act at any price which so soon overtakes me in periods of frustration. I let go of Mars. Behind us a pair of double doors opened into the temple. I satisfied myself with a glance that they were real doors and that the temple had a real interior. Then I began to study Hugo's stance. These rapid preliminary studies can be very important in Judo. Notice where your opponent's weight is placed and at what point a pressure will mostly readily upset his balance. I ran over various moves in my mind and decided that the most appropriate would be some version of the O Soto-Gari throw, as we term it. Then in a leisurely way I rose to my feet.

I stood on the top step beside him. "Hugo!" I said sharply. He half turned toward me. As he did so I took hold of his right arm between the wrist and the elbow and forced it strongly away to my left, so drawing him to face me. At the same time I hooked my right leg behind the bend of his right knee. As one firm unit my body swung smoothly round my left hip joint, while my right hand grasped Hugo's belt and drew him into the circle of my movement, pushing and lifting at the same time. As he began to collapse I took two or three steps backward and we fell together through the double doors, and went rolling into the interior of the temple. The doors closed behind us, but not before Mister Mars had squeezed through and sat down in front of them as if on guard.

Hugo and I picked ourselves up, Hugo rubbing those parts of his anatomy which had suffered in transit. The inside of the temple was dark, lit only by light which filtered through a narrow grating under the angle of the roof. It was empty, except for a wooden box on which after a moment or two Hugo sat down. I joined Mars by the door and sat cross-legged. We looked at Hugo. Mars clearly wasn't quite sure what sort of attitude he ought to adopt towards him, and kept looking at me for a cue. He growled softly every now and then as if to try to keep the situation under control without giving any serious offence. I took out my cigarette packet, selected a cigarette and lit it. I waited for Hugo to say something.

"Why did you do that, Jake?" said Hugo.

"I told you I wanted to speak to you," I said.

"Well, there's no need to be so rough," said Hugo. "You nearly broke my neck."

"Nonsense," I said. "I knew exactly what I was doing."

"What did you want to tell me?" said Hugo. He seemed quite resigned to being kept a prisoner.

"A great many things," I said, "but first of all this." And I told him rapidly what I knew of Sadie's plans.

"Thank you for telling me this," said Hugo. He didn't seem very surprised or even very interested.

Then he added, "I see you've got Mister Mars with you." He didn't seem surprised at that either.

I was about to reply when an enormous din began to break out behind us.

The sound of stampeding feet mingled with confused shouts and cries. The ground shook and the building shivered about us.

"What is it?" I asked. Mars began to bark.

"The United Nationalists said they were going to break up the meeting," said Hugo. "That's probably them arriving. The next thing will be the police."

As he spoke we heard a whistle shrilling in the distance. "Let's go out and look," said Hugo.

We emerged together. A wild scene met our eyes. The crowd which a few minutes before had been so orderly was split into a chaos of struggling groups. Everywhere we looked a fight seemed to be in progress. The whole mass swayed to and fro like a vast Rugby scrum, into the midst of which every now and then a man would leap from the scaffolding or from one of the camera cranes scattering friend and foe alike. Out of this undulating pile of punching, kicking and wrestling humanity there arose a steady roar in which cries of pain and anger were inextricably merged. Upon this scene the arc lamps blazed with unabated fierceness, costing the Bounty Belfounder Company some considerable sum of money per hour, and showing us with an astonishing clarity the enraged faces of the combatants. In the distance we could see Lefty, still mounted on his chariot, still gesticulating, his mouth opening and shutting, while round about him, as about the body of Hector, the battle raged to and fro with particular ferocity. Nearby the long banner which said SOCIALIST POSSIBILITY rose and fell upon the surge. Now one end of it descended as the standard bearer fell before an onslaught, and now the other, but eager hands soon raised it once more to flutter its thoughtful message above the scene.

The police whistles were sounding now at the very entrance to the studio. There was no time to lose. Even when I don't know which side I am on I hate to watch a fight without joining in; but on this occasion I had no doubt of my sympathies nor did it occur to me to question Hugo's.

"Which ones are which?" I asked Hugo.

"I'm afraid there's no way of distinguishing them," he said.

Since this was clearly the case the most sensible thing to do was to go and defend the one person whose identity we were sure of, and that was Lefty. I told Hugo this, and set off, keeping a close grip on Mars, who was beginning to look as if he wanted to bite somebody. Hugo followed me. We made our way with difficulty through the battle in the direction of the chariot. The din was appalling; and behind us there stood out against the gathering night the brilliantly illumined skyline of the Eternal City, swaying very gently to and fro as the ground trembled under a thousand stamping feet.

It took us some time to reach Lefty. It was necessary more than once, in defence of our right to proceed, to deal violently with some person or persons who disputed this right. So we lashed out, hoping that our blows were falling by and large upon the unrighteous. I got through more or less unscathed, but Hugo received a blow in the eye which seemed to enrage him considerably. As we approached the chariot, Lefty, who had been resisting the attempts of the enemy to drag him down, suddenly leapt with a yell of fury on top of one of his foes, and the two rolled on the ground. At the same moment two toughs, clearly friends of Lefty's antagonist, closed in upon them— and it would have gone hard with Lefty had not Hugo and I dashed forward and flung ourselves upon the heap with the abandon of swimmers entering a summer sea. Mars, whom I had let go of some time ago, pranced around the outside of the skirmish, nipping the legs of this and that person rather indiscriminately. The struggle, in the course of which I was able to put in some good ground work, and use one or two particularly rare and exquisite leg locks, lasted only a few minutes. Lefty was fighting like a wild cat, while Hugo, looking more than ever like a bear, was standing erect, his feet wide apart, and his arms whirling like a windmill. For myself, I prefer to get my opponent onto the ground as soon as possible. The enemy fled. We picked up Lefty, who looked a little the worse for wear.

"Thanks!" said Lefty. "Hello, Donaghue, nice to see you. I didn't know you were here."

"I didn't know you knew Lefty," said Hugo.

"I didn't know *you* knew Lefty," I said.

But there was no time to discuss these interesting discoveries. "Look!" said Lefty. We turned toward the studio entrance and there, advancing upon the battle, which still raged with undiminished fury, was a large force of police, some on foot and some on horseback.

"Damn!" said Lefty. "Now they'll arrest everyone within sight, especially me—which will be pretty inconvenient just now. Is there a way out at the back?"

We retreated into the streets of Rome, which were already invaded by a small number of combatants who were, however, more concerned with mutual assault and battery than with the possibility of escape. We passed under a brick archway.

"I don't think there's any way through," said Hugo. "It all ends at the wall."

The city was really much smaller than it had appeared to be on my first view of it. In a moment or two we had reached the city wall, a high structure of spurious red brick which was surmounted at intervals by watch towers and gave the impression of tremendous thickness. It swept round behind the buildings in an unbroken semicircle. Lefty struck it with his fist.

"No use!" said Hugo. It was as smooth as a chestnut and too high to climb.

"We're trapped!" said Lefty. The din in the arena had taken on a new note and we could hear the police shouting instructions through loud-speakers. We looked round us frantically.

"What shall we do?" I said to Hugo.

He was standing there with his eyes glazed. He turned his big head toward me slowly. The noise was coming nearer and already one or two policemen were to be seen hurrying under the archway.

"Leave it to me!" said Hugo. He fumbled in his pocket and brought out a small object.

"Belfounder's Domestic Detonator," he said. "Invaluable for shifting tree roots and clearing rabbit warrens." The object ended in a point, which Hugo plunged into the base of the wall. Then he brought out a box of matches. In a moment there was a fierce sizzling sound.

"Stand back!" cried Hugo. A sharp explosion followed, and like magic a hole about five feet in diameter had appeared in the wall, through which in the early darkness we could see a ragged field scattered with corrugated-iron sheds and bounded by a low fence and a Bovril advertisement. Beyond it was the railway. As I took this in Lefty had already passed us and like a circus dog going through a hoop sped gracefully through the hole, and we could see him a moment later leaping the fence and diminishing across the railway lines under the twinkling red and green lights.

"Quick!" said Hugo to me. But something else was happening. The shock of the explosion must have dislocated something in the fabric of the city. For now suddenly the whole structure was beginning to sway and totter in the most alarming fashion. I looked up and saw as in a dream the brick and marble skyline vacillating drunkenly while there was a slow crescendo of cracking and splintering and rending.

"Damn, that's torn it!" said Hugo. "It's all right," he added. "It's only made of plastic and Essex board."

We seemed to be surrounded by shouting policemen. In the distance I could see columns heeling slowly sideways, and triumphal arches crumbling and sagging and finally collapsing like opera hats. There was a menacing sound like an earthquake tuning up. For a moment I watched petrified; then I turned toward the hole in the wall. But it was already too late. Directly above us the wall began to lean inwards. To see what looks like fifty feet of solid brickwork descending on you is an unnerving sight, even if you have been told that it is only made of plastic and Essex board. With a sickening roar it began to fall. I threw Mars to the ground and hurled myself down, one arm clutching the dog and the other protecting the back of my neck. Next moment, with an apocalyptic clatter, the whole thing was on top of us.

The world blacked out and something struck me violently on the shoulder. I had made myself so flat I almost bored into the earth. Somewhere the shouting and the splintering continued. I tried to get up but something was pinning me down. I became panic-stricken and struggled madly, and then I found myself sitting up with the remains of the wall, in pieces of various sizes, scattered round me. I looked about wildly for Mars, and soon saw him crawling out from under a pile of debris. He shook himself and came toward me with nonchalance. No doubt his film career had familiarized him with incidents of this kind. We surveyed the scene.

All was changed. The whole of Rome was now horizontal and out of its ruins an immense cloud of dust was rising, thick as a fog in the glare of the lamps. In the arena, like a formal picture of the battle of Waterloo, stood a mass of black figures, some mounted on horses, others standing on top of cars, and others on foot marshalling into neat groups. A voice was saying something blurred through a loud-speaker. The foreground looked more like the moment after the battle. The ground was strewn with legless torsos and halves of men and others cut off at the shoulders, all of whom, however, were lustily engaged in restoring themselves to wholeness by dragging the hidden parts of their anatomy out from under the flat wedges of scenery, which lay now like a big pack of cards, some pieces still showing bricks and marble, while others revealed upon their prostrate backs the names of commercial firms and the instructions of the scene shifter. As I shook myself free I saw Hugo rising like a surfacing whale and thrusting his monumental shoulders through the wreckage as if it had been cardboard. He rose to his feet, showering the fragments to right and left. For an instant he was outlined against the sky, and then he shot off in the direction of the railway and was to be seen in the dim light, leaping across the lines like a stampeding buffalo, and disappearing into the distance.

I staggered up and was about to follow him when Mars created an unfortunate diversion. All about us, like a nest of disquieted wood-lice, policemen were crawling out from underneath pieces of boarding. Whether this stirred some memory in Mars's simple mind I know not; but evidently some strong reflex was set off. He was doubtless so accustomed to rescuing people from predicaments such as this that the simultaneous sight of so many eligible rescuees was too much for him. He dashed at the nearest policeman and seizing him by the shoulder began to pull him vigorously into the open. This gesture, which I admit I may have misinterpreted, was certainly taken in bad part by the policeman, who seemed to imagine that Mars was attacking him, and fought back fiercely. I watched for a

F*

little while, until I began to be afraid that Mars might get hurt. Then I interfered and pulled him off, explaining as I did so to the policeman that, in my view, Mars's intentions had been kindly, and not, as the other thought, aggressive. The policeman answered impolitely—and rather than prolong the discussion I turned, taking a firm grip on my necktie which was still trailing from Mars's collar, and prepared to follow in Hugo's footsteps, trains or no trains.

Imagine my dismay when I saw that between me and the railway line, across the piece of waste ground from one side of it to the other, there now stretched a thin but regular cordon of police. To run the gauntlet of both police and trains was more than I could bear. The immediate requirement, however, was to get away from the vicinity of the attacked policeman, so I set off at a run with Mars, skirting the edge of the studio and hoping that I might find a gap where the studio wall ended before the police began. But there was no such gap; and I found myself coming back toward the front of the studio, where the erstwhile combatants now stood in docile groups, a mass of uniforms barred the exit, and a superhuman voice was saying NO ONE IS TO LEAVE. It then occurred to me that really the police could hardly be wanting to arrest everyone, and as I had nothing on my conscience I might as well wait peacefully to be dismissed instead of rushing about the scene and drawing attention to myself. Then as I looked down at Mars it became clear to me on second thoughts that now was not the ideal moment to fall into the arms of the law.

I stopped running and started thinking. As I thought I kept on walking in the direction of the front entrance, where the thickest mass of police were gathered beside the labyrinth of office buildings.

I addressed Mars. "You got me in to this," I told him. "You can get me out." I led Mars into the shadow of one of the buildings and looked about me. From that point I could see down one of the side lanes the gates of the main entrance. They stood open, and a troop of mounted police were just riding into the yard. Through the gates I could see a crowd outside who were peering in and the flashing cameras of newspaper men. In between, by the gate itself, was a small group of police to whom the battlefield was invisible because of the buildings, so that I could assume that they had not been witnesses of my recent antics. I turned to Mars. The crucial moment had come.

I stroked him and looked into his eyes, to command his attention for something of the utmost seriousness. He returned my gaze expectantly.

"Sham dead," I said. "Dead! Dead dog!" I hoped that this word was in his vocabulary. It was. In a moment Mars's legs sagged and his body became limp and he slid to the ground, his eyes turning back and his mouth hanging open. It was terribly convincing. I was quite upset. Then I collected my wits and took a quick look at the gate. No one had seen us. I knelt down, and levering Mars from the ground I lifted him over my shoulder. It was as if he weighed a ton. The inertia of his body seemed to glue it to the ground. Bracing my hand against the wall I rose slowly to my feet. Mars's head, with his tongue hanging out, lay swaying against my chest, and his hindquarters were bumping the small of my back. I set myself in motion.

As I approached the main gate I came into a focus of attention, not only from the police who were keeping the gate, but also from the crowd who were standing outside. As soon as we were well in view a murmur of sympathy arose from the crowd. "Oh, the poor dog!" I could hear several women saying. And indeed Mars was a pathetic sight. I quickened my pace as much as I could. The police barred my way. They had their orders to let no one out.

"Now then!" said one of them.

I strode resolutely on, and when I was close to them I cried out, in tones of urgency, "The dog's hurt! I must find a vet! There's one just down the road."

I was in mortal terror all this time lest Mars should tire of the game. He must have been extremely uncomfortable hanging there with the bones of my shoulder pressing into his stomach. But he endured. The policeman hesitated.

"I must get him attended to at once!" I repeated.

A cross murmur began to rise from the crowd. "Let the poor chap out to get his dog looked after!" said someone, and this seemed to express the general sentiment.

"Oh, all right, out you go!" said the policeman.

I walked through the gates. The crowd parted with respectful and sympathetic remarks. As soon as I was clear of them and saw in front of me the wide open expanse of New Cross Road, unenclosed and empty of police, I could bear it no longer.

"Wake up! Live dog!" I said to Mars; as I knelt down he sprang from my shoulder, and together we set off down the road at full pelt. Behind us, diminishing now in the distance, there arose an immense roar of laughter.

Thirteen

IT was hours later, or so it seemed to my feet, and we were still walking along the Old Kent Road. It was some time now since my triumph at having escaped so cleverly had given place to dejection at finding that I had no money and that there was nothing for it but to keep on walking north-ward. There had been a moment when I had thought of taking a taxi and making Dave pay at the other end, and the reflexion that Dave had already paid for one taxi for me that evening and might have no more ready cash would not have deterred me had I been able to find a taxi; but to those southern wastes the cruising taxi never comes and it was long since I had dismissed this as a hopeless vision. I would have telephoned for help, only I had already foolishly spent my last pence on a copy of the *Independent Socialist,* the next day's edition of which was already being sold to the crowd coming out of a cinema. The paper carried a report of the meeting at Bounty Belfounder and some pictures of the fight. A dramatic photograph of me and Mars coming out of the main gate was captioned: *A Canine Victim of Police Brutality.* The pubs had been shut for a consider-able time and the road was deserted. The cinema crowd had been the last sign of life. Even Mars looked dejected; his head and tail drooped and he followed along at my heels by scent alone, never raising his eyes. Perhaps he was hungry. I certainly was. I thought sadly of the pork chop which we had left behind on Sammy's stairs. Maxim: never tread under foot the food which you can put in your pocket.

It was well after midnight when we were trudging across Waterloo Bridge. I had the impression that I had had an extremely long day; and when we reached the north side of the bridge it was clear to me that I could go no further. It was another cloudless night, with air like warm milk, and we stood for a while looking at the river, not to admire its beauty but because it was necessary to stand still. My feet felt as if they had suffered centuries of attrition, and my body was present to me in a variety of aches and pains which made the external world almost invisible. Then Mars and I jolted wearily down the steps.

If you have ever tried to sleep on the Victoria Embankment you will know that the chief difficulty is that the seats are divided in the middle. An iron arm-rest in the centre makes it impossible to stretch oneself out. I am not sure whether this is an accidental phenomenon or whether it forms part of an L.C.C. campaign against vagrancy. In any case it is very inconvenient. Various systems are possible. One may try to use the arm-rest as a pillow, or one may lie with one's knees raised over it and one's feet on the other side. Or again one may resign oneself to curling up on one half of the seat. This is a very cramped position even for someone as short as myself; but if one is a restless sleeper, as I am, this is probably the best method, and it was this that I chose. Before reposing I wrapped the pages of the *Independent Socialist* carefully round my legs, and tied them into position with my tie and my handkerchief. Newspaper is a good insulator, as every vagabond knows. I only wished I could have afforded two copies. Then I lay down. Mars got up onto the other half of the seat. We slept.

I awoke and it was still night. The stars seemed to have moved a long way. I was feeling stiff with cold. Then Big Ben struck three. Only three! I groaned. I lay for a while in an agony of stiffness. I tried chafing my limbs, but the effort to do so was so painful that it hardly justified the results. I sat up feeling totally miserable. Then I thought of Mars. He was still there, sleeping soundly and snoring gently as he slept. Shivering and solitary I sat looking at him, while on either side the deserted pavements stretched away under lofty street lamps which lit a lurid green in the motionless leaves of plane trees and revealed below them the rows of empty seats each one as uncomfortable as ours. Naked as a bridge in a picture on which no one will ever tread, Waterloo Bridge brooded over the river. I stood up and the blood ran thick and painful into my feet.

Mars was an image of Sleep. At first I just felt annoyed that he should be sleeping so peacefully while I was awake and cold. Then I began to remember stories of men in life-boats who had been saved by being kept warm by faithful dogs. Indeed I'm not sure that I didn't get this idea from one of Mars's films. With some difficulty I wakened Mars and made him move up sufficiently for me to lie beside him. It was true. His body was radiantly warm from nose to tail. For a while we shifted about, trying to find a position which suited us both. At last we settled down with my face thrust into the loose fur of Mars's throat and his hind legs curled into my stomach. He licked my nose. It must have been like licking a block of ice. I stretched out a random hand and drew it over his head. Out of *his* ears it would have been no hard task to have made silk purses. And as I fell asleep I was remembering how much in my childhood I had wanted to have a dog and how thoroughly my elders had made me feel this wish to be extravagant and unseemly until it had faded sadly into a secret dream, and been replaced in about my ninth year by an equally profound yearning to be the owner of an Aston Martin.

The police moved us on at about six a.m. This is the hour when, for some reason, one begins to be a menace to law and order. These things I learnt in days when I was even less successful than I am now. After a rest in Trafalgar Square, which is another place where the police don't like one to lie down, Mars and I presented ourselves at Mrs Tinckham's shop just as it was opening. There, under the scandalized gaze of half a dozen arched and prickling cats, the hero of *Five in a Flood* consumed a large bowl of milk, and I borrowed a pound. Finn opened the door for me at Goldhawk Road and led me straight to the bed which he had vacated. I slept again for a long time.

*   *   *

I woke up and it was the afternoon. I woke with a dull and oppressed consciousness, as when a holiday is over and there is an accumulated pile of work waiting to be done. I pulled myself out of bed. It was raining. I stared for a while at this phenomenon. Changes of weather always take me by surprise, nor can I when the climate is set one way at all bring to my imagination what it is like for it to be set the other. I had quite forgotten about rain. I opened the window. Then for about four minutes I did some diaphragmatic breathing. To do this one opens the lungs to their fullest extent, placing the hands on the lower ribs and slowly expanding the diaphragm; one holds the breath while counting eight at moderate speed and then releases it quietly through the mouth with a low hissing sound. It is unwise to do this for too long as it may induce unconsciousness. I was taught diaphragmatic breathing by a Japanese who claimed that it had transformed his life, and although I cannot say that it has transformed mine, I can recommend it as being harmless and conceivably beneficial, particularly for someone who is as suggestible as I am.

I got dressed and put my head cautiously round the door to look for Finn. I was in no hurry to confront Dave, who I feared might have some heavy remarks to make about the Mars episode. Finn, who had heard me getting up, was hovering about and came at once. I asked him if he would go and buy some horse meat for Mars, but it turned out that he had already done this. Finn doesn't like dogs, but he is a considerate man. Then he handed me a bunch of letters. The only one of these which was of any interest from the point of view of the present story was one which contained a cheque for six hundred and thirty-three pounds ten. For a moment or two I stared at the cheque in bewilderment, wondering who could have made such an odd mistake. Then I drew out of the envelope a typewritten sheet on which were listed the names: Little Grange, Peter of Alex, Hal Adair, Dagenham, Saint Cross, Queen's Rook. They were like names out of history. At the foot of the statement Sammy had written—*You put it down and you pick it up! Suggest you back Lyrebird next time out.* I blushed. When Finn saw me blushing he left the room. Perhaps he thought I had a letter from Anna. But there was no letter from Anna.

Sammy's honourable behaviour put me in a fever to settle the question of Mars. I strode at once into the living-room, where Dave was sitting at the typewriter and Finn was leaning thoughtfully in the doorway. Dave was writing an article for *Mind* on the incongruity of counterparts. He had been working for some time on this article, which he wrote sitting in front of a mirror, and alternately staring at his reflexion and examining his two hands. He had several times tried to explain to me his solution, but I had not yet got as far as grasping the problem. He stopped tapping as I came in and looked at me from under his eyebrows. Finn sat down unostentatiously, like someone taking his place at the back of the court. Mars, who had been lying on the rug, gave me an ecstatic welcome. When this was over I led off quickly.

"Perhaps it *was* a bad idea," I said, "but the question is, what to do now. I want you and Finn to help me to write a letter."

Dave stretched out his legs. I could see he was not going to be hurried into omitting anything. "How you are an amateur, Jake!" he said.

I thought this was just a bit unkind. "Let us be practical," I said. "The first thing, I suppose, is to let Starfield know in whose hands Mars is and for what purpose he was taken. It seems pointless to conceal our identity. Sammy would guess it anyway as soon as we announced our terms."

"In answer to that," said Dave, "I have two observations. Primo, that I do not like this use of *we*. I am not a thief of this dog. Secundo, that naturally Finn and I have already informed Starfield by telephone of the identity of the kid-napper."

"Why?" I asked him, amazed.

"Because," said Dave, "as should be obvious to a black-mailer of even mediocre ability, it was advisable that

Starfield should if possible be prevented from alerting the police. That our information in fact restrained him from doing so is suggested by the fact that you are still at large. I notice that you took the trouble to get your picture into all the papers."

I sat down. When I saw how much Dave relished my predicament I lost the misgivings which I had been beginning to have about inconveniencing him by my antics.

"I appreciate your concern for me," I said coolly. "You overlook the fact that this premature revelation makes it pointless for me to spring on Sammy the proposal to exchange Mars for the typescript. By now Sammy could have had the thing photostated a hundred times over."

"You are naïve," said Dave. "Can you imagine that he would not have done it already? For one like Starfield a thousand typists toil day and night. Not for more than a minute would he let an important document exist in one copy."

"I'm sure from the way he spoke that there was only one, in the afternoon anyway," I said.

"You cannot know," said Dave, "and in any case what was certain was that the police could lay their hand on you blindfold. When will you learn not to travel in taxis?"

I didn't think that I would really have been so easy to catch, but I let that pass. "Well, then," I said, "as a result of your well-meaning move we shall have to modify our proposal. The proposal now is that we exchange Mars, not for the typescript, but for a document guaranteeing me a suitable compensation for its use."

"You are raving," said Dave, "and it is clear that you have not thought the thing out at all." He pushed his typewriter aside and cleared a space in front of him on the table.

"We must first analyse the situation," he said. "Let us consider it under two headings: one, what are your powers, and two, how will you use them. It is useless to consider two until you have first considered one, isn't it? You must be logical, Jake. All right?"

"All right," I said. I felt as the victims of Socrates must have felt. It was impossible to hurry the man.

"Under one," said Dave, "I distinguish two questions, A, how urgently does this Starfield need this dog, and B, how far is this Starfield legally in the wrong about your translation. Now perhaps you can tell us what you know about A?" Dave looked at me, affecting to expect that I had special information about it.

"I've no idea," I said.

"No idea!" cried Dave, simulating surprise. "So in fact, for all you know, this Starfield may not need the dog for weeks or months? Or perhaps he is not yet sure whether he will use the dog at all?"

"I read in a Gallup poll," said Finn, "that the public are sick of animal pictures."

"In any case," said Dave, "it is not clear that Starfield will be in a hurry. And meanwhile he can afford to let you keep the dog. Think of the money that will save him! How many pounds of meat a day did you say it needed, Finn?"

"One and a half pounds a day," said Finn.

"Ten and a half pounds of meat a week," said Dave, "not counting extras."

We all turned and looked at the enormous carnivore. It was fast asleep.

"It ate two pounds to-day," said Finn.

"But at least," I said, "he'll be troubled about the welfare of the brute. He'll want to get it back intact."

Dave regarded me with pity. "What will you do to frighten him?" he asked. "Cut off its tail? Even if it were not that you are one whose character is written on his face, your Sadie knows you well enough to know that you would not hurt an earthworm let alone a big dog."

This was a fact. I was by now beginning to feel myself that my first essay in *chantage* was turning out rather badly.

"It is of course possible," said Dave, "that they will want the animal urgently, but it is not certain. So much for A. Now perhaps you could make a statement on B. Did you personally own the translation rights of Breteuil's books?"

"No, of course not," I said, "I just made a separate agreement with the publisher for each book."

"So!" said Dave, "then so far as anyone's interests are threatened here it is the publisher's interests and not yours. But let us see what the threat is. What is it?"

I ran my fingers through my hair. I felt that whatever I said now would sound simple-minded. "Look, Dave," I said, "what has happened is that they have stolen my translation and are showing it to Mr Pringsheim to persuade him to make a film of the book."

"Exactly," said Dave, "but so far they have not made any other *use* of the translation. If the thing were published they could buy a copy in the shops."

"But it's not published," I said, "and they pinched my typescript."

"The felony," said Dave, "is another question. At any rate it seems that so far there has been no infringement of copyright. This American, who has no French, glances at your translation; that is all. If they decide to make a film they will negotiate the details with whoever owns the film rights, presumably the author."

"Well, at any rate," I said desperately, "there was a theft."

"That's not so clear," said Dave, "morally, yes—but could this be shown? Your friend Madge hands this thing to Starfield. Starfield will say that he had no idea that you would mind. Your Madge in the witness box will say the same, together with any details of how well she knew you which the defending counsel can draw out of her."

I was imagining this. "All right!" I said. "Yes, yes, yes, all right."

"Shall I sum up?" said Dave.

"Go ahead!" I told him bitterly.

"It is unlikely that they need the dog, anyway in the next few days," said Dave. "After these days, after this American has seen the book, they will return you politely the typescript and ask for the dog. If you refuse to give him up they go then to the police. What charge could you possibly bring against them? This American will know and care not whose translation he saw. If you press the matter you are lost in a labyrinth. All that is clear is that you stole the dog."

"But," I said, "if they are not afraid to have their actions questioned, why is it that they haven't gone to the police already? Assuming that you're right in thinking that we'd know it by now if they had."

"Can you not work that out?" said Dave with scorn. "They are just being kind to you. Starfield might well have the police on you. But your friend Sadie will laugh and say that you are perfectly sweet and so you are let off."

This conjecture enraged me the more because I saw at once that it was very likely to be correct. "You've succeeded in showing that I'm a fool," I said. "Let's leave it at that. I'm going out for a walk."

"But no, Jake," said Dave. "We have not yet discussed the second heading."

"I imagined," I said, "that since it turns out that I have no bargaining power the question of what I am to do with it would not arise."

"It is not certain that you have no bargaining power," said Dave, "though I think it very likely that you have none. But you have the dog. And what do you propose to do with him? Send him back to Starfield?"

"Never!" I cried, "so long as there's any alternative!"

"Well, then," said Dave, "let us discuss number two." He sat there, relaxed and reflective, as if he were giving a seminar, except that there was a very sharp gleam of enjoyment in his eye.

"You can still try to bargain," said Dave. He was now changing over from making the worst of the affair to making the best of it. "It is conceivable that they might indeed need the dog at once, or they might be worried about its welfare and make you an offer so as to get it quickly. And to make you an offer might be their best course if they are at all uneasy about the felony question. Whether they are uneasy may depend upon an unknown factor, which is the behaviour and state of mind of your Madge."

I think I felt more pessimistic at this point than Dave did. "It's hopeless!" I said. "All I wanted was to prevent them from using the typescript. Since that's impossible, I'd better start thinking about what I'm going to say in court!"

"Nonsense!" said Dave. "Try to bargain, if only to save your face. You might appeal here to the sporting spirit of this Starfield."

This made me wince. I had no further wish to be beholden to Sammy's sportsmanship. "I had rather deal with Sadie," I said.

"Well, write to her," said Dave; "we will compose the letter together. But first we must decide in what *persona* you are writing, whether as an injured party or as a simple blackmailer. And remember," he added, "with whom we have to deal. It is my view that if these people at any moment want back their animal they will not trouble with bargains or with the police, they will discover where it is and send four strong men in a car to get it."

We were cut short at this point by a thunderous knocking at the front door.

"Police!" said Finn. I thought it was more likely to be Sammy's strong men. We looked at each other. Mars growled, his fur rising. The knocking was repeated.

"We'll let on not to be in," said Finn in a whisper. Mars let out a couple of deafening barks.

"That's given that away!" said Dave.

"Let's go and look at them through the glass of the door," I said, "and see how many there are."

I was ready to fight for Mars, unless of course it should turn out to be the police. We walked softly out into the hall. The stained glass of Dave's front door gave us a jagged image of what lay beyond it. There seemed to be only one person there.

"The rest are in wait on the steps," said Finn.

"Oh, damn this!" I said, and opened the door.

"Two wires for Donaghue," said a telegraph boy.

I took them, and he disappeared down the stairs. Finn and Dave were laughing, but I shivered with apprehension as I tore open the first telegram. At that moment everything was alarming. I read it through several times. Then I walked back into the sitting-room. What it said was: *Come Paris Hotel Prince de Clèves at once by air for important talk stop all expenses paid stop thirty pounds immediate outlay under separate cover Madge.*

"What is it?" said Finn and Dave, following me. I gave it to them to read. The other wire was the order for the thirty pounds.

We all sat down. "What will this be for?" asked Dave.

"I haven't got the remotest notion," I said. What in the world could Madge be up to now? It was all curiously unreal. Except for the thirty pounds. That was real; like the next morning object which proves that it wasn't all a dream. What was Madge doing in Paris? A fever of curiosity was already raging in my blood. In an instant I had run over a dozen possibilities without finding one that was plausible.

"I shall go, of course," I said thoughtfully to the other two. Madge's wire was from every point of view a very welcome development. It wasn't that I was exactly bored with my blackmail scheme; but it had turned out to be rather disappointing and its final stages were likely to be frustrating and mechanical. Perhaps indeed the best thing would be to abandon it altogether. I need small persuading to go to Paris at any time; least of all now, when Anna was there. Or rather Anna might be there. But no, she *must* be there, I felt, so charged with her presence was the image of that city which now rose up before me; and already in my mind I was walking with Anna along the Champs-Élysées, while the warm breeze of an eternal Parisian spring blew into our faces like drifting flowers the promises of a coming felicity.

"And you would leave us to hold up the baby?" Dave was incoherent with indignation. "You commit stealing and blackmail and when all is confusion you go off to Paris and leave here your stolen property to be found by the police, no?"

"All expenses paid," said Finn.

"Look," I said, "I won't stay long, only half a day if need be. I'll just see what Madge wants. If trouble breaks out here you can cable me and I'll be back in a few hours."

Dave calmed down a little. "Can you not wait?" he said.

"It sounds so urgent," I told him, "and there may be money in it." The all expenses paid aspect had suggested this to me very strongly.

This made Dave more thoughtful. "All right," he said, after a little more discussion, "you may as well earn your bail. But first we must decide what letter to write, and second, you must leave us much money to feed the animal and in case there is a crisis."

"There's no difficulty about money," I told him, nursing a secure feeling about Sammy's cheque.

Then a dreadful thought spun me round like a bullet in the shoulder. Of course, as soon as Sammy had heard who it was that had kidnapped Mars he would have stopped the cheque. I leapt out of my chair.

"What is it now?" said Dave. "You are getting on my nerves."

How far would Sammy's sporting instincts extend? Not that far, I was pretty sure. Or would it depend how angry he was? A mental picture of his sitting-room as I had last seen it rose before me and I groaned. The only possibility was that he might have forgotten about the cheque altogether.

"You spoke to Sammy personally on the phone?" I asked Dave.

"Yes," he said, "from a call box, of course."

"And was he angry?"

"He was murderous," said Dave.

"Did he say anything special?" I asked.

"Now I come to think of it," said Dave, "he did. I meant to tell you earlier. He said, tell Donaghue he can have the girl and I'm keeping the cash."

I could have wept. Then of course I had to tell them all about it. I went and fetched the cheque and we looked at it together. It was like viewing the corpse of a loved one.

Finn said he had never seen a cheque for so much money. Even Dave was moved.

"Now I *must* go to Paris!" I said. With the world owing me so much money something radical had to be done at once.

Finn was studying Sammy's statement of account. "There's still Lyrebird," he said. "He can't take that back."

"It only hasn't won yet!" said Dave.

"You two watch the papers," I said. "I've got about sixty pounds in the bank. How much can you put up, Finn?"

"Ten pounds," he said.

"And you, Dave?" I asked.

"Don't be a fool!" said Dave.

Finally we agreed that a stake of fifty pounds should go on the horse from the three of us. We were all a little unhinged still by the loss of the six hundred and thirty-three pounds ten.

After that we discussed the question of the letter. I maintained my view that our dealings should be with Sadie. I was still wounded by Dave's conjecture, and I recalled with some distress how Sadie had said that she liked me. If there had been more time I would have speculated about whether this had influenced my decision. It wasn't, however, a moment for indulging in analyses of motive. If one has good reasons for an action one should not be deterred from doing it because one may also have bad reasons. I decided that scruples were out of place here. Sadie was more intelligent than Sammy, and as far as this adventure was concerned Sadie was the boss. Also she had not had her curtains wrenched out of the wall and her sitting-room turned upside down. That Sadie might still fancy me was neither here nor there. I didn't like it, all the same, and I was impatient to be off.

We agreed finally that Dave should write a simple letter over my signature to Sadie proposing an exchange of Mars for a formal recognition of my status in the matter of the translation and an adequate compensation for the use which had been made of it. We argued for some time about what compensation we should demand. "What are you after," as Dave put it, "restitution, damages or revenge?" Finn thought that we should make it a straight case of blackmail and ask for as much as we thought we could get by the detention of Mars together with veiled hints about a possible deterioration in his health, and suggested five hundred pounds. Dave thought that we should only ask whatever might have been the fee charged for a preview of the translation. He said that he had no idea what this would be, and that strictly it was owed to the publisher and not to me, but that in the circumstances and in order to uphold my dignity I might ask for fifty pounds. I thought that I needed to receive not only the regular fee but also compensation for the theft of the typescript, and suggested modestly two hundred pounds.

In the end we fixed the sum at a hundred pounds. I felt this was very tame; but I was now thoroughly obsessed by the idea of going to Paris and I would have agreed to anything. I signed my name at the foot of a number of sheets of paper, on one of which Dave was to type the letter when he had drafted it along the lines we had agreed upon. Dave wanted me to suggest some endearments or personal touches which could be added to make the letter look more authentic; but I insisted that it must remain completely impersonal and businesslike. I very reluctantly gave Dave a blank cheque. Then I set off to Victoria to catch the night ferry, in order to save money and because I am nervous of air travel.

Fourteen

I FIND that sea voyages promote reflexion. Not that the night ferry can strictly be called a sea voyage in the ordinary sense. A necessary element in the experience of travelling by boat is the smell; whereas one of the special features of the night ferry is that one encounters the kinaesthetic sensations of a boat combined with the olfactory sensations of a train. It was in the midst of such a *déréglement de tous les sens* that I now lay thinking about Hugo.

My interview with Hugo could hardly be said to have been a success; on the other hand it hadn't exactly been a failure either. I had acquainted Hugo with something which he needed to know, and we had exchanged not unfriendly words. We had even had an adventure together in the course of which I had acquitted myself at least without shame. In a sense it could be said that the ice was broken between us. But it is possible to break the ice without burying the hatchet. As I had been rather busy since my meeting with Hugo I had not yet had time to brood upon my impressions. I now gathered them all together and began to turn them over one by one. I remembered vividly my first sight of Hugo, as he stood there at the top of the steps, like the czar of all the Russias. He seemed to me now, as I lay upon my undulating pillow, an image of mystery and power. I felt more than ever certain that we had not finished with each other. To whatever effect the threads of my destiny might be interwoven with his, the tangle had yet to be unravelled. So strongly did this come upon me that I found myself regretting that I had to go to Paris and surrender, even for one day, the possibility of seeing him again.

What had not been made at all clear by our interview, and from this point of view it could be said to have been a failure, was Hugo's present feelings toward me. He had not, it is true, displayed any overt hostility. His behaviour had been, if anything, rather casual. But was this a bad sign or a good sign? I recalled in detail Hugo's expression, his tone of voice, his gestures even, and compared them with earlier memories, but without reaching any conclusion. How fed up Hugo was with me still remained to be seen. I then thought about *The Silencer* and could not help wishing that Sadie and Sammy could have chosen some place other than Sadie's kitchen for their conspiratorial talk. I would, all things considered, have preferred to have retrieved the book and been without the information, and so been spared a great deal of trouble, past and to come; for I didn't seriously imagine that my warning to Hugo had any importance save as a gesture of good will. As for the book itself, it figured in my mind, not only as a *casus belli* between myself and Hugo, but as a constellation of ideas which I could no longer be so disloyal as to pretend to be discontinuous with the rest of my universe. I must reconsider what I had said. But where could I find a copy now? It occurred to me that I might perhaps take off Jean Pierre, if he still had it, the copy which I had sent him on publication and which I could be fairly certain that he had never opened. The thought of Jean Pierre led me on to thoughts of Paris, beautiful, cruel, tender, disquieting, enchanting city, and on these I slept and dreamed of Anna.

Arriving in Paris always causes me pain, even when I have been away for only a short while. It is a city which I never fail to approach with expectation and leave with disappointment. There is a question which only I can ask and which only Paris can answer; but this question is something which I have never yet been able to formulate. Certain things indeed I have learnt here: for instance, that my happiness has a sad face, so sad that for years I took it for my unhappiness and drove it away. But Paris remains for me still an unresolved harmony. It is the only city which I can personify. London I know too well, and the others I do not love enough. Paris I encounter, but as one encounters a loved one, in the end and dumbly, and can scarcely speak a word. *Alors, Paris, qu'est-ce que tu dis, toi? Paris, dis-moi ce que j'aime.* But there is no reply, only the sad echo from crumbling walls, *Paris.*

When I arrived I felt in no violent hurry to see Madge. I was for letting the usual spell bind me; life has so few moments which announce themselves as sacred. Later on would be soon enough to start thinking the thoughts, whatever they might be, which my interview with Madge would compel me to think; and as I wandered toward the Seine I felt sure that, wherever the line was to be drawn between appearance and reality, what I now experienced was for me the real. The prospect of Madge paled like a candle. It was that time of the morning when mysterious rivers, guided by bits of old sacking, flow round and round the gutters of Paris. The cloudless light drew a wash of colour along the grey façades of the *quais* and made them look as soft and deep as icing sugar. There are details which even the most tender memory will mislay. The shutter-softened houses with their high foreheads. I leaned for a long time, looking into the mirror of the Pont Neuf, whose round arches make with their reflexions a perfect O, in which one cannot tell what is reflected and what is not, so still is the Seine with a glassy stillness which the tidal Thames can never achieve. I leaned there and thought of Anna, who had made this city exist for me in a new proliferation of detail when, after having known it for many years, I first showed it to her.

At last I began to want my breakfast. I began walking in the direction of Madge's hotel, and sat down *en route* at a café not far from the Opéra. Here I began to notice the more mundane details of the busy city; and after I had been sitting there for a while a sort of stir upon the pavement just beside the café began to catch my eye. Several men in shirt sleeves were standing about as if they were expecting something. I looked at them with vague interest; and I soon divined that they were emanating from a bookshop which

stood next door to the café. I wondered for a while
what it was they were waiting for. They hung about,
looking down the street, returned into the bookshop, and
then came out again and waited all agog. After a while I
turned to study the shop, and there I saw something which
explained the scene. The main window was completely
empty, and across it in enormous letters were written
the words PRIX GONCOURT. When the big literary prizes
are awarded each year the publishers of books which are
thought to be hopeful candidates stand by, ready to turn
out at a moment's notice a huge new edition of the winning
book. This work, reprinted in tens of thousands, is then
rushed pell-mell to the bookshops, so that before the news
has lost its savour the public can gorge its fill of this hall-
marked piece of literature. In preparation for this event all
bookshops which have any intellectual pretensions clear their
best windows and stand ready to welcome in the winner as
it arrives with the break-neck speed of a stop-press edition.

I sat drinking my coffee and watching this scene and
reflecting on the difference between French and English
literary *mœurs*, when there was a screaming of brakes and a
lorry drew up sharply at the kerb. The shirt-sleeved men
precipitated themselves upon it, and in a moment they had
formed a chain along which bundles of books were tossed
rapidly from hand to hand. Inside the shop I could see
that others were anxiously setting up the cardboard display
cases in the empty window which, in a few minutes, was
to be crammed from end to end with the monotonous and
triumphant repetition of the winner's name. The whole
episode had the hasty precision of a police raid. I watched
with amusement as the lorry was emptied; while behind
me now the window was whitening with books. I turned
to inspect it; and there I saw something which stopped my
smile abruptly.

Across the whole window, with the emotional emphasis
of a repeated cry, I saw the name of Jean Pierre Breteuil;
and underneath it in parallel repetition, NOUS LES VAIN-
QUEURS NOUS LES VAINQUEURS NOUS LES VAINQUEURS. I

started from my seat. I looked again at the notice which said PRIX GONCOURT. There could be no doubt about it. I paid my bill and went and stood by the window, while under my eyes the message was repeated ten, a hundred, five hundred times. *Jean Pierre Breteuil* NOUS LES VAIN-QUEURS. The mountain of books rose slowly in front of me; there was not one dissentient voice. It rose to a peak. The last book was put in place on the very top, and then the shop assistants came crowding out to see how it looked from the front. The name and the title swam before my eyes, and I turned away.

It was only then that it struck me as shocking that my predominant emotion was distress. It was a distress, too, which went so deep that I was at first at a loss to understand it. I walked at random trying to sort the matter out. I was of course very surprised to find Jean Pierre in the role of a Goncourt winner. The Goncourt jury, that constellation of glorious names, might sometimes err, but they would never make a crass or fantastic mistake. That their coronation of Jean Pierre represented a moment of sheer insanity was a theory which I could set aside. I had not read the book. The alternative remained open, and the more I reflected the more it appeared to be the only alternative, that Jean Pierre had at last written a good novel.

I stood still in the middle of the pavement. Why was this absolutely unbearable? Why should it matter to me so much that Jean Pierre had pulled it off? I went to a café and ordered cognac. To say that I was jealous was to put it too simply. I felt an indignant horror as at some monstrous reversal of the order of nature : as a man might feel if his favourite opinion was suddenly contro-verted in detail by a chimpanzee. I had classed Jean Pierre once and for all. That he should secretly have been changing his spots, secretly improving his style, ennob-ling his thought, purifying his emotions: all this was really too bad. In my imagination I was already lending the book every possible virtue, and the more I did so the more I felt a mingled rage and distress which drove every other idea from my mind. I ordered another cognac. Jean Pierre had no right to turn himself surreptitiously into a good writer. I felt that I had been the victim of an imposture, a swindle. For years I had worked for this man, using my knowledge and sensibility to turn his junk into the sweet English tongue; and now, without warning me, he sets up shop as a good writer. I pictured Jean Pierre with his plump hands and his short grey hair. How could I introduce into this picture, which I had known so well for so long, the notion of a good novelist? It wrenched me, like the changing of a fundamental category. A man whom I had taken on as a business partner had turned out to be a rival in love. One thing was plain. Since it was now impossible to treat with Jean Pierre cynically it was impossible to treat with him at all. Why should I waste time transcribing his writings instead of producing my own? I would never translate *Nous Les Vainqueurs*. Never, never, never,

It was striking ten before I remembered Madge. I took a taxi to her hotel, and as I went my rage was curdling inside me and turning into a sort of rash vigour, which hardened my sinews and lifted my head. I did not slink into the Hôtel Prince de Clèves as I would normally have done. I strode in, making receptionists and porters cower. They did not need to affect to ignore, for I think they truly did not see, the leather patches on my elbows, such is the power of the human eye when it darts forth its fire. I commanded to be led to Madge; and in a moment or two I was at her door. The door opened, and I saw Madge reclining on a *chaise-longue* in an attitude which she had clearly taken up some time ago in expectation of my arrival. The door was closed softly behind me as behind a prince. I looked down at Madge; and it came to me that I was more pleased to see her than I had ever been before. Under my look her dignity dissolved, and I could see unfolded in her face how deeply moved, relieved and delighted she was to see me. With a whoop I fell upon her.

*   *   *

Some time later it was necessary to start talking. I had been struck as I came in, only the impression had been submerged at once, by a further alteration in Madge. Now as she powdered her nose I sat and took this in. Her clothes were quieter and sleeker and desperately well cut, and her coiffure was completely transformed. The undulating English perm was gone, and her hair fitted her now like a scalloped cap. She seemed slimmer and more piquant; even her movements were more gracious. Clearly somebody new had taken Madge in hand, somebody far more expert than Sammy. She watched me out of the corner of her eye as she blocked in the tenderly proud mouth of a woman who knows that she is desired; and as I went to kiss her she turned her head and offered me with a regal movement the perfumed and artificial bloom of her cheek. It was unnerving to see someone transforming herself so rapidly : like seeing the stars moving or the world turning.

"Madge, you are beautiful," I said. We sat down.

"Jakie," said Madge, "I just can't tell you how glad I am to see you. I just can't tell you. You're the first human face I've seen for ages."

I was already beginning to wonder what sort of faces Madge had been seeing lately; there would be time enough, however, to get this out of her. We had a great deal to tell each other.

"Where shall we start?" I asked.

"Oh, darling!" said Madge, and threw her arms round me. We put off starting for a bit longer.

"Look," I said at last, "let's begin by establishing what we both know: for instance that Sammy is a scoundrel."

"Oh dear!" said Madge, "I was so miserable about Sammy!"

"What happened?" I asked.

Madge plainly wasn't going to tell me. I could see her selecting an evasion. "You don't understand Sammy," said Madge, "he's an unhappy muddled sort of person." This is a standard remark made by women about men who have left them.

"Was that why you made him a present of my translation?" I asked.

"Oh, *that*!" said Madge. "I did that for your sake, Jakie." She kept me at bay with her big eyes. "I thought if anything came of it Sammy could help you. But how did you know he had it?"

I then gave her a highly selective version of my own recent adventures. I could see Madge hated the bits about Sammy and Sadie.

"What a pair of crooks!" she said.

"But surely you knew about Sammy's plan?" I asked her.

"I had no idea until two days ago," said Madge.

This was clearly false, since she must have known more or less what Sammy was up to when she gave him my typescript; but at that time she had doubtless been under the impression that it was herself and not Sadie who was to be the woman in the case. Indeed, perhaps Sammy had thought this too, to begin with. On the occasion of our sporting afternoon he had certainly manifested what had appeared to be a genuine interest in Madge. That Sammy was muddled was possible after all. Whether he was unhappy I neither knew nor cared.

"Well now, suppose you tell me a few things?" I said. "What's this important talk you wanted?"

"It's a long story, Jake," said Madge. She poured me out a drink, and then stood looking at me reflectively. She had the withdrawn feline look of a woman who is conscious of power and seeing herself as Cleopatra. "Would you like to earn three hundred pounds down and a hundred and fifty a month for an indefinite time?"

While I considered this I contemplated Madge in her new role. "Other things being equal," I said, "the answer is yes. But who is the paymaster?"

Madge walked slowly across the room. Her sense of drama was acute enough to electrify the whole atmosphere. She turned quietly to face me, with the quietness of somebody who knows that quietly is how they are turning.

"Oh, cut it out, Madge," I said, "and come clean. This isn't a screen test."

"A person," said Madge, choosing her words with care, "who has made a great deal of money out of shipping or something in Indo-China, is proposing to put this money into the creation of an Anglo-French film company. It will be a very big enterprise. The people who are to control it are looking round for talent. Naturally," she added, "all that I say to you now is in confidence."

I stared at Madge. She had certainly been to school since I had last seen her. Where could she have picked up words like "enterprise" and "in confidence"?

"This is very interesting," I said, "and I hope that the eye of the talent-spotter has lighted favourably upon you; but where do I come in?"

"You come in," said Madge, "as a script-writer." She poured out a drink for herself. The timing was perfect.

"Look, Madge," I said, "I appreciate this. I appreciate *all* your kind efforts on my behalf. But one can't just walk into a job like that. Script-writing is highly technical—I should have to learn it before anyone in their senses would pay me the sum you mentioned. Anyway," I said, "I'm not sure that it's the sort of job I'd care for. *Ce n'est pas mon genre.*"

"Stop acting, Jake," said Madge. She had obviously been stung by my earlier remark. "You're panting for that money. Let me just tell you what you have to do to get it."

It was true that I was not unmoved. "Give me another drink," I said, "and tell me how you propose to drag me in."

"You don't need to be dragged in," said Madge. "You come in quite naturally because of Jean Pierre."

"My God!" I said, "what has Jean Pierre got to do with it?" I seemed to be up to my ankles in Jean Pierre that morning.

"He's on the board of directors," said Madge, "or he will be when everything's signed. And just guess what our first production will be," she said, with the air of someone whipping out a conclusive argument. "An English film based on his latest book!"

I felt sick. "You mean *Nous Les Vainqueurs*?" I said.

"That's the one," said Madge, "the one that got the what-not prize."

"I know," I said, "the *Prix Goncourt*, I saw it in a shop as I came along."

"It would make a marvellous film, wouldn't it?" said Madge.

"I don't know," I said, "I haven't read it." I sat looking at the carpet. I felt more like crying than I had for a long time.

Madge watched me as I sat there with my head drooping. "What's the matter with you, Jake?" she cried. "Aren't you well?"

"I'm fine," I said. "Go on telling me things."

"Jake," said Madge, "everything has worked out wonderfully. You just haven't seen it yet. This is better than anything we ever dreamed up in Earls Court Road. That it should be Jean Pierre! It's all come out in a beautiful pattern."

I could see that it had come out in a pattern. "Madge," I said, "I'm not a script-writer. I know nothing about the cinema."

"Darling," said Madge, "that's not the point, and it doesn't matter."

"I rather thought it wasn't the point," I said.

"You haven't understood," said Madge. "It's all fixed. The job's yours."

"Is this job in your gift?" I asked.

"What do you mean?" said Madge.

"I mean, can you give it to anyone you like?"

We looked at each other. "I see," I said, and settled back into my chair. "Fill up my glass, would you?"

"Jake, stop being difficult," said Madge.

"I want to have things clear," I said. "You're offering me a sinecure."

"I'm not sure what that is," said Madge, "but I expect it's that."

"A sinecure is when you get money for doing nothing," I said.

"But isn't that exactly what you've always wanted?" said Madge.

I looked into the amber depths of my glass. "Perhaps," I said, "but I don't want it now." I wasn't sure if this was true. It remained to be seen whether it was true.

"Anyway," said Madge, "it won't be for doing nothing. You may have all kinds of things to do. There's translating the book, which you'd do anyway."

"You know perfectly well that that's another matter," I told her.

"You must be jolly glad," said Madge, "that he's written a decent book at last. Everyone says it's marvellous. Particularly since it got the what-not prize."

"I shall translate no more books for Jean Pierre," I said.

Madge stared at me as if I were mad. "What do you mean?" she said. "At Earls Court Road you were always complaining at having to waste your time translating such bad stuff."

"That's true," I told her, "but the logic of the situation is odd here. It doesn't follow that I would regard it as less of a waste of time to translate better stuff."

I got up and went to look out of the window. I could hear Madge following me across the thick carpet.

"Jake," she said close behind my ear, "stop this. You've got the chance of a lifetime. Maybe at first you wouldn't have much to do, but later it would be different. And you must drop this nonsense about Jean Pierre."

"You wouldn't understand," I said. We turned to face each other.

"Your girl friend's gone to Hollywood," said Madge after a moment's silence.

I took hold of Madge's limp and unresponsive hand. "It's not that," I said. "Incidentally," I said, "I wish you wouldn't refer to Anna as my girl friend. We haven't met for years, except for one time last week."

Madge said "Oh!" rather sceptically.

"Anyway," I added, "she *hasn't* gone to Hollywood." It wasn't till that moment that I felt absolutely certain of it. "You don't *know* that she has, do you?" I asked Madge.

"Well, not exactly," said Madge, "but I'm told she has. And everyone goes to Hollywood if they can."

I made a gesture expressive of contempt of a world in which this was so. But I had already displayed too much emotion and I wanted to change the subject. "How will this company of yours relate to Bounty Belfounder?" I asked.

"Relate to it?" said Madge. "It'll wipe it off the face of the earth." She spoke with cruel satisfaction. I shrugged my shoulders.

"And don't pretend," said Madge, "that that matters tuppence to you. In fact, you'll be doing a great service to your friend Belfounder. There's nothing he wants so much as to lose all his money."

This startled me. Madge had evidently been moving in circles where Hugo's character was dismissed. "He can do it without my help," I said, turning away.

I felt a sort of confused lassitude. I was being offered a great deal of money; and it was not at all clear to me why I was refusing it: if what I was doing was refusing it. What was more important, I was being offered the key to the world in which money comes easily, and where the same amount of effort can produce enormously richer results: as when one removes a weight from one element to another. As for my conscience, I could catch up with that in a few months. In time I could earn my keep in that world as well as the next man. All I had to do was to shut my eyes and walk in. Why did the way in seem so hard? I was in anguish. I seemed to be throwing away the substance for the shadow. What I was preferring was an emptiness of which I could give no intelligible account whatever.

Madge watched me with increasing distress.

"Madge," I said, just for something to say, "what will happen about the *Nightingale*?"

"Oh, that'll be all right," said Madge. "Someone from Sadie did approach Jean Pierre about it, but he put them off. And now our company has got the film rights of all his books."

This was cool. I smiled at Madge, and saw her smiling too with relief. "So Sadie and Sammy have had it," I said.

"They've had it," said Madge.

I began remembering how sorry I'd felt for Madge, and then it occurred to me that Madge had probably started double-crossing Sammy even before she knew that Sammy was double-crossing her. It takes time to make the Hôtel Prince de Clèves. This was so funny that I began to laugh, and the more I thought of it the more I laughed until I had to sit down on the floor. At first Madge laughed with me, but then she stopped and said sharply, "Jake!" I recovered.

"So Sammy will have to make animal pictures after all," I said.

"As for that," said Madge, "Sammy's been sold a pup there too. Or rather he hasn't been sold a pup."

"What do you mean?" I asked.

"Phantasifilms cheated Sammy," said Madge. "Do you know how old Mister Mars is?"

A sad finger touched my heart. "I don't know," I said. "How old?"

"Fourteen," said Madge. "He's on his last legs. He could hardly get through the last film he made. Phantasifilms were going to retire him anyway. Then Sammy got interested in him, and they sold him without telling his age. Sammy ought to have looked in his mouth."

"You can't tell a dog's age by looking in his mouth," I said.

"So Sammy's one down there too," said Madge.

I didn't care. I was thinking about Mars. Mars was old.

He would do no more work. He would not swim flooded rivers any more, or scramble over high fences, or fight with bears in lonely places. His strength was waning and his intelligence would avail him nothing. He would soon die. This discovery completed the circle of my sadness; and with it my resolution crystallized.

"I can't do it, Madge," I said.

"You're insane!" said Madge. "Why, Jake, why?"

"I don't know very clearly," I said. "I only know it would be the death of me."

Madge came up to me. Her eyes were as hard as agate. "This is real life, Jake," she said. "You'd better wake up." And she struck me hard across the mouth. I recoiled slightly with the sudden pain of the blow. We stood so for a moment, and she sustained my gaze while the tears gathered slowly in her eyes. Then I received her into my arms.

"Jake," said Madge into my shoulder, "don't leave me."

I half carried her to the settee. I felt calm and resolute. I knelt beside her and took her head, brushing her hair back with my hand. Her face rose toward me like a lifting flower.

"Jake," said Madge, "I must have you with me. That was what it was all for. Don't you see?"

I nodded. I drew my hand back over her smooth hair and down onto the warmth of her neck.

"Jake, say something," said Madge.

"It can't be done," I said. Madge was *lancée*; nor could I know after describing what parabola she would finally return to earth. There was nothing I could do for her. "There is nothing I can do for you," I said.

"You could stick around," said Madge. "That would be everything."

I shook my head.

"Look, Madge," I said, "let me be simple. I might tell you that I cared for you too much to be willing to stand by while you go to bed with the men who can help you to become a star. But that wouldn't be true. If I cared for you a bit more perhaps I should want to do precisely that. The fact is that I must live my own life. And it simply doesn't lie in this direction."

Madge looked at me through real tears. She played her last card. "If it's Anna," she said, "you know that I wouldn't mind. I mean, perhaps I'd mind, but that wouldn't matter. I just want you near me."

"It's no use, Madge," I said, and I stood up. At that moment I loved her deeply. A few minutes later I was going down the stairs.

Fifteen

I CROSSED the road and walked automatically toward the river. I collided with people on the pavements and was nearly run over several times. My legs were trembling under me. When I reached the Seine I sat down on a seat. I took off my coat, and found that my shirt was drenched with sweat. I unbuttoned my shirt and ran my hand about my chest and under my arms. I wasn't at all sure what it was that I had done, but I knew that it was something important. Just then it felt like committing a murder when drunk. As I looked about me, Paris recomposed itself like a reflexion which ceases to waver as the water becomes still. At last it was as still as glass. What *had* I done?

Refused a net sum which, on the assumption that it would have taken me at least six months to get the sack, could be reckoned at twelve hundred pounds. Refused an easy step out of the world of continual penury into the world of perpetual money. And what for? For nothing. At that moment my action seemed to me completely pointless. In Madge's room I had seemed to see some reason why it was necessary. Now I couldn't for the life of me think what that reason could have been. I got up and walked across the iron bridge. The clock at the Institut said ten past twelve. And as I walked a great truth became apparent to me. Nothing in the world was more important than money. Why had I not understood this before? Madge had been right when she had said that it was real life. It was the one thing needful; and I had rejected it. I felt like Judas.

I stopped to look at Paris. Its gentle colours awoke for me, clear but not violent under the July sun. The fishermen were fishing, and the *flâneurs* were flaning, and the dogs were barking down at the steps where people try to persuade them to swim in the Seine. How strangely it excites people to see their dogs swimming! Beyond the green trees the towers of Notre-Dame rose tenderly like lovers rising from the grass. "Paris," I said aloud. Once more something had slipped through my fingers. Only this time I knew very well what it was. Money. The heart of reality. The rejection of reality the only crime. I was a dreamer, a criminal. I wrung my hands.

As I reached the left bank I began madly to want to drink; and at the same instant I realized that I had hardly any cash. I had thrust into my pocket as I was leaving the few notes which I had had left over from my last trip. I had intended to borrow something from Madge. But no one with any aesthetic sensibility would have tried to borrow five thousand francs off somebody from whom he had just refused to accept twelve hundred pounds. And anyway I didn't think of it. I cursed. I walked as far as the Boulevard St Germain wondering what to do. Then a second need, equally expensive, began to make itself felt: the need to communicate my sorrow to some other person. I balanced the two needs against my assets and against each other. The need for communication was the more profound. I made for the post office in the Rue du Four and addressed a wire to Messrs Gellman and O'Finney which ran as follows. *Just definitely refused minimum sum of twelve hundred pounds. Jake.* Then I went to the Reine Blanche and ordered a pernod, which although it is not the cheapest of *apéritifs* is the one with the highest alcohol content. I felt very slightly better.

I sat there for a long time. At first I kept thinking about the money. I brooded on every aspect of it. I turned it into francs. I turned it into dollars. I shifted it around from one European capital to another. I invested it avariciously at high rates of interest. I spent it riotously on *château* wines and *château* women. I bought the very latest make of Aston Martin. I rented a flat overlooking Hyde Park and filled it with works of the lesser-known Dutch masters. I lay on a striped divan beside a pale-green telephone while the princes of the film world poured fawning, supplication and praise along the wire. The exquisite star, the idol of three continents, who lay like a panther at my feet, poured me out another glass of champagne. "It's H. K.," I murmured to her, putting my hand over the mouthpiece; "what a perfect bore!" I tossed her an orchid which lay on the table; and clasping my body with her sinuous hands she began to pull herself up to lie beside me, as I told H. K. that I was in conference and that if he would contact my secretary in a day or two no doubt a meeting might be arranged.

When I was tired of this I began to think about Madge, and to wonder who it was who had installed her in the Hôtel Prince de Clèves and whose unseen presence had hovered in the background of our interview. Was it the man who had owned ships or something in Indo-China? I pictured him, white-haired and heavy, battered by winds and stained by the oriental sun, with power and intelligence breaking through the lines of his face of an old Frenchman who had seen, in his time, many things. I liked him. He was wealthy beyond the dreams of avarice. The years which had passed since he had pursued money with passion could now be counted by the score. He had had his fill of money: he had loved it, struggled with it, suffered for it and made others suffer; he had bathed in it until it had filled his head and eyes with gold; finally he had tired of it, and cast it from him fortune by fortune. But money will never leave a man who has endured enough for its sake. He had become weary, he had consented. He lived with it now as with an aged wife. He was come back to France, tired and detached, with the detachment of one who has gratified every wish and found every gratification equally transitory. He would watch with a gentle indifference the launching of his film company, in a scene where every actor except himself was driven mad by the smell of money.

Or perhaps Madge's protector was some shrewd Englishman: a middle-aged man, I pictured him, with long experience of the film business. Perhaps a failed director who had turned his artistic talents into the business side of the industry, consoling himself by making money for the loss of a vision of beauty which would nevertheless haunt him all his life, and make him short-tempered whenever he came near the set and saw other men struggling with the problems which had given him ecstasy at twenty-five, and sleepless nights at thirty, and finally brought him to despair. Where had Madge met him? Possibly at one of those parties of "film people" which Sammy had said that Madge frequented on the occasion when he had warned me that not letting them out of your sight was the only way.

Or perhaps—the devastating thought struck me at last—perhaps Madge's friend was Jean Pierre himself? I absolutely hated this idea. But it was by no means impossible. I had never introduced Madge to Jean Pierre although she had often asked me to do so. Some instinct of caution had deterred me from promoting this particular juxtaposition. There are Englishwomen for whom Frenchmen are, as it were, *ex officio* romantic, and I think I suspected Madge of being one of these. Madge was, however, perfectly capable of having introduced herself to Jean Pierre without telling me. I remembered the familiar way she had referred to him by his Christian name in our recent talk; and although she might have simply picked this up from me, or from her new milieu, it was also possible that she had in fact cast Jean Pierre in the role of her fortune-maker. He was not my idea of a charmer, but women are funny.

I thought about this a bit longer and then decided that after all it was unlikely. Of my three hypotheses the second one was doubtless the most probable. A while later I felt that I didn't care anyhow. One glass of pernod had taken me some way; a second glass took me further still. The sun began to rise over my intellectual landscape and I saw at last, in an outburst of clarity, the real shape of that which had before so obscurely compelled me to what had seemed to be a senseless decision. It wasn't just that I didn't want to enter Madge's world and play Madge's game. I had so

littered my life already with compromises and half-truths. I
could have picked my way through a few more. The twist-
ing halls of falsehood never cease to appal me, but I constantly enter them; possibly because I see them as short
corridors which lead out again into the sun : though, perhaps, this is the only *fatal* lie. I didn't care for the role of
valet de sentiment which Madge had prepared for me, but I
could perhaps have supported it because I really liked
Madge and because of the cash prizes, if there had been
nothing else at stake. I had said to Madge that it wasn't
Anna, and I think that that was true. What my relations
with Anna might or mightn't compel me to do in the future
remained to be seen. I felt, indeed, almost fatalistic about it.
If Anna was strong enough to draw me to her over every
obstacle she was strong enough to draw me, and the ob-
stacles would be overcome at the proper time. Meanwhile Madge was in no position to make complaints. It
wasn't that.

When I asked myself what it *was*, there rose authori-
tatively before me the shop window which I had seen
earlier that morning surmounted by the words *Prix Goncourt*. As for the *Prix Goncourt* itself, *je m'en fichais*, that
was just a label. What mattered was what Jean Pierre had
done. Or rather even that didn't matter. Even if *Nous Les
Vainqueurs* turned out to be just as bad as Jean Pierre's
other books, this was of no importance either. All that
mattered was a vision which I had had of my own destiny
and which imposed itself upon me as a command. What
had I to do with script-writing? When I had told Madge
that it was not my *genre* I had not been thinking what I was
saying; but it was true all the same. The business of my life
lay elsewhere. There was a path which awaited me and
which if I failed to take it would lie untrodden forever.
How much longer would I delay? This was the substance
and all other things were shadows, fit only to distract and
deceive. What did I care for money? It was as nothing
to me. In the light of that vision it shrivelled like autumn
leaves, its gold turning to brown and crumbling away into

dust. When I had had these thoughts a profound contentment filled me, and I resolved at the same instant to go and look for Anna.

There was, however, one immediate difficulty, which was that I hadn't enough money to pay the bill. I seemed somehow to have consumed four glasses of pernod to a tune of several hundred francs. Even not counting the tip, I was about fifty francs short. I was considering whether I wouldn't ask the *patron* to charge it to Jean Pierre, who is well known at the Reine Blanche, when there hove up on the horizon a cadger of international repute who was an old acquaintance of mine. He bore down upon me with glistening eyes; and a few minutes later I had the satisfaction of taking off him the thousand-franc note which shame and the remembrance of hundreds of drinks which I had bought him in at least three capital cities could not permit even him to withhold. I left him a poorer but a better man.

My conviction that Anna was still in Paris was after all rather irrational. It was, however, very strong; and when I had got well round the corner I made for a telephone. I telephoned first of all to the *Club des Fous*, a gay but enlightened *boîte* where Anna had made her Paris *début* some years earlier. But no one there had any news of her. They knew she had been in Paris, but whether she was still there, or where she was to be found, no one could say. I then rang up various individuals who might have come across her, but they all said the same thing, except one who said that he thought she had sailed on the previous day, unless it had been Edith Piaf, he couldn't remember. I then started phoning hotels, first the ones at which I had stayed with Anna, in case sentiment might have led her back to them, and afterwards more luxurious hotels which I knew Anna knew of, in case comfort had triumphed over sentiment or sentiment had worked in a contrary way. It was all in vain. No one had seen her, no one knew where she was. I gave up, and started walking disconsolately. It was very hot.

If Anna were in Paris, what would she be doing? She might be with somebody. If she was with somebody I was done for anyway. I must work on the assumption that she was alone. If she was not with any of the song or theatre people, what would she be doing here all by herself? The answer, from my knowledge of Anna's character, was clear. She would be sitting in some place which she found beautiful and meditating. Or walking very slowly along a road somewhere in the fifth or sixth *arrondissement*. Of course she might have gone to Montmartre; but she always used to complain so about the steps. Or to Père-Lachaise; but I didn't want to have to think about death. If I made a tour of our shrines on the left bank I might stand some small chance of finding her. The alternative was to get drunk. I bought a *tartine* and set off for the Luxembourg gardens.

I went straight to the fontaine des Médicis. There was nobody there; but the spirit of the place held me at once and I could not go. When I had been in Paris with Anna long ago we had used to come here every day; and now when I had stood in silence for a moment I could not but believe that if I waited she must come. There is something compelling about the sound of a fountain in a deserted place. It murmurs about what things do when no one watches them. It is the hearing of an unheard sound. A gentle refutation of Berkeley. The pied plane trees enclosed the place. I approached slowly. To-day there was hardly a trickle down the green steps and the tall grotto swayed only slightly in the water on which a few large leaves floated lotus-like. On the steps fantail pigeons waded in to drink deeply. Above them the lovers lay immobile, she in a pose of abandoned shyness exposing an exquisite body, while he cups her head in a gesture which is too concerned to be called sensual. So they lie, petrified into stillness by the one-eyed gaze of huge rain-marked, weather-stained, pigeon-spattered, dark-green Polyphemus, who leans over the rock from above and sees them. I stood there for a long time, leaning against a marble urn and meditating upon the curve of her thigh. How her

right leg is drawn under her, and her naked left leg out-
stretched in that pure undulation which can lift contemplation and desire almost together to the highest point of awareness, the curve of a reclining woman's thigh. There she lies,
braced and yet relaxed, superbly naked and smiling faintly
with closed eyes. I waited a long time, but Anna did not
come.

Then I recalled to mind all the things and places which
Anna had liked most in Paris. She had liked the chameleons
in the Jardin des Plantes. I went next and looked at the
chameleons. Very very slowly they were climbing about
their cage, their long tails curling and uncurling with
unspeakable deliberation as with a scarcely perceptible
motion they stretched out one of their long hands to grasp
another branch. Their squinting eyes would stare quietly
for a while until one of them would swivel very gently
to another angle. I liked them very much. This is the
real tempo of the world, they told me, as with an almost unbearable slowness they brought another limb into play, and then relaxed into a rigid immobility. Watching
them, my sense of duration slowed down and almost
stopped; and I stayed there too for a long time, where
every second was lengthened out into a minute, and
motion and rest almost completely reconciled. Anna did
not come.

I left the Jardin in haste and ran along the *quais*. I
dashed into the churches, one after the other, St Julien, St
Severin, St Germain, St Sulpice, in case I should find Anna
there, her head thrown back, feeding some sad wish. Nobody. I went to the garden behind Notre-Dame where the
church bears down like a ship and we had often fed the
sparrows. I crossed to the right bank and went to the garden with the cascade, behind the Grand Palais, which is
open all night. Nobody. Then I went to St Eustache and
wandered in a forest of multiform pillars. After that I gave
up. It was late in the afternoon. Outside the *halles* they
were cleaning the pavements with hoses. Fruit and vegetables coursed along the gutters. I bought some bread and a

Camembert, and through crowds of fat women nibbling the ends of the long loaves which they were taking home, my feet began automatically to carry me back toward the *quartier* St Germain. As I walked, and the vision of Anna faded a little from my eyes, I began to notice that the city was more than usually decked with *tricolores,* and down side streets I saw little strings of flags which ran from house to house across the roadway. Some fête was on. Then I remembered that it was the fourteenth of July.

When I got as far as the Brasserie Lipp I felt ready to sit down. So I sat down and ordered vermouth. The events of the morning already seemed far away, and equally far away the moment of insight which had succeeded them. In so far as I felt anything now concerning these things it was a sort of dull stupid pain which may have been regret for the money, or may have been simply the after-effects of too much pernod at lunch time. But my need of Anna had not lost its sharpness. Where was she at this moment? Perhaps not half a mile away, sitting on the bed in some hotel room and looking at a half-packed suitcase. As I pictured the sad angle of her head I began to find the idea unbearable. No, doubtless she was on the sea, leaning on the rail with her eyes already full of America. I could not decide which of these thoughts was the more unpleasant.

I hadn't been sitting in the Brasserie Lipp for more than a few minutes when I heard one of the waiters calling out "Monsieur Dohnagoo, Monsieur Dohnagoo." I have had my name called on the *terrasses* of cafés all over Europe, so that I was ready for this. I waved my hand. The waiter approached me holding a telegram. My first irrational notion was that it must be from Anna in New York. I seized it. It was from England; it was from Dave, who knew my partiality to the Brasserie Lipp and evidently sent the wire there on the off chance of its finding me. It read—*Never mind Lyrebird won to-day at twenty to one.*

Paris was beginning to tremble with the excitement of the *quatorze.* I started to walk along the Boulevard St Germain. I was in my shirt sleeves, but still feeling extremely hot, although the day had softened into evening. I walked slowly, passing Diderot, where he sits amid the acacia trees looking with understandable dubiety in the direction of the Café de Flore. There were a great many people walking up and down, and a confused hum of voices and laughter rose above the traffic. All Paris was out of doors. When I reached the Odéon I saw that the cafés had spread themselves over half the road, and in the Rue de l'Ancienne-Comédie people were already dancing to the sound of an accordeon. Above them strings of coloured lamps were burning in the evening daylight. I sat down for a while to watch.

If like myself you are a connoisseur of solitude, I recommend to you the experience of being alone in Paris on the fourteenth of July. On that day the city lets down its tumultuous hair, which the high summer anoints with warmth and perfume. In Paris every man has his girl; but on that day every man is a sultan. Then people flock together and sweep chattering about the city like flights of brilliantly coloured birds. Amid unfurling of streamers and bursting of rockets and releasing of pigeons and popping of corks the unit of gaiety becomes, as the evening advances, larger and larger. No one is left outside; until the whole city has turned into one enormous party. To be alone in such a carnival is a strange experience. I decided to refrain from drinking. After a few drinks I knew that a sentimental loneliness would begin to spoil my detachment. Whereas to be the cool and collected spectator of scenes of mad revelry, the solitary man who brushes aside with a wan smile the women who accost him and the coloured streamers in which the enemies of solitude hasten to entangle him; this was the pleasure which I promised myself for that evening, and I had no mind to let such rarely compounded moments of contemplation be ruined by miserable yearnings for a woman I could not find.

With these good resolutions I picked my way through the dancers and began walking down the Rue Dauphine. I wanted to be by the river. As I came near to it the crowd

increased, their voices flying about like bats in the thick
evening air. A feeling of expectancy came over me. My
feet were led. I walked out onto the Pont Neuf. It was not
yet dark, but the flood-lighting had already been switched
on. The Tour St Jacques stood out in gold like a tapestry
tower and the slim finger of the Sainte Chapelle rose mys-
teriously out of the Palais de Justice, with every spike and
blossom clearly marked upon it. High in the air the Eiffel
Tower cast out a revolving beam. Down in the Vert Galant
there was shouting and laughter and the throwing of things
into the river. I turned away from this. I needed to see
Notre-Dame. I walked through the place Dauphine and
regained the mainland at the Pont St Michel. I wanted
to see my darling from across the river. Jostled by revellers,
I fixed myself to the wall and looked at its pearly towers
behind which the night was beginning to gather. How
curiously this church is dwarfed by its beauty, as some
women are. I began to make my way towards it, until I
could see mirrored beneath it in the unflecked river a
diabolic Notre-Dame, sketched there but never quite motionless, like a skull which appears in a glass as the reflexion of
a head. Very gently the illumined image bulged and frag-
mented, absorbed in its own quiet rhythm, ignoring the
crowds which across all the bridges were streaming now in
both directions.

I was leaning on the parapet. With no diminution of
warmth the darkness was coming, in a granulation of deeper
and deeper blues. A cart passed by with an accordeon band,
and a crowd running at its tail. A man in a paper hat ran
up to me and threw confetti in my face. Some students were
singing on the Pont St Michel. A little crowd came marching behind a flag. I began to think that perhaps after all I'd
have a drink. So precarious is solitude. When suddenly,
high up in the air, there was a sizzling explosion tailing
away into a murmur. I looked up. The fireworks had
started. As the first constellation floated slowly down and
faded away a delighted "aaah" rose from thousands of
throats and everyone stood still. Another rocket followed

and then another. I could feel the crowd gradually solidifying behind me as people began to come out onto the *quais* for a better view. I was crushed against the parapet.

I am afraid of crowds, and I should like to have got out, but now it was impossible to move. I calmed myself and started watching the fireworks. It was a very fine display. Sometimes the rockets went up singly, sometimes in groups. There were some which burst with a deafening crack and scattered out a rain of tiny golden stars, and others which opened with a soft sigh and set out almost motionless in the air a configuration of big coloured lights which sank with extreme slowness as if bound together. Then six or seven rockets would come shooting up and for an instant the sky would be scattered from end to end with gold dust and falling flowers, like the chaos on a nursery floor. My neck was getting stiff. I rubbed it gently, letting my head resume its usual angle, and I looked idly about upon the crowd. Then I saw Anna.

She was on the other side of the river, standing at the corner of the Petit Pont, just at the top of the steps which led down to the water. There was a street lamp just above her, and I could see her face quite clearly. There was no doubt that it was Anna. As I looked at her, her face seemed suddenly radiant like a saint's face in a picture, and all the thousands of surrounding faces were darkened. I could not imagine why I had not seen her at once. For a moment I stared paralysed; then I began to try to fight my way out. But it was absolutely impossible. I was in the thickest part of the crowd and pinned firmly against the wall. I couldn't even turn my body, let alone struggle through the packed mass of people. There was nothing for it but to wait for the end of the fireworks. I pressed my hand against my heart which was trying to start out of me with its beating, and I riveted my eyes upon Anna.

I wondered if she was alone. It was hard to tell. I decided after watching her for a few minutes that she was. She remained perfectly motionless, looking up, and however deep the murmur of delight which this or that exceptionally splendid rocket evoked from the crowd, she did not turn to share her own pleasure with any of the people who stood about her. She was certainly alone. I was overjoyed. But I was in anguish too in case when the crowd disintegrated I should lose her. I wanted to call out to her, but the murmur of voices all about us was so strong and diffused that my call would never have reached her. I kept my glance burning upon her and called out with all the power of my thought.

Then she began to move. The crowd on the other bank was less dense. She took two paces and hesitated. I watched in terror. Then to my relief she began to descend the steps to the riverside walk directly opposite to me. As she did so she came fully into my view. She was wearing a long blue skirt and a white blouse. She carried no coat or handbag. I was moved to the point of frenzy and I called her name. But it was like shooting an arrow into a storm. Thousands and tens of thousands of voices covered up my cry. The steps were covered with people sitting and standing on them to watch the fireworks, and Anna was finding it quite hard to pick her way down. She paused halfway, and with an unutterably graceful and characteristic gesture which I remembered well, gathered up her skirt from behind and continued her descent.

She found a vacant place on the very edge of the river, and sat down, curling her feet under her. Then she looked up once more to watch the rockets. The river was black now under the night sky and glassy, a black mirror in which every lamp raised a pole of light and the conflagration in the sky above dropped an occasional piece of gold. The line of people on the other bank was clearly reflected in it. Anna's image was quite still beneath her. I wondered if in the river, which at that point on the left bank came fully up to the wall of the roadway, my own reflexion was as vividly shown. I agitated my hands, hoping that either I or my image might attract Anna's attention. Then I took out a box of matches and lit one or two close to my face. But in such a galaxy of lights my little light could not attract much notice. Anna continued to look up. While I flapped and waved and flung the upper part of my body about like a ridiculous puppet, she sat as still as a spellbound princess, her head thrown back and one hand clasping her knee; while a stream of stars fell from the sky almost into her lap. A moment later something dropped with a sharp clatter onto the parapet beside my hand. Automatically I picked it up. It was the stick of one of the rockets. As I lifted it, in the light of the next star burst, I read the name which was written upon it : BELFOUNDER.

I held it for a moment in a kind of astonishment. Then taking a careful aim I threw it into the water so that it fell directly into Anna's reflexion, and at the same time I waved and called. The image was scattered and the glass disturbed for a long way between the two bridges. Anna lowered her head; and while I leaned towards her until I nearly toppled head first into the river, she fixed her eyes upon the rocket stick which was now moving very very slowly in the direction of the sea, offering thereby a sensible proof that moving water can render an impeccable reflexion. Then someone behind me said *"c'est fini!"*; and I felt the pressure beginning to lessen at my back.

Poised, I watched to see what Anna would do. The people on the other bank were beginning to go up the steps at both the bridges. Anna got up slowly and shook out her skirt. She bent down and rubbed one of her feet. Then she began to make her way back toward the Petit Pont. I struggled along in the same direction. I could see her mounting the steps. Then I lost sight of her. I crossed the bridge against a stream of people. Voices and laughter were blowing like a gale. Under the bright lights faces pressed for a moment against me, were each one wrenched to a smile, and then whisked away. I got to the other side and began to move toward the Pont St Michel. I saw a golden coronet of hair some way ahead, and followed it; and as I crossed the Boulevard du Palais I could see that it was indeed Anna who was ahead of me in the crowd. I felt less anxious now. I could have caught her if I had struggled very hard, but I let the crowd carry us both along, and waited until it should clear a little. In this way we went the length of the island.

Anna crossed the Pont Neuf to the right bank, and so we came to the pavements beside the Louvre which were very much less packed; and when we had got past a crowd which was gathered at the Pont des Arts she was only about sixty yards ahead of me and showing as clear as day in the brightness of the floodlight façade. I could see that she was limping a little, perhaps her shoes were hurting her; but she was walking nevertheless with strength and determination, and it then occurred to me for the first time that she was not walking aimlessly. I could now have caught her easily. But something made me pause. It would do no harm to see where she was going. So I continued to walk behind her until at the Pont Royal she turned inland.

What was Anna seeing, what filled her golden head at that moment, I wondered. What image of sadness or of promise blotted out for her the scene into the centre of which she kept moving with a dreamer's pace? Was she thinking perhaps about me? Was Paris as full of me for her as it was full of her for me? It was partly in the foolish hope of receiving some sign that it was so that I restrained myself from running up to her. Something which Anna and I had often used to do was to go into the Tuileries gardens at night. The Tuileries are impregnable from the *quais,* the Concorde, and the Rue de Rivoli, but if you approach them from the Rue Paul Deroulède they are guarded only by a grassy moat and a low railing. On ordinary nights there are *gendarmes* whose task it is to patrol this vulnerable region: a hazard which gives to the Tuileries by night the dangerous charm of an enchanted garden. To-night, however, it was probable that the ordinary rules would be relaxed. As I saw Anna turning toward the gardens my heart leapt up, as the heart of Aeneas must have done when he saw Dido making for the cave. I quickened my pace.

The roadway was glowing with light. On one side the Arc du Carrousel stood like an imagined archway, removed

from space by its faultless proportions; and behind it the
enormous sweep of the Louvre enclosed the scene, fiercely
illumined and ablaze with detail. On the other side began
the unnatural garden, with its metallic green grass under the
yellow lamps, and its flowers self-conscious with colour and
quiet as dream flowers which can unfold and be still at the
same moment. A little distance beyond the railings the
garden ran into trees, and beyond the trees an explosion of
light announced the Place de la Concorde, above and beyond which was raised upon its hill the floodlit Arc de
Triomphe, standing against a backdrop of darkness, with
an enormous *tricolore* which reached the whole height of the
archway fluttering inside the central arch.

Anna was already walking upon the grass, still limping
slightly, and passing among the white statues which popu-
late these lawns with laurelled foreheads and marble buttocks in various poses of elegant asymmetry. She came to the
railings, just behind the bronze panthers, at the point where
we had so often climbed over. She had mounted the grassy
bank and hitched up her big skirt, and I was so close to her
then that before she was across the railing I saw the flash of
her long leg up to the thigh. As I vaulted over she was
thirty paces ahead of me, walking between flower beds.
Only a little further and the grass ended and the trees began. I saw her outlined against the forest like a lonely girl
in a story. Then she stopped walking. I stopped too. I
wanted to prolong the enchantment of these moments.

Anna bent down and took off one of her shoes. Then she
took off the other one. I stood in the shadow of a bush and
pitied her poor feet. Why did the silly child always wear
shoes which were too small for her? As I stood still and
watched her the perfumes of night were rising from the
ground and swirling about me in a cloud. She pawed
the cool grass with her white feet. She was wearing no
stockings. Then very slowly she began to walk along the
grass verge carrying her shoes. As one set in motion by
a tow-rope I followed. In a moment we should be entering
the wood. It stretched before us now, very close, its rows

and rows of chestnut trees, the leaves clearly showing in
the diffused light, those tiny leaves that seem peculiar to
the chestnut trees of Paris, etched with clarity and turning
golden brown along the edges as early as July. Anna walked
into the wood.

Here the grass ended and there was a loose sandy soil
under foot. Anna stepped onto this surface without any
hesitation. I followed her into the darkness. She advanced
a short way down one of the avenues and then she stopped
again. She looked around at the trees; and going up to one
of them she thrust her two small shoes into a cavity at its
root. After that she walked on unencumbered. This thing
moved me enormously. I smiled to myself in the obscurity,
I very nearly laughed and clapped my hands. When I drew
level with the place where Anna's shoes were I could not
but pause and look at them, where they lay half hidden and
curled up together like a pair of little rabbits. I looked at
them for a moment and then obeying an irresistible urge I
picked them up.

I am not a fetishist and I would rather hold a woman any
day than her shoes. But nevertheless as my grip closed upon
them I trembled. Then I walked on, holding them one in
each hand, and in the sandy avenue my feet made no sound.
At the moment when I had paused to pick up the shoes,
Anna had turned aside into another avenue. Diagonally
now through the trees I could see her white blouse like a
pale flag in front of me. We were now in the thickest part
of the wood. I began to make haste. That she was thinking
of me now, that she was ready for me, I could not after this
long pursuit any longer doubt. This was a rendezvous. My
need of her drew me onward like a physical force. Our
embrace would close the circle of the years and begin the
golden age. As the steel to the magnet I sped forward.

I caught up with her and spread out my arms. "*Alors,
chérie?*" said a soft voice. The woman who turned to face
me was not Anna. I reeled back like a wounded man. The
white blouse had deceived me. We looked at each other
for a moment and then I turned away. I leaned against

a tree. Then I set off running at random down one of the avenues, looking to left and right. Anna could not be far away. But it was extremely dark in the wood. A moment later I found myself beside the steps of the Jeu de Paume. Beyond the iron grille were the blazing lights of the Concorde, where in a mingled uproar of music and voices thousands of people were dancing. The noise broke over me suddenly and I turned my head away from it as if someone had thrown pepper in my eyes, and plunged back under the trees.

I ran along calling Anna's name. But now suddenly the wood seemed to be full of statues and lovers. Every tree had blossomed with a murmuring pair and every vista mocked me with a stone figure. Slim forms were flitting along the avenues and pallid oblique faces caught the small light which penetrated through the forest. The din from the Concorde echoed along the tops of the trees. I cannoned into a tree trunk and hurt my shoulder. I sped along the colonnade toward a motionless figure which confronted me with marble eyes. I looked about me and called again. But my voice was caught up in the velvet of the night like a knife-thrust caught in a cloak. It was useless. I crossed the main avenue, thinking that Anna might have gone into the other half of the wood. A man's face stared at me, and I stumbled over someone's foot. I ran to and fro for some time like a lost dog.

When at last I paused in exhaustion and desperation I realized that I was still holding Anna's shoes. I turned about, and with a renewed hope I went plunging back toward the place where we had first entered the avenues of trees. The exact place was hard to identify, as each avenue so precisely resembled the next one. When I thought I had found the place, I began to search for the tree with the cavity at its root. But every tree had a cavity at its root; and yet no one of them looked quite like the one where Anna had left her shoes. I began to think that I must have mistaken our point of entry. I went back onto the grass and tried again, but with no greater certainty. I decided after

a while that all I could do was to wait and hope that Anna
would come back. I stood there leaning against a tree, while
whispering couples passed me by in the darkness, and I
called out. Anna's name from time to time in tones of increasing sadness. I began to feel tired, and sat down at the
foot of the tree, still clutching the shoes. An indefinite time
passed; and as it did so a very sad stillness descended on me
like dew. I stopped calling and waited in silence. The night
was getting colder. I knew now that Anna would not come.

At last I rose and chafed my stiff limbs. I left the
Tuileries gardens. The streets were strewn with the dis-
carded toys of the evening. Through a sea of coloured paper
tired people were making their way home. The party was
over. I joined the procession; and as I walked with them
in the direction of the Seine I wondered to myself with what
thoughts and down what streets, perhaps not far from here,
Anna was walking homeward barefoot.

Sixteen

I WAS waiting for the sun to set. I had been back at Goldhawk Road now for several days. The sunlight moved
very slowly on the white wall of the Hospital, casting a long
shadow from a ledge halfway up the wall. Longer and
longer the shadow grew, and as the shadow moved my head
turned upon the pillow. The wall was glaring white at mid-
day, but toward evening the glare was withdrawn and a
softer light glowed as if from within the concrete, showing
up little irregularities in the stone. Occasionally a bird flew
along between the windows and the wall, but looking always
more like a false bird on a string than a real bird that would
fly away somewhere else when it had passed the Hospital
and go perhaps and perch upon a tree. Nothing grew upon
the wall of the Hospital. Sometimes I tried to imagine that
there was vegetation growing on the ledge : damp plants
with long fingery leaves, that drooped from crevices and
opened into spotted flowers. But in reality there was nothing
there, and even in imagination the wall would resist me and
remain smooth and white. In two hours the sun would have
set.

When the sun was set I might perhaps go to sleep. I never
let myself sleep during the day. Daytime sleep is a cursed
slumber from which one wakes in despair. The sun will not
tolerate it. If he can he will pry under your eyelids and prise
them apart; and if you hang black curtains at your windows
he will lay siege to your room until it is so stifling that at
last you stagger with staring eyes to the window and tear
back the curtains to see that most terrible of sights, the broad
daylight outside a room where you have been sleeping.
There are special nightmares for the daytime sleeper : little
nervous dreams tossed into some brief restless moments of
unconsciousness and breaking through the surface of the

mind to become confused at once with the horror of some waking vision. Such are these awakenings, like an awakening in the grave, when one opens one's eyes, stretched out rigid with clenched hands, waiting for some misery to declare itself; but for a long time it lies to suffocation upon the chest and utters no word.

I was afraid to go to sleep. Whenever I began to feel drowsy I would move to some less comfortable position: which was not difficult since I was lying on Dave's camp-bed, which resumed innumerable possibilities of discomfort. It was one of those beds in which the canvas is slung in a rectangle of rigid rods supported by four W-shaped steel legs. At the junction of the legs with the rectangle there are bulging joints into which the rods supporting the canvas also fit. By shifting my body about I could make one or other of these joints bore into my ribs or back. So I would lie for a time contorted, while the haze of sleep was dispelled and replaced by an aching stupor which I knew from experience could continue indefinitely without ever darkening into unconsciousness. My pillow was propped up on a rucksack of Dave's which contained a coagulated mass of boots and old clothes which had not been taken out for years; and sometimes the pillow would fall off, and leave me propped against the rucksack and bathed in its aura of the perspiration of long ago. I needed to see the window. The sun was still moving.

Mars was somewhere in the room. He would lie so silent for long periods that I would think that perhaps he had gone away, and start looking for him with my eyes; only to find him lying close to me and looking at me. Occasionally he would attempt to lie on the bed beside me, but I discouraged this. His warm fur had an aroma of sleep which made me afraid. Then he would stretch out near me on the floor and for a time I would dangle my hand upon his neck. Later on he would poke about the room in a bored way until he threw himself down in a far corner with a grunting sound. Later on again I would hear his claws click on the linoleum and he would come and thrust his long nose into my face

and give me a look of anguish which came so near to
transcending his nature that I would push his face away and
ruffle up the fur of his back to satisfy myself that he was
only a dog.

I was worried that he was getting no exercise. Dave, it is
true, took him out every morning and evening as far as
Shepherd's Bush Green, and there, Dave would tell me, he
would race about like a mad thing until it was time to come
home again. But this could not be enough for such a big
dog; and Dave, who was due to start teaching at a summer
school in a day or two, would then have even less time to
devote to him. I wondered if Mars was unhappy; and then
I wondered whether, supposing that he could not be said to
know that he was unhappy, he could properly be said to be
unhappy. I decided to ask Dave about this sometime.

Dave was often in during the day, and I would hear the
distant sound of his typewriter. Then there would be silence.
He brought me a meal at midday and in the evening. We
did not speak. Sometimes in the afternoon he would open
the door and look at me for a while. I saw him as one sees
someone through the wrong end of a telescope. Then much
later I would remember that the door had shut and he was
gone. Dave had seen me like this before. The bed creaked
and shivered as I turned upon it restlessly. I was dressed in
my shirt and pants, and although it was a sunny day I had
two blankets drawn over me. I felt cold in the marrow of
my bones. I retrieved my pillow and balanced it again upon
the rucksack. I turned away from the window. No sun
came into this room, but in the reflected light from the
Hospital wall everything was revealed with an abnormal
clarity, as if an extra dimension had been added to space,
and objects projected and receded with a sharpness which
made them almost unbearably present. I lay looking at my
shoes and wondering what could have happened to Finn.

I had come back from Paris on the morning of the
fifteenth. I had found Dave and Mars at Goldhawk Road
and heard from Dave the story of how he and Finn had
spent the previous afternoon at Sandown Park where

Lyrebird had obliged us all by winning at such fancy odds. They had placed the bet at the course, and as soon as Dave collected the money he had given Finn his share, which amounted to two hundred and ten pounds. Finn had stowed this sum, which was largely in five-pound notes, in odd pockets all over his person. This he had done in silence, somewhat with the air of a man donning a parachute for a dangerous jump. After that he had shaken Dave mutely by the hand for some time. Then he had turned and disappeared into the crowd. He had not returned to Goldhawk Road that night, and Dave had thought it possible that he had gone to join me, until I had arrived on the following morning and, after looking about for Finn, asked for news of him. Since then he had not reappeared. I was not yet seriously worried. Finn was probably on the drink. I had known him go off once before on a blind which lasted for three days and from which he was brought home in an ambulance. I didn't imagine that anything serious could have happened to him. All the same I wanted him very badly to come back.

After my arrival I had written at once to someone at the *Club des Fous* asking him to try to find out where Anna was and to let me know. But I had not had any reply. I had also tried fruitlessly to contact Hugo. There was no answer from his flat, and the studio said that he had gone into the country. Dave had shown me a copy of the letter which he had sent to Sadie about Mars, which was a masterly compound of friendly argumentation and menace. But so far Sadie had shown no sign of life either. I had written to Jean Pierre congratulating him on his success. After that I had lain down on the camp-bed. The day of my appointment with Lefty had come and gone, and since then he had rung up twice and asked for me; and Dave had told him that I was ill, which I suppose was true.

The Hospital wall was now almost entirely in shadow. There was only a triangle of gold at the top of the window where I could still see it touched by the evening sun. Dave opened the door and called to Mars, and I could hear him dancing and barking in the hall at the prospect of his evening walk. When Dave brought Mars back I might consider going to sleep. Or perhaps it would still be too early; and so I might sleep and wake again before the night had really started. I had a horror of this. I rose and tidied my bed just to wake myself up a bit. I lowered myself slowly back onto the bed and lay very still until it had ceased to tremble. Mars was back, looking closely into my face, and bringing with him a disquieting freshness from the outside world. His wet nose and his eyes were shining, and the light brown markings upon his brow gave him a perpetual look of expectation. He barked once. "Be quiet!" I told him. The disturbing sound rang in my ears for long afterwards as the structure of silence recomposed itself.

It was the following morning and I was waiting to hear the postman come. I did this every morning now. My watch had stopped, but I could tell the time from the Hospital wall. It was nearly time. It was time. Then I heard his feet on the stairs and the rattle of the letter box, and a moment later a heavy bump. There must be a lot of letters this morning. I heard Dave going into the hall. This was the only real moment of the day. I waited. There was silence. Now Dave was approaching my door. He looked in.

"Nothing for you, Jake," he said.

I nodded my head and turned it away. I could see that Dave was still standing in the doorway. Mars had pushed past him into the hall.

"Jake," said Dave, "for the Lord's sake get up and do something, anything at all. I'm a nervous wreck thinking of you lying there all the time. I can't do philosophy when you are making me feel so nervous." I said nothing.

Dave waited a little longer. Then he said, "Don't mind me, Jake. Who am I to speak? But you ought to get up for the sake of yourself."

I shut my eyes, and a bit later I heard the door close. Then I heard Dave going out with Mars. Then it was later still and Mars was in the room again, and Dave had gone away perhaps to his summer school. I decided to get up.

At first I couldn't find my clothes. The room seemed to be a chaos of unrelated objects. I found myself automatically beginning to unpack Dave's rucksack. I kicked it away. Then I saw my trousers in a heap in the corner where Mars had been using them as a bed. They were covered with short black hairs. I shook them out and put them on. Then I opened the window wide and did some breathing exercises. The heat wave was over and it was a brisk rapid day with a summer wind. I leaned out and looked up at the sky, far off above the top of the Hospital wall, and saw the blue and white haste of the small clouds. Mars was prancing round me and whining with pleasure and jumping up at me with his rough paws. When he stood on his hind legs he was almost as tall as I was. But then, as I mentioned before, I am not very tall. I tidied the room a little. Then I found my coat and left the house with Mars.

Goldhawk Road was hideous. The traffic made a continual jagged uproar and the pavements were crowded with people jostling past each other in front of shop windows full of cheap crockery and tin cans. I managed to get with Mars as far as the Green, and I sat down under a tree upon the hard earth which had tried to produce a little grass and all but failed. Mars ran about and played with some other dogs. He kept coming back to assure me that he had not forgotten me. I fixed my eyes upon the sky above the Shepherd's Bush Empire. With an extraordinary speed the curdling masses of white cloud were tumbling down behind the roofs. The whole sky had put on a gigantic and harmonious haste which made the scurrying of the people in the streets about me seem nervous and paltry. I got up and walked several times round the Green, escorted by Mars. Then I took him back to the flat. It made me too anxious to have him with me in the middle of so much traffic, and I had forgotten to bring his lead. I telephoned to Hugo's flat and to the studio, but with the same negative results as before. After that I went out again and walked about by myself until the pubs opened.

As I was coming back toward Dave's flat I found myself

passing the front of the Hospital, and I paused. The Hospital is a great white concrete structure with regular square windows and a flat roof. It was built not long ago and pictures of it appeared in the architectural reviews. There are a number of wings or transepts which jut out in different directions from the main block and cunningly divert the eye from its monotony of line. In the wells or gullies created by these transepts they have planted gardens, with grassy lawns and small trees which will one day be large trees, the preservation of which will be a matter debated endlessly by hospital committees torn between the therapeutic benefits of the charms of nature and the need to let a little more light into the wards on the lower floors. I stood for a while watching the cars coming and going in the square courtyard in front of the main entrance. Then I crossed the road and went in and asked for a job.

Seventeen

IT amazed me, in retrospect, when I considered how readily I had been engaged : no questions put, no references asked for. Perhaps I inspire confidence. I had never in my life before attempted to get a job. Getting a job was something which my friends occasionally tried to do, and which always seemed to be a matter for slow and difficult negotiation or even intrigue. Indeed, it was the spectacle of their ill success which, together with my own temperament, had chiefly deterred me from any essays in this direction. It had never occurred to me that it might be possible to get a job simply by going and asking for it, and in any normal state of mind I would never even have made the attempt. You will point out, and quite rightly, that the job into which I had stepped so easily was in a category not only unskilled but unpopular where a desperate shortage of candidates might well secure the immediate engagement of anyone other than a total paralytic; whereas what my friends perhaps were finding it so difficult to become was higher civil servants, columnists on the London dailies, officials of the British Council, fellows of colleges, or governors of the B.B.C. This is true. I was nevertheless feeling impressed, at the point which our story has now reached, and not only by my having got the job, but also by the efficient way in which I turned out to be able to perform it.

I was what was termed an orderly. My hours were eight to six, with three-quarters of an hour for lunch, and one day off a week. I was attached to a ward which specialized in head injuries and was called "Corelli" in accordance with the Hospital custom of calling its wards by the names of wealthy benefactors: Mr Corelli having been a soap manu- facturer from Sicily whose son once received a fractured skull through driving his Lancia when under the influence

228

of drink in the Uxbridge Road. His child restored, the elder
Corelli had acted with suitable generosity, and hence the
name of the ward in which I had now been working for
four days.

My tasks were simple. When I arrived at eight a.m. I took
a mop and bucket and cleaned three corridors and two
flights of stairs. These surfaces were easy to clean, and I
achieved spectacular alterations of colour with the help of
a little soap. After this, I washed up the crockery of the
patients' breakfast which was stacked up waiting for me by
now in the ward kitchen. Corelli occupied three corridors,
one on the ground floor called Corelli I, and two on the first
floor called Corelli II and III. The ward kitchen was in
Corelli III, and it was here that my activity centred, and in
a cubby hole next to the kitchen that I left my coat, and
retired to sit and read the newspapers should there ever be
a spare moment. After the washing up I went and fetched
the cans of milk from the main kitchen, which was known as
the Transept Kitchen, and took them back to Corelli III on
a trolley which I brought up on a special service-lift. I
enjoyed this bit very much. To reach the Transept Kitchen
I had to walk quite a long way through the corridors of
other wards with strange names; and as I walked quickly
along, passing unfamiliar people in white coats, they on
their tasks and I on mine, I felt like a man entrusted with an
important mission. When I got back to Corelli I was
allowed to perform an operation of almost clinical significance, that is to warm the milk on the big electric stove
and pour it into mugs which the nurses took to those of the
patients who were allowed to have it. After that I cut bread
and butter and then washed up the mugs and saucepans and
cleaned the kitchen.

I was still more than a little nervous of my colleagues and
superiors and very anxious to please. With the nurses, who
were mainly young Irish girls without a thought in their
heads, unless obsession with matrimony may be called a
thought, I immediately got on very well. They were calling
me "Jakie" on the second day, and treating me with an

affectionate teasing tyranny. I noticed with interest that none of them took me seriously as a male. I exuded an aroma which, although we got on so splendidly, in some way kept them off; perhaps some obscure instinct warned them that I was an intellectual. With the Ward Matron I got on well too, though in a different way. The Ward Matron was so august a person, so elderly and austere and with such a high notion of her own dignity, that the possibility of certain frictions was removed simply by the social distance which lay between us. My personal peculiarities could not offend her since she was totally uninterested in my pretensions to be a person. The only question which I raised was whether or not I did my work well and kept out of the way; and as I did these things she showed her approval by ignoring me, except that on the first occasion on each day when we passed each other in the corridor she would turn her head very slightly with a faint intensification of expression which if produced almost indefinitely might have become a smile.

Beyond the Ward Matron into the stratosphere of the Hospital hierarchy my vision did not extend. It was with the intermediate portions of my small society that my relations were most uneasy. Under the Matron were three Sisters, one for each of the Corellis, and it was from these beings that I directly received most of my orders. The lives of these women, already far advanced, were made a misery, on the one hand by the Matron, who treated them with unremitting despotism, and on the other by the nurses who repaid them with continual veiled mockery for the pains which the Sisters, in order to recoup their own dignity, felt bound to inflict upon those beneath them. The Sisters found me hard to understand. They suspected me of wanting to score off them, not only because of my friendly relations with their enemies the nurses, but because, more than anyone else with whom I had contact in the Hospital, they divined something of my real nature. I presented them with a problem that made them nervous; and for them alone of all the women with whom I had to do in that place, I indubitably existed as a man. An electrical current passed between us, they continually avoided my eye, and when they gave me orders, their high-pitched voices went a semitone higher.

I was particularly fond of the Sister of Corelli III, which was the one with whom I had most to do, who was called Sister Piddingham and known to the nurses as The Pid. The Pid must have been about fifty, or perhaps more, and many years might have passed since she had started dyeing her long grey hair black. Her voice and eyes, made sharp by verbal warfare and professional habits of critical scrutiny, followed me continually as I worked in the kitchen. Her very anxiety to criticize me made a bond between us; I should have liked to have done something special and unexpected to please her, such as bringing her flowers, but I knew that she took me seriously enough to be capable of construing this as an act of condescension and hating me for it. For the sad mystery of her mode of existence I felt a respect which almost amounted to terror. The only other Hospital people of whom I saw anything were a man called Stitch, who was a sort of resident head-porter, who was very stupid and hated me heartily, and one or two ward maids who were more or less semi-deficient.

Every day at lunch time I would buy sandwiches at the Transept Canteen and then go and fetch Mars from Dave's flat: sometimes then I would catch a glimpse of Dave, from whose face the astonishment that had appeared there when I had first told him of my job had not yet completely faded; and I would tell myself that the whole thing would have been well worth it even if it were only for the sake of giving Dave such a jolt. Then I would return with Mars to sit in the garden outside Corelli I and eat my sandwiches. The garden here consisted of a long smooth lawn with two rows of cherry trees planted in the grass. I knew they were cherry trees because the nurses were always exclaiming about what the garden looked like in the spring. I would sit under one of the trees, while Mars bounded about close by, giving his attention now to one tree and now to another, and the young nurses of Corelli would come and gather round me like nymphs and laugh at me and say that I looked like a wise man sitting cross-legged under my tree, and admire Mars and make much of him, and defend me against Stitch, who would have liked to have forbidden me to have Mars in the garden at all. I enjoyed these lunch times.

It was in the afternoon that I managed at last to see something of the patients. But this wasn't until the late afternoon. I looked forward to this all day. In my apprehension of it, the Hospital declined through a scale of decreasing degrees of reality in proportion to the distance away from the patients. They were the centre to which all else was peripheral. The patients in Corelli were all men, and all in a variety of conditions resulting from blows on the head. Some of them had concussion with or without fractured skulls and others had more mysterious capital ailments. They lay there with their turbans of white bandages and their eyes narrowed with headache, and watched me as I mopped the floor; and I felt for them a mixture of pity and awe, such as an Indian might feel for a sacred animal. I should have liked to have talked to them, and once or twice I did begin a conversation, but on each occasion one of the Sisters came and stopped it. It was felt to be improper for orderlies to address patients.

What contributed yet more to the numinous aura with which the patients were surrounded was the fact that although I was close to them all the day I never saw them except in their full dignity of sick people, lying there solitary and silent with idle hands, privately communing with their pain. That at other times they were washed and fed, used bed pans, and had bloody and pus-soaked dressings removed from their shaven heads, I knew only at second hand by inference from the dirty dishes and other less savoury objects which entered more directly into my day's work. When the nurses and doctors were engaged on their priest-like tasks the doors of the rooms were religiously closed and notices displayed forbidding entrance. It was only occasionally that I would pass in the corridor one of the patients being wheeled to or from his bed on a trolley; and whenever I heard the dull rumble of the trolley wheels, with a heavy sound of rubber on rubber, I would contrive to emerge from wherever I was and catch a glimpse perhaps of some new arrival, whose face and newly bandaged head, still fresh with astonishment from the outside world, would convince me that after all the patients were men like myself.

After I had cleaned the rooms there was an interval in my work, during which I would retire into my cubby hole where there is just room to sit, and read the evening papers by a dim electric light. There was no window in the cubby hole, and as all the walls were covered with people's coats hanging on pegs, it was rather like the inside of a wardrobe. I didn't mind this, as the insides of wardrobes have always had, since childhood, a peculiar fascination for me, no doubt for reasons known to psychoanalysts. I did, however, dislike the dim light, and on the second day provided, at my own expense, a more powerful electric light bulb : which was confiscated on the third day by Stitch and the dim one put back again. There I sat, perusing the *Evening Standard*, and, as I read, the rumours of the outside world came to me like distant cries or the sounds of battles far away in time and space. Lefty's name occurred quite often; and once a whole editorial was devoted to him, couched in terms designed to suggest simultaneously that he was a serious public menace and that he was a petty street-corner agitator who was beneath contempt. I noticed that a grand meeting was to be organized by the Independent Socialists in West London in a day or two, and it was apropos of this that the editor was calling on the *optimates* to exercise this peculiar blend of negligence and strong measures. Homer K. Pringsheim had held a press conference in London at which he had said that the British and American film industries had much to learn from each other, and had departed for the Italian Riviera. Other names which I looked for were not there.

I enjoyed this part of the day too. By this time I could combine a considerable feeling of tiredness with a feeling which was almost entirely new to me, that of having *done* something. Such intellectual work as I have ever accomplished has always left me with a sense of having achieved nothing: one looks back through the thing as through an empty shell; but whether this is because of the nature of intellectual work as such, or whether it is because I am no good, I have never been able to decide. If one no longer feels in living contact with whatever thought the work contains, the thing seems at best dry and at worst stinking; and if one does still feel this contact the work is infected through it with the shifting emptiness of present thought. Though it may be that if one had any present thoughts that were at all considerable they would not have this quality of emptiness. I wonder if Kant, as he conceived his Copernican Revolution, said to himself from time to time, "But this is *nothing, nothing*"? I should like to think that he did.

I had decided to wait for the weekend before making another attempt to contact Hugo. The sense of my own destiny, which had so curiously deserted me during the days when I had been lying on Dave's camp-bed, had now returned, and I felt sure that whatever god had arranged for me and Hugo to have deeply to do with one another would not leave his work unfinished. On this matter I felt for the moment a certain calm. I was more anxious about letters from France, and perhaps most anxious of all about Finn, of whom there was still not a breath of news. Dave had said that we ought to start making enquiries, but this was impossible for the simple reason that there was nowhere where we could enquire. Finn had no friends in London, so far as we knew, except ourselves, and concerning his present whereabouts we could not even get as far as framing a theory. Dave had suggested going to the police, but I was against this. If Finn was drinking himself to death somewhere, that was Finn's business, and it would be my last sad act of friendship to leave him to it. This worried me all the same, and I thought a lot about Finn during those days.

The other unsolved problem which I had upon my hands was the problem of Mars, and about this I worried in fits and starts. Sadie and Sammy had still made no move, and their silence was beginning to get on my nerves. I felt tempted at times to go and see Sadie and talk the whole thing over. But I felt afraid of this too, partly because, *au fond*, I was a bit afraid of Sadie, especially now when I had put myself in the wrong, and partly because I didn't fancy the idea of Mars being taken from me. I didn't want Mars, in his old age, to fall into the hands of someone, viz. Sammy, whom I suspected of having little enough respect for an unexploitable life, even if it were a human one. So I did nothing and waited.

A day or two passed, and it was some time in the late afternoon. In about half an hour my day's work would be over. Owing to my exceptional diligence it was virtually over now, only although there was nothing further for me to do I could not leave the building until six o'clock had struck. In a few minutes, I was thinking to myself, I would go and mop the kitchen floor; one could never mop round that kitchen floor too often. But for the moment I was in no hurry. I felt very tired; and it was becoming clear to me that this was indeed the main drawback of this otherwise fascinating job, that it was extremely tiring. At some time in the future, I decided, I would arrange to work, whether here or elsewhere, only half-time. Then in the other half of the day I might do some writing. It occurred to me that to spend half the day doing manual work might be very calming to the nerves of one who was spending the other half doing intellectual work, and I could not imagine why I had not thought before of this way of living, which would ensure that no day could pass without *something* having been done, and so keep that sense of uselessness, which grows in prolonged periods of sterility, away from me forever. But all this was for the future. Just then I had no idea but to continue with my tasks and wait for my destiny to catch up on me. That it would do so I felt confident; though as I idly turned the pages of the *Evening Standard*, standing up because the light was so bad, I had no notion how fast it was galloping at that very moment to overtake me.

I saw from the paper that Lefty's great meeting had taken

place earlier that day, not without considerable disturbance and the final interference of the police. There were several pictures of mounted policemen controlling crowds. Some-one had thrown a magnesium flare and two women had fainted. Lefty had made a speech which, so far as I could see, was filled with harmless and boring remarks about the technicalities of affiliating left-wing organizations to each other. A well-known Trade Union leader who was a mem-ber of Lefty's party had made another speech, also a woman M.P. who was not a member but very pretty.

As I was looking this over I heard the swing doors which led onto the main corridor being opened, and then the rumble of the trolley wheels. A new patient was being brought in. Through the glass door of the cubby hole I saw The Pid pass by, and heard her black heels click away down the ward corridor. I opened the door and held it ajar, standing just inside. Stitch was pushing toward me the trolley on which, under a red blanket, a figure lay prostrate. Stitch caught my eye and jerked his head angrily to indicate that I had no business to be hanging around and watching. He did not speak to me, in accordance with an unwritten rule that hospital servants do not speak while they are wheeling patients along corridors; but his eyes spoke volumes. I returned his look with all the insolence I could muster. Then I lowered my eyes to the face of the man on the trolley, which was at that moment passing in front of me. The man on the trolley was Hugo.

His face was dead white and his eyes were closed. A darkly stained bandage encased his head. I stood there rigid. Then the trolley had passed. I stepped back inside the cubby hole and closed the door and leaned against it. A conflict of emotions filled me. My immediate feeling was one of guilt; like Hamlet confronted by the ghost of his father. I had a curious sense that it was because of some neglect of mine that Hugo had been struck down. Together with this I experienced immediately a certain gratification at the thought that as soon as I had ceased to look for Hugo he had been knocked on the head and brought to me. I was still smarting a little from his casualness to me at the studio. But this idea had no sooner formed than I was overcome with remorse, and nothing mattered to me except the question of how badly Hugo was hurt. I came out into the corridor.

They had put Hugo into a single room right at the far end. I saw The Pid emerging and coming back. I followed her into the surgery.

"What's the matter with the big fellow?" I asked. "Is it anything bad?" There was nothing unusual about this question; I asked it about every new patient that came into the ward.

"I've told you before not to come into this room," said The Pid. She would never call me by any name.

"I'm sorry," I said, "I'm just going. But is it bad?"

"You ought to be doing your work," said The Pid. "I shall ask Stitch to see that you have more to do." I started to go. Then when I was half out of the door she added, "He had a brick thrown at him at that meeting. He's got concussion. He'll be here about five days."

"Thank you!" I said, and slid out as smoothly as a fish. A great concession had been made.

I went into the kitchen and started mopping the floor. Stitch came in and made a number of remarks which I scarcely heard. I was wondering what to do. I had to see Hugo. It was an odd trick of fate that although we had been brought together it was under circumstances which made communication virtually impossible. We were placed here in the one relationship that totally debarred any exchange. I ran over a hundred possibilities. By an unfortunate chance to-morrow was my day off; so that if I wanted to see Hugo in the ordinary course of my duties I should have to wait until the time when I should clean his room on the afternoon of the day after to-morrow. Even then I should only be able to be with him for, at the most, fifteen minutes; and in any case this was too long to wait. It was always possible that by then, if Hugo's injuries turned out to be very slight, he might have left the Hospital; but quite apart from this, I could not bear the idea of waiting so long. Hugo had been brought to me and I had to see him at once: but how? There then occurred to me a further difficulty, viz. that Hugo was unconscious.

I cursed to myself as I ran the mop savagely in under the cupboards. Stitch had gone away. I wondered if it would be possible to alter my day off, or to offer to work to-morrow in any case; and then to creep into Hugo's room some time during the morning. This would be very difficult, with nurses and doctors continually on the prowl. And would I be allowed to work to-morrow, even if I offered to? The matter would be referred to Stitch, who would be certain to divine that I wanted it, and so to declare it impossible. If I had had a bit more time I might have thought out some way of inveigling him into imposing it on me as a penalty: but it was too late for this now. As I was debating one of the nurses came in. She was the most Irish of the nurses, with a voice that constantly reminded me of Finn. I asked, "How is the big fellow?"

"He's after shouting for a meal!" said the nurse.

When I heard this I made up my mind what to do; and indeed there was only one thing possible. That was to come back to the Hospital in the middle of the night. This idea filled me with a kind of religious terror while at the same time it fascinated me very much. I had never seen the Hospital at night, though I had often tried to picture it. To the terrors of its imagined silence and solitude was added the sense that my presence there at such an hour would be a sort of sacrilege. If I were discovered I would, I felt sure, be shot down at sight. There could be no mercy. But it was necessary to come. The proximity of Hugo was already raising in me a tornado which could only be stilled by his presence. I had to see him.

I put away the mop and took off my white overall, thinking fast. It was now after six. I had to contrive the details of my plan at once, for if there were any preparatory steps that needed taking they must be taken now. How was I to get into the Hospital? I pictured the place, and it seemed to me like an impregnable fortress. The main entrance was open all night, but very brightly lit, as I knew from having passed it by at all hours when going to Dave's flat. A night porter would be certain to be on duty and would stop me and ask my business. I thought of various lies I might tell, but none of them seemed plausible enough to ensure my being allowed in without anyone else being put on my track. Then there was a back door which led out of Corelli I into a yard where coal and bicycles were kept. This was the door which I normally used. But I knew, from something that Stitch had said, that this door was locked at ten; and doubtless the same applied to any other back doors the place might turn out to have. There was always of course the entrance through the Accident Wards, where emergency cases were brought in. But this entrance would be garrisoned too, so that there would be precious little chance of slipping through unobserved; and one mistake would be fatal. The only possibility was to come in through a window; and if I were going to do that, I must decide which window to use, and go and open it straightaway.

I put on my coat and began to walk slowly down the main stairs. My head was in a turmoil. The side of the building which faced the bicycle yard had lights upon it which were kept burning all night. Anyone trying to enter from the yard would be clearly in view from the street. The ends of the Transepts came into the radius of the street lamps, and the main building had its own row of lamp-posts which encircled the main courtyard. There remained the Transept gardens, which were wells of darkness. Most of the windows which opened onto these gardens were the windows of patients' rooms. It was impossible to think of entering through one of these; for even if I had had the nerve to go now and satisfy myself that one of these windows was open, I had certainly not the nerve to re-enter through it at two a.m. and run the risk of being pursued by the screams of some nervous inmate. There were other possibilities, such as the scullery window of Corelli I. But this would fall too much under the eye of the Corelli I Night Sister, whose room was next door to the scullery; and the same objection applied to the other windows which led from the garden into the administrative rooms of the ward. My only hope lay in the more anonymous and public parts of the Transept, round about the Transept Kitchen. It was true that there was likely to be somebody in and around the kitchen all night; but there was a number of cloak rooms and store rooms round about which seemed to be derelict and unvisited even during the day, and whose windows lay at the very end of the garden, where it would be darkest.

On reaching the bottom of the stairs I turned, with an air of conspicuous casualness, toward the Transept Kitchen. When I am up to something I find it very hard to realize that I probably *look* no different from the way I look on other occasions. I felt sure that the expression of my face must be betraying me, and whenever I passed anyone in the corridor I turned this tell-tale surface in the other direction. I walked firmly past the door of the kitchen. The upper half of the door was made of plain glass, and out of the corner of my eye I could see figures moving about within. I selected a door two or three further on, and turned into it sharply. I had remembered right. It was a store room, against each wall of which the iron frames of bedsteads were leaning ten deep. I closed the door quietly behind me, and walked down the aisle in the middle of the room. In a square of sun and shade the garden was revealed and the rows of cherry trees. The shadow from the Corelli side fell sharply across the lawn, and cut it into two triangles of contrasting greens. I stood for a moment looking out. Then I unlatched the window.

It was a simple casement window with one catch halfway up the frame and a perforated bar at the bottom which regulated the aperture. I unpinned the window and undid the catch, opening the window an inch or two, so that the catch rested against the glass on the outside. I didn't want the window to look as if it were undone; and on the other hand I wanted to be certain that I should be able to pull it open from the outside when the time came. It took me some minutes to satisfy myself that both these conditions were met. Then I marked the position of the window carefully in relation to the rows of trees. After that I went back and listened at the door until I was sure that there was no one in the corridor. I emerged, closed the door, and walked back toward Corelli. No one had seen me. A moment later I was leaving the building.

Eighteen

THE first thing I did after that was to take a stiff drink. My heart was beating like an army on the march. I would never do to enroll in a conspiracy. Then I went back to the flat and fetched Mars. I took him on a bus to Barnes, had beer and sandwiches at the Red Lion, and then walked with him on the Common until the light was failing. By the time we got back to Goldhawk Road it was nearly dark. I left Mars at the flat; there was no sign of Dave. He was out at some meeting. Then I started walking at random in the direction of Hammersmith. I just wanted the hours to pass and be quick about it. The pubs were just closing, and I put down as much whiskey as I could in the last ten minutes. I walked until I was nearly at the river. I wasn't thinking about anything in particular during this period, but my mind was simply dominated by Hugo. It was as if from his bed in the hospital Hugo were holding the end of a cord to which I was attached, and from time to time I could feel it twitching. Or else it was as if Hugo brooded over me like a great bird; and I took no pleasure in the prospect of our imminent encounter, save a sort of blind satisfaction at the downrush of the inevitable.

I looked at my watch. It was after midnight, and I was standing on Hammersmith Bridge, not far from the place where we had released Mars from his cage. I looked up stream and tried to make out where in the mass of buildings on the north bank the Mime Theatre lay. But it was too dark to see. Then a panic overtook me in case I should arrive back at the Hospital too late. I set off walking briskly and hailed a taxi at Hammersmith Broadway which took me back to the Goldhawk Road. But now it was still too early. I walked up and down the street several times, passing the Hospital. It was not yet one o'clock, and I had resolved not to try to enter before two. I kept walking away from the Hospital, but something kept drawing me back again. I had to set myself little tasks: this time I would walk as far as the Seven Stars before I came back again; this time I would stand under the railway bridge as long as it took me to smoke a cigarette. I was in anguish.

At about twenty past one I could bear it no longer. I decided to go in. But this time, as I approached, the whole scene appeared to be most damnably exposed. The street lamps were blazing and the building itself seemed to be covered in lights. As I came near I could see people standing in the entrance hall, and there were lights in the windows of all the stairways, and lights too in some of the wards. I had not foreseen this degree of nocturnal illumination. The Transept gardens, it is true, were plunged in darkness, and as far as I could see there were no lights in Corelli, except for one glimmer which doubtless came from the room of the Night Sister. To reach the Transept gardens, however, meant crossing the wide gravel walk and the lawn which ran the whole length of the Hospital on either side of the courtyard, and all this area was lit up by the indefatigable street lamps. Low posts with chains swinging between them divided the gravel walk from the street. The darkness seemed a long way away.

I chose a point as far from the main entrance as possible and I looked carefully both ways along the street. The scene was deserted. Then I took a quick run and sprang over the chains and darted straight across the gravel and diagonally across the main lawn. I ran very lightly, my toes hardly touching the ground; and in a moment I had reached the darkness of the Transept garden. I stopped running and stood still on the grass to get my breath. I looked back. No one. A great silence surrounded me. I looked up at Corelli. There was only that one light burning on the first floor. I began to walk along the grass, touching the cherry trees one by one as I passed. Now that I was away from the glare of the street lamps it occurred to me that it was a very light night. From the road the garden had looked pitch black;

but in the garden itself the darkness was not dense but diffused, and as I walked quietly along I felt that I must be clearly visible from all the windows, and I expected at any moment to hear a voice challenging me from above. But no one spoke.

From outside everything looked very different, and it took me some time to identify the window of the store room. When I did find it I was surprised to discover how high it was from the ground. I pulled at the window very gently, holding my breath. To my relief it came open without any check and without a sound. I looked about me. The garden was empty and motionless, the cherry trees turned toward me, quiet as dancers in a tableau. There was still no one on the road. I opened the casement wide, and then hooked my fingers firmly onto the steel frame of the opening on each side. But the foot of the window was just too high for me to reach it with my knee. There was no sill on the outside. I stood back. I hesitated to spring up, for fear of making a noise. Then I thought that I heard footsteps approaching along the road. Quick as a flash, I put one hand into the opening and sprang. The steel edge of the frame caught me at the hip, and next moment I was heeling over gently onto the sill on the inside, and drawing my legs after me. I stood dead still on the floor of the store room. There was a silence into which it seemed to me that I had just let loose a vast quantity of sound. But the silence continued.

I drew the window to, leaving it unlatched as it had been before. Then I walked down the middle of the room, feeling rather than seeing the dark bulks of the iron bedsteads on each side. Here it really *was* pitch black, with a dense darkness which seemed to coat the eyeballs. I fumbled for the handle of the door, listened for a moment, and then stepped into the corridor. The bright lights and the white walls broke through the door and dazzled me. My eyes, laid open by the dark, winced at this inrush of light, and I covered them. Then I turned in the direction of Corelli, my feet padding dully on the rubber composition floor. Here concealment was impossible. I simply had to hope that some kindly deity would see to it that I met nobody.

The Hospital was deserted, yet strangely alive. I could hear it purring and murmuring like a sleeping beast, and even when at times there came as it were a wave of silence I could still sense within it its great heart beating. As I passed the Transept Kitchen I averted my head; for I feared that if I encountered any human eye my guilt would write itself so plainly on my face as to cry "Shame!" upon itself of its own accord. I came to the main stairs. They were glittering, deserted, immense. The small sound of my footfalls echoed up far above me into the great well of the staircase, and looking up I saw the superimposed rectangles of the banisters diminishing almost to a point many floors above. By now there was no thought in my head at all, not even the most general notion of Hugo, and if anyone had stopped me I would have gibbered like an idiot. I came to the door of Corelli III.

Here I paused. I had no very clear conception of how the ward was organized at night. If there were any nurses sleeping in the ward they would be downstairs. In Corelli III there would probably be nobody over and above the patients, except the Night Sister. Of this person I knew only by report, and she had figured in my mind, even before I had planned this escapade, as a sort of nocturnal goddess, a Piddingham of the underworld. Now as I thought of her, with my hand upon the door, I was taken with a fit of trembling, like a postulant approaching the cave of the Sibyl. I opened the door quietly and stepped into the familiar corridor of the ward.

One or two lights were burning in the corridor, but the patients' rooms were all in darkness. The kitchen and the Administration Rooms were dark too, except for the Sister's Room, and from this a light was streaming through the door, the upper half of which was made of frosted glass. Through this semi-transparent medium I feared that the Night Sister, to whom I was ready to attribute supernatural powers, let alone any ordinary human acuteness, might see me passing by; so I manœuvred the first part of the corridor on my hands and knees. When I was well past her door I stood up and glided on, and as I went I could not hear myself making a sound. An uncanny stillness was drinking me up. I was now at the door of Hugo's room. I took hold of the handle, which consisted of a sloping steel bar which had to be depressed in order to open the door. I wrapped it firmly in my hand as if to master it into silence and I depressed it with a strong smooth movement. Holding it well down I pushed the door. It opened like a dream door as quietly as if it were giving way to my thought. I held the handle until I was well through the doorway and then took hold of the handle on the inside with my other hand. I closed the door firmly behind me and released the handle. There had been no noise.

I was in semi-darkness. In the door at about the level of the human head there was a small rectangular window about eighteen inches square through which some light came from the corridor. I could see the red of the blankets and a humped shape upon the high bed. An instinct of caution made me fall on one knee. Then the shape stirred, and Hugo's voice said sharply, "Who is it?"

I said, "Sssh!" and added, "It's Jake Donaghue."

There was a moment's silence and then Hugo said, "My God!"

I wanted to get out of the light. I swivelled to a sitting position and propelled myself upon my buttocks through underneath Hugo's bed. I had thoroughly cleaned the floor of this room on the previous afternoon before Hugo's arrival, and I slid upon it now as smoothly as a jack on the ice. I came to rest on the other side of the bed, where I sat against the wall with my knees drawn up. I felt completely calm.

Hugo's eyes looked for me in the dark and found me. I smiled, inclining my head.

"This is a bit much!" said Hugo. "I was asleep."

"Don't speak so loudly," I told him, "or the Night Sister will hear."

He lowered his voice to a whisper. "I wish you wouldn't keep following me about!"

This annoyed me. "I'm not following you!" I whispered back. "I work here. The last thing I expected was that you'd be brought in."

"You *work* here?" said Hugo. "What do you do?"

"I'm an orderly."

"Good heavens!" said Hugo. "Still, you might have waited till to-morrow."

"It would have been very hard to see you during the day when I'm on duty," I said.

"So you're not on duty now?" said Hugo.

"No."

"So you *are* following me."

"Oh, go to hell!" I told him. "Look, Hugo, I want to talk to you about a number of things."

"Well, I can't get away this time, can I?" he said.

He settled back into the bed and for a few moments we looked at each other in the way that people look when they cannot see each other's eyes.

"What are you so upset about, Jake?" Hugo asked. "I felt it at the studio. For years you make no attempt to see me, and then suddenly you start chasing me about like a mad thing."

I felt I had to be truthful. "I've seen Sadie and Anna and this reminded me of you," I said.

I could see Hugo closing up like a sea anemone. "How did you meet those two again?" he asked in a cautious voice.

I felt I had to be desperately truthful. "The girl I was staying with threw me out, so I looked for Anna and she passed me on to Sadie."

I could see Hugo shiver. "Did Sadie say anything about me?" he asked.

"Nothing in particular," I said, uttering the first lie. "But I got some news of you from Anna." I wanted to get back to the subject of Anna.

"Yes," said Hugo, "Anna told me she'd seen you. You came to the theatre one night, didn't you? I wanted to see you afterwards. I was sorry when Anna said you'd gone. You evidently weren't very anxious to see me *then*."

I felt unable to comment on this in detail. "I was afraid to see you, Hugo," I said.

"I can't understand you, Jake," said Hugo. "I don't see how anyone could be afraid of me. I never could see why you cleared off like that before. I wanted to talk to you very much then. There was never anyone I could discuss with like you. We might have discussed that stuff of yours."

"What stuff?" I asked.

"That book of yours," said Hugo. "I forget when it came out, but it must have been some time after you cleared off from Battersea, or else we would have talked about it, and I don't remember talking of it with you."

I leaned my head back and pressed it hard against the wall, as one might do to ease a crisis of drunkenness.

"Do you mean *The Silencer*?" I asked.

"Yes, that thing," said Hugo. "Of course, I found it terribly hard in parts. Wherever did you get all those ideas from?"

"From you, Hugo," I said weakly.

"Well," said Hugo, "of course I could see that it was about some of the things we'd talked of. But it sounded so different."

"I know!" I said.

"So much better, I mean," said Hugo. "I forget really what we talked about then, but it was a terrible muddle, wasn't it? Your thing was so clear. I learnt an awful lot from it."

I stared at Hugo. His bandaged head was silhouetted in the light from the little window; I could not see his expression. "I was ashamed about that thing, Hugo," I said.

"I suppose one always is, about what one writes," said Hugo. "I've never had the nerve to write anything. I hope you made some money out of it anyway. Did it sell well?"

"Not very," I said. I wondered for a moment if he were mocking me; but it was impossible. Hugo was incapable of mockery.

"Too highbrow, I suppose," said Hugo. "People never like original stuff when they first see it. I hope you weren't put off. Are you writing another dialogue?"

"No!" I said, and added, just to keep the conversation going while I collected my wits, "I thought of looking the thing over lately and developing one or two of the ideas, but I couldn't get hold of a copy."

"A pity! You could have borrowed mine," said Hugo. "I keep one in the drawer of my desk and look at it sometimes. It reminds me a bit of our talks. I used to enjoy them so much. My brain's quite gone to seed since then."

"I came to your flat one night last week," I said, "and you'd left a note saying *Gone to the pub*, and I went round the pubs looking for you."

"You can't have gone far," said Hugo. "I was in the King Lud."

"I went eastward," I said. "I met Lefty Todd that night."

"Of course, you know Lefty, don't you," said Hugo. "I saw him to-day at the meeting, before someone chucked the brick at me."

"How *is* your head, by the way?" I asked.

"Oh, it's all right," said Hugo. "I've just got a raging headache—which but for you would be raging in my sleep. But, Jake, you haven't told me why you cleared off. Did I do something to offend you?"

"No," I said patiently, "I did something to offend you. But I see now there was a misunderstanding. Let's skip it."

I could see Hugo looking at me intently. The bulky bandage gave him an enormous head. "The trouble with you, Jake," said Hugo, "is that you're far too impressed by people. You were far too impressed by me."

I was surprised. "I *was* impressed," I said, "but I didn't know you knew."

"Everyone must go his own way, Jake," said Hugo. "Things don't matter as much as you think."

I felt exasperated with Hugo. "I don't know what you mean," I said. "You thought *something* mattered enough when you took so much trouble with that theatre in Hammersmith." I wanted to draw him on the subject of Anna.

"Oh, *that* . . ." said Hugo, and was silent for a moment. "I did that to please Anna, but it was a foolish thing."

I held my breath. I had to step carefully now if I was to get out of him the full confession for which I thirsted; and as I inhaled slowly I could smell Hugo's thoughts.

"You mean, it didn't really please her," I asked coaxingly.

"Well, it *pleased* her, of course, yes," said Hugo, "but what was the use? Lies don't get one anywhere. Not that this was exactly a lie. After all, we both understood the situation. Yet it was a sort of a lie."

I felt a little out of my depth here. "You mean that she wasn't really interested in it, that she was somehow imprisoned in it?" I asked.

"No, *she* was interested all right," said Hugo, "but *I* wasn't really interested. And then she would introduce all that oriental junk, heaven knows where she got it from!"

"She got it from you!" I said with as much incisiveness as I could put into a whisper.

"That's nonsense!" said Hugo. "She may have picked up some vague notions from me, but they didn't add up to *that*."

"Why did you act in the mimes then if you thought the whole thing was bad?" I asked.

"You're right; I oughtn't to have," said Hugo, "but I did it to please her—and after all she did seem to be *making* something there."

"Yes," I said, "she can create things."

"You can both create things, I mean you and Anna," said Hugo.

"Why do you say it like that?" I asked.

"It just strikes me," said Hugo. "I never made a thing in my life," he added.

"Why did you destroy the theatre?" I asked.

"I didn't destroy it," said Hugo. "Anna did. She suddenly began to feel that it was all pointless, and she went away."

"Poor Hugo!" I said. "So then you gave it to NISP."

"Well," said Hugo, "NISP were urgently wanting a place and I thought they might as well have it."

I felt sorry for Hugo. I pictured him standing alone in the theatre after the being had departed that had been its life. "I didn't know you had any political views," I said. "You must have developed them since I last saw you."

"I haven't exactly got any political views," said Hugo, "but I think Lefty's ideas are *decent*." This was a very high term of praise in Hugo's vocabulary.

"Are you working with him?" I asked.

"Good heavens, no!" said Hugo. "I wouldn't know how. I just give him money. That's all I can do."

"I suppose Rockets are still going strong," I said. "I notice that the municipality of Paris is a customer of yours."

"Oh, Rockets," said Hugo. "I've sold the factory, you know."

"I didn't," I said. "Why?"

"Well, I don't really believe in private enterprise," said Hugo, "at least I *think* I don't. I'm so bad at understanding these things. And if one's in any doubt about a racket one ought to clear out, don't you think? Anyhow, while I had the factory I just couldn't help making money, and I don't want that. I want to travel light. Otherwise one can never understand anything."

"I've always travelled light," I said, "and I don't see that it's ever helped *me* to understand anything. But what about films, or are they different?"

"I'm clearing out of that too," said Hugo. "There's a new Anglo-French show that's going to take over Bounty Belfounder, and good luck to them."

"I see," I said. I felt moved. "But you'll still be a rich man, Hugo," I added.

"I suppose so," said Hugo. "I'm reluctant to think about it. I expect I'll get rid of the money somehow. I'll give a lot to Lefty. You can have some too, if you like."

"You're a strange man, Hugo," I said. "Why this sudden urge to strip yourself?"

"It's not sudden," said Hugo. "It's just that I've been cowardly and muddled. I don't suppose I should have made up my mind to do anything even now if it hadn't been that my life had got into such a ghastly mess that even I can't overlook it."

I thought of Anna. "You've been very unhappy?"

"That, of course," said Hugo. "I've been nearly demented. But that was no excuse for behaving so badly. By the way, I'm sorry I cut you off that day on the phone when I rang up Welbeck Street. I was so taken aback when I heard your voice, it made me feel so ashamed of myself that I rang off."

I couldn't understand this. "What were you so ashamed about?" I asked.

"Oh, well," said Hugo, "things I'd been doing, and things I intended to do. You think far too well of me, Jake. You're a sentimentalist."

"Sssh!" I said to him sharply, and we both fell silent.

There was a sound of feet in the corridor. I realized with a shock where I was. The soft sound of the footfalls drew nearer. Perhaps our voices had been heard, as in the excitement of the discussion they grew louder. I moved quietly up against the edge of the bed, to make sure that I was invisible from the door. Perhaps it was simply the Night Sister on her rounds, and we had not been heard after all. The steps came to a stop outside Hugo's door, and the square aperture was darkened. I pressed my face into the red blanket and held my breath. I wondered suddenly if Hugo would denounce me to the Night Sister, and for a moment I felt him to be capable of it. But Hugo lay rigid, and I could hear him breathing deeply. Then a moment later the face was withdrawn and the footsteps went slowly onto the next room. I relaxed, and still leaning against the bed looked up at Hugo while my thoughts reassembled

I felt that I was playing a big fish. Hugo was communicative. Now, it was only a matter of saying the right things and he would tell me all.

I broke the silence with a low whisper. "Anna's stopped singing."

Hugo was silent for a moment. "Anna's all right," he said, rather shortly.

I felt that this had been a wrong move. I tried something more direct. "Hugo," I said, "what was it that you felt ashamed of when you rang up there and I answered the phone?"

Hugo hesitated. I could see him fiddling with his bandage and looking past me. "I behaved badly to her," he said.

"How?" I breathed out the question, reducing my presence to a minimum. I wanted Hugo to soliloquize. I saw Anna's fleeing figure.

"Oh, I persecuted her terribly," said Hugo.

"Did she love you?" I murmured, and the air all about me was trembling.

"Oh, no," said Hugo, "it was hopeless. You know," he said, "I sometimes thought that she was keen on you."

The muscles relaxed one by one all over my body like little animals falling asleep, and I stretched out my legs. I felt sorry for Hugo as for a moment or two I brooded upon the picture he had conjured up. But now there was no time for brooding. I must get the facts; theories could come later. My mood at that moment was almost scientific. "What made you think that?" I asked. "I mean, that she was keen on me."

"She talked about you a lot," said Hugo, "and asked me questions about you."

"What a bore for you," I said, and I smiled to myself. Nothing is more maddening than being questioned by the object of one's interest about the object of hers, should that object not be you.

"I was glad to be of service to her," said Hugo, with a disgustingly humble air.

Was Hugo being frank with me? I suddenly wondered. "When will you see her again?" I asked. "Is she really going away?"

"I don't know," said Hugo. "I really don't know what she plans to do. She's like the weather. One simply never knows with Sadie."

"You mean Anna, yes," I said.

"I mean *Sadie*!" said Hugo.

The names of the two women rang out like the blasts of a horn which echo through a wood. A pattern in my mind was suddenly scattered and the pieces of it went flying about me like birds.

I rose to one knee and my face was close to Hugo's. "Who have we just been talking about?" I asked him.

"Sadie, of course," said Hugo. "Who else do you imagine?"

My grip closed upon the blanket. Already my thought, turned back the other way, was showing me an entirely different scene. "Hugo," I said, "can we get this absolutely clear?"

"Be quiet!" said Hugo, "you're talking almost out loud."

"Who is it that you're in love with?" I said. "Which of them?"

"Sadie," said Hugo.

"Are you sure?" I asked.

"Bloody hell!" he said. "I ought to know! I've suffered more than a year of misery about that woman! But I thought you knew all this?"

"She told me," I said. "She *told* me! But, of course, I didn't believe her." I sat back onto the floor and rocked my head in my hands.

"Why 'of course'?" said Hugo. "After all, she called you in to defend her against me, didn't she? Only you walked out!" He spoke bitterly.

"She locked me in," I said. "I couldn't stand that."

"My God! I wish she'd locked *me* in!" said Hugo.

"I couldn't believe her, I couldn't!" I said.

"Did she tell you I'd been awful?" said Hugo.

"Well, she said something vague about your possibly bursting in."

"She's a kind woman," said Hugo, "if she told you no more than that. I behaved like a mad thing. I broke in once in the night, and another time I came during the day while she was at the studio and looked for letters and took away some of her things. I was absolutely insane about her. I tell you, Jake, my life's been a perfect chaos for nearly a year. That's why I've got to clear myself out of it all and begin again."

"But, Hugo, it's not possible!" I said. "You *can't* love Sadie!"

"Why not?" said Hugo. He was angry.

I felt incoherent. The impossibility of Hugo's loving Sadie loomed over me inexpressibly, and as I stared at the fact of Hugo's loving Sadie I could only babble. "She isn't worth it" was on the tip of my tongue, but I didn't say it. That wasn't the reason, anyhow. "But you knew Anna," I said. "How could anyone know Anna and prefer Sadie?"

"I'll tell you one reason," said Hugo, and his voice was edged with fury. "Sadie's more intelligent!"

I had a confused sense of something terrible raising itself up between us. Hugo saw it too, and added immediately, "Jake, you're a fool. You know anyone can love anyone, or prefer anyone to anyone."

We were silent, I still clutching the blanket and Hugo half sitting up in bed. I could feel his legs close to my hand and they were rigid.

"I still don't understand," I said at last. "It isn't just that I thought the thing impossible. But everything was pointing the other way. Why did you take all that trouble about the Mime Theatre?"

"I've told you," said Hugo, "it was to please Anna."

"But why, why?" I struggled with this idea.

"Well, I don't know," said Hugo impatiently. "I probably oughtn't to have. Nothing can come of these concessions. One is just telling lies."

His words entered dully and blankly into my mind. Then quite suddenly I realized the truth. I stood up. "Anna loves you," I said.

"Yes, of course," said Hugo. "She's as crazy about me as I am about Sadie. But I thought you were in on all this, Jake?"

"I was in on it," I said. "I knew everything. I got it all the wrong way round, that's all!"

I walked to the door and looked out through the little window. I saw a row of white doors opposite me and a red floor. I turned back toward Hugo, and saw his face clearly for the first time. He was still very pale, and as he looked up at me anxiously from underneath the bandage, his face wrinkled and intent, he looked like Rembrandt.

I came back to the other side of the room. I wanted Hugo's face darkened. "I didn't realize all this," I said. "I might have behaved differently."

I couldn't at the moment think just in what way I would have behaved differently; all I knew was that I had had a wrench which dislocated past, present and future. Hugo was looking at me hard, and I gave him my face though not my eyes. If he could read the truth there, good luck to him. I knew that for myself it would take a long time to become clear.

"Just say something more about Anna, would you, Hugo?" I said. "Say anything that comes into your head. Anything might give me a better understanding."

"Well, I don't know what to say," said Hugo. "I'm terribly sorry about all this, Jake; it's like life, isn't it? I love Sadie, who's keen on you, and you love Anna, who's keen on me. Perverse, isn't it?"

"Come on, Hugo," I said, "say something about Anna. Tell me when all this started."

"It was long ago," said Hugo. "I ran into Anna through Sadie, and she took one look, Anna, I mean."

"Don't worry about the pronouns!" I said, "it's all clear from now on."

"At first she pursued me," said Hugo. "She stopped doing everything else and simply pursued me. It was no use my leaving London and staying at a hotel. In a day or two she would turn up. I was frantic."

"I find this hard to believe," I said to Hugo. "I don't mean that I think you've invented it. I just find it hard to believe."

"Well, have a try," said Hugo.

I was struggling to recognize in this frenzied maenad the Anna that I knew, the coolly tender Anna who was forever balancing the claims of her admirers one against another with the gentle impartiality of a mother. I was in considerable pain.

"You said 'at first'," I said. "What happened then?"

"Nothing much ever *happened*," said Hugo. "She wrote me hundreds of letters. Beautiful letters. I kept some of them. Then she became more sensible and I saw a bit more of her." I winced. "I liked to see her," said Hugo, "because I could talk to her about Sadie."

"Poor Anna!" I said.

"I know," said Hugo. "I've been a brute to both of them. But now I'm clearing out. I advise you to clear out too," he added.

"I don't know what you mean," I said, "but I'm damned if I will!"

"Some situations can't be unravelled," said Hugo, "they just have to be dropped. The trouble with you, Jake, is that you want to understand everything sympathetically. It can't be done. One must just blunder on. Truth lies in blundering on."

"Oh, to hell with truth!" I told him. I felt very confused and very ill.

"It's odd," I said. I was picking about among the things I had just learnt. "I was so sure the theatre was all your idea. It seemed so like you. 'Actions don't lie, words always do.' But now I see that this was all a hallucination."

"I don't know what you mean by 'like me'," said Hugo. "The theatre was all Anna's idea. I just joined in. She had some sort of general theory about it, but I never understood properly what it was."

"That was just what was yours," I said. "It was you reflected in Anna, just as that dialogue was you reflected in me."

"I don't recognize the reflexions," said Hugo. "The point is that people must just do what they can do, and good luck to them."

"What can you do?" I asked him.

Hugo was silent for a long time. "Make little intricate things with my hands," he said.

"Is that all?" I asked.

"Yes," said Hugo. We were silent again.

"What will you do about it?" I said.

"I'm going to become a watch-maker," said Hugo.

"A *what*?" I said.

"A watch-maker. Of course, it'll take me many years. But I've already arranged to be apprenticed to a good man in Nottingham."

"In *where*?"

"In Nottingham. Why not?"

"I don't know why not," I said. "But why this at all? Why a watch-maker?"

"I've told you," said Hugo. "I'm good at that sort of thing. Remember how clever I was with the set pieces? Only there was so much nonsense about set pieces."

"Isn't there nonsense about watches too?" I asked him.

"No," said Hugo, "it's an old trade. Like baking bread."

I stared into Hugo's darkened face. It was masked, as ever, by a sort of innocence. "You're mad," I said.

"Why do you say that, Jake?" said Hugo. "Every man must have a trade. Yours is writing. Mine will be making and mending watches, I hope, if I'm good enough."

"And what about the truth?" I said wildly. "What about the search for God?"

"What more do you want?" said Hugo. "God is a task. God is detail. It all lies close to your hand." He reached out and took hold of a tumbler which was standing on the table beside his bed. The light from the door glinted on the tumbler and seemed to find an answering flash in Hugo's eyes, as I tried in the darkness to see what they were saying.

"All right," I said, "all right, all right, all right."

"You're always *expecting* something, Jake," said Hugo.

"Maybe," I said. I was beginning to find the conversation a burden. I decided to go away. I got up. "How's your head now?" I asked Hugo.

"It's rather better," he said. "You made me forget about it. How long do you think they'll keep me in this place?"

"About five days, the Sister said."

"Good God!" said Hugo. "I can't have that ! I've got all sorts of things to do."

"Perhaps they'll let you out sooner," I said. I wasn't interested. I wanted to sit somewhere quietly and digest what Hugo had told me. "I'm off," I said.

"Not without me!" said Hugo, and he began to get out of bed.

I was scandalized. I seized him and began pushing him back. The hospital ethic was already deep in me. A patient must do what he is told and not presume to behave like a free agent. "Get back at once!" I said in a loud whisper.

For a moment we struggled. Then Hugo relaxed and drew his feet back into the bed. "Have a heart, Jake," he said. "If you don't help me to get away now I may not be let out for days. You know what these places are. They take your clothes away and you're simply helpless. Where are my clothes, anyway?"

"In a locker at the end of this corridor," I answered foolishly.

"Be a sport. Go and get them for me," said Hugo, "and show me the way out."

"You're not well enough to move," I said. "The Sister said it would be dangerous for you to move."

"You've just invented that this moment," said Hugo. "In fact I'm perfectly fit, and I know it and you know it. I've *got* to get out of this place. There are very urgent things I have to do to-morrow, and I'm damned if I'm going to be imprisoned here. Now go and get my clothes."

Hugo was speaking now with a sudden air of authority, and I noticed with distress a strong tendency in myself to obey him. Resisting it, I replied, "I work here, Hugo. If I do this I'll lose my job."

"Does anyone know that you're here?" asked Hugo.

"Of course not."

"Then no one will know that it was you who helped me."

"We shall be caught on the way out," I told him.

"You needn't come with me," said Hugo.

"I'd have to," I said. "You couldn't find the way alone."
I was cursing Hugo heartily. I didn't want to take this risk
for him, and I could see now that I was going to.

"Do this thing for me, Jake," said Hugo. "I wouldn't ask
if it wasn't urgent."

"Damn you," I said.

I went to the door and examined my watch. It was just
after four. If I was to act I must act at once. I looked at
Hugo's nocturnal face. I knew that I would do whatever he
wished. I had to. "Damn you," I said again, and I took hold
of the door handle. I swung the door open quietly and left it
ajar. I stood for a moment in the corridor getting used to the
light. Then I began to walk quietly. The Locker Room was
next door but one to the Sister's Room, on the side nearest
to me. It contained lockers in one-one correlation to the
number of patients in Corelli III, each locker being assigned
to a particular bed. The keys of the lockers were kept there
too, in a drawer. Once I could get into the room there
would be no difficulty in finding Hugo's clothes; but of
course the room itself might be locked. I found myself
hoping sincerely that it might. "Oh, let it be locked!" I said
to myself, as my hand touched the door of the Locker
Room. It was not locked. The door opened for me noiselessly. As I stood inside in the semi-darkness I had a rapid
debate as to whether I wouldn't go back and tell Hugo that
the door had been locked. It might have been locked. It
might *easily* have been locked. I struggled with this idea,
not certain whether or not I ought to regard it as a temptation. I tried to conjure up some sense of obligation to the
Hospital; but it was too late to call upon these reserves. If
I had been going to be moved by any bond or contract with
the Hospital the time for that was four minutes ago. I was
now embarked upon helping Hugo. I was committed to

Hugo. To lie to him would be an act of treachery. I put my hand on the keys.

I opened the locker and very quietly removed its contents piece by piece onto the table. Hugo's old check shirt, his even older corduroy trousers, a newish sports-coat that smelt of soap, a Jaeger vest and pants, socks with holes in, and dirty boots. Small objects jingled in Hugo's pockets. I held my breath and began to load myself, piling the garments up in my embrace and putting the boots on top, so that I could hardly see out over the armful. Then I found that I had left the locker door open and the bunch of keys hanging in the lock. One by one I replaced the things on the table, closed the locker, and returned the keys to the drawer. Not that it mattered, since the disappearance of Hugo could be noticed almost as soon as the theft from the locker; but I like to be neat. Then I loaded up again and shuffled toward the door. As I went I kept having auditory images of what it would sound like if one of Hugo's boots were to fall off onto the floor. But there was no mishap. I glided down the corridor with a feeling in my back as if someone were pointing a Sten gun at it. The door of Hugo's room was ajar and I sidled in and decanted the pile of clothes onto the bed with a soft bump.

Hugo had got up and was standing by the window, dressed in a shapeless white nightgown and biting his nails. "That's colossal!" he said. He seized on his clothes with glee while I shut the door again soundlessly.

"Hurry up!" I told him. "If we're getting out let's get out." I had never felt less sympathy and consideration for Hugo than at that moment. I noticed that as he dressed he kept putting his hand to his head, and I wondered idly whether this escapade mightn't really do him some serious harm; but this possibility no longer interested me, either as a debating point, since the time for debate was over, or as a factor in Hugo's welfare, since any concern I might have had about the latter was thoroughly driven out by more poignant worries about myself. I felt extreme irritation with Hugo for having put me in the position of being disloyal to the Hospital, and great anxiety about our prospects of getting out unobserved. As to what would happen to me if we were caught I felt a terror which was augmented in proportion to the vagueness of my conceptions. I trembled.

Hugo was ready. He was tidying up his bed in a futile way. "Leave that!" I told him with as much brutality as I could. "Look," I said to Hugo, "we have to get past the Night Sister's room, which has glass in the door, so we shall have to crawl that bit. You'd better take those boots off. They look ready to make a noise all by themselves. Follow me and do what I do. Don't speak, and for heaven's sake see that there's nothing likely to fall out of your pockets. All right?" Hugo nodded, his eyes rounded and his face beaming with innocence. I looked at him with exasperation. Then I put my head out of the door.

There was no sign of life from the Night Sister and not a sound of any kind to be heard. I slid out and Hugo followed, making a noise like a bear, a mixture of grunting and lumbering. I turned back and frowned and put my finger to my lips. Hugo nodded enthusiastically. The light was still on in the Night Sister's room, and as we approached it I could hear her moving about inside. I crouched down and scudded past, keeping well below the level of the glass. Then I turned to watch Hugo. He was hesitating. He obviously didn't know what to do with his boots, which he was carrying one in each hand. We eyed each other across the gap and Hugo made an interrogatory movement. I replied with a gesture which indicated that I washed my hands of his predicament, and walked on to the door of the ward. Then I turned back again, and nearly laughed out loud. Hugo had got his two boots gripped by their tongues between his teeth, and was negotiating the passage on hands and feet, his posterior rising mountainously into the air. I watched anxiously, wondering whether the attention of the Night Sister might not be caught by the movement of this semicircular surface which must be jutting out well into her field of vision. But nothing happened, and Hugo joined me by the door with the saliva dripping into the inside of his boots. I shook my head at him, and together we left Corelli III.

Now there was no protection, only hope. We walked down the main stairs, Hugo crowned with bandages. It was blatant. The Hospital lay about us quietly, and focused its brilliant lights upon us, like a great eye watching us, into the very pupil of which the pair of us were walking. I waited for the echoing call from many stories above which should accuse us and tell us to halt; but it did not come. We left the stairway, and now we were approaching the Transept Kitchen. To my joy I saw that the Kitchen was dark; there was no one there. In a moment we should be free. Already my heart was beating with the joy of achievement and my thoughts taking to wings of triumph. We had done it! Only a few steps now separated us from the door of the store room. I turned to look at Hugo.

As I did so, a figure appeared round the corner of the corridor some fifteen yards in front of us. It was Stitch, wearing a blue dressing-gown. All three of us stopped dead. Stitch took us in and we took in Stitch. Then I saw Stitch's mouth beginning to open.

"Quick, this way!" I said to Hugo out loud. These were the first words which I had uttered aloud for many hours and they rang out strangely. I leapt to the store-room door and pushed Hugo through it.

"Through the window!" I called after him. I could hear him blundering ahead of me and I could hear Stitch's feet scrabbling on the floor of the corridor. I slammed the door of the store room behind me, and as I turned toward the window, with a sudden inspiration I seized hold of a stack of bedsteads on one side and gave it a violent pull toward the centre of the room; I felt it move to the vertical, totter, and begin to fall inwards. I sprang to the other side and in an instant I had set the stack in motion there too. Like two packs of cards meeting, and with a clatter like the day of judgment, the two piles met and interlocked across the door. I heard Stitch cursing on the other side. I followed Hugo.

Hugo had left the window wide open. I sprang through it like Nijinsky, and cannoned into Hugo, who was hopping about on the lawn.

"My boots! My boots!" cried Hugo in anguish. He had evidently put them down inside the window as he was getting out.

"Never mind your bloody boots! Run for it!" I told him. Behind us there rang out the metallic din which was Stitch trying to open the door and being prevented by the barricade of bedsteads. I threw back my head to run, and saw with surprise that the garden was clearly revealed in the grey morning light; and as we sped along between the cherry trees it would not have surprised me if someone had opened fire on us from an upstairs window.

We crossed the lawn and the gravel and leapt over the chains and bolted along the pavement in the direction of Goldhawk Road. Hugo's bandage was coming undone and flapped behind him like a pennant. Before we turned the corner I looked back; but there was no sign of pursuit. We slowed down.

"And how's your head *now*?" I said to Hugo. We must have been doing a good twenty miles per hour.

"Hellish!" said Hugo. He leaned against a wall. "Damn it, Jake," he said, "you might have let me pick up my boots. They were special ones. I got them in Austria."

"You'd better see a doctor some time to-day," I told Hugo. "I don't want to have any more on my conscience."

"I'll see a chap I know in the City," said Hugo. We walked slowly on in the direction of Shepherd's Bush.

The light was increasing fast. It must have been after five, and when we reached Shepherd's Bush Green the sun was shining through a mist. There was no one about. We stopped once to fix Hugo's bandage. Then we padded along in silence. As I looked at Hugo's big feet, which were bulging through various holes in his socks, I could not but think of Anna; and with this thought I suddenly felt for Hugo a mixture of compassion and anger. What a lot of trouble the man had caused me! Yet none of it could have been otherwise.

"You've made me lose my job," I told him.

"You may not have been recognized," said Hugo.

"I *was* recognized," I said. "That fellow that saw us works in Corelli. He's my enemy."

"Sorry," said Hugo.

We were walking along Holland Park Avenue. It was broad daylight and the mist had cleared. The sun, just risen over the houses, gave us sharp shadows. We passed by sleeping windows. London was not yet awake. Then one or two workmen's buses passed by. Yet still we walked. Hugo's head was down, and he was biting his nails and looking sightlessly at the pavement. I observed him closely as one might observe a picture or a dead man. I had a strange sense of his being both very distant and yet closer to me than he had ever been or would be again. I was reluctant to speak. So we went for a long time in silence.

"When are you going to Nottingham?" I said at last.

"Oh," said Hugo vaguely, lifting his head, "in two or three days, I hope. It depends how long it takes to wind things up here."

I looked at his face, and although no line of it had changed I saw it as the face of an unhappy man. I sighed. "Have you anywhere to live up there?"

"Not yet," said Hugo. "I shall have to find digs."

"Can I see you again before you go?" I asked him.

"I'm afraid I'll be very busy," said Hugo. I sighed again.

It then occurred to us at the same moment, both that this was the end of our conversation and that it was going to be very difficult to take leave of each other.

"Lend me half a crown, Jake," said Hugo. I handed it over. We were still walking.

"I must dash on, if you'll excuse me," said Hugo.

"O.K.," I said.

"Thanks a lot for helping me out," he said.

"That's all right," I said.

He wanted to be rid of me. I wanted to be rid of him. There was a moment of silence while each of us tried to think of the appropriate thing to say. Neither succeeded.

For an instant our eyes met. Then Hugo said abruptly, "I mush dash. Sorry."

He began walking very fast, and turned down Campden Hill Road. I followed him at my ordinary pace. He drew ahead. I walked after him along the road. He turned into Sheffield Terrace, and when I turned the corner he was about thirty yards ahead. He looked back and saw me and quickened his pace. He turned into Hornton Street; I followed at the same pace, and saw him in the distance turning into Gloucester Walk. When I got to the corner of Gloucester Walk he had disappeared.

Nineteen

As I walked through Kensington the day began. There was nothing to do in it. I wandered along looking into the windows of shops. I went into Lyons' and had some breakfast. That took up quite a long time. Then I set off walking again. I walked down the Earls Court Road and stood for a while outside the house where Madge had lived. The curtains on the windows had been changed. Everything looked different. I began to doubt whether it was the same house. I moved on. Beside Earls Court Station I had a cup of tea. I thought of ringing up Dave, but couldn't think that I had anything particular to say to him.

It was the middle of the morning. At the Hospital they would be washing up the mugs in the kitchen of Corelli III. I went into a flower shop and ordered a grotesquely large bunch of roses to be sent to Miss Piddingham. I sent no note or message with them. She would know very well who they were from. At last the pubs opened. I had a drink. It occurred to me that I had something to say to Dave after all, which was to ask whether there was any news of Finn. I telephoned the Goldhawk Road number, but got no answer. My need of Finn began to be very great and I had to force my attention away from it. I had some more drinks. The time passed slowly.

During this time I didn't at first think of anything special. There was too much to think about. I just sat quietly and let things take shape deeply within me. I could just sense the great forms moving in the darkness, beneath the level of my attention and without my aid, until gradually I began to see where I was. My memories of Anna had been completely transformed. Into each one of them a new dimension had been introduced. I had omitted to ask Hugo when exactly it was that Anna had encountered him and, as

he so horribly put it, taken one look. But it was very likely
that since Hugo's acquaintance with Sadie dated back such
a long way, Hugo's acquaintance with Anna might well
overlap with the later phases of my relations with her,
before our long absence from each other. At this thought,
it seemed that every picture I had ever had of Anna was
contaminated, and I could feel my very memory images
altering, like statues that sweat blood.

I had no longer any picture of Anna. She faded like a
sorcerer's apparition; and yet somehow her presence remained to me, more substantial than ever before. It seemed
as if, for the first time, Anna really existed now as a separate
being and not as a part of myself. To experience this was
extremely painful. Yet as I tried to keep my eyes fixed upon
where she was I felt toward her a sense of initiative which
was perhaps after all one of the guises of love. Anna was
something which had to be learnt afresh. When does
one ever know a human being? Perhaps only after one has
realized the impossibility of knowledge and renounced the
desire for it and finally ceased to feel even the need of it.
But then what one achieves is no longer knowledge, it is
simply a kind of co-existence; and this too is one of the guises
of love.

I began thinking about Hugo. He towered in my mind
like a monolith : an unshaped and undivided stone which
men before history had set up for some human purpose
which would remain forever obscure. His very otherness
was to be sought not in himself but in myself or Anna.
Yet herein he recognized nothing of what he had made.
He was a man without claims and without reflexions. Why
had I pursued him? He had nothing to tell me. To have
seen him was enough. He was a sign, a portent, a miracle.
Yet no sooner had I thought this than I began to be
curious again about him. I pictured him in Nottingham
in some small desolate workshop, holding a watch in his
enormous hand. I saw the tiny restless movements of
the watch, I saw its many jewels. Had I finished with
Hugo?

I left the pub. I was somewhere in the Fulham Road. I waited quietly upon the kerb until I saw a taxi approaching. I hailed it. "Holborn Viaduct," I said to the driver. I lay back in the taxi; and as I did so I felt that this was the last action for a very long time that would seem to me to be inevitable. London sped past me, beloved city, almost invisible in its familiarity. South Kensington, Knightsbridge, Hyde Park Corner. This was the last act which would provoke no question and require no reason. After this would come the long agony of reflexion. London passed before me like the life of a drowning man which they say flashes upon him all at once in the final moment. Piccadilly, Shaftesbury Avenue, New Oxford Street, High Holborn.

I paid the taximan. It was the middle of the afternoon. I stood upon the Viaduct looking down into the chasm of Farringdon Street. A pigeon flew up out of it, moving its wings lazily, and I watched it flying slowly south toward the spire of St Bride's. The sun was warm on my neck. I dallied. I wanted to hold on, just a little longer, to my last act. A premonition of pain made me delay; the pain that comes after the drama, when the bodies have been carried from the stage and the trumpets are silent and an empty day dawns which will dawn again and again to make mock of our contrived finalities. I put my foot on the stair.

It was a long way. When I was halfway up I stopped to listen for the starlings, but I could hear nothing. It is toward evening that they sing and chatter. The question of whether Hugo would be there or not was one that I had hardly even asked myself. On the penultimate landing I paused for breath. The door was shut. I came up to it and knocked. There was no reply. I knocked again, very loudly. The place was completely silent. Then I tried the door. It opened, and I stepped in.

As I entered Hugo's sitting-room there was a sudden wild flurry. The room was whirring and disintegrating into a number of black pieces. I grasped the door in a fright.

Then I saw. The place was full of birds. Several starlings which had not found the window in their first dart fluttered madly about, striking the walls and the glass panes. Then they found the opening and were gone. I looked about me. Hugo's flat seemed already more like an aviary than the abode of a human being. White dung spattered the carpet, and through the open window the rain had come in and made a deep stain upon the wall. It looked as if Hugo had not been there for some time. I walked through into the bedroom. The bed was stripped. The wardrobe was empty. I pondered for a while on these phenomena. Then I went back into the other room and lifted the telephone. I had a strange fancy that I should find Hugo at the other end of it. But it appeared to be dead. Then I sat down on the settee. I was not waiting for anything. Some time passed. A clock in the City struck some hour. Then other clocks followed. I did not try to count.

My gaze, after wandering vaguely about the room, fastened on Hugo's desk. I looked at it for a while. Then I got up and approached it. I opened the top drawer. Inside the drawer, half hidden by a pile of empty files, was a copy of *The Silencer*. I took it out. On the first blank sheet Hugo had written his name in large letters. I turned over the pages. Here and there Hugo had underlined passages, put crosses and question-marks in the margin; and at one place there was a pencilled note, *Ask J.* This filled me with pain, and I closed the book and thrust it into my pocket. I glanced at the other contents of the drawers, and then I opened the top of the desk. It was crammed with letters and papers. I began very quickly to turn these over. As I delved further into boxes and pigeon holes a flood of papers began to cascade onto the floor. I could not find what I wanted.

Old letters and bills and blunt pencils and sealing-wax and boxes of matches and many kinds of paper clips and half-empty books of stamps and obsolete cheque-books streamed through my fingers. In a small drawer I came upon a collection of sinister-looking objects which I identified as Belfounder's Domestic Detonators, of a rather smaller variety than the one which had liberated us from the film studio. Another drawer contained a pearl necklace: perhaps a gift bought with tender care and destined for Sadie, which now would never reach her; or which she had returned, and it had arrived one morning in a registered packet and lain there for days because Hugo had not had the heart to undo it. But I could not find what I wanted.

I sat down and took an empty sheet of paper. I wanted to write a letter to Hugo. I took one of Hugo's pens and Hugo's ink. A starling flew in at the window, saw me, and flew out again. There was a soft chattering on the balustrade. I looked up at the blue sky above it. *Hugo,* I wrote on the paper. Then I could think of nothing more to say. I thought of putting *Send me your Nottingham address,* but this sounded too weak and impersonal and I didn't write it down. In the end I just drew a curving line across the page, and signed my name at the bottom of it, adding the address of Mrs Tinckham's shop. I put the note in an envelope and balanced it on the bookcase and prepared to leave. As I turned, something caught my eye in the wall behind the bookcase. It was the green door of a safe.

I paused, and then moved the bookcase out a little from the wall. I pulled at the safe door, but it was locked. I stood looking at it pensively. Then it was clear to me what I must do. I went back to the desk and took from the drawer one of Belfounder's Domestic Detonators. I fingered this small explosive, wondering how powerful it was. I wondered this in a detached sort of way as I fumbled in my pocket for matches. The detonator was cone-shaped. I ran my finger over the door of the safe, trying to find some crack into which I could fit the point of the cone, but the whole thing was as smooth as a bishop's hand, even the hinges were stowed away inside. There were no crevices, neither were there any protuberances on which I might have tried to balance the detonator. Eventually I took a roll of stamp paper from Hugo's desk and with this I glued the object on at what seemed to be the point of maximum vulnerability on the lock side of the door. A small cotton fuse protruded from the blunt end, like the blue paper of a firework. I applied a lighted match to this and retired to the other end of the room. I watched thoughtfully. I think I would not have been either very surprised or very moved if the whole wall had suddenly disintegrated in a cloud of wood and plaster, revealing the open sky and a view of St Paul's.

There was a bright flash and a crack. I shut my eyes. The room was filled with smoke, and a cloud of starlings flew up from under the balustrade. When I opened my eyes I saw through the sulphurous mist that the door of the safe had swung open and was dangling toward the floor on one hinge. No other damage had been done. I came forward and looked inside the safe. Its interior consisted of two deep shelves. On the lower shelf there was what appeared to be a great deal of money, done up in bundles of one-pound and five-pound notes. On the upper shelf I saw what I wanted.

There were two packets of letters. I took them out. There was a small packet, in a neat self-conscious hand which I recognized as Sadie's. The other packet was very much larger. I flicked it over as one flicks a pack of cards. All these letters were from Anna. "Beautiful letters," Hugo had called them. Guilt and triumph and despair battled in me as I clutched them. I sat down on the settee. Now I would *see* that which I had been unable to imagine. I drew out the first envelope.

At that moment I heard the sound of a vehicle drawing up, with a great screeching of brakes, in the street outside. I hesitated. I was blushing and trembling. I got up and climbed onto a chair and put my head out of the window, still holding the letters in my hand. A lorry had drawn up outside the door. I watched it for a moment, but nobody emerged, so I got down again. I looked at the envelope; and as I did so I saw as in a vision the dark wood and the figure of Anna stepping into it barefoot. My fingers fumbled with the letter inside. It was a letter of many pages. I began to unfold it. Then I heard the sound of a car. It approached with a strong crescendo and then stopped. I stood rigid, cursing to myself. I climbed onto the chair again. Far below I saw Hugo's black Alvis. It was drawn up in the road just behind the lorry. An emotion which was neither pleasure nor fear but a mixture of both made me watch the car with a fast-beating heart. I shivered. Hugo was imminent.

Someone got out of the car. But it was not Hugo. I stared for a moment. Then I recognized the fair head and slim figure of Lefty. I watched with parted lips, gripping the edge of the window. Lefty was standing on the pavement, consulting with two men who had just climbed out of the lorry. The strong sun cast their tall shadows upon the pavement. Then I saw across the windscreen of the Alvis the letters NISP. And I understood. I leapt down from the chair. I whirled about and looked at the room as a man might look for a foothold upon a crumbling mountain-side. I snatched up my note to Hugo and put it in my pocket. I stood for a moment paralysed. Then far below I could hear feet upon the stairs. I took in the scene: the rifled desk, the open safe. I looked at the letters which I still held in my hand, and I slipped the one which I had been opening back into the packet. I held them for a second longer and made as if to put them into my pocket. But it was impossible. They were burning my hand. I hurled them back into the safe. Then I selected the largest of the bundles of one-pound notes and thrust it inside my coat. "That's something the Revolution won't get!" I said out loud; and I made for the door.

I crossed the landing in three strides, and as I entered Hugo's kitchen I could hear Lefty's voice on the stairs. I opened the kitchen window and vaulted out onto the flat roof. I walked firmly across the roof. The skylights of the next door office building were propped wide open to the summer afternoon. I lowered myself through one of them, and found myself on a deserted landing. I began to descend the stairs, and a minute or two later emerged from a door into a side alley. I walked back onto the street and crossed the road; and as I walked nonchalantly past Hugo's house on the other side they were already carrying out the Renoirs.

Twenty

Mars was delighted to see me. He had been shut in all day. I fed him, and made up the rest of his meat into a parcel. Then I packed some of my clothes into a bag. There were a few letters and a package for me in the hall; I stuffed them into the bag too without looking at them. I wrote a note to Dave, thanking him for his hospitality, and I left the house with Mars.

We got onto an eighty-eight bus. Mars provoked a flood of remarks from the conductor. We sat in the front seat on top, the seat in which I had sat not so very long ago thinking about Anna until I had had to get off the bus and go looking for her. And as I looked down now on the crowds in Oxford Street and stroked Mars's head I felt neither happy nor sad, only rather unreal, like a man shut in a glass. Events stream past us like these crowds and the face of each is seen only for a minute. What is urgent is not urgent forever but only ephemerally. All work and all love, the search for wealth and fame, the search for truth, life itself, are made up of moments which pass and become nothing. Yet through this shaft of nothings we drive onward with that miraculous vitality that creates our precarious habitations in the past and the future. So we live; a spirit that broods and hovers over the continual death of time, the lost meaning, the unrecaptured moment, the unremembered face, until the final chop chop that ends all our moments and plunges that spirit back into the void from which it came.

So I reflected; and was reluctant to get off the bus. But when we reached Oxford Circus I rose and pulled Mars after me down the stairs. It was the rush hour. I threaded my way through the crowd with the dog at my heels, and turned down Rathbone Place. Soho was hot and dusty,

sulky idle and senseless with the afternoon. People stood
about waiting for opening time. In an upper room someone was playing a piano. Someone else picked up the tune
and whistled it, going away into the distance. I walked
along Charlotte Street. The scene trembled and shimmered
before me perhaps with the heat or perhaps with fear. Like
one pursued I quickened my step.

Mrs Tinckham's voice came to me out of the wreaths of
tobacco smoke. She seemed to have been expecting me.
But then she always expected me. I sat down at the little
table.

"Hello, dearie," said Mrs Tinck, "you've been a long
time."

"It took a long time," I said.

Mars sniffed discreetly at one or two of the nearest cats.
They seemed to have got used to him and merely turned
away their delicate heads and blinked. Behind Mrs Tinck
they rose, tier upon tier, and I could see their eyes through
the smoke like the lights of a railway terminus in the fog.
Mars lay down at my feet.

I stretched out my legs. "What about a drink?" I said to
Mrs Tinckham. "It's nearly opening time."

"Whiskey and soda?" she said. I could hear the glass
clinking under the counter and the gurgle of the whiskey
and the fizz of the soda. Mrs Tinckham passed it to me and
I threw my head back and closed my eyes. Very distantly
the wireless was murmuring like the voice of another
world. The sounds of a Soho evening came in through
the doorway. I could feel Mars leaning against my foot. I
took two gulps of the whiskey; it ran through me like quick-
gold and, almost physically, I felt a sort of shiver of possibility. I opened my eyes and found Mrs Tinckham looking at me. She had something on the counter under her
hand. I recognized it as the parcel containing my manuscripts. I reached out for it and she passed it over without a word.

I laid the parcel on the table. Then I extracted from my
bag the small pile of letters which I had brought from

Dave's. I saw at once that there was a letter from Sadie among them, and I set that one aside.

"Do you mind if I read my letters?" I said to Mrs Tinckham.

"Do what you please, dear," said Mrs Tinck. "I'll get on with my story. I'm just at the exciting part."

I didn't want to open Sadie's letter first. So I took up a letter with a London postmark and an unfamiliar hand and opened it. It was from Lefty. I read it through several times and I smiled. Lefty wrote in an elegant and faintly rhetorical manner with colons, semi-colons and parentheses. His first paragraph dealt with our night beside the Thames: a midsummer night's dream Lefty said it had been for him; he only hoped that he had not played the ass. He seemed to remember talking his head off. He went on to say that he was sorry to hear that I had been ill. He suggested that when I felt better I should come and call on him : and if I felt I could do any sort of political work he would be glad, but that I should call anyway; after all, life wasn't entirely a matter of politics, was it? I got a good impression from this letter; and although I doubted whether Lefty really entertained the final sentiment I felt that here I had to do with a man.

I pocketed Lefty's letter and turned my attention to the package. I had already noticed out of the corner of my eye that it came from France. I began to tear it open. It was from Jean Pierre and it contained a copy of *Nous Les Vainqueurs* with an extremely Gallic superscription addressed to myself in Jean Pierre's flowing hand. I looked at the book with some emotion. Then I drew out my penknife and opened the first few pages. Before I knew what had happened I had read as far as page five. The impression was startling. Jean Pierre had always been a deft story-teller. But I felt at once that there was more here than deftness. The style had hardened, the manner was confident, the pace long and slow. Something had changed. Starting a novel is opening a door on a misty landscape; you can still see very little but you can smell the earth and feel

the wind blowing. I could feel the wind blowing from the
first pages of *Nous Les Vainqueurs* and it blew strongly
and tasted fresh. "So far," I said to myself, "so good."
Something had changed; it would be time enough later
on to decide what it was. I looked at Jean Pierre's name
on the cover—and felt for the first time that perhaps after
all we were entered for the same competition. And as I
found myself thinking this thought I shook my head and
laid the book aside.

I selected next a letter in an unknown hand with an Irish
stamp on it. I opened it. There was a brief and nearly
illegible note inside. It took me a long time to realize that
this letter was from Finn. When I did decipher the signature I felt distressed and shocked. It was an odd fact that I
had never before received any communication in writing
from Finn. We normally communicated by phone or telegram when we were not together; and indeed some of my
friends had once had a theory that Finn couldn't write.
What Finn's letter said was the following.

DEAR JAKE,

I am sorry I went off without seeing you. It was just when
you were in Paris. I thought it was time to go back then
because of the money. You know how I often thought of
going back before. I'll be in Dublin now and the Pearl Bar
will always find me. I think they forward letters, I haven't
got a place to live yet. Hoping to see you when you come
over to the Emerald Isle. Remember me to David.

yrs.

P. O'FINNEY

This letter upset me extremely and I exclaimed to Mrs
Tinckham, "Finn's gone back to Ireland!"

"I know," said Mrs Tinck.

"You *know*?" I cried. "How?"

"He told me," said Mrs Tinck.

The notion that Finn had made a confidant of Mrs
Tinckham came to me for the first time and rushed in an
instant from possibility to probability. "He told you just
before he went?" I asked.

"Yes," said Mrs Tinckham, "and earlier too. But he must have told you he wanted to go back?"

"He did, now I come to think of it," I said, "but I didn't believe him." And somehow this phrase had a familiar ring. "I'm a fool," I said. Mrs Tinckham didn't dispute this.

"Did he have any special reasons for going?" I asked her. I felt pain and indignation at having to ask Mrs Tinckham questions about Finn; but I needed to know. I looked at her old placid face. She was blowing smoke rings; and I knew that she would tell me nothing.

"He just wanted to go home, I suppose," said Mrs Tinckham. "I imagine there were people there he wanted to see. And there's always religion," she added vaguely.

I looked down at the table, and I could feel on my brow a gentle pressure which was the gaze of Mrs Tinckham and half a dozen cats. I felt ashamed, ashamed of being parted from Finn, of having known so little about Finn, of having conceived things as I pleased and not as they were. "Well, he's gone," I said.

"You'll see him in Dublin," said Mrs Tinckham.

I tried to imagine this; Finn at home and I a visitor. I shook my head. "I couldn't," I said. I knew that Mrs Tinckham understood.

"You never know what you won't want to do when the time comes," said Mrs Tinckham in the vague tone in which she utters those remarks of hers which may be deep counsel or may be senseless. I looked up at her quickly. The wireless murmured on and the cigarette smoke drifted between us like a veil, shifting its layers very gently in the slow summer air from the doorway. She blinked at me and her pupils seemed narrowed to vertical slits.

"Well, we'll see," I said to her.

"That always the best thing to say, isn't it, dear?" said Mrs Tinckham.

At last I took up Sadie's letter. I was extremely nervous of it. I felt sure that it would contain something unpleasant. Mars stirred at my feet and snuffled against my shoe. I

opened the envelope. There were two enclosures which I set
aside and unfolded a long perfumed sheet down which a
narrow column of writing flowed in Sadie's elegant hand.
Her letter read as follows.

DARLING JAKE,

About that *wretched* dog—you must think me awful not to
have written sooner, but the truth is that your letter got
mixed up with the most *enormous* pile of fan mail. (What a
problem that is! One never knows whether to look at the
stuff or not. Just to see it there is *rather* uplifting for the
ego—though I suppose it does undermine the character a
bit. Not that I'd ever dream of reading it even if I had time.
My secretary just classifies it into cretins for, cretins against,
cranks, professionals, intellectuals, religious, and offers of
marriage!) I must say, I was just a *little* hurt by the tone
of your letter—that is, until I realized that of course you
didn't write it. (*Did* you, darling?)

Yes, now about the dog. The fact is, S. and I have so
much on our hands at the moment we really can't cope with
the brute. (You've no *idea* what a bother an animal picture
is. The most impossible men in tweeds come in and wander
about the set—and the next thing is the Dumb Friends'
League are sending in spies disguised as continuity girls.) S.
thought the easiest thing would be for you to keep him if
you'd like to. That is, we'd expect you to buy him, of course.
(Sorry to be a business girl, but one has to watch the cash,
with the cost of living and partly living what it is, and one
income tax people absolutely inventing ways to make one
poor. Anyway, it's S.'s thing, you know, not mine. I'm
just writing on his behalf.) I should say £700 and call it
quits. That covers all film rights, book rights, ad. rights,
and so on. (You've no idea how many rights there are in
this business! Talk about the Rights of Dog!) Of course
he's a *bargain* at the price. But S. got him cheap in fact, and
we only want to cover our costs. If you'd like to buy, perhaps you'd get in touch with my solicitor—I enclose his
card, if I've remembered to do so. If you don't want to buy
perhaps you'd get in touch anyhow and make some arrangement about returning the animal. Sorry not to look after
this in person; I'm *madly* busy getting ready to go to the

States. By the way, if you do decide to buy the dog, don't forget to work the ads. I enclose (ditto) a letter from the dog-biscuit people, I forget their name. They want to use photos or something. Whatever they offer, ask for twice.

Forgive this fearful scribble. It was good to see you. Let's meet again, shall we, when the hurly burly's done. Tho' heaven *only* knows when that will be. Perhaps in a year or two. I have a long and tender memory.

Yours ever,

SADIE

P.S. S. seems to have a typescript of yours which some woman lent him. I'll get him to lodge it chez my solicitor, so you can pick it up when you call about the dog.

This letter absolutely delighted me. I didn't know which pleased me most, its gentleness or its cunning. I had no doubt that Sadie thought it quite possible that I would be fool enough to buy Mars, she probably wasn't sure whether I knew the secret of his age, she must think it unlikely that she would find a better buyer in her own well-informed milieu, she asked a sum of money which was about the maximum that I would be likely to be able or willing to cough up, she then hastened to indicate a way in which I might manage to recoup myself; and the final paragraph clearly came from the heart, or whatever cool yet sensitive organ Sadie kept in place of one.

I looked at the two enclosures. One was the card of Sadie's solicitor, which I stowed away in my pocket. The other was the letter from the dog-biscuit people. I glanced at this and then tore it up. "Your public career is over!" I said to Mars. Then I took out of my coat the bundle of notes which I had taken from Hugo's safe. I began to count them. Mrs Tinckham watched with interest, but made no enquiry. The bundle contained exactly a hundred pounds. I tied them up again and put them away.

"Could you sell me some writing-paper and envelopes?" I asked Mrs Tinckham.

She handed them over. "These are on the house," she

said. "I shall never manage to sell them." They were yellow with dust and age. Inside the cover of the pad I made a short calculation. My winnings on Lyrebird amounted to six hundred pounds. This, with Hugo's hundred pounds, and what I had in the bank, brought my credit up to about seven hundred and sixty pounds. I looked at this figure for a while, but more in sorrow than in hesitation. Of course I had to buy Mars. I didn't need to pause to ask myself whether or even why. It was written in the heavens, and not to do it would be to prove myself an underling. Nor did it occur to me to try to beat Sadie down. The formal properties of the situation left me with no choice. I must pay up, and without argument or comment. This was no moment for haggling with destiny. I would only allow myself the luxury, when it had all been settled, of one brief note to Sadie : a note which she would *not* pretend to have mislaid among her fan mail. As I thought this I knew that Sadie concerned me. There was no doubt that we should meet again. But that was for the future. The future—it opened for a moment before me, a land of hills and far distances; and I closed my eyes. Sadie would *keep*. There is only one thing which will make a woman *keep*, and that is intelligence. Sadie had it. Hugo was right.

I wrote the cheque. I reckoned that this left me with just about as much cash to my name as I had had when I left Earls Court Road at the beginning of this story. I sighed a little over this, and for a moment the spectral fortunes which I had been so near to winning rose about me in a whirl till I was blinded in a snowstorm of five-pound notes. But the tempest subsided; and I knew that I had no deep regrets. Like a fish which swims calmly in deep water, I felt all about me the secure supporting pressure of my own life. Ragged, inglorious and apparently purposeless, but my own. I completed the letter to Sadie's solicitor, and asked him to send the typescript to me care of Mrs Tinckham. I could raise money on that as soon as I wished. There would be no more translating. I began to undo the parcel of manuscripts.

I spread them out on the table; and as I touched them my hands were trembling like the hands of a water-diviner. I began to glance through them, looking with surprise on what I had done. There was a long poem, the fragment of a novel, a number of curious stories. It seemed to me that I had written them long ago. These things were mediocre, I saw it. But I saw too, as it were straight through them, the possibility of doing better—and this possibility was present to me as a strength which cast me lower and raised me higher than I had ever been before. I took out Hugo's copy of *The Silencer*, and the sight of it gave me joy. This too was only a beginning. It was the first day of the world. I was full of that strength which is better than happiness, better than the weak wish for happiness which women can awaken in a man to rot his fibres. It was the morning of the first day.

I stretched and yawned, and Mars stretched too, shaking each limb. I spread out my arms and smiled at Mrs Tinckham. She smiled back through the haze like a Cheshire cat. But as I stretched my body out, trying to embrace the world, there was a strange whisper going on in my head, as if someone I knew were murmuring into my ear, as if someone I loved were trying to tell me a secret; and I stiffened slowly as one who is listening.

"There's a friend of yours on the wireless," said Mrs Tinckham.

"Who?" I asked.

"Name of Quentin," said Mrs Tinckham. She passed me the *Radio Times*, and as I fumbled with the pages she suddenly turned the wireless on full.

Like a sea wave curling over me came Anna's voice. She was singing an old French love song. The words came slowly, gilded by her utterance. They turned over in the air slowly and then fell; and the splendour of the husky gold filled the shop, transforming the cats into leopards and Mrs Tinckham into an aged Circe. I sat quite still and held Mrs Tinck's eyes, as she leaned there with her hand frozen upon the knob of the wireless. It was very long since I had heard Anna sing; and as I listened I saw her, and saw the little streak of grey in the coronet of her hair. The song ended. "Turn it off!" I said, for I could bear no more.

The shop was suddenly silent. Mrs Tinckham had turned the wireless off completely, and for the first time since I had ever come to Mrs Tinckham's shop I could hear the animals breathing.

Anxiously I turned the pages of the *Radio Times* until I found the place. "Anna Quentin," it said, "relayed from the *Club des Fous* in Paris, in the first of a series of ten broadcasts entitled *Qu'est ce que la Chanson?*" I smiled with a smile which penetrated my whole being like the sun.

"You see," said Mrs Tinckham.

"I see," I said. I wondered what she meant. We looked at each other.

"Mrs Tinck," I said, "I'll tell you something."

"What?" said Mrs Tinckham.

"I'm going to get a job," I said.

I didn't expect her to look surprised, and she didn't. "What can you do?" asked Mrs Tinckham.

"I shall find a part-time job in a hospital," I said. "I can do that." I am very conservative by temperament.

"But first I must find somewhere to live," I said.

"You could look at the board outside," said Mrs Tinck. "There may be a room advertised, I forget."

I got up and went outside. Mars ambled after me and stood leaning lazily against my legs, scanning the street for mobile and chaseable cats. I examined the board. It was covered with more or less ill-written postcards, which were pinned there for a weekly fee. One, neater than the rest, caught my eye, advertising a ground-floor room near Hampstead Heath, with *no petty restrictions*. This obviously referred to women; I wondered if it might be extended to cover dogs.

"Who put that one up?" I asked Mrs Tinck.

"An odd kind of man," said Mrs Tinckham. "I don't know him particularly."

"What's he like?" I asked.

"He's rather tall," said Mrs Tinckham.

I knew that I should have to go to Hampstead to find out what was odd about him. "You've nothing against him?" I said.

"Oh, nothing at all," said Mrs Tinck. "Why don't you go and look at the room?"

"I'll do it to-night," I said.

"If you're stuck for a bed you can come back and sleep here," said Mrs Tinck.

This was an extraordinary concession. "Thank you, Mrs Tinckham," I said, "but where shall I sleep?"

"I'll make you a bed behind the counter," said Mrs Tinckham. "I'll move Maggie and her kittens into the back room."

"How are Maggie and her kittens?" I asked politely.

"Come and see," she said.

Feeling that I was stepping onto sacred ground, I came round behind the counter. In the corner at Mrs Tinckham's feet, in a cardboard stationery box, lay Maggie with four kittens curled against her striped belly. Maggie was blinking and yawning and looking the other way while the kittens struggled into her fur. I looked, I looked closer, and then I exclaimed.

"Yes, you see," said Mrs Tinckham. I knelt down and began to lift the kittens one by one. Their bodies were as round as balls and they squeaked almost inaudibly. One of them was tabby, one was tabby and white, and two of them appeared to be completely Siamese. I studied their markings and their crooked tails and their fierce squinting blue eyes. Already they seemed to be squeaking more huskily than the others.

"So Maggie's done it at last!" I said. Mars thrust his head under my arm and sniffed at the little beasts with condescension. I put them back in the box.

"What puzzles me," said Mrs Tinckham, "is why those two should be pure Siamese and the other ones quite different, instead of their all being half tabby and half Siamese."

"Oh, but that's how it always is. It's quite simple," I said.

"Why is it then?" said Mrs Tinck.

"Well," I said, "it's just a matter of . . ." I stopped. I had no idea what it was a matter of. I laughed and Mrs Tinckham laughed.

"I don't know why it is," I said. "It's just one of the wonders of the world."

Iris Murdoch

THE BLACK PRINCE

With an introduction by
Candia McWilliam

Shortlisted for the Booker Prize

'Iris Murdoch's marvellous, heroic novel...A gloriously
rich tale'
The Times

'Miss Murdoch here displays her dazzling gifts at the full
tide of her powers in a novel which will delight her admirers'
Sunday Times

A story about being in love, *The Black Prince* is also a
remarkable intellectual thriller with a superbly involved
plot, and a meditation on the nature of art and love and the
deity who rules over both.

Bradley Pearson, its narrator and hero, is an elderly writer
with a 'block'. Encompassed by predatory friends and
relations – his ex-wife, her delinquent brother and a
younger, deplorably successful writer, Arnold Baffin,
together with Baffin's restless wife and youthful daughter –
Bradley attempts escape. His failure and its aftermath lead
to a violent climax; and to a coda which casts a shifting
perspective on all that has gone before.

VINTAGE

Iris Murdoch

THE PHILOSOPHER'S PUPIL

With an introduction by
Malcolm Bradbury

'The most daring and original of all her novels'
A. N. Wilson

In the English spa town of Ennistone hot springs bubble up from deep beneath the earth. In these healing waters the townspeople seek health and regeneration, righteousness and ritual cleansing.

To this town steeped in ancient lore and subterranean inspiration the Philosopher returns. He exerts an almost magical influence over a host of Ennistonians, and especially over George McCaffrey, the Philosopher's old pupil, a demonic man desperate for redemption.

'We are back, of course, with great delight, the land of Iris Murdoch, which is like no other but Prospero's'
Sunday Telegraph

'Never for a moment does one want to stop reading...I don't think that Iris Murdoch has ever written better prose'
Daily Telegraph

VINTAGE